D1201200

HIS FATHER'S SON

Baen Books in this series:

Keeper of the King by Nigel Bennett & P.N. Elrod
His Father's Son by Nigel Bennett & P.N. Elrod
Quincey Morris, Vampire by P.N. Elrod (*forthcoming*)

HIS FATHER'S SON

NIGEL BENNETT
P.N. ELROD

HIS FATHER'S SON

A Baen Books Original

Baen Publishing Enterprises
P.O. Box 1403
Riverdale, NY 10471
www.baen.com

ISBN: 0-671-31981-7

Cover art by Jaime Murray

First printing, April 2001

Library of Congress Cataloging-in-Publication Data

Bennett, Nigel, 1949–
His father's son / by Nigel Bennett & P.N. Elrod
p. cm.
ISBN 0-671-31981-7
1. Vampires—Fiction. I. Elrod, P.N. (Patricia Nead) II. Title.

PR9199.3.B3782 H57 2001
813'.54—dc21 00-065092

Distributed by Simon & Schuster
1230 Avenue of the Americas
New York, NY 10020

Production by Windhaven Press, Auburn, NH
Printed in the United States of America

10 9 8 7 6 5 4 3 2 1

To Michael & Sam

with thanks to:
Charles Ballard
Gail Hassell Forestieri
Kath Henebry
Nancy Hill
Nick Marcelja
Helen Mesquita

remembering:
Deborah Heinrichs &
Vashti of the Flaming Tresses—Ruth Woodring

and a special thanks to:
Teresa Patterson & Kevin Topham

Chapter One

Normandy, the Beginning

He awoke in a meaningless half light that could have been dawn or dusk, and in all truth it did not matter. His eyes pierced the gloom easily; to him the inside of her tent was as bright as day. He lay on fur and beneath fur, and the small of his back was wet with sweat. He shifted sleepily and became aware of her next to him. He turned his head and saw she had her back toward him, only partly covered by the stifling fur. Her dark hair, long and lustrous, tumbled away from her shoulders and across the pillows. The side of her neck was bare, and his gaze followed the line of her body from that point, over the rise of her shoulder along the slope of her side and up the sudden sharp rise of her hip. By the slow steady beat of her heart she was still sleeping.

He smiled at the memory of the long hours of love and passion and pure pleasure with her. He'd lost count of how often they'd coupled and ridden together toward that little death, surrendering willingly to it. Each time he'd thought it the ultimate ecstasy, and each new encounter had proved him wrong. They'd kissed and tasted and sucked and stroked. Their sweat and juices had mingled; every moment was perfect.

He reached out and caressed her thick, heavy hair, absently

straightened it, smoothing it down, and yet his touch was so light, so gentle that she did not wake. Her skin was alabaster cool and delicate as that of a babe, and he traced her spine with a finger down to the deep cleft between her cheeks. He cupped their firmness, then slipped his hand around to the flat wonder of her belly, and her thatch of dark curls. She was still wet, and as he stroked, a soft low moan escaped her.

He hardened quickly and feeling it, laughed under his breath in surprise at the strength of his desire. He pressed closer and buried his face in her hair. It smelled of blossom and earth and sky and moonlight, and he breathed in deep. He was fully erect now, hard along her spine, and she pushed back against him, shifting her legs. Without effort, he was in her, once more held in her sweetness, and he closed his eyes and gasped at the feeling, at the warmth, at the sense of wholeness.

She moaned aloud now and as one, they began to slowly move against each other, caught up in the rhythm of creation. She did not open her eyes. Perhaps she slept still, and this was all a dream to her. He did not know. One of her breasts filled his questing hand, hard-nippled, compelling, and he found himself pushing deeper, deeper into her. All his being was centered on her, her every reaction to his touch. They moved together so slowly, so languidly.

Sweat seeped from his brow and disappeared into her hair. He kissed the soft nape of her neck, tickling the fine skin there with his tongue. Lips parted, she murmured something; it sounded like a prayer. Her hands pressed against his as he held her, enjoining him to further exploration. He took his time, touching and fondling, until her breath came short and fast, grew harsh with desire. He brought her right to the edge of it, then without warning the animal took him as well. A desperate urgency seized his being, and he thrust harder into her slick wetness, anticipating the coming explosion, wanting it, needing it. In her sleep she pushed back, equally urgent, arching against him. He was so deep inside her, yet felt himself opening, spreading wide as a rose in the sunlight. Then, spasming, quite out of control, at one with his spirit, and out of his body, he burst within her. Once more she moaned, this time from fulfillment, not longing, and he glimpsed a smile as it flicked across her sleeping face.

Dear Goddess, could there be any greater pleasure?

And inside his head came an answering voice, clear as church bells on a summer's day.

No.

They slept together, he still inside her, softening slowly, until they were once again apart. Yet he held her close, she, he, they, as one in their shadowy heaven.

He dreamed, and in his dream, she came to him, held his face gently in her hands, and spoke. "It will be ever thus, my love, ever thus. I am of thee and thou of me. We are truly one and will never sunder."

He smiled in his sleep, and as she watched him, eyes wide in the darkness, a single tear slid down Sabra's cheek and melted into the pillow.

The thick oaken doors of the great hall of the Castle Orleans creaked open on their mighty hinges, swirling the smoke-laden air into delicate spirals that disappeared upward into the fading golden light of sunset, and Richard d'Orleans strode through. The rushes on the stone flags crackled under his boots as two weary servants hauled hard and pulled the doors slowly shut again, sealing him in the vast, dim space. He pushed back the thick protective hood of his long cloak and looked about at the wreckage of triumph.

The smell that arose all around him would have given many a man cause to retch. The feasting after the great tourney had gone on for several days; the floor was littered with rotting food, spilled wine, pools of vomit. None of the scullions had yet attempted any cleaning. They'd indulged as liberally as any. The collective sickness pressed heavily upon the whole of the stagnant keep. Richard noted and ignored its near-physical presence, immersed as he was in his own thoughts and fears.

He'd been summoned by his father, Duke Montague d'Orleans. Sabra had insisted that he answer to the old man, and Richard could no more refuse her than stay his breathing. So he'd dressed in the fine linen and leather that she'd laid out for him with her own hands, kissed her chastely on the forehead, and gone for her sake, not the duke's.

As things stood now, he had no need to obey the savage old despot ever again. So far as Richard was concerned, he was free of him, of all the past, free of everything except his loathing for it.

How mightily his life had changed since the great tourney, since his ignominious defeat at the hands of that damned boy. Only a few days had passed, yet in that time Richard d'Orleans had been—quite literally—reborn into a new and never-ending life. While he waited in the empty room, looking idly at familiar tapestries covering the cold stone walls, the events of the past few days came back to him with startling clarity. From the depths of defeat and despair he'd risen to a fresh beginning given to him by his lady, Sabra of the Lake. He was changed, from mere mortal to something much more.

His heart raced, and he caught his breath at the thought. The impossibility of it was almost too much to take in, but on his left hand he bore the undeniable truth that it had indeed happened to him. His third finger had been severed by a dagger thrust at the tourney, but because of his change a healing such as he'd never imagined had taken place, magically reversing the maiming. Though the scar that went around the base of his mended finger was not like to go away, he felt no twinge of pain from it. Indeed, its white ring was constant and absolute proof that no injury could truly harm him, that no enemy could ever strike him down again. He had inhuman strength and the skill to use it to withstand anyone now. He clenched his restored hand into a fist and smiled openly as the raw power surged within him. He was what he'd always longed to be: a true champion, afraid of none, invincible, free.

Yet there was a price to pay. Sunlight was now his enemy, as too was flowing water. He discovered that the first day after his change; Sabra had warned that these would kill him if he lingered in either for too long. Like her, he was a creature more of night than day, a creature of earth and darkness and shadow like the Hounds of Annwyn, their progenitors.

But the most important, and most dangerous, price of all was that his appetite, too, had changed. Like Sabra, like all their kind, he drank blood and only blood to live.

Richard d'Orleans was *vampire.*

This utterly set him at odds to all that he'd been taught; he'd become a depraved thing to be feared, abhorred, and destroyed. Blood was precious, sacred, not to be spilled or taken by such monsters.

Or so he'd always been told.

We are not monsters, he thought with quiet certainty. No mindless beast could love as he loved Sabra, as she loved him. No evil could possibly abide in her, nor would she allow it near her. That being so, then he was not as others might see him, but something well beyond their limits. They would only perceive him as an unnatural threat though, and act according to the dictates of their fears. Absolute secrecy was necessary for his survival against such deadly ignorance, but it seemed a small enough price to pay for what he'd gained. He was a servant of the Goddess now, a protector of her ways. So long as he was careful and kept silent about the truth behind his new existence, he was ageless and deathless. That was the Goddess's gift to him, bestowed through his beautiful Sabra.

They'd awakened together the day before from a long afternoon of sleep and fleshly enjoyment in the shelter of her pavilion, but this time Richard's first thought and desire was not for more love.

"You hunger, do you not?" Sabra had asked, raising up on one elbow in their bed to look down at him.

"I feel its hold upon me." He ran a hand over his face and lightly touched his corner teeth. They were not extended yet, though he felt the potential to do so tingling in their roots.

"But not as strongly as that first craving?"

"Nay, 'tis but a shade to it, but still . . ." He licked his dry lips, recalling the first glorious red rush of fulfillment he'd taken from the veins of one of Sabra's servants. The old eunuch had given up his life that Richard might live, given it up to be with the Goddess they all served. "Must I kill again to satisfy this need?" Though troubled by the prospect, he was willing to do so if it meant a never-ending eternity with Sabra.

"But surely not," she replied, smiling at his concern. "Killing each time we must feed would call attention to us, and we would be hunted down and killed ourselves by those who have the knowledge. There is a simple way to satisfy our wants and a pleasing one. I will show you."

Sabra rose from their nest of cushions and wrapped herself in a long loose robe of the same rich brown color as her hair. She went to the tent opening and untied the flap, carefully keeping clear of the rays of the lowering sun that lanced through the cracks. She called to someone outside and soon a young servant girl hurried in. Richard hastily covered his nakedness with a blanket.

"This is Ghislaine, she has helped me many times," said Sabra.

Ghislaine stood in a modest, respectful pose, hands folded and eyes down for the most part, but stealing quick darting glances at her surroundings, at him. Richard could hear the swift patter of her heart. Sabra crossed to her, putting an arm around her shoulders to lean close and whisper something, smiling as she did.

The girl flushed deep crimson and stifled a giggle, nodding.

Sabra whispered again, and the girl shuffled a curtsey at him, smiling coyly. Fresh as a peach, she could not have been much past fifteen, but already had the fullness of a woman's body. By her manner she certainly possessed a woman's experience of the flesh, yet at the same time she seemed to retain a measure of innocence. Richard found the combination highly appealing and felt a predictable stirring within.

Sabra stepped away from the girl and gazed steadily at him. "Now you must tell her what you want."

"What do you mean?"

"With your mind, with your words, you may beguile her to your will."

"I-I know not how, my lady," Richard began, but was stopped from further protest by Sabra's piercing stare. He could not look away. And then he heard her as clearly as if she had spoken to him, though she had not, for he could well see that her lips did not move.

You have the power as I do. Her voice sounded in his head: warm, sweet, seductive. *Will her to do as you wish.*

He blinked, recovering his own thoughts amid those she'd imparted to him.

Try, and learn in the trying, my Richard.

"But is this speaking to the mind not your own Gift of Sight?" he asked. "You told me I did not share in that."

"True, you do not," she said aloud. "What I would have you master now is very like to it, though. It's part of your new nature. You're capable of bringing others to agreement with your desires. If you learn to use it carefully and to your advantage, with prudence and wit, you will always be safe. No one will ever suspect you differ from any other man, for you can put all such wonderings from their heads."

He thought he understood what she wanted of him. He gestured at Ghislaine. "What must I do?" If she followed the meaning of their talk, she gave no sign.

Bend your thoughts, your will upon her, Sabra whispered. *Call her to you.*

Facing the girl, he looked deep into her eyes, not knowing if it really would work. "Come to me," he murmured so softly that he had doubts she could have heard him. "Come, Ghislaine."

With no change of expression, she glided toward him. Was she merely obeying her new master's order or truly responding to his will? He wasn't sure.

"Sit beside me," he said, testing. No servant, no matter what their ranking, would dare take their ease thus in the presence of their betters, but Ghislaine did exactly that, sinking upon the cushions next to him as though she owned them. He looked at Sabra, half smiling in wonder. "I did it."

Indeed, my love. Now lull her to sleep.

With Sabra's approval to bolster his confidence, he focused on Ghislaine and spoke soothingly, willing her to submissiveness and finally slumber with his soft words. God, it was so easy. Her eyelids slipped shut, and she slumped against him. He eased her down by his side on the cushions.

Sabra sat next to her as well, looking at him across the girl's reclining form. Again, she spoke out loud. "In the deepness of her throat or at the crook of her elbow, the blood flows close to the surface and is easy to get to. There are many such places, but 'tis better to take from the arm when you can, for the marks you leave will be less noticeable to others. Bite gently, and take only as much as you need. You will find you want but little and seldom. It is rich elixir and filling."

Richard lifted the unresisting girl's arm, and pushed up the loose sleeve of her simple gown. The skin was white and clear. Blue veins lay just below the surface, and he traced them with his fingertips. He could smell the blood through her flesh. Unbidden, his corner teeth budded, long, sharp, wolflike, and he felt the warm flush as his eyes reddened. His heart began to pound heavily with anticipation, and he could hear the sound of another heart, Sabra's, rising to match its rhythm.

Sabra's voice purred in his ear, and she stroked the side of his face, her touch like fire. "She will feel little, and what she does will be naught but pleasure, I assure you."

For us both, my lady, he thought, lowering his head. He paused to taste the smooth young flesh, running his tongue over the pulsing vein. As he did, Ghislaine's breath became deep and ragged, her lips opening slightly, showing even white teeth. Richard recognized arousal when he saw it and turned to Sabra, silently questioning.

"Take her," she urged, her own eyes gone red.

His teeth broke easily through the tender skin, and a gasp escaped the girl's lips, followed by a long, delectable moan. Blood gushed into his mouth, and eyes closed, he sucked hungrily. Ghislaine's heartbeat sounded like close thunder to him. His hand strayed to her chest to feel the throb of it as he fed. She shifted under his touch, gasping again as his palm smoothed over the firm rise of one of her breasts. Through the light fabric of her gown his thumb teased at her nipple. Not too surprised, he realized he was hard, erect. He sought release by taking more blood.

The heat of it stole over him, more potent than the headiest wine. The sheer *pleasure* roaring through his body was almost beyond bearing; he wanted to shout in celebration, but could not tear away, not yet. What came out was a smothered groan of ecstasy.

Ghislaine writhed, drawing her legs up, pressing her head into the cushions. He felt her young body trembling, then shuddering as he fed. Her back arched, and he had to hold her down. She breathed out the name of the Goddess in her crisis, once, twice, before uttering a long wordless cry of exultation. The tension abruptly departed from her, and with a little sigh, she went completely limp. Disturbing for a moment, it gave him pause, but her heart still beat strongly; her blood still flowed to him.

He took in another fiery draught.

Sabra's hand was on his shoulder, fingers digging into his bare flesh. Now was he able to break off, lifting away to open his eyes. Sabra's dark head was bowed over the girl's other arm as she drank from the same fount. The sight excited him in a manner he'd never known before. He instantly understood what he wanted to do next, but wasn't certain how to bring it about.

As if in response to his thought, Sabra raised herself, her blood-flushed gaze meeting his before sliding down to his hard manhood showing beneath the blanket.

No use trying to deny it. "Forgive me, my lady, I—"

There is nothing to forgive. She leaned forward, her warm lips brushing his like a butterfly's wings. She left behind the taste of Ghislaine's blood.

"Have you had enough?" she asked, drawing his blanket clear.

"No," he answered, decisively reaching for her. He stripped away the robe and lifted her small body effortlessly, pulling her right across the slumbering Ghislaine and onto him. Her legs straddled his hips and she gasped as he entered her. She fell forward upon his chest. His mouth on hers, he kissed and licked at the blood there until it was quite gone.

Not enough.

He was aflame like a fever victim. This was no languorous, dream-filled lovemaking, but a primitive and frenzied coupling, as needs he'd never been aware of took him over. Sabra seemed caught up in it as well as her kisses became deeper, more intense, more fierce. She rode against him with bruising force, nails clawing his chest. Then her mouth fastened on his throat, and he felt the sharp dent of her teeth breaking his skin. He pressed her close, panting as she drank. It was almost the same as when she'd killed him to bring about his change, only this time he stayed gloriously awake as his red life went into her.

She suddenly drew back, eyes shut, her body convulsing in time to his thrusts. He watched her face, reveling in her rapture, taking it for his own. When her moans ceased, he pulled her close again, pushing her head to one side to make taut the skin of her neck. His mouth yawned, his teeth piercing one of her surface veins, and he drew hard at the wounds until all that he'd shared rushed back to him again. It overwhelmed all his senses, stealing away the last of his control. Then came his own explosive release as his seed drove into her; the combined impetus of it and the blood gusted through him like a firestorm. It swept him up and out of himself, his soul tumbling helplessly in the searing heat.

The last thing he heard in the chaos was his own laughter as he embraced the red wind.

Sabra's lithe body gradually slipped away from his, leaving him sprawled on the cushions, puffing and slick with sweat, invigorated and at the same time exhausted. She lay next to him, apparently in much the same state. With a lazy hand he touched his throat. It was sticky with fresh blood, but completely healed. He saw Sabra's skin had also knitted, wholly unmarked but for a few telltale smears. Some minutes later she recovered first and sat up to examine the still sleeping Ghislaine.

"Is it well with her?" he asked drowsily. "She is not hurt?"

"The wounds are small and bled little once we were finished. Mind that you always cleanse them afterward, yourself as well." Sabra got up, drawing her robe on again and went to a table holding a slender wine vessel to pour some onto a square of cloth. She used it to wash away the stains on her lips and throat, then tended to those marring the girl's arms. "Fresh water from a swift stream or rain will do, but wine is best; the sting prevents the flesh from corrupting. Fill a cup for her; she'll need a restorative."

Richard rolled slowly to his feet and did as he was bidden,

handing the cup to her, then followed her example and cleaned himself. He found and pulled on a long tunic before dropping onto the bed again. Sabra touched the girl gently on the side of her face, speaking her name. Ghislaine's eyes fluttered open, and she looked about with some confusion, then alarm, struggling to rise.

"My lady, I'm sorry, I did not mean to—"

"Hush, child," she said, keeping her in place. "'Tis natural. Rest yourself a moment. Lord Richard is"—she glanced at him, the light of mischief in her eyes—"a demanding man. Drink this, then you may go to your supper and bed. You're excused from your duties until the morrow."

Sabra's soothing voice had its effect on the girl, and Ghislaine obediently emptied the wine cup, her gaze straying over its rim to Richard. He wasn't sure how he should respond to what looked to be nascent adoration, and tentatively settled on a smile and nod of appreciation. Apparently it was enough; Ghislaine finished, curtsied low to them both, and departed without another word, leaving him alone with Sabra.

"Will she not speak of this?" he asked.

"She will remember little of what happened here, simply that you and she gave each other pleasure." Sabra's gaze wandered to his still ample manhood outlined under the thin cloth. "A great portion of pleasure, it seems."

He began to blush at his body's betrayal of his still-active desire. "Forgive me, my lady, she means nothing to me, I assure you. I know not why it happened."

"You may say you know not, but I do, sweet Richard. It is our nature to enjoy their lives and flesh in all ways, and I take joy in your delight. She is a pretty creature, after all, deserving of appreciation."

"You are not jealous?"

"No more than you should be of me when the blood calls to my hungers . . . all my hungers."

That gave him pause, the implication being that of Sabra feeding from another man. Richard didn't care for the idea, but had no wish to spoil the moment. Better to deal with the subject later.

He pulled Sabra back to the comfort of their bed, wrapping his arms protectively around her as she lay her head on his shoulder.

"Will all my feedings be thus?" he asked, murmuring into her thick hair. It smelled of flowers.

"Not always. I thought your first one should be memorable, though."

"My lady is the soul of kindness."

"Sometimes you may feast slowly, others will be catch-as-may as you go along with no time for dalliance. No matter what befalls, make certain the one you choose remains unaware, and that none chance to see you. It could mean your death."

He grunted in short reply, knowing the truth of it. The consequences of what had transpired over the last hour had anyone observed them did not bear contemplation. "I will take care, I promise."

"One other thing, and mark this well: beware of attachments to them, my love."

"What mean you?"

"These fragile children abide with us but a little while and then are gone, and I would not have thee heartsick from the loss. You are ever my true love, and I yours. We two will endure long after Ghislaine is dust. That is the way. That is why the Goddess chose thee, for strengths even you may not yet know about yourself."

"Then you must tell me about them, sweet lady."

"When the time allows . . . and we have more of time than anything else."

Certainly while waiting in the empty feast hall away from Sabra's intoxicating presence Richard had had an abundance of it to think everything through. He was mildly surprised to determine that from a loss that should have saddened him, a transformation that should have terrified him, a craving that should have disgusted him, he could see nothing but goodness and bold promise for his future.

His *eternal* future . . . with Sabra.

He shut his eyes, holding the wondrous image close lest it fly away from him in this chill and hollow place.

But his gladness was interrupted when an apologetic servant

hurried into the room bearing a single candle and placed it on the table. Richard's vision was such that he'd not noticed how dark it had gotten.

"Does the duke summon me yet?" he asked, staying the man's excuses for being late.

"I know naught of it, Lord Richard," he said, ducking his head. "Do you wish anything?" Cold was settling in for the night and the man shivered in his tattered clothes. The castle was always cold, even this far into spring.

"I thank you, but no. Be off to your bed."

He stared at Richard for a moment.

Richard met his gaze calmly, but felt a twinge of doubt within. *Does he see the change in me?*

If he did, he kept it to himself and quickly departed the way he'd come, leaving the door ajar. As he hastened along, Richard's sensitive hearing followed the whisper of his footsteps, probably back to the stinking smoky warmth of a pallet by the kitchen hearth.

Then another kind of sound came forth from the entry and suddenly two of the castle's great hounds bounded noisily into the feasting hall to scavenge the leavings. They were huge hunting beasts, and Richard knew them both well; he'd been right there in the stable at their whelping. He'd watched their growth from clumsy pups to graceful adults and trained them himself for the chasing down of game in the forests. They'd often been his only companions for many long weeks at a time. Of all things and people living in his father's castle, these hounds were the only souls he could trust and count as friends.

He clapped his hands and gave a short whistle. "Merlin! Prince!"

The two dogs checked in mid-bound, recognizing the voice, looking around for its owner in the dimness.

"Prince! Merlin! Here, lads, here." Richard stepped forward, hands out as the animals whined an anxious greeting and tore over the flags toward him, tongues lolling as though from laughter. "Come to heel, come on."

Merlin reached him first. Richard was almost close enough to touch the massive head, but paused at an unexpected shift in the dog's reaction to him. Merlin froze an instant, then backed away so quickly that he blundered into Prince, halting him in turn.

Both dogs milled in confusion, sniffing and growling at Richard before settling into a guarded stance. The hair along their backs stood straight on end, and they lowered their heads threateningly. With ears laid flat, teeth bared and snarling, they were primed for the kill.

Instinctively, Richard backed away, hefting a heavy wooden stool as defense. The dogs had recognized him; what was wrong? Had they gone mad, inexplicably perceiving him as an enemy? He'd seen the damage that these two could inflict many times and wanted none of it. Who had turned them against him?

He spoke their names again, firmly, not letting the alarm he felt color his voice. Instead, he brought to his tone all the displeasure he could muster, slamming the stool on the floor with a bang. He held fast to it, though, in case his ploy at dominance failed.

The noise startled them, and his voice seemed to break through before they could charge. First one then the other stopped and began to whine piteously, eyes averted, as though afraid to look at him. They spun around uncertainly, tails between their legs, urinating in fright. Richard lowered the stool and took a step forward, speaking softly. Perhaps his new clothing had masked his familiar scent. But the dogs backed away from him, yelping with fear, then turned tail and fled.

He stared open-mouthed at their retreat, then belatedly understood the why of it. With the cold breath of the Hounds of Annwyn forever upon him, what other reaction could he expect from ordinary canines? Merlin and Prince had sensed the difference all too sharply. What surprised Richard was the enormity of the hurt he felt from their unexpected rejection. Sabra had not warned him about this particular price for his change.

Perhaps this won't be as easy as I thought.

He released his hold on the stool and finally seated himself on it rather than pace the filthy floor. He stared at the entry where the dogs had retreated, mourning their loss. He'd have had to leave them behind, anyway, for all in the castle and lands around belonged to the duke, but this wasn't the sort of parting Richard might have wished for.

Richard had tenuously held his place in the household by strength of arms, bringing honor to the family name with each victory. That had ended with his defeat at the tourney, though, and he knew exactly why he'd been summoned. It was time for the duke to give his hated child a final censure and banish Richard from his house with less consideration and far more rancor than would be heaped upon the lowliest of the servants.

Richard watched the shadows cast by the candle flame twist and jump in the draughty air, remembering how he'd snapped a curt dismissal to the duke's command in Sabra's pavilion earlier that day.

"You must go," she told him.

"I think not." Richard had no desire to forsake her safe, dark sanctuary for a walk in the burning sun only to face his father's own searing wrath at the end of it.

"You must. It is necessary."

"Is it not enough that I've endured a lifetime of abuse and humiliation from him? Can we not simply leave for Britain?"

"For one, you must obtain his release from your oath of service to him. Without it he has the right to hunt you down like an escaped serf."

He ground his teeth, for she was perfectly correct. "And for another?"

"We few of us know how to properly say farewell." Sabra held his hand in hers as she spoke. "It is a necessary and important thing. It is the finishing of the round. Without it, whatever we do from then on can be flawed. Like it or no, he is your father; he is in you always. You owe yourself that acknowledgment and the closing of the circle."

Richard started to protest that he could not remember a single occasion upon which Montague d'Orleans had behaved in any way like a father, but stopped, realizing the humble truth of her words. "He will belittle me."

"That he will."

"And he will shame me and say that I am no son of his. I know it."

"And you are right."

Richard thought for a moment and turned her hand over in his, finally kissing her palm. "Does your Sight tell you what will happen, what will come of this?"

Sabra did not answer.

"Does it?"

The look in her brown eyes as she regarded him could melt the hardest stone. "Dear Richard, what is to be will be. What will happen is within you. You'll find it in your heart. You must be your own guide in this, make your own path for right or wrong."

"What is it you tell me? That I've a choice to make? What sort of choice?"

"I'll say only that we often have to reach through the thorns to pluck the rose. There is always pain if we choose to seize it. Just remember that I am with you through all." She loosed his hand and stepped back from him. "Now go to your father. He has summoned you, and you must give him that one last obedience."

He wanted to ask more, but knew she would not—or could not—answer. Her Sight was clear and truthful, but sometimes it revealed too much, showing her more than one future, each dependent upon actions made in the present.

Perhaps that was what awaited him. If so, then might he not make a mistake, choose the wrong path? The wrong future?

She'd raised herself on her toes to kiss him lightly on the mouth, and he returned it, pressing his lips to her brow. He wrapped his heavy cloak close to shield his vulnerable skin from the sun and left.

And now here in the darkness, lit by a single sputtering candle he sat, waiting to discover the meaning of her words. Out of love for her and trust in her wisdom and judgment he could put himself through one more hour of his father's malice, though not much more than that. Richard had his limits.

Most of that hour had passed already, according to the tolling of the church bell. It was full night and vespers had come and gone by now, though it was doubtful that the chapel had been very full. Perhaps a few had attended to pray for recovery from their revels.

How like his father to keep him waiting thus. It was a very old game he played, and he never tired of it: Summon the despised son, then keep him without. It was an obvious insult, one he'd seen his father use often and to great effect. Richard might be here for hours, even all night if it pleased the duke.

This is the last time for me. It must *be the last time.*

Finally giving in to a portion of impatience, Richard stood and stretched and paced once around the great room. He realized that he did not need the candle. He could see quite well, indeed. The change in his vision was such that this darkness was very much like day. Turning back to the candle, its small light seemed almost as bright as a bonfire.

The moon had risen, the silver-blue glow pouring through the high windows, creeping its way down the wall opposite to make the tapestries and banners there shimmer. It was so beautiful. Everything was heightened since his transformation. He could see more, smell more, feel more. The sounds of the night from both within and without the castle came to him very clearly when he paid mind to them. He cocked his head toward the entry but could pick up nothing to indicate his wait was ending. True, he could cut this nonsense short by bulling into the duke's sanctum, but past experience made him reluctant to try. The old man was king in everything but name here, with the power of life and death over all. To incur his wrath was to risk dire punishment. Richard had dared to cross him on this very point, once. The beating he'd gotten some dozen years past had left an indelible impression on his spirit long after the bruises healed. The lesson stuck.

He could beat me now—could try—for all the good it would do him.

The power of his dark rebirth surged through Richard once more, warming him. The past should be—was—less than nothing to him. Perhaps that was what Sabra wanted him to learn from this. If so, then he could do as he pleased with no fear of reprisal. But if not, and he made the wrong choice, whatever that might be . . .

He decided he could wait a little longer.

He righted one of the long benches and sat at the table, idly toying with an abandoned trencher. There was a time that he would have gladly picked at the remaining food, indeed, eaten his fill from the leavings here, but not now, and never again.

Free. I am free of this.

A sudden noise from the doorway to his father's inner chamber along the hall jolted Richard from his musings, and he stood to meet his sire. The door down there opened sure enough, but all that came out was a string of curses and the unmistakable scrabblings of the two terrified hounds. The dogs pelted into the feast hall, seeking escape from the shouting and then from Richard, finding none. They finally took shelter beneath one of the far tables, whimpering.

More cursing from the entry. A familiar voice, but not one belonging to a friend. Richard had no friends here.

First the dogs, then another kind of cur arrived, as Dear Brother lurched into the vast room. Richard braced inwardly, his face settling into the usual blank mask he tried to maintain when forced to deal with his abrasive oldest sibling.

Ambert d'Orleans was the proud firstborn of the great lord, and had never let Richard forget it. At first glance, he and Richard could have almost been twins, so similar were they. In their youth many had mistaken them as such. Both over six feet in height, fair-haired, with icy blue eyes, and both strong and valiant on the field—but that was in their youth. Their differences had grown with the passing years and were not just those of physical change. Richard could look at himself and without blush know he was principled and intelligent with a strong sense of honor; Ambert, on the other hand, was ever a bully and a braggart and, worst of all, a cunning backstabber. Richard had learned the best way to deal with him was simple avoidance whenever possible.

Excess in all things was beginning to take its toll on Ambert, for his belly now far exceeded his chest in girth. He had to balance carefully as he made his way into the dim hall, pausing at the head of the table. His once handsome face was bloated and red from too much wine and fits of temper, and his fine blue eyes were rheumy and bloodshot. His bleared gaze quickly fastened on

Richard, regarding him with the usual measure of contempt, Ambert's idea of a superior look.

He bore a goblet in hand, and swaying a little, extended it imperiously in Richard's direction. "Wine, brother," he said, as though addressing a servant. There was an open cask on the table before him, but he made no move toward it.

Knowing the uselessness of argument, Richard crossed to him and took the goblet away. There being no ladle, he tipped the cask with care. It was nearly empty and the wine threatened to spill as it slopped about. He got it steady enough to control the pouring of a thin stream.

"Don't stint with it, you fool." Ambert shot his hand out and upset the cask. It was an old trick, the object being to add stains to Richard's clothing. The elegant new garments he wore now had obviously not escaped Dear Brother's notice; the temptation was irresistible. The result was different this time, though, for Richard quickly moved out of the way, letting the thing crash to the floor. The wine flew in all directions, a goodly amount of it splashing onto Ambert. He gasped and snarled, but only for a moment. The startlement was clear on his face when he saw just how far out of the way Richard had taken himself in the merest blink of an eye. He was at the other end of the long table.

"That was clumsy, wasn't it?" said Richard, calmly surveying the damage. "Your fine coat is all spoiled."

"Bastard," Ambert spat, throwing him a murderous look.

"That's the whole point for you, isn't it? I'm not a bastard. If I were, you wouldn't be so afraid of me."

"I fear you not, sweet Dickon. 'Tis only wisdom to keep a sharp eye on the ambitions of the third-born."

"And so you always cast upon me what you'd want yourself were our stations reversed. A tiresome game it's become. You know I've no desire for your share."

"So you say to all within hearing. You've said it too much, too loudly. No one believes you."

"I'm thinking no one gives a bloody damn anymore. You've provided our father with a grandson; your position is secure."

"Aye, but brats die so easily. Three times it took before that bitch finally birthed something that lived. How you must have prayed otherwise."

Richard held to an immobile face, but his hand, still clutching the empty goblet, compressed into a sudden fist. There was a crumping sound of strained metal. He looked down. The cup portion was crushed in, the shape of his fingers clearly defined in the thick brass. He felt a brief smile twitch over his features and carefully set the ruined object on the table where Ambert could see it.

Dear Brother's eyes went wide at the sight, and for once in his life Ambert seemed to have nothing to say.

"Sorry," said Richard, offering him a thin, insincere smile.

"You—you'll pay for that," Ambert finally spluttered out. "God's death, but you'll pay for that before you leave."

"With what, pray?"

Ambert took the offered bait, seizing it for a new weapon. "Aye, you lost all at the tourney, to the disgrace of our house."

"You've a new champion to take my place. The honor of the house is safe."

"With that overgrown pup?"

"At least he's a true bastard, so you've no need to worry over his ambitions. They probably don't extend much past his next meal and place to sleep, which he's already gotten from me." The boy had been quick enough to claim Richard's weapons, armor, and other gear for his winnings. He was welcome to all of it now.

"You're not suffering from what I see." Ambert nodded at Richard's new clothing, the finely woven wools, leather boots, the thick blue cape with gold embroidery along the hem, and the jewel-trimmed knife in his belt. "Mayhap you'll get the payment from that rich whore you've been riding in her grand pavilion by the lake."

That Ambert would know of his liaison with Sabra was no surprise; Dear Brother always kept himself abreast of all the gossip. That he would try for the easiest of insults was not unexpected either. Richard held to his smile, refusing to react. He looked at the remains of the goblet and tapped it lightly with his fingers a few times before flicking it over. It made a thump against the wood.

Ambert stared now with raw hate, but mastered himself after a moment, replacing it with a sly look. "Mayhap," he drawled, "mayhap I should see to collection myself. I have heard she is most fair of face. If she will not part with any coin, then she'll trade something else to me instead."

He has everything; why does he need to be cruel?

The answer came from within as Sabra's sweet voice stole gently into his mind. *The cruelty hides the emptiness of his spirit*, she murmured, her voice so clear she might have been next to him. It gladdened him to know that in this dreary place he was not as alone as he'd thought. *Alas for his pain*, she added plaintively.

It was easy enough for her to be kind, she'd not had decades of Ambert's torment, but for her sake Richard decided to modify his initial harsh reply. "You're drunk, Dear Brother, else you could think of better ways to provoke me."

Ambert puffed out a short guttural curse. It had the strange sound of agreement in it. "Oh, but I have, sweet Dickon. Your new whore is a riddle to all who have heard of her. No one knows aught of her, and her people keep to themselves like lepers, speaking to none if they can help it. I would know who she is and who she serves. Before the next hour is gone I'll have a dozen armsmen through her tents to drag her here to give full answer to that riddle."

It was no idle threat, not when he used that tone. By right of his place in the household he had the authority to carry it out and the wit to justify all to the duke later.

"How does *that* please thee?" he demanded.

A few days ago Richard would have swallowed his anger and suffered whatever humiliation Ambert cared to heap upon him to prevent such a disaster.

No more. No more ever again. He's like a boy throwing stones at a chained wolf to show how brave he is. He knows not that this wolf is free.

Richard made his shoulders slump with defeat, let his gaze fall to the floor, and slowly closed the distance between them, his bearing such as to not give any hint of a threat. When he was but a pace away, only then did he raise his head and look his brother full in the eye.

"What would please me, dear Ambert, is for you to forget all about it," he whispered. "Do you mark me?"

Ambert winced as though in pain and drew a hand over his brow. "How—how d-dare you speak thus to me?"

Richard puzzled for a moment over this surprising resistance. Certainly Ambert had more reason to defy his will than would a compliant young girl, but he was still made of the same ordinary flesh. Perhaps drunkenness had befuddled his mind, making him more difficult to influence. Richard bent all his concentration upon his brother, eyes focused so hard and steady he thought he could almost see past the bloated face to the pitted vestige of his soul.

Ambert gave a shudder, breaking into a sweat, and this time he did not look away.

"You will forget all about disturbing the lady by the lake," said Richard, his voice calm, but brooking no argument. "You have no interest for her or her people, none at all."

Dear Brother's lower lip sagged, trembling, but no words came forth.

"Forget her. Completely."

He flinched as though each utterance held the sting of a wasp and still did not look away.

Richard eased back slightly, fascinated a moment by this evidence of his own power, then finally released his invisible hold.

Ambert staggered, clutching at the table to steady himself.

"Have a care, brother, the drink is besting you tonight," said Richard. He was once more standing several yards away. He watched and waited for Ambert's reaction . . . which was only to shake his head as though to clear it. Not one sign of what should have been red-eyed fury. Oh, but this was *most* wonderfully interesting.

"I've not had enough is the problem. What's become of my cup?" He stared peevishly about, but missed his crushed property amid the litter on the table.

"Does my lord the duke send you to fetch me?" Richard inquired, hiding his amusement and satisfaction. This ability to sway others to his will was very useful indeed.

"Please you to wait," grumbled Ambert. "You'll see him soon enough and like it not when you do. You'll like it not at all." He then burst into a harsh laugh, pushed from the table, and tottered back the way he'd come. Down the hall a door closed with a bang; by its sound it was the one to the duke's inner chamber. Ambert would have gone there to apprise the old man of the presence of his other son. Either the wearisome task of waiting would soon end or Richard would be out here the rest of the night.

The two hounds whimpered, still hiding under a far table. Richard bent to look at them.

"Come on, my lovelies. Am I not better company than Ambert? When did I ever kick and curse you, eh?"

Merlin whined, head pressed to the flags, but gave a tentative wag of his tail.

"Come and be friends again. I'll not hurt you." He put forth first his hand, then his will, to see if it might also work on animals. "Come, now, come to heel, there's a good boy. . . ."

Whether it was his voice or his influence that coaxed Merlin out, Richard could not be sure, but after much hesitation the great dog did finally emerge, slowly followed by Prince. With halting steps they came close enough to touch. Richard ruffled their coarse fur, praising and reassuring them. As if shamed by their previous fear of him and wanting to make up for it, they licked his face and hands, tails still tucked, but wagging.

"You're all right, now, aren't you? Good, good lads. What a pity Ambert and I can't get along as well as you two."

They rolled on their backs for him to scratch their bellies, friendship restored. Richard sealed it by finding some choice scraps from the table to give them.

A door opened somewhere. As one, Richard and the hounds swung their heads in the direction of the noise, alert.

Light spilled into the feasting hall from the entry. Richard heard a rustle and grunt from his father's chamber followed by the sound of slippered feet. Perhaps his long wait was nearly over.

"Go on, lads. You won't want to be here." He pushed the dogs off and found a place to stand in the darkness well away from the candle.

A large shadow fell across the floor as his brother's ample frame obscured the entry light. For a moment, Ambert peered across the apparently empty hall, saying nothing before moving forward, his steps hesitant and faltering. He picked up the abandoned candle, holding it out ahead of him.

"Richard . . . ?"

Richard remained quite still.

"Are you there, or have you run away like the craven you are?"

The silence that followed must have convinced Ambert that what he thought was indeed the case, and his courage grew proportionately.

"Well you may run, sirrah, for you are of no worth here," he spat to the room. "The midwife should have strangled thee!"

He turned to go back, but gave a sharp cry when the candlelight shone on Richard, who was suddenly in the way. Ambert started, letting the candle fall, only to see it caught in midair by his brother, who calmly raised it to illumine their faces once more. They were close enough that, had he been so inclined, Richard could have counted the broken veins on his brother's nose. Ambert shivered, and his face twitched into what should have been a scowl, but his fear spoiled the attempt. He jerked his chin in the direction of the hall.

"Fa—Father wants . . ." But he did not seem to be able to finish. His words sounded too thick to escape the trembling portal of his mouth.

"I await only my lord's pleasure, dear Ambert," said Richard evenly.

"Damn you," he choked out in return.

Richard placed the flickering light back in Ambert's shaking grasp. "Have a care, brother. One fallen candle on these rushes could cost you your castle."

A booming voice from down the hall cracked through the still air like a whip. "I would speak with you, Richard!"

Their father's voice. Even the favored eldest son cringed at the sound.

"Let me see you, boy!"

Richard turned and, released from his sway, Ambert hurried ahead to disappear into another twisting of the hall. It had always been one of his greatest skills, not being in the wrong place at the wrong time, and he practiced it now to perfection. Light spilled brightly from the chamber ahead, and like a moth to the destructive flame, Richard went toward it.

The duke's sanctum was quite large. Torches in their sconces along the walls provided some heat for the cheerless room, along with all the light. Their smokes rose high, adding to the soot already coating the ceiling. Several embroidered arras covered portions of the walls. Some stirred gently, doing their work of cutting down drafts coming from the doorways they concealed. Off to the right was a huge oaken table. Benches ran along each side of it, and at the far end where Montague now stood, crouched a massive thronelike chair. No one ever dared to come near it. When he was a child, Richard had once been foolish enough to crawl up and sit there, pretending to be a king of his own castle and lands. His father had seen, and the outcome was a beating of such severity that many thought the boy would not live. Even now as Richard looked at it, a tremor ran through him at the sick-making memory. It had been the first of many other beatings, so many he could not count, but that particular one stood out by its right of place.

The room, full of its vile memories, was empty of people apart from the duke. That was a blessing. At least there would be no witnesses to the coming censure.

Montague d'Orleans was a giant of a man in all ways: in stature, in reputation, and in deed. He was the most powerful man in Normandy, and there was answerable for his actions only to God, and then but rarely. He was a brutal pragmatist, a survivor. He had no time for failure, hating it as if it were a contagious disease that might be spread to him and cause his downfall. Now more than ever before, he had no regard for Richard, for his son had become a carrier of this contagion since the tourney.

"My lord." Richard's greeting was murmured low, and he bowed from the waist delivering it. "Father."

Montague had his back to his son, and did not turn. "Who is it that calls me father?"

Richard stepped into the golden light cast by the torches, dropped to his knees, and spoke the words of old ritual that were required of him. "It is I, Richard, your son. You sent for me and, as ever, I await your pleasure."

"My pleasure? My pleasure!" The old man turned and leveled what Richard could only assume was meant to be a murderous look upon him. Unfortunately, the effect was ruined by the slurring of his voice and a decided stagger as he came forward. He was very drunk. "My pleasure was to have the champion of all the land within my own household. Within my own family."

Richard kept quiet. Comment would only draw out the process.

The old man loomed over his kneeling son, blood in his eye, building in his anger. "Once it was so. By some miracle or witchcraft you were champion, but no longer. Now, I have only shame to distinguish my household. My reputation lies in the dung heap!"

Richard stared straight ahead, keeping a stony face. He could not trade words here as he'd done with Ambert. That would not stop or deflect the flow of bile.

Montague reeled to one side to refill his empty tankard from a keg on the table and swilled back a mighty draught. "Explain yourself, boy."

"I cannot." Richard replied honestly, for although he knew that Sabra had had much to do with the outcome of events that day, he also knew he would never disclose any of it. It would mean immediate death both for him and his lady. "I was beaten."

His father lurched toward him and bent until his face was close; the rank stench of his breath filled Richard's nostrils. "Clearly, you were never beaten enough!" He suddenly righted himself.

Richard saw the blow coming. His reactions were sharper, faster since the changing, and he could have easily avoided it, yet something within him made him hold his ground and brace for it. No stinging open-handed slap, Montague used the full power of his fist. The force of it knocked Richard flat on the floor, but surprisingly, he hardly felt any pain. It was no more to him than a sigh of air on a summer's day.

Am I beyond being hurt or grown so used to it that I feel it not?

He waited a moment, expecting next to be kicked, but the old man drew away and gulped down more drink. Richard got slowly to his feet, brushing at his clothing. He felt cold inside, very, very cold. Like the dead.

"You've disgraced me, brought humiliation to my house," the duke continued. "Wise you were to skulk away afterward. You missed all the sly looks, the hidden laughter from the others when I had to give the purse to that damned bastard pup. That you yielded at all was defaming enough. Couldn't you have had the wit to cede to a full-grown man?"

He stared without expression at Montague.

"Well, boy? Give me answer!"

"The new champion will serve you honorably and with much heart," said Richard, astonished at how steady his voice sounded.

"That is no answer. Why did you yield?"

"He offered me quarter. I accepted rather than—"

"Rather than die," Montague concluded for him. "Aye, showing the world the kind of coward I sired."

Richard clenched his jaw hard to keep back the sudden protest that wanted to spring forth at this unfairness. He'd begun the tourney as one of a hundred other fighters and managed to last until but two remained: himself and the boy. To survive for so long in such a struggle was not the achievement of a coward. He took a deep breath, releasing it slowly. *This is of no matter. There could have been a thousand of us and the duke would still speak to me so.*

"You don't deny it, either. Pah!"

"I am my father's son," Richard muttered. "But what part of you is in me?"

"What say you? What was that?" he snarled, pausing in the act of raising his tankard.

"I await my lord's pleasure," Richard said more clearly, hoping the duke would soon finish his ravings and make his formal dismissal.

"Your lord's pleasure would be to see you dead."

How often has he voiced that wish? It's come true and he knows it not. Richard hadn't lost his life in battle, but in the throes of passion with Sabra to make his rebirth possible—something the old man would never understand.

"You smile? Do you mock me, boy?"

"No, my lord." *I'm five and thirty years, old enough to have sons and grandsons of my own, and still he calls me boy. Is it to belittle me or to keep his own age and death at bay? Or both?* For Richard's father was ancient, being a few years past fifty. Many thought the only reason he'd not yet died was that heaven wouldn't have him, and the Devil didn't want to contest with him for the rule of hell.

But he will die eventually, and I will continue. The realization got him through the next few moments as his father ranted on. Richard no longer heard the words, but looked long at the man whose blood flowed in his veins, the man who had given him life, and saw only another whose cruelty shielded a sad, empty spirit. For all that, Richard could feel no pity, only contempt.

"*Well, boy?*" Montague's last words rang through the stillness of the castle and into Richard's consciousness. "What do you have to say?"

That he'd not listened mattered little; any reply would be the wrong one. "I've nothing to say, my lord."

"Pah!"

The hair abruptly stood on the back of Richard's neck as he became aware they were no longer alone. He could sense another presence here, another drawing of breath, another scent on the smoky air. Out of the corner of his eye he glimpsed the slightest movement of the heavy arras covering the wall to his left. It was not a draught or a trick of the torchlight. Someone had come silently and was listening, watching. Richard relaxed as he comprehended who it was, and knew that there would be no interference.

"My lord, as I have failed thee, I ask leave to depart from your service." There, it was out at last. The old man could rail all he liked, but eventually he must grant his permission. This had been coming for years.

"Ceding again, are you?"

"My lord the duke is above keeping company with those who displease him. I would shame you no more and depart quietly."

"Think you such flattery will make favor with me?"

"I seek no favor—"

"Only escape." The old man backed his way unsteadily to his massive chair and dropped into it, glaring at Richard all the while. "I know what dreams fire you, boy. There's nothing you'd like better than to leave this place. You'd hoped to do it with that bag of tourney gold, but failed. Now you hope to run off with that rich whore camped by the west wall. Aye, there's fitting toil for you, playing whoremaster, or have you sold yourself to serve in her house instead? Will she finish the work you started on the field? Make a eunuch of you to disport with her sodomites?" He paused, apparently awaiting a reply.

Richard could find none to give, but stifled the beginnings of a shiver. It was as though ice had taken the place of all his bones, chilling him from the inside out. The duke was trying to provoke him to make an excuse to punish him, another of his old tricks, but Richard felt too cold for anger. *Sabra, what is the choice I must make?*

But she was silent.

Montague leaned well back in the chair and looked at him over the expanse of his belly, all but smacking his lips at some inner satisfaction. "Well, you can put that out of your mind, boy—I've no intention of releasing you from your oath to me."

Now did Richard manage to find voice again, and it was choked with disbelief. "*What?*"

"You will remain here."

"Why? My lord wishes me dead, banishing me from your house is the next best thing to that."

"Aye, so you can run off to a life of ease with that woman? I'll not have it. I'll not have you nosing after the bitch and the two of you laughing at me for giving you leave to go."

"Wh-what does my lord require of me, then?" It was the question he would be expected to ask, and Richard's guts turned over for he was certain of the answer.

Montague deigned to smile. Unpleasantly. He spoke slowly, softly. "I *require* you retrieve that which you lost: the honor of my house. You will stay here—I'll put you in chains if need be—but you *will* stay until the next grand tourney."

Richard felt a swell of black despair. It surged upon him like smothering death until he remembered himself. Such feelings belonged to the man he had been, not the man he'd become. He was immune to such threats, now. The feeling faded, replaced by new strength.

The duke continued unaware. "There you will fight that damned upstart and kill him—or die yourself in the trying."

I think not. Richard's mouth twitched, the only sign of his amusement.

Montague's bloodshot eyes went narrow, on guard for any hint of an attack; his hand moved to rest on the hilt of his dagger. "You smile again, boy? What pleases you so much?"

"That my lord has such an excellent way with a jest," he replied, mindful of the other ears in the room.

"Jest?" said Montague, his tone beginning to rise.

Richard held his breath, all his attention on the duke. He did as before with Ambert, as before with Ghislaine, pouring all his hard concentration into it, striving this time to get past the monumental barrier of his father's anger, hatred, and drunkenness. A small pain formed behind his eyes from the effort. "Indeed," he whispered after many long moments. "You did but jest, did you not?"

Montague's reply was tardy. Richard held out, the ache in his skull growing, but in the end he got a small, near imperceptible nod in response. His father's wide face was shiny with sweat.

"It was most clever, but now you will release me from your service."

"R—release . . . ?" The old man's lips quivered.

"Say it, my lord, say that you release me. Say that I am free of my oath to you."

And the words came out, halting at first, and then in a steady stream of ritualized speech. "I, Montague, Duc d'Orleans, release you, Richard d'Orleans, from all oaths of fealty and service to my house. You are free to go and make thy way in the wide world, in honor and grace . . ."

"Excellent," said Richard, when it was all finished. "You'll not go back on this. No one will be able to change your mind on it. I shall leave soon, and you'll allow no one to hinder me or the people I travel with. They are of no interest to you; you've better things to worry about. Is your understanding clear on this?"

"Yes . . . I—"

"That is good." Richard withdrew a few steps and waited.

It took only a little time for the duke to regain himself, and when he did his first action was to rise and fill his tankard again, growling like a bad-tempered bear. He shot a belligerent glare at Richard. "Well? Why do you tarry? You've leave to go, take it!"

Richard pressed his hand to his brow, and the ache there lessened. The beguilement had been difficult, but worth it. Relief washed over him, and he recalled the other reason why he'd come. "Then I give you my farewell, Lord Montague."

The old man sneered. For all his lapse bending to Richard's will, he was well recovered back to his original foul humor. "Keep your farewell. I want it not, and will be glad to see you gone."

Richard blinked once at this brusque dismissal. *What did I hope for? A fond embrace? A fallen tear?* Pushing away the old and futile hurt, he bowed deeply and backed a pace or two toward the main door before turning.

"Bad riddance to thee!" Montague threw after him. "You should never have been born."

How often had he heard that one? *Never again, God 'a mercy.* He kept going.

"In all of your miserable life, you've brought me nothing but grief from the very beginning," the duke continued, his voice rising. "I curse the day you were conceived and the day you came forth." It was his favorite torment, though he usually took more time to work up to it. His drunkenness must have altered the pattern. "The day you took my wife from me!"

The effect of this all-too-familiar attack on Richard was immediate and impossible to hide behind his usual wall of silence and nonreaction. He knew where the duke was leading and how impossible he was to stop.

"Better if you had died instead, you murdering—you were the one that did it. You killed your own mother!"

No! I did not kill her! I did not! I did not! His steps faltered as the old agony seized him once more.

"Killed her, I say. Ripped her from the inside and left her screaming with her blood pouring out."

In all the years that he'd been lashed by the tale, Richard had held himself in check. He'd endured every kind of variation, delivered by every kind of utterance from whispered baiting to blistering shrieks, time and time again, knowing that any objection, denial, or rage to the contrary would only make it worse. As a child, he'd seek solitude and weep out his grief; as a man, he'd swallow back the anger to release it on the practice field with fighting, or get drunk.

But *now* . . .

For want of a sword, his hand sought the dagger on his belt. In that moment he wanted nothing else but to stop the tearing rasp of the old man's voice. A quick strike, slide the blade through his throat and watch the blood spurt . . .

He felt the heat sear his face and with it came blinding, unquenchable fury born of the helpless anguish he kept within his soul. Always he'd been able to hold it back—but it was . . . was *different* now.

"Your fault—"

Far, far different.

"You damned—"

His corner teeth . . . budding . . .

"—murdering—"

Richard came to a stop, bewildered by his body's unexpected response to the torment. A hot breath seemed to touch his brow, clouding his vision. The torches burned steadily, but the golden cast of their light appeared to be tainted with crimson. He closed his eyes tight, knowing that they'd gone red as hellfire, and lowered his head, giving in to a shudder as he fought what was happening inside.

"—coward!"

He raised his hands, palms out as though to push the words away, and placed all his thought upon mastering himself. *I will not let him win. Not after all this time.*

"*Your* fault!"

I will be the strong one, not he. But it was so hard. So many, many years of blame to carry, to struggle against. It had ever and always been the one fight he could not win.

Then clear within his mind he heard Sabra's voice, full of love and comfort. *Ah, the poor man. He grieves for her still. He loved her so.*

And suddenly Richard's hot rage cooled. He felt a stillness take hold of his pounding heart, gently slowing it. Holding his breath, he listened for her to speak again, but no more came. What had been said was all; it would have to be enough. Was, indeed, enough. He was in control of himself again and very, very calm.

He'd always believed the old man's anger over his wife's death had been about being deprived of one of his prized possessions. It never occurred to Richard that his father could have loved a woman, might still love her. *If he felt about her as I feel about Sabra . . .* He shook his head at the idea, finding it a difficult thing to take in, then turned and looked at Montague, trying to see him afresh.

But nothing about him seemed different. The duke stood hunched forward, a hand on the table to hold himself steady, his bloated face flushed and mouth set. "Well, boy?" he demanded, once more insisting on an answer to the impossible.

He is the same; it is I who am changed.

"Well?"

Richard shook his head as comprehension seeped into him. "I thought you the greatest in all the land. You were a noble warrior, strong and valiant—and *you* were *my* father. I'd have done anything to show my love for you. I tried everything I could think of to prove it, yet nothing worked. Whatever I did was never enough."

The old man snarled as he poured more ale, yet his disdain meant nothing to Richard. Not anymore.

"I have ever been loyal. I fought and bled and killed for you. I have been a fine and faithful son. That you could never see this makes your loss of me all the greater."

The duke peered at him more keenly now. This was verging on criticism. This was verging on revolt.

"I have seen my father change over the years. I have seen his nobility vanish, his strength turn to cruelty, his valor become bitter self-interest."

The tankard crashed to the floor, spraying ale.

"I've watched him degenerate into the drunken old man who totters before me now. You are pathetic, and the worst of it is that you know it not."

The duke's face went purple. His whole body quivered, and he worked his mouth until white spittle flecked his lips.

He looks like to die, and in truth, I care not.

Montague gave a half-choked bellow and lurched blindly forward, fists swinging. Richard put his arms up to ward them off, but one blow landed full in his face, bloodying his nose. A second followed, but with a speed born of his changing, a speed impossible for a mortal man, Richard caught the massive fist in midair, stopping it dead. He pulled the old man close and, staring eye-to-eye with him, tightened his grip, and began to squeeze . . . hard. He could clearly hear the sound of muscles tearing and bones snapping. The old man's face paled in an instant to a sickly gray, and a grunt of pain escaped him. He tried to pull free. Richard held on. For one of eternity's long, silent seconds the two stayed exactly as they were, father and son striving for control.

"Yield, Montague," he whispered.

"To . . . hell . . . with you." Montague's gray flesh faded to white; his knees began to crumble. Breath hissing, he struggled to stay afoot, pressing to throw off Richard's balance. Richard held firm, until he felt a sudden shifting between them. Montague's eyes gleamed with unholy delight as his free arm made a short, forceful movement.

Richard thought he'd only been struck somewhat more bruisingly than before until the burning started. He looked down and saw the duke had drawn his dagger and put it to use. It was buried to the hilt in Richard's leg, just below its join to his body. The blade had cut deep, severing the flow from his heart. Blood pumped from him like a river.

Its warmth soaked his clothes, then the pain set upon him in earnest, and he fell. He found the floor with a jolt, twisting awkwardly to avoid jarring the dagger. The soot-black ceiling spun once and seemed to swoop down toward him, blotting out the world. He didn't care. Despite all the beatings, humiliations, the thousand daily censures, he'd not foreseen this, not really.

He dares. God in heaven, he dares. He would kill his own son!

Pressing his hands hard against the wound, Richard managed to slow the bleeding. It was bad. On the battlefield he'd seen men die in but a few swift moments from such piercings, their life gushing out to be soaked up by the cold earth. He'd felt such a death once in a vision Sabra had given him. A hard lesson it was and frightening in its reality of pain.

But the agony of his father's act transcended that of the knife in his flesh, and for a time all he could do was lie unmoving as this last betrayal tore him to the soul.

He dimly saw Montague tower over him, wheezing and holding his injured hand . . . but grinning. He was actually grinning down at his dying son.

Sabra, did you see this, too? Why did you not warn me?

Unless a warning was not needed. He was changed. Stronger. The natural way of things held no sway over him, now.

Nor did his father, it seemed.

So that was it.

I'll not grant you this wish, old man.

Richard's fingers gingerly grasped the hilt of the dagger. He hissed at the touch, but held fast. There was no way to prepare himself; hesitation would make it worse, so he simply carried through and pulled as fast as he could.

The shock of it dragged a cry from him even as he dragged the blade clear. More blood flowed, but for naught but an instant before the cut sealed itself up. The burn flared and blazed, then gradually diminished. After a few moments it ceased altogether, and he breathed normally again, marveling at the miraculous healing he knew must be taking place. Sabra had told him such things would be quick. Not pleasant, but quick.

He waited it out, staring up at Montague, who had not budged. Indeed, he was taking vast amusement from Richard's seeming futile efforts to save himself.

He dares to laugh.

Richard's reaction surged up from his deepest being: a rage powered by strength such as he'd never known before, a rage he'd never allowed himself to express. Rage at the lifetime of mistreatment and of blame for something not his fault. He rolled and got his hands under him and pushed the floor away, found his feet, and stood.

The blunt astonishment for this was plain on Montague, his surprise so consuming that he did not move even as Richard closed on him. Richard wrenched him around and slammed him upon the great table, bending him backwards with both hands fastened around his throat.

He knew his eyes were red and his teeth were out, but Richard cared not. All that mattered was the fact that his trembling hands could free him from all the tyranny by snapping Montague's neck as easily as a dry summer twig. He wanted to; he had the power and the will to do so.

Montague gagged and clawed, his heels drumming against the flags. He was helpless, probably for the first time in his life. Panic limned his eyes, and his tongue bulged as he fought to draw air.

Richard squeezed all the more. How little effort it would take to finish things. But within him the beast hungered. He had a better use for the old man . . .

He clawed at the duke's tunic, ripping the stained wool away to bare his throat. The old man cried out as Richard bit down through the thick folds of skin to reach the nectar within.

Your blood is already in me, Father, but you will render more.

Montague did not struggle, perhaps too far gone from being choked.

Richard drank deeply, replacing that which had been taken, relishing the bitter taste of the man's horror.

You wanted a death, dear Father, then I shall deliver it to you.

He would smother that grating voice forever and for him it would be forever. He'd have his freedom—true freedom—once and for all from the past, from a lifetime of misery.

He pulled away to look at Montague, at the face he'd tried so hard not to hate. His father's head lolled weakly away, lips slack, eyes staring.

Richard encircled that fat bleeding neck with his hands, savoring the satisfaction it would bring, the vast, singing joy.

Forever. Think on it!

A dozen times over he set himself to finish things. But each time he refrained, kept himself from taking that last terrible step, delighting in the anticipation for its own sake.

He hovered on the edge for a hundred heartbeats.

Think on it.

For good or ill, this death above all others would be with him for the rest of his life. What a long journey it would be to always carry such a burden. Light for now, but how heavy in a year, a hundred years hence, or a thousand?

Then he came to know he could not, would not be able to bear it. Strong as he was, he was not that strong.

He eased his grip. *You won't win this way, either, old man.*

But the rage still lived and needed expression. He roared, a great, angry, monstrous sound torn from the maddened beast within that reverberated through the chamber, blasting everything else to utter silence. He hauled Montague up from the table and, with a mere flick of his hands, hurled him into his great chair so hard that both nearly crashed to the floor.

The duke roused himself but made not a sound, as much from his awe of Richard as from his injuries. He trembled in his chair, gasping and rubbing his throat. Richard thought that now the old man finally looked different, smaller . . . no, not that, not smaller; it was something else.

Montague was *afraid.*

Yes, it was fear that Richard perceived in those once-hard eyes—cold, naked fear. He'd gone his whole life waiting to see that look but until this moment had never before realized it. And with realization came revelation.

He is a rock, but I am a river. And the river shall triumph always, for a river cannot be pushed, and does not wear away. The heavens shall feed me, renew me forever, and I will be here long after he is gone and forgotten.

Sweet calm returned to his soul in a soothing rush. Richard was master of himself once more. His teeth were normal again, his eyes their usual disturbing wintry blue. He looked at his father and understood suddenly just how close he'd come. How very, very close . . .

So *that* had been the choice.

He shook his head and gave a small laugh. No wonder Sabra had said nothing of what was to happen. How could she? In matters of life and death Richard had to follow his own conscience—and know he would have to live with the results of his actions, for good or ill, always.

"You will never see me again, old man," he said.

Not a murmur from Montague.

"It will be best for all concerned."

Richard turned to leave. This time he made it to the entry door before pausing. There was one last matter requiring his attention.

With preternatural speed he darted toward the arras. He could hear a swift heartbeat now and scent the terror there. Thrusting an arm behind the heavy tapestry he hauled Dear Brother blinking into the light. He squawked as Richard hoisted him off his feet and slammed him against the wall, holding him there with one arm under his chin. Sweating profusely, Ambert began to whimper. There was a new smell in the heavy air of the room. What was it? Ah, yes, Ambert had wet himself.

Richard leaned close and purred a sympathetic noise. "What ails thee, Dear Brother?"

When Ambert made no reply, Richard glanced once over his shoulder at Montague, then back again. "Disappointed I didn't kill him for you?"

Ambert's face told all, confirming what Richard already knew.

"Oh, but you are indeed your father's son."

Richard stepped away, but instead of merely releasing Ambert, he thrust him hard across the room to land in a heap at the foot of the great chair. As this new truth dawned for him, their father's malevolent glare suddenly returned, now directed down at his utterly appalled firstborn.

What comes next is not something I want to see, thought Richard, turning away. It was not likely to be agreeable.

With a short, mirthless laugh, Richard left them to it.

The moonlight was bright outside the castle, bright enough to cast a clear shadow before him as Richard walked. Innumerable stars speckled the heavens, and his breath clouded in the cold spring air. As he neared the campsite at the foot of the castle's west wall, he observed that Sabra's pavilion and the other tents were gone, struck and loaded onto heavy wagons by her people. He approved of the haste; there was no reason to linger. Soon he would join them on their trek to the coast and thence to Britain, to assume a new name and start his new life.

Richard paused for a moment to breathe deep of the night air and take in the beauty of the setting. The moon was still high, its light dusting the stone towers with silver. Except for the usual sounds of night everything was silent about him, as though the land itself slept. Not all those who walked it rested, though. In the dark shadow of the castle he saw Sabra astride her horse, holding the reins of another, waiting for him. Without his new powers he would never have been able to find her.

Were that true, then she would have found me.

Yet he did not go to her, but stood awhile beneath the trees.

She'd been right about saying good-bye. Any parting, whether for an hour or a lifetime, made a change within, and few were aware of the fact. He was glad he'd gone, but at what price?

As he stood hugging the shadows of what had been his only home, the cold hand of staved-off sorrow clawed its way up his body and gripped his throat, shaking him.

It shook him with sudden sharp memories of the childhood he'd survived and gave him a clear knowledge of what his childhood might have been like had his mother lived—and the unbridgeable gulf between the two.

It shook him with the realization of what he had done to his father and what he had wanted to do.

How very, very close . . .

And though he'd not given in to the temptation, he still felt pain. All the lost and lonely years piled upon his shoulders. His knees buckled, and he slumped to the damp earth, head bowed low. How he wanted the pain to stop.

"My love?" Sabra now stood beside him. He'd not heard her approach. "Richard?"

I don't want her to see this.

Then he felt her hand caressing the side of his face; her gentle touch of compassion and kindness shattered his reserve as nothing else could, and he began to weep. Not an easy thing, his first sobs hurt like that dagger. He'd not allowed himself such utterance since childhood. Sabra held him, saying nothing. The worst of it eventually passed, and he regained a measure of composure, but the pain still gripped him.

He glanced up at Sabra. She voiced no question, but the desire for an explanation was in her expression.

"I have killed my father," he finally whispered.

She was silent for a few moments, carefully taking in the red stains and tears on his clothing. "How can this be? You fought, but I know he still lives."

"You know well. I—I . . . did things." Richard wiped his face roughly with the back of his sleeve. From his lips it came away with traces of the blood he'd taken. "The duke lives, yet my father is dead. In my heart I have killed him."

She shivered once, as though feeling his anguish.

"The man I bade farewell to is no longer my father; he is dead. For that loss I must grieve."

Sabra lifted his chin with her fingertips to make him look at her. Her face shone in the moonlight. Her eyes were full of love. "You had to go to him, my Richard, it had to be done."

"Perhaps so."

"I have the Sight, and it showed me what was needed before

you could leave. You may not know it, but tonight was a great triumph, for you have freed yourself from a lifelong yoke, and *you* have done it, not your new powers, not I. This was your greatest victory." She pressed her palm against his chest, over his beating heart, then kissed his forehead.

She was right. He was free. The word rang through his very being like a great bell. Yet with the exultation a deep sadness lay heavy on him.

"It will pass, my love," she said, responding to the words of his soul. "It will pass."

He stood, and for a long time Richard held her tight within his arms, soaking in her warmth and strength, taking it for his own. Another kiss, this time returning it to her own forehead. Holding her hand, he led the way back to the wall where the horses were ground-tethered. Lying at their feet were two great hounds.

"Who are they?" she asked in wonder. "They have no fear of us."

"Old friends of mine," he said, suddenly pleased. "The white one is Merlin and the brindle is Prince. They must have followed me. Good lads, come here and meet your new mistress."

The dogs bounded over, sniffing cautiously. Sabra won them to her in a matter of seconds. "Amusing it is that one of them is named Merlin," she said.

"Why is that?"

"I'll tell you as we ride."

He boosted her up on her horse, mounted his own, and with the dogs trailing along, they set off down the castle's wide hill toward the west and their future. They carefully forded a shallow place in the lake, following the road as it climbed the steep slope of another hill on the other side. The chill breeze ruffled Richard's hair as they reached its crest, and he stopped. He knew this spot well. It was his favorite view of the castle, and he'd seen it in every manner in every season over the years. With torchlights peeping out through the narrow windows, the cold stones would be perfectly reflected in the calm water along with the farmlands and outbuildings around it.

Though she was already well ahead of him he heard Sabra's voice floating back in the still air. "One thing more, my Richard, and I tell you this so that you may one day cast your sadness away and be happy. You will never have the childhood you wanted, you can only have the childhood you had."

Her simple words echoed many times through his mind, and regrettably he knew that they were true.

Nothing would change what had been.

But . . . he could make sure that it did not ruin what was to be.

He spurred his mount to catch her.

And he did not look back.

Chapter Two

Toronto, Canada, the Present

The warm fingers of sleep held him tight and did their best not to let him go, but in the end they slipped away, and his eyes fluttered open in the quiet darkness of his room. For a second or two, he didn't know quite where he was, for his last dream had been comfortable, serene, and not of this place or time. He blinked sluggishly and wondered what exactly it was that had stirred him from slumber. A drowsy glance at the glowing green numerals of his clock radio told him that it was not the alarm. What then? He was normally a deep sleeper, even at night, and this unknown interruption irked him. Damn it, but he'd put head to pillow not more than twenty minutes ago. Then, distant in the house, he heard it again.

As he fought to full wakefulness, Richard Dun reached for the bedside lamp and flicked it on, wincing against its soft golden luminescence. The dim light demolished the gloom of his bedroom and seeped through the half-open door into the hallway beyond. The noise that had disturbed him came from out there somewhere. He couldn't quite place it and knew that he should be able to, that for some reason it was important.

It was not the sound of an intruder who had somehow gotten

past the house security. Even without clamor Richard would have sensed such a person long before he heard him. This disturbance was mechanical and muted, as if coming from far away. Definitely not a fire or burglar alarm, but something very similar and just as urgent. Then with a cold swoop of dismay he realized exactly what it was, and was suddenly quite wide awake and moving.

The sound repeated as though in reproach for his tardiness. He arose quickly, pulling a long blue bathrobe over his naked body, tying the belt loose around his waist as he hurried from his bedroom, padding silently along the hall. Down the stairs he rushed toward his office and his computer. It was from there the sound originated.

He didn't bother with lights this time for he could see well enough without and was now fully alert. The pale glow of the computer screen spilled out like a beacon to guide him, pulsing gently in the gloom. That was another disturbing thing. It shouldn't have been pulsing; it should have been on the screen saver. The sound grew in intensity as he approached and, rounding the corner of the doorway, hit him with its full force. It wasn't really loud, simply insistent and impossible to ignore, like the cry of a baby. Then he saw the screen, and it confirmed what he already knew. His stomach turned to ice.

The screen was blank save for one thing, a letter, flashing on and off, the letter *S*.

Richard dropped heavily into the leather office chair and cut the sound. It was Stephanie, an emergency e-mail. This was the private alarm system he'd set up just for her, her cry for help to use when everything else failed. In all the years since he'd arranged the program, she'd never had cause to employ it. In fact, she had laughed when he'd explained it to her, chiding him for being such a worrier, then gently listened and promised that if she was ever in trouble she would use it. She'd understood the deep caring behind his worry.

"But I'll never need it," she said lightly, so full of sweet innocence that she honestly believed herself.

He knew too much of life and she not enough, but he did not

gainsay her, not on this of all days. Not for the world would he hurt her more than he'd done already.

And she kissed him chastely on the cheek, and they went back inside to her wedding reception, she to her new husband, he to his own gut-wrenching sadness. Yet another that he had loved and lost, that he'd had to give up because of his nature and fate. Immortality did indeed have its harsh price.

Richard closed his eyes and sank his head into his hands from the photographically clear recollection. He thought that he'd forgotten the pain of her loss, that he'd grown beyond wanting her so much and that his heart was all healed. Wrong.

But this was no time for self-pity or sad reflection. Stephanie using this method of contact meant that something was awfully, terribly amiss. She had all his phone numbers, and could get in touch with him at any time no matter where he might be on the globe. Why had she not simply called? She would have—unless she feared a line tap at her end. That was entirely possible.

Richard punched in the access code to tell the computer to begin the complex retrieval of the message. He chafed at the brief wait; then it was on the screen, a scattering of random-seeming numbers and symbols. He hit one last command key, and the mess instantly deciphered itself into readable words.

Richard, something is wrong. It's lots of little things—gates left open, mail coming late, and there's been a lot of static and clicks on the phone. Luis says to ignore them but I think it's Alejandro. I don't know what to do. I'm afraid. Can you help us? S.

He read it twice, his mouth going dry. For Stephanie, always cool-headed and so self-possessed, this was close to gibbering panic. Stephanie, Luis, Alejandro, how those names brought the memories crowding back upon him. Such memories. He rubbed his eyes reflexively and entered a simple response to the plea.

Of course. On my way ASAP. Hold on. R.

How in hell had Alejandro found them? Richard had set their new lives up using every trick he'd ever learned and a few he'd invented himself. A vast expense, but worth it where Stephanie and the children were concerned.

Richard checked the miniature clock face at the bottom corner of the screen. It read six minutes short of four A.M., confirming the temporary futility of his reply. Nothing was flying at this hour, nor would be for several more. By the time he woke people up and arranged for a charter, the commercial flights would be running. Would Stephanie know that? She must, but it was nearly three in her area, and he knew how worry and lack of rest could erode common sense and feed one's fears in the darkest hours of night. He could picture her hovering by the glow of her own computer screen, biting her lip, waiting for his answer to come.

She'd have it now. His turn to wait for her to respond.

Two minutes crawled by. He gave in to impatience and hammered out another message.

Tell me more, he sent.

Another minute. Then: *Take too long. I don't want Luis to know I've asked for your help.*

Well, that explained her desire for secrecy. Her husband Luis, despite all civilized protests to the contrary, must still possess a lingering apprehension about Richard. Understandable. It would take a most remarkable man indeed not to be jealous of his wife's one-time lover. After the marriage Richard had certainly never given Luis cause to doubt Stephanie's faithfulness, nor had she. She took monogamy very seriously indeed, but some men were born insecure. Stephanie was aware of it and reluctant to stir things up, especially now if Alejandro was back.

Get to a public phone and call me. Richard demanded, craving more details.

I don't dare leave the house. Don't call here, either. Think the lines are tapped. Just hurry.

Will be on the first flight in if I have to bump the pilot himself. I'll be there in the morning. Noon latest.

Nonono. Come to house at NIGHT!

Hurry, but wait???

Make it look like one of your visits. I'm sure we're being watched. Safer for all.

Tell me more, he repeated.

The reply was quick in coming. She sent only one frustrating line:

Tomrow nite Luiis awake havve too go

He frowned at the haste the misspelled words implied. Why was she afraid of keeping this cry for help secret from her own spouse? Was it to protect herself from his reproach or spare Luis's ego? Probably a combination of the two. It was an old, old dance.

Richard had seen a thousand and more variations of such tensions between couples in as many years, taking all forms, ranging from mild annoyance to violent murder, inspired by insecurity or obsession or both, resulting in infinite degrees of soul-destruction. It was love's dark side, having transmuted from initial delight with one's partner into a form of mutual slavery, something Sabra had wisely banished between herself and Richard from their very first night together. She'd apparently been less successful with Luis. Why in God's name did people let themselves get caught in so intimate a trap? And choose to stay? Fear of loneliness, perhaps, but there were worse fates than being alone. Most of the time, he guessed, they didn't know any other way to live, couldn't even imagine it.

But Stephanie had always been so strong within herself and independent. That was one of the many things he'd loved about her. However motivated she might be to spare Luis's feelings, for her to be snared the same as so many others angered and saddened Richard. How could she let herself change? How could Luis do that to anyone he professed to love?

Richard made himself break off his speculation. What's done was done. Much as chivalry and preference inspired him to take Stephanie's part, he did not know all the facts. He was, in the end, an outsider to their marriage and would ever be so. Basing such imputations toward her husband on a single line of words only revealed to Richard how deep his own feelings still ran for her.

Stephanie was long married to another and gone. He could be a good friend to her now, but nothing more. Sabra's words often came back to him over the years, her tender warning against becoming too attached to another's swift-passing life.

But dammit, time and again, he just couldn't help himself.

Stephanie . . . Luis . . . Alejandro.

And himself.

It was all Bourland's fault.

There had been an embassy party some dozen years before. Richard was recently arrived in Toronto, complete with a new life background and in need of VIP contacts to establish his security business in the right levels. Such a gathering was the perfect means to do so, otherwise it was the last place he would willingly take himself. His height, crown of blond hair, and good looks made him memorable, and there might still be some aging political codgers around from the last time he'd opted for a moderately high-profile position. If he was spotted, then he could always pass himself off as his own son or grandson. It wouldn't be the first time, but it was often difficult keeping his stories (and generations) straight.

One of his past connections in Britain had recommended him to Philip Bourland, who held a nondescript civil service post in the Canadian government. Out of habit Richard had researched him prior to their first meeting, turning up a long, if somewhat bland career—that did not precisely fit the man. He found Bourland's drawling speech pattern and lazy demeanor were at odds with his sharp blue eyes, and the expensive, hand-tailored suit on his back certainly did not jibe with what should have been a humble salary. After a few minutes of hypnotic questioning—which Bourland never later remembered—Richard confirmed his suspicions. Bourland was rather more than a simple civil servant when it came to his range of government duties. He'd created a unique niche for himself within the various hierarchies, and over the course of time he proved to be an exceedingly valuable contact indeed.

But these were still the early days yet. A slight nudge of a suggestion and Richard secured an immediate liking between them. That would probably have happened anyway; they were similar enough in attitude and goals to assure it. Long after his initial suggestion wore off Richard became aware of a trust and a deeply felt kinship he felt for Bourland that surprised him, though he made no mention of it. It was the way Bourland reminded him of certain knights whom he'd served with in the past. Bourland was honest, responsible, and deeply committed to ideals beyond his own personal ambitions. A rare combination in any age. Definitely a man to be cultivated.

Bourland proved to be most cooperative and useful from the start, coming up with the idea of their attending the embassy party himself and offering to extend his invitation to cover Richard.

"I'm not sure it's my sort of function," Richard hedged. "I'm trying to set up as a security consultant. Low visibility is preferable for someone like me."

"There'll be hundreds of people there far more concerned with you noticing them than the other way around. What's one more man in a tuxedo?"

He had a point there.

"Besides," Bourland drawled on, "while they're all jockeying to get next to the politicians, I'll introduce you to the people who really run things around here."

That decided it. "Then I'll be glad to come, thank you."

"Bring a date if you like."

Richard flashed a regretful smile. "I haven't been in town long enough to make any friends."

"We'll cure that tonight, then. If she likes you, you can borrow my secretary for a dance or two. Normally I'd be taking my daughter, but she's studying for a law exam or something, so Stephanie fills in for her at social functions. They're both good girls."

Richard took that last little tidbit to mean Bourland's secretary was hands off. Fine with him, he had to concentrate on work, anyway.

He arrived on time, found his name had indeed been included on the guest list, and drifted into the crowd, artfully avoiding offers of champagne and hors d'oeuvres. His practiced eye picked out the security people as a matter of course before Bourland found him and began introducing him around. From that point Richard was all affable business, shaking hands and committing a dozen or more names and their attendant jobs to memory for later recall and use. He projected the polished charm and confidence necessary to such encounters and made sure (with a subtle hypnotic nudge here and there) that the people he met would remember him as well—with a very positive cast to the memory.

Throughout the evening Richard had purposely avoided sitting at Bourland's table so as to skip the whole awkward business about not eating and drinking. Several young women congregated there, and one of them broke away to join them now on the edge of an area set aside for dancing, lightly taking Bourland's arm. He did the honors and introduced his secretary.

"Assistant really," he said, presenting her to Richard. "More. God knows how I'd manage without her. She's an absolute gem."

Stephanie Andersson held out her hand for Richard to shake, but he took it gently and kissed it instead, adding a gallant little bow that put him very close to her. She didn't flinch or go self-conscious at his courtly manner, as many women in the New World were wont to do, and merely smiled, gracious as royalty.

"A pleasure, Mr. Dun," she said in a honey-smooth voice.

Richard did not reply. He was far too busy drinking her in with his eyes. She was a vision. Her milky skin and black hair, cropped close like a latter-day Mia Farrow, were most striking when matched with the palest blue eyes that he had ever seen. Her ancestors had come from Iceland, he later learned.

Her hands were long and slender, the nails short and perfectly manicured. She wore a light silver sheath of a dress and clearly very little else beneath it except for a spectacular figure. He noted almost in passing her lack of jewelry, and knew instinctively that she was well aware she needed none. A vein pulsed gently in her throat.

"I have a distinct feeling that I'm rather superfluous here." Bourland's voice cut through the uncanny silence that had established itself between them in the midst of the party noise.

Richard became aware that he was still holding her hand near his mouth, and disconcerted, released it and straightened.

"Let me know if you need a ride home," Bourland said to her in a dry tone.

"I will," she murmured. She continued to smile at Richard.

Bourland was a perceptive man. He shot Richard a piercing look, one brow slightly raised. The message was clear: *Make her cry and I'll murder you.* He then kissed her briefly on the cheek and disappeared into the swirl of people, leaving them alone.

Richard made a slight motion toward Bourland's retreating back. "Are you and he—?"

Stephanie shook her head, her smile turning rueful. She'd obviously fielded this question many times before. "No, nothing like that. We're close; my late mother and his late wife were good friends, and I'm best friends with his daughter. He's more of a father or an uncle to me than anything else."

"Ah." Now, that was excellent news.

"And he's usually rather more protective."

"Indeed?"

"He always warns me about the predators who work these parties looking for a tasty morsel like myself."

Richard pursed his lips, then puffed out a single soft laugh. How very, very apt. "Well, perhaps he trusts me to be a gentleman with you."

Her gaze flicked over him, appraising and approving. "I certainly hope not."

"Ah," he said again, which seemed to be more than enough for the moment.

"Do you dance?" she asked. The music, geared toward the preferences of a mature crowd, was balanced somewhere between slow big band and jazz. It had enough of a beat to attract couples onto the floor.

"I've picked up a few steps in my misspent youth," he modestly admitted.

"Show me," she said. From anyone else it would have been an order, but from her it was a guileless request that only a fool would refuse, and Richard was no fool.

He recalled the time he once told Oscar Wilde about dancing being a vertical expression of a horizontal desire. Never before had he felt so right about that particular observation as he swept the beautiful Stephanie into his arms. She followed his lead as though they'd rehearsed for years.

And the rest of the night passed for him in that wonderful magical lightness that is the start of falling in love.

Stephanie had not needed a ride home. Not from Bourland, anyway.

They dated for months, but despite the warm intimacies of bed, intense mutual affection, and—for Richard—occasionally feeding from her, nothing permanent was ever established between them. That, of course, was an impossibility.

Stephanie remained unaware of Richard's true nature; he made sure of that. It was for the best for them both. Over the course of centuries he'd had many lengthy affairs with exceptional women, though none of them could ever approach the wholeness of bonding he shared with Sabra. Whether it was mentioned or not, most of those women sensed or knew he wasn't entirely free. The ones who wanted more from him he gently discouraged by means of hypnosis, seeing to it that they always parted as friends. In Stephanie's case, even for her, he could make no exception no matter how much his heart ached.

She'd wanted marriage and children, neither of which Richard could provide. Even with hypnotic help to ease things, the blunt fact of it hurt her deeply, and their relationship entered a long cooling stage. Though he would have liked continuing things for decades, her biological clock was running, so he finally stepped back. It did not take her long to meet another man at another embassy party.

Thus did Luis Trujillo enter her life. Bourland made the introductions then, as well. A CEO in a major coffee exporting business, Luis was charming and intelligent, tall, with dashing good looks and gracious humor. He fell for Stephanie in that hard and heavy way that only a Latin can, courting her with tender and wholehearted attention. Talk of marriage was almost immediately in the air.

Richard made it his personal business to check Luis's background and found it disgustingly clean. Colombian by birth, he made his permanent home in Toronto. His years at Harvard getting a business degree had solidified his connections in the international community through its own "old boy network." He came from a good family that eschewed the easy profits of drugs for a more honorable and safer trade. He was wealthy, but not ostentatious about it, well-liked by his peers, and even his ex-girlfriends had kind things to say of him. Though none would recall being questioned on such intimate matters, Richard ascertained from them that Luis's sexual habits were healthy, his attitude toward his lovers considerate and gentle.

It would be an excellent match if Stephanie decided to accept his suit.

Damnation.

She gave Richard a final chance. She came to him in one last achingly unhappy night, waiting, wanting for him to ask the question, and he had once more simply not asked it. Instead, they made love slowly, with infinite care and sadness, each knowing that it was the last time, and each wanting to remember it, remember it forever. She kissed him in the morning, and held him tight, pressing her lithe body against him.

Still he said nothing.

Tears silently flowing, she left. Instead of a question, she had gotten an answer.

Richard, relegated now to the role of friend, eventually heard through Bourland all the painful details as Stephanie allowed herself to wholly fall in love with Luis. The wedding date was announced shortly after, and Richard had truly been happy for her, though he also carried regret heavy in his heart.

He'd tried to warm to Luis, but found it difficult, putting it down to understandable jealousy for still loving Stephanie himself. For her sake he put on a convincing show of cordiality and managed to attend the wedding with good grace. Why, he hardly felt a twinge when Bourland, standing in for her long-dead parents, gave her away.

As always, things became easier with the passage of time, especially after the birth of her first child, Michael, a close eight months after the wedding. To some, he'd arrived with unseemly haste; to Stephanie he was a greatly longed-for joy. Much to Richard's delight, he was named as the boy's godfather. The christening photo of him holding the baby had a central place on his work desk. Two years later, he once more stood in the church as godfather to her twin girls, Elena and Seraphina, and another photo adorned his desk. He couldn't have been happier or more proud than if he'd been their father himself. Stephanie documented their childhood with hundreds of pictures, always sending duplicates to Richard along with plenty of stories.

The good days were short-lived, though. Three years into the marriage, in a messy and highly publicized sting operation, Luis's export business was revealed to be little more than a cover for another far more lucrative one. Within the bags of coffee beans that arrived regularly from his home country was another cargo, that white mistress of energy and despair, cocaine.

Luis seemed relieved to be caught and quickly turned Queen's evidence, hoping for sanctuary in Canada. His story was that he was little more than an unwilling pawn paid to look the other way on certain shipments. The true kingpin of the operation, the real drug lord, was his brother, Alejandro.

Left with a small fish instead of the big one, the Queen's prosecutor wanted nothing to do with Luis, no matter how eager he was to save his skin. He was richly cooperative and helped to shut down or seriously damage a dozen other drug operations, but couldn't convince the authorities to provide him with sufficient protection. Death threats from the raging Alejandro came regularly by phone and mail. In desperation, Stephanie had called Richard, begging him to do something, anything to protect them all.

He was furious with Luis, of course, but even more so with himself for not discovering the truth earlier. Had he been more thorough in that background check, he could have spared Stephanie from making a hideous mistake. Too late now. Her chosen lot was to stand by her husband, for she did still love him. With three small children and a spouse powerless to shield them, Richard could no more refuse her than stop his own breathing.

He did not merely pull strings, he hauled them until his hands bled, calling in and promising favors with reckless abandon. Once the prosecutors had squeezed every last drop of information possible from Luis, they agreed to release him into Richard's custody. Bourland had also brought his silent but massive influence to bear, and between the two of them they managed to make the whole family disappear.

At his own expense Richard set up their quiet transplantation to Texas. New names, new backgrounds, new location, new jobs, their past was utterly buried.

Or so they had all thought.

Richard now stared intently at the screen as it scrolled with information long forgotten on the Trujillo case. What had he missed? How could this breach have happened? He racked his brains for any detail that he had overlooked. He'd missed nothing. They had been perfectly hidden, perfectly safe, and yet, somehow, Alejandro had found them. Over the years he had patiently searched and searched from the safety of his Colombian fortress, and finally . . .

In other witness protection programs it was often the witness himself who gave away his location to the hunters by reverting to old habits and preferences. Some had even been foolish enough in their enforced isolation to openly contact old friends and family. Though Luis may have been easily intimidated by brother Alejandro into his crimes, he wasn't a stupid man. He'd been warned again and again what to avoid. He liked French cooking, but switched to Italian restaurants. He was a great soccer fan, but would only attend basketball games. The same rules applied to Stephanie. She had a passion for ice skating, but abandoned it for horseback riding. Her love of rock concerts was restricted to watching them at home on cable. They'd both been more than careful, not just for themselves, but for the sake of their children.

Could Bourland have possibly slipped up? Certainly not in an intentional way, for Stephanie was a second daughter to him, but perhaps in some passive sense. Alejandro was determined enough to make an example of his brother and capable of arranging the most astronomical of bribes in the right places. All he needed was one person able to get to the crucial records of his case. But Philip Bourland had carefully obliterated everything concerning the relocation. Only he and Richard knew the details; nothing was on paper or in any computer.

Then it came to him in a cold white light of sickening realization.

There would be phone records of the few and far between long distance calls.

And mail.

Alejandro had no need to search the rest of the world for his brother; he had only to watch Richard and Bourland. The postal service would have been the easiest to crack. Even without a return on an envelope all he had to do was have someone check all the cancellation stampings and note their origin. He would have them all traced. Phone company records could be gotten to by any moderately talented hacker, and Alejandro could afford to buy the best. It would take him a long time, for he couldn't keep at it steadily without being spotted. And then there was the lengthy, ongoing task of sifting out anything useful from the irregular accumulation of data, but he was a patient man. He would have been at it for all these years, looking for patterns, comparing Richard's records to Bourland's and eventually finding what he wanted. A little on-site investigation in Texas, and he'd have an exact address fast enough.

The most insignificant of details could have led Alejandro to his goal. As resignation seeped in down to the bone, Richard saw the truth of it, and his heart sank with the knowledge that he'd once more failed Stephanie. He'd let sentiment get the better of his judgment. He should have severed *all* ties to her. Harsh for everyone, but safer, much safer.

Their cover was blown, and he had to move fast.

Richard snapped out of his reverie and glanced at the clock on his computer screen. Nearly an hour had passed. It was still early, but he was close to the margin of actually being able to do something constructive concerning transportation. The problem with the rest of the diurnal world was its inability to fit itself with any sort of convenience to his own personal timetable.

He made one call and informed the voicemail of his travel agent that he would urgently need to leave for Dallas as soon as a flight—any flight—became available. He left his cell phone number, then settled in front of his computer screen. First he wrote an e-mail to Deborah Heinrich, his secretary, apprising her of his sudden trip and lack of a solid return time. He hazarded that he might be away for at least a week. She was used to such disappearances by her employer and would reschedule appointments accordingly.

Then he copied all the files, both official and otherwise, concerning Alejandro, dropping the disk into a lead-lined pouch that went into his briefcase. Leaving the computer pulsing gently, silently in the gathering dawn, he locked the case and went to his bedroom to pack what few things he would want for his trip. Long practice meant that he inevitably took little: a change of clothing, shaving kit, passport, a walletful of credit cards, and some loose American cash. If the trip proved a long one, he could always buy whatever else he needed.

Once showered and dressed, he wound his way down to the Jaguar E-Type slumbering in his garage, opened the trunk and deposited the briefcase, carelessly flicking his overnight bag in on top of it.

His mouth twitched as he slammed the lid shut.

Oh, for an early flight.

The trip to Pearson Airport was thankfully uneventful. For once, there was no construction to delay the flow of dawn traffic through which the E-Type Jag moved with catlike ease, slipping past the lowlier vehicles, heading away from the rising sun. It promised to be a hot and brilliant day, and even through the dark tinted windows of his car, Richard felt his skin prickle in protest at the coming light. Had he remembered sun block? Yes, there it was, reassuringly in his coat pocket as always. How easeful it would be to go back to the days when he'd fully shielded himself with armor before departing on a quest. It may have been like wearing an oven, but there was nothing to match metal and leather for stopping a deadly sunburn.

His cell phone came to sudden life, warbling insistently. He flipped it open, cradling it to his ear. A voice on the other end of the line identified itself as belonging to Sasha with Ulysses Travel. For a brief second, his mind raced until he registered her face in his imaginings. She was a pretty young thing, tousle-haired and wide of smile, with freckles. How he loved her freckles. He might have been interested in her, as she certainly was in him, but something always stopped him from pursuit. For an instant he wondered what it could have been, and dismissed the thought. He had enough on his mind without pondering the intricacies of his admittedly flexible conscience. Sasha's voice purred in his ear, turning her bald facts into a lush seduction, not unlike listening to Marilyn Monroe give a weather report.

"The first available flight is at seven twenty-five from terminal three and gets you into Dallas at nine fifty-one. The best they have is business class."

"No first?"

"Doesn't exist on this one. It's Canadian."

Richard scowled, his eyes following the graceful curve of the road as he left the Q.E.W. and headed north on 427.

"And the price will be pretty steep for such short notice," she added.

"Just put it on my account as usual and book me in."

A pause at her end. He thought he could hear the swift clicking of her keyboard as she worked. "It's set up. You can claim your ticket at the counter."

"Well done, thanks."

Her voice murmured back to him, loaded with what he was sure she thought was subtle innuendo, "My pleasure, Mr. Dun. Whatever you want."

He smiled as he slid the E-Type out of the center lane to pass a gently rusting Camaro, and flipped the phone shut. Why was it that each succeeding generation thought that it was the one that had first discovered sex? If only they knew. His long existence at vampiric unlife had taught him many things, but most of all it taught him that in the whole of the world, there was *nothing* new.

He pushed the accelerator to the floor, feeling his heart leap at the pure power he controlled. What wonderful cars these were. A quarter century gone and he'd still not tired of the model. He surged past the other traffic, safe in the knowledge that no speed cop would be able to give him a ticket, one of the advantages of his hypnotic ability, and was soon at the required terminal. He parked in his usual reserved space, and took out the scant baggage he'd packed. Then he locked the door, activated the alarm, and was gone.

The land throbbed in the heat. Not a breath of wind stirred the air. The sun glared down from the noon sky, daring anything to move, and nothing took up the challenge. The song of cicadas rasped loud in pure concert.

Richard was surprised that he wasn't burning. Clearly, the combination of a long overcoat, fifty-plus sun block, sunglasses, and a wide-brimmed Stetson worked well for him. Sweat prickled on his upper lip, though, and ran down salty into his mouth. He should have been blistering by now. Best not to push things. He'd be of no help to Stephanie if he let himself get careless in the open furnace of a Texas summer.

He had difficulty making out the lines of her vast low house in the heat shimmer. Determined to get under its shade, Richard started toward the building, moving silently, as only he knew how. Dust spiraled up from his boots in tiny talcum gusts as he stepped carefully between rocks and clumps of cactus until reaching the white edge of the gravel driveway. He caught a single flash of movement as a lizard scurried frantically under a stone, then heard the solitary scream of a turkey buzzard circling impossibly high in the pale blue above.

Richard had watched for a long time before breaking cover, satisfied that the whole area was clear of all intruders except for himself. It seemed safe enough to announce his presence. He stepped carefully onto the back porch, grateful for the relief of the sheltering overhang that ran around the whole of the house. He knocked at the flimsy screen door, making quite a racket as it banged in place, and waited.

No one answered. The inner door beyond the screen remained unopened. The knob would not turn in his hand.

The window shutters, once a proud deep shade of blue, now faded to the same color as the sky, were tightly closed, blocking any view within. Not unexpected if Stephanie anticipated trouble.

He tried one gingerly. It was locked from the inside. He did not attempt to force it, as he easily could, but moved instead around to the front of the building and its large, ornately carved door.

That was a new addition since his last visit. Its quasi-medieval style didn't match with the informality of the rest of the place, but it did look sturdy. He had seen one like it somewhere else, in some other time he could not immediately recall. The memory—or lack of it—bothered him. He tried the heavy iron handle, but found it, too, was sensibly locked.

"Stephanie?" He knocked firmly enough to be heard through the thick oak. His heart beat fast with impatience to see her again. Perhaps she was no longer his, but he couldn't help his feelings or his anxiety for her. He needed to know that she was all right.

The cicadas turned up the volume, thwarting his effort to listen for sounds within the house. The damned things were everywhere, surrounding him, screaming in their frenzy of noise. But screaming what? The buzzings rose and fell with annoying irregularity, a language he did not know and could never learn.

Against the aged blue paint of the door he noticed a streak of bright red rust running down from one of the bolts that held the great hinges in place. Once aware of it, he saw another, and another. Instead of a long dried trickle, the rust trails were still fresh and liquid, as though from a recent rain. But it couldn't have rained here for weeks. Entranced by the anomaly, he watched the red threads dance their way down the furrowed wood. Amazing that even here, in this arid heat, iron rusted so.

The trickles thickened, grew darker and more substantial in their flow.

That was wrong . . . very wrong.

The longer he stared the worse it got, until a steady stream of red welled forth. It made a viscous pool near his boots, and he stepped backward to avoid it.

Oh, no.

Now thin red streaks ran from the cracks between the boards of the door, which had begun to shudder. He sensed some great force pressing against it, trying to break free. The stout wood beams, fused together by metal and age, were actually bending outward like so much rubber.

No.

As they bent, more streaks appeared and more rust flowed forth. Only it wasn't rust, he could see that now.

He could smell it.

All but taste it.

Dear Goddess, no!

The door bellied out to the breaking point, and the buzz-saw rasp of the cicadas sliced into his head, and the red streams ran swift, gathering on the planks of the porch in gleaming lakes that blazed in the sun like fire. He went suddenly weak from the unbearable heat and fell to his knees, one hand out to keep from dropping flat. He clutched his free arm against his heaving stomach in a vain attempt to still the abrupt cramp there.

The closeness of the flow filled all his sight. It covered his supporting hand; the dark stains crept up his sleeve and soaked through to his skin. He made himself straighten and brought his trembling fingers to his lips.

Despite the pain, he felt his eyes flush red with vampiric lust, his manhood going hard, pushing urgently against his clothes; his corner teeth were fully extended. The rich scent around him teased and tormented his hunger, awakening his beast.

No!

Then the thick boards of the door groaned and abruptly split into kindling that shot past him with deadly force. A great, warm wave crashed into him and over him, sweeping him back. He thrashed for balance. His mouth was full of the stuff, and he roared, raising his hands as though to catch more as a second surge burst forth from the house like a sea tide. It overbore him, and he fell splashing as it swept him away. It was miles deep now, the undertow trying to pull him under.

The cicadas screamed, and the buzzard shrieked high overhead as the scarlet sea drowned him, and he tasted it, *how* he tasted it.

It was blood . . .

And it was *good.*

Chapter Three

Richard awoke with a heart-hammering start as his flight was called in the business lounge. Sweat slicked his face. He could smell his own cold fear and looked around quickly to see if anyone had noticed. Clearly no one had. The click of computers and the low voices of last-minute calls to the office or home hummed through the air. The normal humans surrounding him had no time to spare from their own private crises for a solitary traveler having a restless nap in his chair.

He moved hurriedly out of the patch of sunlight that had crept up on him unawares. His body was geared for sleeping late into the day, so giving in to the needs of interrupted rest was understandable, but the dream . . . Whatever was waiting for him in Texas had him thoroughly alarmed—or maybe it was just the prospect of another hated flight. He'd see it through, of course, to get to Stephanie, but that didn't mean he had to like it.

Still shaky, he picked up his carry-ons and made his way to a rest room. The face that glared apprehensively back at him from the mirror was even paler than usual. He splashed water on the sweat, and washed his hands carefully, illogically checking his cuffs for stains. Damn, but he could still almost smell the blood.

A dream, my lad, and nothing more, he told himself. He did not possess Sabra's Gift of Sight, and was therefore mercifully spared glimpses of the future—or futures—but oftimes hideous dreams did plague him. Anxieties welling up from his subconscious, Freud had once told him. Richard took them seriously as warnings. He'd seen too much not to, but how frustrating it could be when unable to carry out immediate action against them. That was yet hours away when the sun was gone.

He dried off with a paper towel that felt like fine emery paper, snagged his bags, and left for the long nervous walk through that awful tunnel to the waiting plane.

He approached the yawning door of the winged beast, and a pretty attendant checked his boarding pass. She must have assumed from his demeanor that he'd never flown before, and also could not read, for she slowly enunciated the information that he was two rows down on the left.

Richard gave her a wan smile and moved to his seat. He stowed his meager baggage in the overhead bin, and slumped wearily next to the window. If anything could be considered fortunate in his situation it was the seating, since it gave him some control over the light coming in. When allowed to do so, he would pull the plastic shade down. In the meantime, he settled back to try, yet again, to relax and let these highly trained people do what they were so highly trained to do.

The plane, filled with happy, stressed, sleepy, and/or oblivious travelers, taxied to its allotted takeoff point, and Richard found himself gripped by the too-familiar heart-racing panic. His rational mind could understand its source, after all; the horrors of that decades-old air disaster he'd survived were still with him. Should it happen again he knew he would probably not be killed, no matter what might happen to the rest of his poor flightmates, yet the terror remained, threatening to overwhelm him. He pushed the memory away, breathing deeply, and reminded himself that the pilot didn't want to crash any more than the rest of them.

As if to gainsay his thoughts, a surge of accelerating power pushed him back in his seat and, obedient to his fear, Richard counted quietly up to sixty. It was an excruciating mantra, but seemed to help. Once past that magic number all would be well for him—or as close as he could get to well given the circumstances.

How he hated, truly *hated* flying.

A sudden loss of height wrenched his guts, waking Richard from an unexpected second sleep. He swallowed back his unease and grimaced. He'd been like a soldier in a foxhole, napping while under fire. The plane was at last on the descent to the Dallas/Fort Worth Metroplex and near the end of this particular piece of torture. This time he'd been spared further bad dreams—or at least from remembering them—but he still felt like a crumpled newspaper ready for the dustbin.

The pretty attendant marched along the center aisle, stopped opposite Richard, leaned across with a smile, and lifted the window shade. He flinched visibly as the southern sun crashed into his part of the cabin. She noticed his discomfort, and apologetically explained.

"FAA regulations."

Richard nodded grimly and shifted to the vacant aisle seat next to him, out of the sun's direct glare. Then the plane banked steeply for its final approach. Far too steeply, he thought, gripping the armrests. Soon it would all be over, and he'd be safe in the confines of the arrivals area, picking up his rental car and driving to his place at New Karnak.

The plane tires squealed as their stillness was rudely disrupted by the rushing tarmac, and reverse thrust pushed Richard forward. The plane slowed quickly and taxied to its terminal slot. He glanced at his watch and saw they were slightly ahead of schedule; it was a quarter before ten in the morning in this time zone. He stayed in his seat, deliberately not joining the crush of tourists and native Texans streaming off the plane. Those not in business suits were in the practical local uniform of light cotton shirts and shorts. He wrapped up in an unseasonable full-length drover's coat, with gloves and a broad-brimmed Stetson. It was one of the many things that he liked about Texas. Even in midsummer such an outfit raised not an eyebrow.

As he stepped into the bright space of the terminal, the first pangs of hunger inconveniently hit him. Damn it, but he'd not fed since before yesterday. In the rush of the morning, and his worry about Stephanie and the trip, such a mundane thing had slipped his mind. Now that the tension of the flight was over, his body demanded replenishment for all that expended energy. A pity he couldn't have brought a plastic packet of blood with him, but it made passing through customs more complicated than necessary, despite hypnotic help.

He'd just have to endure until he could arrange things with his usual local supplier. The insistent, gnawing feeling was yet only the thin end of the wedge, merely a gentle warning of more distress to come if he delayed too long. Out of habit, he cast about for a likely prospect to feed from. There were dozens of them strolling past, but privacy was at a premium at such a busy airport. Better to keep moving toward a surety than take a risk. He could last until then. Probably.

Phoning from the plane, he'd arranged to rent a large luxury sedan, specifying tinted windows and efficient air conditioning. Apparently such conveniences were beyond the resources of the hire firm. What he got was a cramped compact, with crystal-clear windows and a questionable cooling system. The air was rather lukewarm at first and smelled of stale cigars and mildew. After a few moments the flow got colder, but he sensed a subtle internal struggle going on in the unit's mechanical innards.

As he took the northbound exit from the airport, his tongue absently explored his teeth. He could feel the insistent budding of his canines and tried to push them back. The famished beast within him would take no rest until fed. He swung into an open lane and pressed down on the gas pedal. A speeding ticket would again be no problem; unsatisfied hunger would. He'd have to get to his supply stop soon.

When the blast of air coming from the dashboard vents was equal in temperature to that outside, Richard gave up and opened all four windows. It was going to be one of those interminable, hot Texas days when the sun tried its hardest never to set, and an all-pervading tropical humidity drenched wearer and clothes alike. He would achieve no artificial respite from it and vowed to strike the rental firm's name from his electronic travel planner and to hell with their air miles bonus.

The hot wind booming through his open windows died as the morning rush traffic thickened, slowing his pace. Sweat trickled from under his hat, and ran down his cheek and neck, turning the once crisp collar of his shirt into an uncomfortable damp noose.

Welcome to Texas, he thought glumly. And his empty belly gave a sharp twist that made him hunch over, gasping. Damn, he had less of a margin than anticipated, maybe half an hour before the cramp became a constant agony. Perhaps not even that much as the heat steadily sucked moisture from his body. Not for the first time did he regret he couldn't drink water for replenishment the same as everyone else.

The brilliant, shadowless light wasn't helping either.

He was facing east with the new sun streaming in full force, savagely pricking his skin even through the fresh layer of sun block. This particular road was notorious for delays, and he fretted that he didn't know enough about local geography to risk taking an off-ramp to a less traveled corridor toward his goal. He was stuck sitting in the linear parking lot that locals jokingly called a freeway, his patience wearing dangerously thin.

The start-stop-start pattern was slow enough for him to study a one-page area map that had come with his rental packet. He determined the Luna Road exit would get him to Belt Line which would lead him eventually into Addison. There would be lots of signal lights on that route, but he preferred them over his present stagnation. If he stayed on past Stemmons he'd be mired in the worst of it for God knows how long.

The Luna exit was sensibly wide and almost clear. He shot away from the rest of the herd and cut north across the overpass. The roads were still crowded, but at least he was moving. Not good enough for his beast, though. It stirred and rumbled with increasing impatience.

The last few miles stretched long until he hit Addison's restaurant row. He was in familiar territory now. The corporate offices of Arhyn-Hill Oil (which he owned) were very close, located in the infamous New Karnak complex. He could just see the distinctive top of its ten-story structure gleaming bright under the heat-bleached sky.

New Karnak sounded far better than it actually was. It began as the dream of a young entrepreneur in the heady days of the development-happy eighties. He wanted a haven in the big city, an oasis of refinement and quiet only minutes north of the hurly-burly rush of central Dallas. Not being an actual resident of the area, he was rather innocent of the realities of local sensibilities and traffic patterns.

It had gone downhill from there. The entrepreneur in question had a surplus of inherited money and an ill-researched fascination with ancient Egypt, which explained the oddness of the structure that he managed to build. The whole glass-and-steel edifice was shaped like a pyramid, the interior replete with thick stone columns, larger-than-life-size statues of non-existent pharaohs, and gobbledygook hieroglyphics he'd designed himself adorning the inward-slanting walls. There was a formal garden in a cavernous four-story courtyard, dedicated to and occupied by the household gods of old, and finally, brightly painted friezes depicting Cleopatra and Tutankhamen frolicking together in gay abandon. Historical accuracy played a very small role in the decor. It was as tacky as Texas could get.

Richard loved it at first sight.

On a business trip to the area in search of a good location for Arhyn-Hill Oil to open a Dallas branch, the monstrosity was pointed out to him as a joke. Its pink-tinted sides gleamed pathetic in the setting sun, the ugly duckling of the city's northern skyline. Alas, the underground parking garage was empty of cars, the windows dark and deserted, for the money had run out long before the lower floor offices and luxury flats were rented. Those who could afford to live there generally had better taste and a desire for the prestige of private homes or condos since high-rise living was something of a foreign intrusion into the mind-set of the space-loving natives. That, and a minute miscalculation in the hastily excavated foundation had given New Karnak a decidedly slanted view on life. The courtyard swimming pool was a foot deeper at one end than the indicated number painted on the surrounding tile walls.

After some discreet investigation, Richard discovered he'd found the makings of a bargain. A white elephant perhaps, but with some coaxing, it could be made to work. He saw to it that the thing was brought up to safety code, added a few architectural refinements for his own convenience, then Arhyn-Hill Oil took up residence on the lower business floors.

Instead of downplaying the bad taste, he purposely exploited it, appealing to a younger, more adventurous crowd of tenants. The word "eclectic" was often used in brochures and advertising. Those with artistic pretensions, real or imagined, were morbidly delighted, and if the decor inspired groans instead of gasps it mattered not to Richard so long as the rents were timely paid.

The vast apartment he kept for his occasional visits was at the peak of the pyramid, described as the Pharaoh Suite in the selling literature. Not a single outer wall was straight or quite true to angle, but he had a view through the slanted glass of the downtown core that was to die for. And most important, with the security of a private keyed elevator leading straight from garage to penthouse, it was quiet and secluded. No one ever asked anyone's business, especially his. In fact, in all the years that he had owned this unique pied-à-terre, the only person he'd ever spoken to in the residence part of the building was the night security guard, who dozed most of the time in the main lobby. But New Karnak had another distinct advantage for Richard, one not immediately obvious to the regular human observer, yet highly necessary to him. It was very close to his blood supply.

Restaurant row indeed.

His stomach gave another awful twisting. He clutched the steering wheel and fought the cramp, nearly running the compact up on the curb. Behind him an annoyed commuter struck a warning beep on his horn. Panting, Richard snarled an ugly reply and only just managed to center himself back in the lane.

Not long now, he promised his beast, trying not to sound desperate. *Just a little more time.*

Damn, but that last one felt like a knife. He could take more of the same since he had no choice in the matter, but preferred to shorten the torture. He hit the gas, sighting the line that marked Midway Road, his exit. If once he made that . . . but he drew up hard on the bumper of the car ahead and was forced to slam on the brakes yet again.

His head felt swollen and blood pounded sluggishly behind his eyes. Next would come the tunnel vision, and he'd have to work to concentrate on accomplishing simple things, like walking and opening doors. The point where he lost all self-control and could be in danger of attacking some innocent was yet hours off. He hoped. He'd done exactly that not so very long ago, and though his victim hadn't been at all innocent, Richard never wanted to repeat the experience. The problem plaguing him then had been dealt with, but he did not want to push things.

The light ahead changed, and one by one the lines moved forward. The car in front, coughing a cloud of stinking exhaust, reluctantly crawled for a few yards, then stopped. Exactly across the exit lane.

One foot. If the other car just went forward one more foot Richard would have enough clearance to squeeze past and onto Midway.

He touched his horn and got only another thick puff of blue exhaust. He raised his hand to hit a longer blast, then had to double over as the knife dug into his guts with a vengeance. A thin cry tried to trickle out from his clenched teeth. He refused to give his beast the satisfaction. His sight blurred, and he made himself focus on something outside himself in a futile effort at distraction.

The vehicle blocking his exit was of a seventies vintage, and from its size clearly guzzled gas at a rate well beyond the national average. Richard could see the back of the driver's head through the rear window, and it occurred to him that the driver too probably guzzled well beyond the national average. His head was a large round ball which connected, seemingly without the benefit of a neck, to massive sloping shoulders. Richard could only assume the rest. He fumbled with a shaking hand to sound his horn, and without turning, the driver of the offending vehicle raised his left arm out of his window, middle finger well extended.

In any other circumstance, the whole thing would have been amusing, but not now. Richard felt the pressing need for blood mounting by the second, and the intransigence of this worthy product of steak and potatoes simply enraged him. He was swimming in his own sweat, feeling the acid bite of the sun, and once more his corner teeth budded uncontrollably. They would not retreat.

Cramp. His beast biting him from the inside out.

Desperate, he pressed the horn again, but the driver was unmoved by the sound, and sat a good dozen feet back from the vehicle in front, clearly in no mood to move and let Richard pass.

Then Richard was out of his car, pain replaced by a scalding wrath that was well beyond the limits of reason and safety. A warning against the danger sounded loud within, but he furiously ignored it. He knew what he looked like striding the few short paces between his car and that of the man ahead. He knew that his eyes were red, that his teeth were fully extended, as surely as he knew that the fat man in the car was going to satiate his agonizing hunger, and to hell with the consequences.

As though through a red mist he saw his hand stretching out to take the door handle, to rip it from its hinges.

Then the car was not there.

Richard blinked against the mist, trying to draw breath in the thick, hot air. Where had . . . ?

Without a backward glance the car and the man in it had simply moved forward as the traffic had moved. He was gone, unaware of his close brush with death.

Richard stood befuddled for a searing moment in the hot Texas sun, slowly becoming aware of other car horns, now directed at him. He trembled from the rush of unused adrenaline and careless action. God, what had he been thinking? He hadn't—that was the problem. He was closer to losing it than he'd estimated.

He walked hastily back to the fragile shelter of his own car and got in. Even the warm breeze from the ineffective air conditioning was a blessed relief. He was back again, in control of himself. His teeth were normal, and his eyes sparked blue in the morning light. But for how long? He turned quickly off the main highway, discovered that the traffic here was mercifully thin, and sped onward toward his sanctuary.

Less than five minutes after his encounter with unreasoning Middle America, Richard stepped from the hire car into the welcoming darkness of New Karnak's underground parking garage. He grabbed up his briefcase and overnight bag from the passenger seat. Half walking and half running, he crossed the patched concrete to the elevator. Inside, he inserted his private security card in the required slot in the control panel, punched "P" for penthouse, and lurched suddenly, sickeningly upward. Were this a normal visit he would have stopped at the lobby to chat with the day security team and announce his presence to the company, but just now he had no time to spare. The hunger that had momentarily retreated was back with a vengeance. He needed blood, and he needed it now.

The elevator doors opened directly onto his living room. Richard stepped out, and almost immediately they hissed shut behind him. The whole apartment was dark and sweetly cool. It had cost him quite a penny to install the automatic metal blinds and the special high efficiency air conditioning unit, and at this moment, he would willingly have paid double. Such soothing relief was truly beyond price.

Without pausing to savor the sensations, he stripped hat, gloves, and overcoat as he crossed to the kitchen, leaving them where they fell. He was sure he had some blood safe in the fridge, but couldn't for the life of him remember how much. He opened the door, squinting against the tiny interior light. There was a single bag left. It would do. He tore the top open and sluiced the contents down his aching and parched throat. It was way past its expire date. The taste was stale, nearly dead, but sufficient to ease his angry beast for a couple of hours. Ample time to arrange a fresh supply.

He leaned against a counter in the clean white kitchen and let the stuff flood through him. The pounding ache finally cleared from his head and with a frown he considered the incident that had almost occurred with the stubborn driver. Was that what they were now calling "road rage"? More like road disaster. Certainly the heat and stress had taken its physical toll on his reserves, but they couldn't account for such a hideous lapse in control.

He'd not been like this since that incident a few months back when his beast had seized charge of him—with fatal results to a would-be killer. Richard still shied away from thinking about it. Perhaps the healing he'd later gone through had restored his command over his beast, but the margin for error was much more narrow than before. He could no longer rely on past experience to measure his present limits. More caution was clearly required.

And more blood.

After squeezing the last barely drinkable drop from the bag, he called his supplier, ordering what would be needed for the next few days. It would be ready when he arrived, the doctor told him. There. One less thing to worry about.

Face washed and with a fresh layer of sun block in place, he dressed again in his protective western garments and strode toward the elevator. He punched the button for the parking garage, the doors sighed shut, and down he went like a damned soul to hell.

The Med-Mission Clinic sat happily and busily in a block of decrepit single-story, cream-colored brick constructions. The building, indeed the whole area, was well past its brief 1950s heyday. What had been built as an example of the best of post-war business, full of hope against an atomic future, had fallen far in its relatively short life. The aging process had been quick, and no one with the patience or money had tried to alleviate it. The end result was rotting wood, graffiti-covered brickwork, windows that would never open again, and hopelessness, a deep unending hopelessness that was echoed in the people of the area, people who had been left behind the times along with their neighborhood.

Those not in the thrall of drugs and crime were certainly good people and proud, but were all crushed by the heavy hand of poverty and need. The trickle-down effect, so popular with economists and distant politicians alike, had certainly not trickled down to this urban war zone. Here, the wealth of the few had absolutely no effect on the many.

And here, in a valiant one-man battle against the forces of ignorance, fought Dr. Samuel Ross George: Samuel for the diarist whom his mother had studied at University, and Ross because she had read *Macbeth* during the later stages of her pregnancy and had fallen in love with the name. To his friends—and he considered all and any of the people who walked through the door of the Med-Mission Clinic as his friends—he was just Dr. Sam.

Richard Dun met him quite by accident—though Sam later insisted that there was no such thing as accident or coincidence—one dangerously chill winter evening some ten years ago.

A cold night in Texas sounded strange to anyone except the natives who took a perverse pride in their weather extremes. Richard had been in Dallas leading a corporate seminar for the newly installed Arhyn-Hill Oil called "Personal Security in the Workplace (The Ongoing Threat)"—whoever made up these names?—and was out late searching for food. The area was exactly the sort he'd just advised the attendees to avoid whenever possible, but it had seemed perfect for the type of young woman who served him well in these instances.

The midnight hunting had not been at all good, for anyone he might have found of interest had long made their money earlier and left to escape the sub-zero wind. The few sad souls left still plying their trade were addicts or drunks, whom Richard strove to avoid. They had enough problems in life without having someone draining away their weak, tainted blood.

Richard was ready to give up and try the more risky prey that frequented the numerous bars. He preferred to avoid the entanglements inherent in such places. A newcomer was always subject to study by the regulars, and since he was often better dressed, it made him a tempting target for mugging. Countless times before, he'd encountered the very old game of the woman sent to distract him while her male accomplice(s) tried to sneak up behind, weapon(s) at ready. He'd grown bored with it centuries ago.

As he turned back toward his car, an altercation across the otherwise deserted street caught his attention. A lumpy collection of old clothes, barely identifiable as an ancient wino, was huddled in the recess of a doorway. Another, much younger black man spoke earnestly to him, his hand out. The gist of the conversation that came to Richard's keen ears was that the night was too bitter and the wino should come along to a shelter. He was either too drunk or uncaring to respond much beyond a muffled grunt.

The young Samaritan was involved in trying to persuade the wino from his folly and did not notice the approach of a decrepit van. It stopped short, headlights beating suddenly on the hapless pair. The doors opened as a number of even younger men emerged. They weren't nearly as drunk as the wino and spoiling for a good time if one could judge anything by their predatory laughter.

Richard knew better than to wait for the gangers to make the first move. The speed of his action took them all by surprise. He was across the street in an instant, screaming a truly bloodcurdling war cry he'd once learned from the Sioux. It had the same effect on the teenagers that it had had on the 7th Cavalry. Some froze with wide-eyed shock, others tried to fight.

Tried.

Of the latter, two were left bleeding and unconscious, and the rest wisely accepted that discretion was indeed the better part of valor and departed the scene as speedily as they could manage. Their van nearly toppled over in the driver's haste to achieve the next corner. Lest the cursing, frustrated brigands return with help, Richard scooped both wino and the astonished young man up and, resisting the temptation to sup on the freely flowing red stuff of the vanquished, left the battlefield.

As Richard followed directions and drove them all to a charity shelter to drop off the still oblivious wino, the rescued Samaritan stumbled out with his thanks and introduced himself. Richard was prepared to dismiss the incident and resume his hunt, but during the course of the conversation learned that Samuel Ross George was a doctor.

Ever on the alert for a practical opportunity, Richard simply smiled, murmured encouragement, and listened as Dr. Sam poured out his story.

To the despair of his middle-class family, he'd eschewed the profits of a more mundane practice and labored long with the unfashionable poor. He had an idealistic desire to help those whom he called his fellow pilgrims, but lacked the means to do anything on a large scale. His tiny practice with its third-hand equipment was barely enough to keep up his insurance payments, much less pay off his medical school loans.

To his delight, Richard found the good doctor was deeply susceptible to hypnotic suggestion, and arranging a supply of whole blood for a very special patient was no problem. Subtly made aware of Richard's special needs, Dr. Sam became a provider of precious nourishment, beginning that night. More than that, he became a trusted friend.

Aware that genuine saints were a rare occurrence and often needed conservancy, Richard soon made true the doctor's dream of a free clinic, generously funding it through Arhyn-Hill. In the decade to follow it grew and flourished. Everyone in the area benefited, and when visiting, Richard was spared from making time-consuming, post-midnight jaunts in search of food.

Richard parked the rental outside the Med-Mission and stepped out. Though it was painfully bathed in broad daylight, the street did not inspire confidence. Several young men, who apparently had nothing better to do, were already checking out the car.

Quickly scanning the neighborhood, Richard saw exactly the fellow he needed no more than ten feet away, lounging against an alley dumpster, taking the brutal sun, seemingly oblivious to the rest of the world, hard eyes missing nothing behind his pale tinted Ray Bans. There were other youths in the area also on the watch, but this one's attitude marked him as their leader.

"Nice wheels, man."

This somewhat ominous comment greeted Richard as he neared the studiously relaxed teenager. He was anywhere between fifteen and twenty, with the life experience of a veteran mercenary. He moved not at all. Only the ragged antics of a toothpick held loosely between his teeth gave any sign of life within. The young man had obviously spent much time perfecting his toothpick repertoire as the slim piece of wood danced from side to side in his mouth. It reminded Richard uncomfortably of a miniature wooden stake. In fact, he'd once seen one packaged as a portable vampire slaying kit. Someone had thought it amusing. Strange humor, that.

"I need a favor," said Richard.

"I'm all out of favors. Cowboy."

What an observant young fellow to have noticed the clothes. "Then I need a service."

The kid merely stared, the unquestioned ruler of his turf, beholden to none, awaiting the next move of this presumptuous intruder.

Such games always irritated Richard, but he knew if he didn't play it exact and to the rules, there would be little left of his car when he came out of Dr. Sam's. He wanted to avoid further irritation.

"I'm willing to pay you," he added.

By some wonderful contraction of face muscles, the sunglasses lowered themselves, and a wary eye peered at Richard over their tops.

"What you want?" Such disdainful suspicion in so few words.

"They are nice wheels," he said agreeably, nodding in the general direction of his transport. "I want them to stay that way. I want the whole car to stay that way. You're the man here, so I come to you."

The teeth snapped the toothpick clean, and the boy spat it out to join a scattering of similarly broken fellows on the sidewalk. He straightened, stretching catlike, right hand resting on the pocket of his baggy jeans. The pocket sagged with the weight of something heavy. Perhaps a knife, but more likely a gun. With a gesture he'd most certainly seen in the movies, he slowly removed his sunglasses, the better to fix his adversary with an intimidating glare.

It was all too easy. One look and immediately Richard had him in his power.

"Watch the car," he told the youth in a mild tone after a moment of stare-down. "Your life depends on it."

Mesmerized, the boy repeated the instructions and the warning. The rental would be safer now than in a police garage. Hell,

Richard could have the kid wash and wax the thing if he ordered it. But there was no time for such satisfying frivolities. The sunlight was prickling, burning hot against his body even shrouded as he was, and he needed fresh blood. Damn, he really did.

As he pushed through the clinic doors, all conversation in the waiting room stopped and every eye, young and old alike, took him in. It was absurdly like an old cowboy movie. A stranger was in town, and the locals could smell it. Certainly he was dressed for the part.

The receptionist, pretty and starched, was alerted by the silence and looked up from her glass-shielded alcove. Moving toward her through the parting waves of suffering humanity, Richard smiled, all warmth, and swept off his Stetson. Being inside was a relief, even in the crowded confines of Dr. Sam's waiting room. The air conditioning was very efficient.

"Hello, Helen."

Remembering her name was easy. There it was on the badge pinned to her very attractive bosom: Helen Mesquita. For a moment, puzzlement showed in her face, but was soon replaced by happy recognition. She'd been there long enough to understand that Richard was some sort of special patron of the clinic. She touched a few spikes of the short, dark hair that kissed the top of one ear, an unconscious primping gesture.

"Mr. Dun. How lovely to see you. It's been so long. Dr. Sam said you'd called." Helen, along with a bright team of nurses and other assistants, kept the unworldly Dr. Sam's endeavor running smoothly amid the chaos of the street and demands of bureaucracy.

She stood, absently brushing the front of her uniform, and hit the door buzzer release, allowing Richard access to the inner areas of the clinic. He'd made sure about installing a good security system since the pharmaceuticals on the premises were a constant temptation to thieves and addicts.

He followed her, appreciative of the view as she led him down the narrow white hall to Sam's office. She didn't have to, he knew the way but chose not to object. Once more he felt the stirring that he always got whenever he saw an attractive young woman like Helen Mesquita, and once more pushed his desires (and hunger) to the back of his mind. However delectable the staff might be, they were strictly off limits. He wanted to keep things simple, which did not include impromptu feeding trysts in the examination rooms.

Nothing wrong with looking, though, he thought.

Helen opened the office door and held it for him. He had to turn sideways to get past, and even then brushed against her gently. A familiar fragrance wafted to him from the pulse point on her throat, and he paused in the doorway, still in light contact with her.

"Freesia," he said, amiably gazing down into her enormous brown eyes.

"I beg your pardon?"

"Your perfume. It's Freesia. One of my favorites. Natural and . . . pure."

Did she actually flutter those lovely eyelashes? Certainly his lingering attention had her heart beating hard and fast. "Why, thank you. It probably is. I never look at what I put on. I'm lucky I don't just smell of ether and rubbing alcohol."

She smiled up at him, backing free in the narrow space, but sliding against his body—deliberately, Richard knew—to return the way she came. Richard's gaze followed her hungrily.

No complications, old lad, he firmly told himself. Not without a degree of regret. She looked to be very tasty, indeed.

"Richard, good to see you!"

Dr. Sam emerged from one of the examining rooms farther along the hall, a delighted grin on his dark face and arms outstretched in greeting. He was slight in build, but wiry in strength. He gripped Richard's hand for a solid shake then a brief, backslapping embrace.

"How are you?" he demanded. "This isn't the time of year for your usual visit. What's going on?" He ushered Richard into his office and shut the door.

"Nothing special, just some business that needs looking into."

"Not this place, I hope."

"Of course not, I trust your accountant." After all, Richard had picked her himself. "I'm in need of supplies, no more than that."

"Got you covered. This should do for you." Sam went to a small refrigerator and opened it wide to display the contents.

Richard eyed the pile of flat plastic bags filled with precious life within. His mouth was suddenly dry and his speech came out as a whisper. "It will, indeed. If you don't mind very much I'd like to . . ."

Sam instantly understood and handed over one of the pint bags. All other aspects of the doctor's life and work were his own, but where Richard was concerned, he'd been carefully primed and programmed to accept and ignore certain things. Watching his patron drinking down a pint of human blood and thinking it to be perfectly normal was one of them. For all the reaction he displayed Richard might have been imbibing a can of soda.

He drained it away in a mere few seconds, hardly regarding the taste. It was better than what he'd had earlier, fresher, more nourishing. Though it could never satisfy as fully as taking directly from a vein it would keep him alive and safe to be around. He allowed himself one small ecstatic shudder as his starved beast finally rolled over and went to sleep.

Until the next time.

"You're looking well, as ever," said Dr. Sam, dropping into a worn chair behind his cluttered desk. Richard took a chair before it. Sated for now, and with the rest of the day to wait, he could indulge himself in a brief visit.

"You, too." Though Richard noticed a few curls of gray making a beachhead in the hair around Sam's temples. They stood out against the deep chocolate color of his skin. How old was he anyway? Richard always thought of him as a very young man. "How are things going?"

"Busy. I'm trying to entice a few more doctors into helping out with the load, but they don't care for the pay. Helen's looking into finding some community support—"

"I'm not here to talk about the money. Arhyn-Hill will give you whatever funds you need to hire whomever you wish, you know that. I want to know how things are going for you."

Sam shrugged as though thinking about himself was not an

especially important activity to him. In his case it was likely to be true. "I'm all right. I take my vitamins and wrap up in the winter."

Still no wedding ring on his finger. Richard harbored a hope that Sam would marry an equally nice girl and make lots of little Sams and Samanthas to spread some of his goodness and cheer in the world. "Are you happy?"

Sam blinked, evidently surprised, but did not say anything right away. The nature of the query and their friendship required something more than a casual answer.

"Are you?" asked Richard after a moment to give the man time to think.

In reply Sam gestured at the office. Its walls were decorated with laminated anatomy charts and grim public service posters bearing warnings against drug abuse, sexually transmitted diseases, and domestic violence. "I'm trying to keep people alive who have to sleep on the floor because some neighborhood bozos think they're hell on wheels with their guns. I've got an eleven-year-old girl whose uncle got her pregnant with twins, and her mother says it's a righteous judgment from God if the delivery kills her. One of my patients died last week from the heat because she was afraid of not affording her electric bill if she ran her fan, and three others came in to find out their test for HIV was positive. I'm operating an improbability in the midst of insanity, Richard, and the sad fact of it is that, yes, I am happy."

This time Richard could not bring himself to speak for a while. Nothing would have been appropriate. He finally rolled up the empty blood bag and dropped it in a waste basket. "How is that possible?"

"Because I know what this place would be like if I wasn't here, doing what I'm doing." Anyone else would have sounded to be in love with his own ego, but not Sam. He simply stated facts.

"It would be worse," said Richard.

"Yes. A hellhole with no ladder out. I've made some things better, thanks to you, and I'd like to cure all of it, but I know that will never happen. There's just too much of the bad stuff and not enough of me. But what I can do is try to ease one disaster at a time and hope it goes out from there."

"You sound like you've had some successes."

"A few. At least I got that little girl out of her abusive environment and had the uncle arrested. The rest of the family's trying to talk sense into the mother. It's not much, but that's what keeps me going."

"You know if you need anything, you've only to call. Collect."

Sam flashed a single, short grin. "Well, since the subject *has* come up . . ."

In less than five minutes, Richard agreed to the purchase of a quantity of new medical equipment, an upgrading of the clinic's computer system, and some special filters designed to trap a particularly virulent bacteria that had been found in the Dallas water system. Its chief prey were AIDS victims and anyone else with an impaired immune system. Dr. Sam wanted the filters installed in the homes of his high-risk patients.

"As many as you want," said Richard. "Have Helen fax it in and get things started. You can have the first shipment by the end of the week."

"You're a saint," said Dr. Sam.

"I don't think so." And Richard refrained from telling the doctor to look in a mirror. It wasn't that the man simply did good works, he really was good in himself, and Richard liked to bask in the glow surrounding him. He'd have to ask Sabra to come down from her near-hermitage in Vancouver and meet the man sometime. She'd like him.

Richard left the clinic slightly humbled as always whenever he had contact with Sam. He freed his untouched, utterly scratch-free rental from the tender concern of the young hoodlum, told him to forget their encounter, then drove back to New Karnak. Very easy. On the passenger seat lay a heavy opaque plastic bag that held a disposable ice pack and three pints of pure sustenance. He'd have to get them refrigerated quickly before the damned heat coagulated the lot to undrinkability.

He swung onto the Dallas tollway and headed for home as fast as the afternoon traffic allowed. The sun now shone nearly directly overhead. His face itched and reddened, yet still that blazing sign of passing time gladdened him. It would soon be night, and he'd be able to leave to see Stephanie. With the easing of his desperate hunger, the worry for her reasserted itself and now took a turn at twisting his guts.

What had happened with her today? And what was she doing now?

Chapter Four

The sun hung blood red just above the horizon for a impossibly long age, as if time itself had stopped to admire its breathtaking beauty. Then slowly, hesitantly, as if trying the water of a bath that she knew would be just a little too hot, the vast orb slid behind the edge of the earth, winked one last good-bye, and was gone.

It was 8:45 according to the dimly glowing clock in the dash of the car. Richard, much relieved physically and mentally from the burden of day, was at last heading north in the still-bright twilight on the final leg of his journey. Faithfully adhering to Stephanie's instruction, he would arrive at her house in the usual manner of past visits, about twenty minutes after sunset, which was how long it took him to get there from New Karnak.

He'd spent the endless-seeming hours alternately healing from his initial journey and restlessly pacing the penthouse in between bouts of research at his computer. The first thing he checked was the e-mail, but no new message awaited him from Stephanie. Disappointing, that. And worry-making. Next he scoured any and all sources available to him for a location on Alejandro Trujillo. The latest unsecured intel had it that he was still in Colombia. No surprises there, also no real confirmation. He would certainly want to stay away from any country that had arrest warrants out for him, but it was not beyond possibility that he could be in the States to personally see to his brother's disposal.

Richard had never been overly impressed with monitoring operations on the drug lords, anyway. A return to some sort of old-fashioned method of reprisal might be more preferable and practical. If it was indeed a war on drugs, then would it not be in one's best interest to try to knock out the generals of the opposing side? The cartels had no restraints when it came to brutally removing their enemies, after all.

Not my problem, thought Richard, though in his own small area of focus he planned to be most conclusive. If Alejandro ever came within his reach he would take some sort of swift—and quite final—action against him. A threat to Luis was a threat to Stephanie and her children. To protect them Richard could and would cheerfully rip Alejandro to shreds.

But he fervently hoped this call from her would only be a false alarm.

He'd resisted the impulse to openly announce his presence to Arhyn-Hill Oil. He owned it, but preferred to turn the actual running of the business over to the specialists. Occasionally he would come down to check on things and remind his CEOs of his existence, but that always stirred things up. Luis worked there and if he was being watched, then it was better for him that Richard continue with a low profile. On the other hand, were this a regular visit, he would always phone Luis, letting him know he was in town. If only Stephanie had provided more information on how best to proceed.

Someone in building security did notice that the penthouse flat was in use, and sent a man up to check. A few hypnotic moments with the fellow were enough to assure Richard a continuance of uninterrupted privacy. By the time he took the elevator down to the garage, all but the live-in tenants had gone home, so his evening departure went as unmarked as his arrival.

There'd been improvements made on the old county highway since his last sojourn. It was now four lanes and boasted stop-lights at the infrequent intersections. For now they only blinked a cautionary yellow, but that looked to be short-lived. Developers were encroaching on once empty fields, and would soon turn farm and grazing land into clusters of apartment complexes the same as those that covered the more urban areas like fungus. When he'd first hidden Stephanie and her family here, the area had been wonderfully isolated, the land little changed from the days of the earliest European explorers. In another year it would be covered with concrete, strip malls, and petrol stations.

But all was empty in the descending darkness for the time being, and now and then his headlights only picked out a startled rabbit darting for cover. He sped by a fearful mess in the center of the road that had once been an armadillo. Odd how one never actually saw the creatures scuttling across to meet with their violent end, only their remains long after the fact. He held his breath until the brief fog of decay cleared from the car.

He slowed for a turn onto a narrow and much older side road and followed it for a mile, then made a final turn-off to a deeply rutted dirt track. The rental bumped badly from side to side, suspension creaking and complaining, tires throwing up huge clouds of pale dust in the darkness. Fifty yards in, amid a wild stand of mesquite, he was obliged to get out to open a gate, drive through, and shut it again. Was this the gate Stephanie had referred to in her first message? Perhaps one of the children had strayed from the house, left it open, and chose not to confess the crime. Michael was a likely suspect, being the oldest and most adventuresome, but Elena and Seraphina were more than capable of egging each other on to great feats of mischief.

He hoped that was all there was to it, just a series of coincidences misinterpreted.

But his dream . . . that damned dream had left him paranoid. When it came to such matters it was better to listen to such nagging fears than dismiss them outright. He would take a little extra time and check things thoroughly before going up to knock on the front door.

The road climbed a slight hill within the property, and Richard pulled to a stop just before topping its flat crest, killed the lights and motor, and got out. He finally divested himself of his drover's coat, hat, and leather gloves, stowing them on the passenger seat. It felt like he'd shed a too heavy and much too tight skin. By contrast the stagnant leftover heat of the day almost seemed chill. Everything was silent save the incessant hum and chirp of the insects, and the air was gently scented with sage, soothing and caressing to his senses. He did not relax, though. Except for being dark, it was still disturbingly like his dream.

Clinging to the edge of the thorny trees, he followed the line of the track down the other side of the hill. Really, it was hardly high enough to be dignified with such a label, but it did serve as a physical buffer between the house and the outside world. One last turning and he caught sight of the satellite structures: a low barn with its corrugated metal roof and attached corral, the pump house, the propane tank. In the backyard on lovingly transplanted grass stood a clothesline and a scattering of brightly colored toys, a swing set, a battered plastic play fort and this year's splashing pool.

Quiet. As it should be.

He made a wide stealthy circle of the entire yard, senses alert for the least sight, the softest sound of intruders, and was greatly relieved when nothing out of the ordinary presented itself. The horses dozing in the corral canted their ears in his direction, but didn't bother to stir. Having the space to indulge her childhood passion, Stephanie had acquired a tiny herd of her own and even dabbled in breeding. She'd sent him many pictures of the children at play on their pony. He couldn't see it offhand and guessed it to be stabled in the barn away from its larger quarter-horse cousins.

A few lights were on in the house down below; it looked normal and peaceful. The sight inspired a flood of memories from that first evening when he'd brought Stephanie here. He'd had every window shining a warm yellow welcome for her arrival.

It had been a long trip from Toronto. They'd traveled for five days, taking a very roundabout route and twice changing vehicles. On the last leg, they'd driven to Kansas, left the cars completely and flown in to D/FW on a charter. Richard had a van waiting for them at the airport and hustled the whole family inside. Luis was worried, the children were fussy and confused, but Stephanie was calm, rising above the clamor with her serenity. Richard understood it to mean that no matter what the circumstances she trusted him to take care of them all. She soothed the girls and talked Richard into a stop for some fast food. That got even Michael settled, putting them in a better mood for moving into a house they'd never before seen.

Richard was fairly confident they would like the place. The outside looked rough, being built completely of logs that glowed golden in the moonlight, the chinking between them yellow-gray with age. It appeared somewhat forbidding in its sturdiness, but the interior was a gem. He'd seen to it himself by hiring a decorator and letting her have her way with updating things. Stephanie would have been grateful for a dirt-floored hovel so long as her family was safe, but it pleased him more than he cared to admit to be able to escort her to a modern Aladdin's cave. If she had to spend the rest of her life in hiding, at least it would be in comfortable surroundings.

Tired from the trip, she moved slowly, and he helped her down from the van as Luis, carrying the twins, walked with young Michael toward the house. Stephanie paused and smiled breathtakingly at Richard, and for a moment he wondered if she was pregnant again, for he thought how true it was that a woman looked even more beautiful in the full bloom of childbearing. And his heart broke a little more. It did not matter her condition, he would always see her in such radiance. He held her hand just a little too long as she steadied herself and smoothed her dress. She only smiled gently at him again, squeezed his fingers, and turned away. Luis was watching from the freshly painted blue door of the house.

Once inside Stephanie had been like a little girl at Christmas, going from room to room, gasping in delight at the rough-hewn wood and heavy low ceilings, and laughing out loud at the apparently antiquated plumbing. The place had been built in the hip seventies by an oil baron wishing to appease his young back-to-nature, flower-child wife, hence the log cabin look in a landscape where large trees were an oddity. He'd imported the lot from out of state, added many additional rooms and filled them with faux Spanish fixtures and shag carpeting. The decorator had thankfully removed those shards of bad taste, but left intact the huge fireplace in the main living room, made of fieldstone and artistically crooked. She'd replaced the hideous avocado kitchen with faux antique fixtures, including a large glowering range, black and dully gleaming, but using propane instead of wood fuel.

Stephanie took joy in everything, allocating rooms as she went, Michael running ahead to call her on to fresh discoveries. She busied herself settling Elena and Seraphina in their new nursery.

That left Richard in the company of Luis. Neither man had avoided or ignored the other for the duration of the journey, both giving and getting courtesy. It had still been uncomfortable, but they'd made the best of things. Richard could respect the man's effort, and found himself unbending a bit.

It had to do with his intimate familiarity with the dynamics of temptation and threat. As both qualities had been amply manifested in and expressed by dear brother Alejandro, Luis's mistake of giving in to him was understandable. He'd committed a crime, but wasn't a criminal at heart, only weak. And frightened.

Would I have done differently were our positions reversed? Richard wasn't sure. It had been centuries since he'd humbled himself for the last time before the long departed Ambert.

Luis seemed distracted and stood alone before the cold fireplace, hands in his pockets, looking bleak and lost. He had committed that most grievous of sins in the drug community: he had gone straight, and worse, had tried to make amends by supplying the authorities with valuable information. The cartels had bled steadily as a result. The men who were after him were not to be trifled with, especially Alejandro. When Luis started to inform against his brother, Alejandro's reaction had been predictable and unwisely public. He'd openly sworn—from the safety of his Colombian fortress—that he would kill Luis like a dog, and a contract had been issued. The largest in cartel history, word had it. No wonder Luis stood closed off from his family and simply stared, dark eyes seeing nothing.

"It will be all right," Richard told him, hoping he was not lying.

"You think so?" There was justified doubt in his question.

"So far as it is in my power to make things safe. Bourland's people had us well covered in Toronto. Anyone watching your old house will think you're still there."

Luis gave an expressive shrug, shaking his head. "Alejandro is no fool and he does not hire fools, only uses them. Like me. They will find out I'm gone soon enough."

"You did the right thing, Luis."

"So everyone tells me, but if I'd kept quiet—"

"You'd be in jail."

"Or safe in Colombia."

"And in thrall to Alejandro for the rest of your life."

"You think this is any different?"

"Oh, yes. Very different."

"How?"

"Because here you can look your wife and children in the eyes without shame."

That made Luis pause. He even managed a small, fleeting smile in acknowledgment of the point, but still had practical worries to voice. "Alejandro is not one to give up. He always had to win even when we were little. He would not stop playing a game until he'd won."

"That may be so, but he has no pieces now with which to play. You have very effectively vanished."

Luis gave a soft snort. "What a good mood he will be in then. He will never cease looking until he's found us."

"Do you think if you spoke with him he'd change his mind? Sometimes a face-to-face talk can change—"

Now Luis barked out a soft laugh. "You are too much the optimist, friend Richard. Where I come from this is a matter of honor and blood. It is no concern that what Alejandro does breaks the law, but it is a great concern that I have broken faith with him. I betrayed my own brother to ruin. He deserves it, but in his world I am the one who is the traitor."

"Then it's best to be removed from such a world. Would you wish your children to learn such twisted rules?"

Luis shook his head and paced slowly across the room, taking it in, perhaps, for the first time. He stopped by a large wraparound sofa that faced an equally large entertainment center. It was not unlike the way Stephanie had arranged things back in her Canada home. Richard had an eye for detail and even managed to provide video tapes of their favorite films and a few CDs and books in the hope their familiarity would ease the shock of moving, of leaving nearly everything behind. To judge by the squeals now coming from the children's playroom, Michael had discovered the cache of toys and storybooks scattered there. Like many other items in the house everything was new, still in their plastic wrappings, but Richard didn't think the child would mind. Michael always took such savage joy tearing into presents it seemed a shame to deprive him of it.

"Daddydaddydaddy!" The boy rushed screaming into the room, his arms full of treasure. He held a stuffed elephant nearly his own size, tripped and fell on it. The plush beast broke his fall, and he was too excited to remember to cry at the sudden tumble. He struggled to his feet holding the animal high trying to show it off to his father.

Luis looked to instantly wake out of his glum mood and gave his undivided attention to his little son. He exclaimed over the toy and tried to coax Michael into correctly pronouncing the word "elephant." The child had inherited his mother's blue eyes but not her dark hair. His pale blond cap had come from her Nordic forebears, the trait having skipped a generation with her. Elena and Seraphina were the same. The childrens' skin had just the faintest dusky hue from their father's side. It would tan dark beneath the Texas sun. When the infant girls became young women they would be even more stunning than Stephanie.

God, they were all so tiny, yet growing so fast. Richard took in the moment from far across the room feeling both joy and the harsh stab of relentless sorrow. Sabra had warned him against attachments, but how could he avoid them? It was his lot to look on their ephemeral lives and know that in a few short decades they would be grown up, grown old, and die. How wonderful it was to see the beginnings, and how heartbreaking to watch the long, agonizing decline. Out of necessity to his own sanity he'd learned to push such dismal anticipations away and live as best he could in the present, but sometimes that was damned difficult. It was only thin comfort to him that however temporary their time was on earth he could try to make it happy for them.

Michael galloped away again, and as quickly returned, this time holding high a red plastic airplane and making appropriate buzzing noises. He'd been highly impressed with the flight from Kansas, his great blue eyes taking in every detail. He was bright for his age and had a talent for charming people, confiding to his father he would fly planes when he grew up. A week earlier he'd wanted to be a soccer champion.

He looked up at Luis and asked, "Is it Christmas? Can I keep the toys?"

Luis automatically corrected the boy's grammar and confirmed everything was his to keep. This was greeted with a piping cheer, then he rushed off to find his mother. The room seemed smaller after his noisy exodus. Luis stared after him in the abrupt silence, his face somber, his eyes unblinking like the dead.

"The children will be all right, too," said Richard, guessing Luis's thoughts.

He looked up sharply. His mouth twitched in a grimace. "I can hope for that . . . and thank you for this." He raised one hand to indicate the house. "But I know you would not do all this for me alone."

"Probably not," Richard admitted.

"And thus by default I am in a debt to you I cannot hope to repay. I have nothing."

Richard shook his head. Time to give his own reassurance to this man who did not seem to remember the priceless worth of what remained to him. "You have Stephanie. And you always will."

Another sharp look from Luis. At last a tiny spark of life returned to his dark eyes. What was that? Resentment or triumph? Both? He was certainly entitled. And he yet held some lingering jealousy toward Richard. He could be civilized and pretend otherwise, but couldn't altogether hide it.

But you were the one to walk away with Stephanie. If only you would realize that. Even if you were gone, she'd still not have me.

Richard sighed and this time did not try to conceal his own sorrow. "Luis, you possess everything that I can never hope to have: a wonderful wife who loves you dearly and three sweet, beautiful children who adore their father. If you want to pay me back, then make them as happy as possible. Give to them that which I cannot and never will be able to give myself."

Then Luis dropped his gaze, and that was the end of the matter.

That evening they'd had a minor celebration, Stephanie readily making use of the supplies in her new kitchen. Richard could not imbibe or ingest with the rest, but played with Michael, distracting him from the adult tensions he must have sensed, but was unable to understand. The boy was especially receptive to such things, and picked up on the underlying brittleness to the general cheer as his parents' future was discussed over his head.

In a few days Luis would begin his new job at Arhyn-Hill Oil—working under another, quite different last name in an executive position that Richard had arranged for him. Whether it was coffee or oil, business was business, and Luis would soon be immersed into his new duties and earning a guilt-free living. Stephanie eventually planned to work there as well when she thought the girls were old enough to face the rigors of daycare with a minimum of trauma.

The party did not last long. They were all tired. Stephanie insisted that Richard make use of the guest room, and he gave in for just the one night. All was quiet, or nearly so. Awake and listening to the unfamiliar sounds of the country he became aware of other, equally primal sounds coming from the master bedroom far down the hall. Weary as they undoubtedly were, Luis had summoned enough energy to reaffirm his husband's claim over Stephanie.

Richard had rolled over in his own bed, crammed a pillow against his ear, and bitterly regretted his decision to stay.

How sharp the memories were in their pain and pleasure despite the intervening years. Time was supposed to cure things like that. For Richard it generally did—when he could bring himself to let things go. He'd not been able to do that with Stephanie.

The house itself sat indifferently defiant, built to outlast man and the elements, its heavy outline picked out by the security lights that Luis had installed himself. The huddled outbuildings were silent, deserted in the night. Scanning the scene minutely, Richard spotted nothing out of the ordinary, and concentrating with his unnaturally acute hearing, could detect nothing wrong. Most reassuring.

He pressed flat against the wall of the barn, hidden by the deep shadows cast by the lights around the house. The horses dozed contentedly, and mice scurried on their busy way. Again he listened and heard nothing untoward from the surrounding area. If any humans were about, he'd have found them by now. He turned his attention full upon the house.

The glow of a light peeped out between wooden shutters in what was the master bedroom, and now that he was closer, he could pick out the thin wailing strains of a steel guitar across the night air. Stephanie must have gone completely native. She'd not expressed much interest in country music when they'd been together.

Satisfied that it was safe to approach, he quit his concealment and went back to retrieve the car. If he just walked up to the house now and banged on the door it might startle them unnecessarily, especially Stephanie. It would be better for her no-doubt-strained nerves that she first hear the sound of his approach. She'd insisted that he come as though it were one of his normal visits, and now that he'd scouted things, he saw no reason not to comply with her wish.

He pulled up some yards away, close to the carport where her new minivan was parked. Luis's sedan was missing, indicating he wasn't yet home. Perhaps he'd stopped on some after-work errand. He'd not be far behind in his own arrival, then. Richard hoped this wouldn't create complications for Stephanie later. Luis would put on a show of welcome, as he always did, but he'd not be too pleased to see the ex-boyfriend in his house, or to hear the reason why. He might resent her calling for help without first discussing it. Or asking permission.

Richard cared nothing for that thought and shoved it away.

He strolled onto the porch, boots noisy against the wood. He half expected the door to be pulled open by Stephanie before he had the chance to knock, but it remained shut. Its once proud blue was quite faded by the unremitting sun, its iron hinges rusted and brown. No blood flowed from them or from the cracks in the wood, he noted with much relief. Damn that dream, anyway.

The music changed, grew louder. It was Willie Nelson crooning out "The Healing Hands of Time." How appropriate. Having been at the receiving end of heartbreak on many, many occasions in his long life, Richard had a vivid understanding and appreciation for the themes of country music. Odd that he could hear it so clearly, though.

Then he noticed that the front door was open. There was a half-inch gap between it and the frame. He felt the cool breath of the central air conditioning escaping into the outside heat.

Mouth dry and fully alert to any waiting ambush, he gave the iron handle on the door a push. His heart sank as the great slab of wood creaked gently open. The entry was but dimly lighted and apparently empty.

Several possibilities ran through his mind, one of which being that the family had left in haste and forgotten to secure things. A foolish idea, but he preferred to grasp at such fragile straws than anticipate anything worse.

Well, if anyone was inside ready to spring upon him, they'd have long heard him by now. No need to be stealthy at this point.

"Stephanie?"

That damn dream again. He'd called to her in just that manner, loud enough for the whole house to hear. The hair on the back of his neck stood on end from the memory.

"Luis? Michael?" There, that broke the pattern.

When no reply came, he moved fast—at the kind of unnatural speed only he could attain. In less than an eye blink he was inside, back pressed against a wall, every nerve alert, every sense straining for information.

Nothing. Only the faint hum of the air conditioning and Willie Nelson with a lush string accompaniment.

Wait, now . . . there was a scent hanging in the entry air. Very faint, with an artificial, chemical quality. Innocuous, but out of place. He couldn't quite identify it. He didn't dismiss it so much as register the puzzlement and put it aside for the moment.

He moved farther into the house, leaving the front door wide. The living room was lighted up, but deserted, as was the hall connecting it to the dining and kitchen areas. The music came from the back of the place.

Another smell abruptly intruded upon him. This one much stronger, very identifiable and entirely alarming. Propane gas. He moved toward the kitchen, taking a deep breath before going in. The deadly smothering stink was so strong that even in the hall he almost gagged. He entered, careful not to flick on the overhead light. He picked out the stove controls in the dimness. They were all on high, the pilot lights blown out.

He cut everything off fast and eased open the back door to allow in fresh air, looking out. Nothing to see, but instinct told him that someone was probably out there watching from cover. Whoever had done the mischief couldn't be far away. The valves hadn't been open for more than a few minutes or else Richard would have detected the explosive poison when first he came in. Perhaps the intruder had gone out the back the moment Richard stepped onto the front porch.

Was that the trap? For him to rush in here, turn on the light, and let the electrical spark do the rest? Possibly, but it was too sloppy, too uncertain.

And there was that other smell . . .

The propane could have been meant to cover it, to keep him from noticing. No normal human would have picked it up, though. A feint, then, a minor distraction to get him stirred up and off balance.

"Stephanie? Where are you?"

He remembered the glow from the master bedroom's window and quit the kitchen, moving fast and silent over the carpeted floor. Just because he couldn't sense anyone else there didn't mean that the house had to be empty. If they kept very, very quiet . . .

Willie's voice grew stronger, as did that almost-familiar odor.

The only light breaking the interior gloom was a narrow streak showing out from the bottom of the bedroom door. All the other doors opening onto the hall—the children's rooms, the bath, an office—gaped onto darkness.

Trap, he thought, his hand resting on the doorknob. Who was on the other side? One of Alejandro's hired assassins, waiting with a shotgun at ready? If so, then he was in for a hellish surprise.

Richard turned the knob. It moved freely. No hindering obstructions. What if opening the door triggered a booby trap of some sort? A bomb?

That smell . . . more concentrated now. It was an unlikely combination, reminiscent of new car interior and petrol, and its source was here.

As was another, intermingled with the first, but instantly familiar to him.

Blood.

Panic flared in his chest. He fought it down. Made himself go slow. Made himself listen. He should be able to hear the breathing, the very heartbeat of anyone in the room beyond.

Nothing. That damned music interfered, masked it all.

Sweat coated him, the slick discomfort of his own fear. If it was only his safety at risk he'd already be inside, but what if the threat was also to Stephanie?

He had to look in, to take that chance with her life.

He slowly pushed the door open, tensed and ready to spring, to fight, ready for anything except the sight greeting him.

They lay in bed together, Stephanie and her twin daughters, fully clothed, yet apparently asleep.

Too still, much too still for that, his mind whispered.

For it was the cold sleep of death holding them, and its freezing grasp closed hard upon his heart, holding him as surely as if he'd been struck dead himself. He was stunned beyond thought, beyond action; all that remained was sickening perception.

The bullet holes were unseemly neat in the smooth skin of the twins' foreheads, at least on the entry side. He didn't need to see the exits to know of the hideous damage there.

Their throats had also been cut. Blood was everywhere. It matted their fair hair, soaked the pillows, and dripped down onto the floor where it puddled on the hardwood. The slaughterhouse stink of it filled the room.

Stephanie's eyes were open and stared at him dully. She had two bullet wounds, one in her stomach, the other squarely over her heart. They weren't enough for her killer; he'd taken care to cut her throat, too.

Then her face blurred as tears filled Richard's vision. A keening cry escaped him, echoing through the emptiness of the house, and Willie's words mocked him from the sound system.

I'll get over you by clinging to the healing hands of time.

He tried to step toward them, hand out as though to offer help, to give comfort, an automatic gesture and quite useless.

He tried to step toward them, but his legs gave way, dumping him in an unceremonious heap on the floor. He couldn't move, couldn't see for the tears. A great sob racked his body, unstoppable.

No time. No time for this!

He fought the tidal rush of anguish and rage, raising up, trying to make his limbs work. He could have lain there forever weeping, but that smell of new plastic and petrol, now redolent of death, pierced his grief like a dagger, and he suddenly understood the true danger all around him.

It was Semtex. Plastic explosive.

No time to look for the bomb. It could detonate any second. They'd been watching for him, waiting for him to find the bodies—

He had to run.

Terror overthrew the grief for a few precious seconds. Just long enough for him to gather himself to crash through the shuttered window. But a stray thought stopped him.

Michael. Where's Michael?

His body was not with theirs.

If there was any chance of the boy being alive, Richard would not leave no matter what the risk. He stared wildly about, then staggered to the closet, the bath.

Empty. Only blood. Blood everywhere.

At vampire speed Richard shot from the room, tore through the house. First Michael's room. Then the rest. He ripped open doors, threw over beds, calling the boy's name in a strangled voice he did not recognize.

Nothing. Not one sign of the child. Richard ran through the rest of the house in a frenzy of fear and doubt.

He tried the kitchen, searching all the cupboards, the pantry. Nothing.

Only the coat closet in the hall remained. He rushed toward it.

The front door was still open. Beyond lay the safety of night, of clear space to run.

Closet. A fleeting look. Empty. Whether that was good or bad . . .

Door.

He made it as far as the threshold.

The universe exploded into flames and dropped away from him. Some terrible force seized his whole body, lifting him effortlessly. The noise was too great to hear, only feel as it pulsed through him like a vast train. He was flying, limbs fluttering, helpless as a rag doll. He tumbled end over end before slamming into the packed earth.

The impact struck the breath from him. He was dimly aware of things hurtling past, like bullets but larger. Great chunks of the house flew around him. He cowered, hands on his head. Futile shields.

Run!

But he couldn't coordinate enough for that.

Nor was he fast enough.

The whole front wall, somehow holding together in spite of the destruction, bellied outward. He had an awful vision of red flames licking through the expanding cracks between the huge logs, and then they were falling onto him, and they were all on fire.

Chapter Five

Amid searing light, he was in darkness.

And pain. So much that the shadows in his mind drew back enough to allow in consciousness . . .

. . . realization . . .

. . . and horror.

Everything around him was in flames. They crackled and roared in obscene greed, flames that must surely consume him if he did not quickly do something.

The darkness that had fallen upon him withdrew as swiftly as it had come, and Richard became aware that he could not move. He tried to turn and see what held him. The effort made his whole body scream, and the blackness at the edge of his vision crept close once more.

He lay facedown on bare earth. He could see his arms. They were bloodied but free. Something pinned his legs. He pushed at the ground, ignoring the agony, and tried once more to turn. Succeeded.

Where the old house had been was now a rumbling, roaring bonfire. Thick rivers of smoke, blacker than the night sky, spiraled high to blot out the stars. The heat hammered against his exposed skin, worse than the sun.

The great logs had been thrown around like matchsticks by the unholy blast. Some lay in jumbled heaps of devilish architecture, others stood upright embedded in the ground like giant nails.

And one huge timber lay across his legs. And it was on fire. He smelled burning flesh and knew it was his own.

He scrabbled at the earth beneath him, digging, clawing frantically for freedom. His hands tore and bled from the sharp stones; he lost several fingernails, ripped from the root. This was what an animal felt as it chewed off one of its own limbs to escape a trap. He dug faster, then twisted his body back and forth until at last something gave way.

The heat grew unbearable as the tinder-dry log that held him burned more rapidly, but at last his legs were coming clear. At least one of them must have been broken, yet still he pushed and pulled for his freedom. Then suddenly he slid out from under the log, dragging himself from the fiery trap.

But flames licked insidiously up his legs; he slapped them out with bare and bleeding hands. Unable to walk, he clawed his way over the baking earth, until the stinging smoke was not so hot in his straining lungs, then collapsed.

He could do nothing for what seemed a very long time. His world had become hell, and he one of the damned souls in eternal torment.

Keeping still, he tried to take stock of his injuries. Something was embedded in his back like a knife, whether wood or iron he knew not. He could feel the wet trail of his own blood running down from the wound. One of his legs was broken, as he had surmised, the thigh bone jutting out through his flesh, ghastly white in the light from the burning wreckage. He was gouged raw with shrapnel and splinters. Hearing was impossible; blood trickled from his ears, from his shattered eardrums. And he was badly burned. The lower front of his broken leg was black and charred, and his reddened hands sprouted ugly white blisters.

Never had Richard known such a wounding, not even in the plane crash. Had he been any closer to the blast or been a normal human, he'd be dead. He could yet die. That he still breathed was hopeful, but he needed time to heal.

And fresh blood. Lots of it.

But from where? This place was truly isolated. He doubted that the explosion, massive as it was, had been noticed by any other than the small animals in the surrounding fields.

The horses.

He could not hear them, but saw their panicked milling in the nearby corral. Distance from the house and the barn's tin roof had spared them from the blast and fire.

Animal blood was not good for him. Sabra had warned him from the very first of the dangers of drinking it, of it being much the same peril as seawater to a parched human, but in a desperate situation it would do. The wretched stuff would keep him alive and give him some strength, though it would not be pleasant.

But before he could even think of doing anything else, whatever was impaled in his back would have to come out. It was worse than his leg and still bleeding freely.

He reached gingerly around and felt behind him. His burned fingers touched something hard projecting from a low angle between his ribs, but he couldn't tell what it was. Slowly, agonizingly, he inched the missile from his flesh. It had punctured a lung; he felt rather than heard the bubbling hiss of escaping air with each breath. Black mist whirled about him, threatening to engulf him. He had to pause between each effort, recover, then brace for the next. The only thing worse than pulling it out was leaving the damned thing in. A fit of coughing seized him. He spat blood and kept working.

He had no idea how long the removal took, only that it was a *long* time, and that every moment was agony. Finally, with a desperate exertion, it slipped free. Richard caved flat with a groan and stayed that way for a while.

When the black mist cleared somewhat he dragged the artifact around to see. It was one of the iron hinges that had held the front door of the house in place, half a yard in length. A third of it was covered with his blood.

He let it drop in the dust. Or rather mud. The ground where he lay was soaked crimson.

He tried to get up and failed. His broken leg. He'd have to set it before the healing could begin or be crippled for the rest of his life. He turned over and lightly touched the end of the broken bone, and immediately arched back, again in agony, biting off his cry. That was no good. It would have to be quick, this straightening of the bone. He'd have to gather every atom of will and force himself through the ordeal. Icy sweat stung his eyes, and he realized that his arms were shaking.

Dear Goddess, give me strength.

Unable to walk or even crawl, he dragged himself once more, covering the infinite distance to the corral and one of its fence posts. Panting and chilled with encroaching shock, he hooked the heel of his useless leg against the post, positioned his good foot over the instep, and made ready to push.

Don't let me pass out before it's over.

He moved quickly, before he could think too much about it. He pushed hard, stretching the break apart, and then reached down and shoved the bone back into the flesh of his leg, so that the two ends were level with each other. They ground back into place and held.

He could not hear himself, but knew that he screamed throughout the whole procedure, an animal's scream that cut through the roar of the fire, the scream of a wolf caught in a cruel steel trap. Then he fell back, gasping and soaked with sweat, white with shock, hardly able to move.

But move he must.

Richard was pitifully weak; he'd never been so feeble and sick, and every moment's delay stripped more strength and blood from his body. All he wanted was rest, just to close his eyes and sleep, to get away from the dreadful pain that racked his existence. Yet if he slept now in this enervated state he might never wake again. Then the rising sun would surely finish him off.

He used the fence to pull himself up. Had to lean on it. The black mist hovered close, drifting across his eyes. He dared not give in to it.

But he was so tired. So hurt . . .

He clung to the wood, praying for the temptation to pass.

Blackness and rest. A few moments of it would help. He could be healing while—

No. To give in was to lose all.

He limped one step, two, and nearly fell. He held to the fence like a drowning man.

Just a little more strength, I beg you.

Two more steps was all he could manage.

Someone would find him like this in the morning, arms draped over the crosspiece, head down, legs sagging. The sun would complete the job begun by the fire.

No . . . please . . . help me . . .

Then he felt it. The surging return of a sometime enemy, sometime friend.

Dazed and unsteady, yet overpowering, relentless in its hunger, it pushed back the blackness with a defiant snarl.

His beast was awake.

Thus it was his red-eyed master that made him raise up and struggle on along the fence line to the gate, to the horses. He had to feed from them or die; it was as simple as that, and the thing inside him would not permit him to stop.

At last, after what seemed an age, he made it to the gate of the corral, and reached over to release the latch. The horses, already panicked by the explosion and fire did not need the threat of his presence to seek escape. The instant there was an opening one of them took it, and the rest followed. He lunged forward to grasp a halter, but their stampede knocked him and the gate away from their flight.

He swung helpless, tears of frustration sheeting his eyes as he tried to hold on. His head throbbed with insidious pain, his vision swam. The darkness at the edge of his mind grew, threatening to overcome even the blood of Annwyn's Hounds. He swayed against the fence, fighting the oncoming faint.

Then through the numbness in his ears, he made out a sound. It seemed very distant, as though coming to him muffled by many layers of padded cloth. There was a thumping and stamping from within the stable and the high-pitched squeal of a frightened animal. Using the fence to keep weight off his bad leg, he edged his way into the smoke-filled building, peering into the dim depths. It was the pony, yet secure in its stall, lovingly cared for with plaited mane and neatly trimmed tail, but clearly filled with fear. Foam flecked its mouth, and sweat darkened its neck and flanks.

Richard hobbled and hopped to it as best he could, but getting close was difficult. The animal kicked out sporadically against the side of the stall. The whites of its eyes showed, and it would not be still. Richard's presence did nothing to help, for as it sensed his opening of the low door behind it, the animal plunged and bucked against its restraints.

Grasping the side of the stall for support, Richard eased around until at last he could take the pony's halter in hand and look the animal in the eye. Summoning his dwindling strength, he willed it to calmness. Most, if not all, creatures were telepathic in one way or another and could be influenced by him if he worked at it. Quiet thoughts, soothing words could overcome the most basic instincts. In moments the pony stopped fighting and came forward, nuzzling his head against him. They might have been in some wildflower meadow on a cool summer evening—that was the picture Richard had tried to project. The pony stretched out its neck, resting its head on Richard's shoulder, and he held it as if in a lover's embrace. Then as gently as he could so as not to disturb the fragile bond he'd made, Richard sank to the stable floor.

He spoke softly, patting the animal to keep it motionless. The veins in its neck were too deep within the flesh for him to reach, so he sought those running just beneath the skin on one leg. The hide was tough as he cut into it, but the bounty would be great.

He buried his fangs deep . . . and fed.

The taste was strange, thick, almost metallic. He dimly remembered that he'd fed so before in another wild and desperate time long ago. When was that? What had happened to him then? No matter. Nothing mattered except the restoration of his life.

The blood welled its way into his mouth, and he drank, greedy and starved, holding on desperately to the pony as the first wave of inner warmth crashed through him. He felt a sweet lightness take him, whether from the ecstasy of feeding or because of his wounds, he knew not. Pounding through his body was the thump of the creature's heart, and he felt his own strengthen as it struggled to match the rhythm, to catch that life.

A glow such as he'd not known since his youth in the sun heated his belly like the most potent wine. It spread out to his limbs; there was a delicious heat gathered at the break in his leg, and a lovely cool tingling at his burns.

The healing. Praise the Goddess and the beast within.

He drank—more than he could have safely taken from a human, but the animal could spare it.

He drank—long and deeply, more than was needed to achieve recovery.

He drank—until the thick blood seemed to go solid in his throat.

And he could not bring himself to tear away.

Not until the dizziness set in and became too much. He choked on his next swallow. His grip loosened, and he fell away coughing, blood bubbling from his nose and mouth as he did, his face a mask of red.

For the briefest time, he could do nothing. He lay helpless in the straw, his head lolling on one outflung arm, feeling the animal's strong life-force coursing through his veins. He found his eyes irresistibly drawn to a small pool of blood on a bare patch of flooring directly below his face. It had dribbled from his lips, and seemed to be taking on the most fascinating and hypnotic shapes, starting as a head in profile. Then it became three, one large and two small. Then it became a gun, held in a large hand.

How curious it all was. Richard moved a little so as to get a better angle on the picture, when it abruptly changed and became a gaping mouth, screaming. He could *hear* the screaming. It was Stephanie.

He thrashed himself upright, trying to find her.

The floor. The scream came from that gaping mouth on the floor.

With an immense effort of will, he wrenched his gaze away, and forced himself to ignore the sound until it faded. When it was gone, he looked down at the blood again and found there was no shape in it at all; it was simply a few drops of spilled redness, and he rubbed that away with one swipe of his hand.

The animal blood was healing him, but at a price.

The pony was recovered from his thrall now, and beginning to stir about once more. Richard reached up and loosened the halter rope. The animal backed away from him and wheeled eagerly toward the barn's open door.

"I thank you, good friend," he whispered as it went skittering out into the safety of the night.

He rested just long enough to decide he could try standing. He had to get to his car before things got any worse. If he could make it home, there was fresh human blood there, enough to flush this lesser nectar from his system.

Surprisingly, his feet held him, but only just. He could not put weight on his leg, but at least it did not blind him with pain each time he moved. On the way out he grabbed up a discarded garden hoe and used it as a cane.

Limping to the open door, he saw that the flames were dimmer now. The full force of the blaze was past, and with its passing the smoking destruction became brutally clear.

Of the house, there was simply nothing left but unidentifiable black lumps and thin remnants of the inside walls amid shards of the collapsed roof. The fieldstone chimney still stood, defiantly pointing skyward, and water jetted up from a ruptured pipe somewhere. Incongruously, the stove stood where it always had, seemingly unscathed, its door open as if expecting a meal to cook. The staunch old house was burned to a complete ruin. Flakes of charred paper flew about haphazardly like obscene snow in the updraft of the leftover heat. The master bedroom and its ephemeral contents were gone, the three bodies buried in a mountain of rubble from the blast.

A wave of nausea passed over him. He'd seen death too many times before to allow himself to react to it in such a manner even under these circumstances. It had to be the alien blood doing this to him, setting him to an uncontrollable shuddering. He had to get back to his car, to New Karnak so he could feed on human blood and fully heal. Then, by all that was holy, by the sacred groves of Avalon, by the Goddess herself, he would find who was responsible. He would avenge those deaths, and his vengeance would be beyond terrible.

He staggered toward his car, lurching like a drunkard. The animal blood was having a bad effect on him mentally, even as it restored him physically. His vision swam, and he saw all manner of strange, distorted things. Shadows leapt out at him, assuming impish shapes before dissolving to nothing. Sounds ebbed and flowed in his ears. Voices rang and mumbled with dire warnings in a language he couldn't quite understand. Then his legs abruptly gave way, and the ground floated up gracefully to meet him. Sweat sprang out on his forehead like spring rain. He lay shaking, his fingers scratching impotently at the hard earth, teeth clenched tight so as not to bite his tongue.

It will pass, it must *pass.*

He felt so tired. His body ached everywhere, and his knitting wounds screamed at him angrily. He tried to shout back at them, but couldn't seem to draw in enough breath. He rolled onto his back and saw the moon, quite new, smiling down at him. Then all at once, it wasn't the moon, but the pale, pock-marked face of his long-dead father Montague grinning at him through broken and discolored teeth. And his voice came clear across the night air.

"What ails thee, Richard? Disappointed you didn't kill me after all?"

That awful night so long, so very long ago, came back to him in haunting detail. He could see it all, his father's face and his brother's distorted with hatred for him and with fear of him. He felt the sharpness of his father's dagger once more and heard his laugh, and tears from the betrayal sprang again fresh to Richard's eyes. But as suddenly as it had come, the vision whipped away, and he knew that the pain was not some long ago wound, but the healing at work, his life renewing itself, the miracle of Sabra's dark gift.

With a grunt, he rolled over onto his knees, and pushed himself upright. Where had that damned hoe gotten to? His leg hurt like hell, and now fresh new pain intruded from one of his burned hands.

He could see them clearly in the pitiless moonlight. Charred skin hung down in papery shreds, and several nails were missing, but beneath was the bright redness of new growth. Then he saw something else. The whole surface of his left hand seemed to be moving, alive. It was covered with what seemed like millions of furiously moving black dots. Ants. Fire ants. He remembered Stephanie speaking often of them. Yet another South American import doomed to create suffering and misery. They were tiny, voracious and mean, with a bite out of all proportion to their size. He looked down at where he'd fallen, and saw a bowling-ball-size mound, its top crushed by his hand. Streams of the angry insects poured out, each one bent on avenging the destruction of their home.

He desperately tried to brush them off, but they seemed to be sticking to him, and all he succeeded in doing was transferring them to his other hand where the rabid biting began anew. Hard red bumps were already evident where the poison had gone in. The pain from them was intense, and Richard groaned aloud at this new suffering. He'd have to wash them off somehow.

He looked around at the destruction, then spied the pump house. It had been out of range of the blast and stood untouched. He'd shown it to Stephanie, explaining that it had been the core of the original water supply for some long vanished homesteader. Within was a large iron hand pump, set imperiously on the wooden cover of a deep well, with a single iron pipe disappearing into the depths below. It squeaked in seeming irritation as he proudly showed her that it still worked. At one time it had stood in the open, as its rusted state attested, until someone had sensibly built a shed around it and the mechanized pump for the well. Richard suggested that the old one be removed and the well closed up for good, but Stephanie resisted, insisting on keeping it exactly as it was.

"You never know when we might need it."

She picked up a rock, and moving a slat of the well's wood cap aside, dropped it into the darkness. They waited a very long time for the splash, and when it came it was from a long way below them.

"No children in here," he pronounced.

Then she quickly hugged him in the sun-streaked darkness, and kissed his ear.

"Thank you, Richard, for everything. Thank you."

The memory had stopped him in his tracks with its vividness, all his pain relegated to no importance by the vision. A lump, hard as coal and twice as black, pushed up into his throat and his breath suddenly came in sobbing gasps.

Why? Why?

The ants brought him back to the present with their incessant biting, and quick as he could, he limped to the pump house. The latch was placed high on the door, well out of reach of small hands. He hit it and stumbled in.

It was cool inside, the iron of the pump cold against his hand. For a second he leaned forward and rested his cheek against the metal, thanking the Goddess for its soothing touch, then hastened to work it.

The thing still squeaked, but the water gushed out strongly, rust-colored at first, then clear. He washed the ants away, then leaned forward and put his head under the icy flow. The cold was intense, a deep-within-the-earth cold, and he nearly pulled away. It was very close to being free-running water.

The uncontrollable shaking took hold of him once again, and he had to stop. He could no longer see. Hot tears streamed down his face as he thought of Stephanie and sobs racked him deep. There was too much pain. His heart would surely break from it. Then his pain gained expression, and he cried all his grief to the mocking moon, the uncaring stillness, the laughing stars.

Your fault, Richard d'Orleans, they told him. *You cannot die, so others must. Your fault.*

They were right. He'd caused his mother's death, and countless others since. And now Stephanie and the girls. Probably Luis and Michael, too. They hadn't been in the house, but must have been caught elsewhere and likely killed first. Luis had done unsavory things in his past, but he would never leave Stephanie in danger if he knew of it. He did love her and his children.

The whole family was gone, and it was all Richard's fault. He'd done something wrong, missed some telling detail, made some simple mistake, and she'd died as a result. She that he had loved . . . did still love. More blood on his already encrusted hands.

The tears drained his remaining strength, and he slumped against the rough wood side of the shed. Again, nausea took hold of him, and he bent double as though cramping from hunger. The walls swam outward away from him, losing their form and substance, then snapped back into place again. He could hear voices, angry, scared. Stephanie's, pleading it seemed, begging, then becoming a scream. He could hear a man's low rumble and children crying. Richard shook his head trying to clear them out. It was all in his mind, an illusion. None of it was real. It was the damned animal blood giving him this waking nightmare.

Then the pain returned. His fingers had swollen to twice their normal size and throbbed horribly. Small dents marked where his nails were growing back, but the ache was as bad as having them torn out, was worse in a way, since he wasn't distracted this time.

The broken leg was mending; he could feel the two pieces of bone literally knitting together with a kind of deep internal itch. He held his hands clear of himself and marked their slow progress back to normalcy. The burns had been washed away with the ants; the new skin felt too tight, but that would pass.

All he wanted to do was sleep, to hide in that blessed darkness from all that had happened in the last . . . how long? He had no idea. It seemed like an eternity and a split second all at once. He had to rest and seriously considered the possibility of giving in to the need. He was safe from the sun in here, and would likely remain unconscious through the day. By then the blood would have done its healing and worked through him. At sunset he could hurry home and replenish himself—

No good. Sooner or later someone would notice the smoke in the morning sky and call the fire department. They were justifiably paranoid about wildfires down here. The last thing he wanted was to be noticed by the local authorities.

But he could rest for a *few* hours. Just a little while would help immeasurably.

As he thought through the possibilities, his gaze fell upon a pile of rags in one corner of the shed. There was something odd about them, about their shape . . .

Then his muzzy senses cleared for a second, and in a cold

moment of realization he knew he was not alone. He could feel another presence in here with him. Despite the pain of his wounds, despite his awful reaction to the animal blood, he was suddenly poised and alert, ready for anything. He listened, straining to the utmost to catch the slightest sound. Then it all broke down and the black mists rolled in once more over his mind. His vision blurred; his senses wandered.

He groaned in frustration. He was trying too hard. The more effort he put into it, the more quickly it evaded him. This was no hallucination, but something real and vitally important.

Just let it come.

He waited and stared until the pile of rags gradually assumed a recognizable shape. A human shape. A child.

It was Michael. He was *alive.*

The boy was hunched across from Richard in the corner, his face turned to the wall, his arms over his head. He made no sound and did not move, yet Richard could now hear the reassuring flutter of his little heart and his soft breathing.

"Michael . . . ?"

There was no reply. The boy did not stir.

Hurts forgotten, Richard eased himself to his knees and tried again. "Michael . . . it's Uncle Richard. Remember? Uncle Richard."

Still no response. Richard crawled toward him slowly. For a terrible moment he doubted his senses, the boy was so still. Had the damned animal blood done this too, blurred his perception into hoping for the impossible, played another trick on him? But it was not so. Now that he was close, it was clear that Michael was indeed real.

Relief nearly made him fall down again. It did make him sob, but he fought that back.

"Everything's all right, Michael. It's Uncle Richard. No one can hurt you now."

Richard reached out and put his hand on the boy's shoulder, then pulled him close. The boy twitched beneath the touch. Then in an instant he was up and fighting, twisting and turning in blind terror, whimpering incoherently. Such was his sudden fear-filled strength that he nearly got away. Richard held him as gently as he could, not feeling the kicks and blows, the scratches, as the terrified child fought for his life against some monstrous enemy. Then as suddenly as the fighting had started, it stopped, and the little body fell slack against him, shaking in reaction. Richard held him tight, rocking, stroking the sweat-tangled white-blond hair.

Dear Goddess, what had the boy witnessed that had done this to him?

"It's all right now, Michael. Nothing can hurt you now. Nothing can hurt you now. It's all right." He crooned the mantra over and over again.

Slowly, ever so slowly, the shaking subsided, the ragged breathing calmed. There were no sobs of release yet; Richard would have felt them. Michael made no sound at all. Richard relaxed his hold, and the boy fell back, his head supported by Richard's arm. Then Richard saw his eyes, and his blood ran cold at the sight. They were bright shining blue—and quite empty. They were like the eyes of a corpse, blank, staring, dead, but in a living body.

Ah, Michael, what did you see?

He had to get them away as soon as possible. The boy needed help. He was deep in shock at the very least, and for all that he was, Richard was no doctor. Then yet another wave of reaction hit him, and he sank down groaning, stomach cramped, vision blurred. Michael lay in his arms like a stone, motionless, heavy. Darkness crept in at the edges of Richard's sight, and he fought it for the boy's sake and his own.

He heard cruel laughter, as though someone outside knew the futility of his efforts. It sounded like his long-perished father.

Then Montague himself appeared in the doorway, not in his dotage as Richard had last seen him, but as a fit young man in his prime. He was tall as a tree, wearing battle armor, and holding a sword.

"What ails thee, boy?" he demanded.

"Go hence," Richard told him in a tongue he'd not spoken in centuries. His tone was astonishingly normal and tinged with annoyance. "You are not real. Leave us in peace."

"I'll leave thee dead, coward," the apparition replied. " 'Tis the only peace left to thee." Montague's sword flashed high, somehow unencumbered by the confines of the shed, and swung down decisively.

In spite of himself Richard flinched in reaction and thought the child in his arms did the same. Montague's ghostly blade cut harmlessly through Richard's body, leaving behind only cold trails. Mere illusion, but for all that still damned unpleasant to simply sit and endure. "Get thee hence! I'll give you no more sport. Thou art dead, gone to dust, and forgot by all."

Montague paused, laughing. "Not all. Here do I live and always will." He bent and pressed one mailed finger firmly on the exact center of Richard's forehead.

Dear Goddess, I felt that!

Then Montague melted away to nothing, only his laughter lingering behind.

Sickened, Richard rubbed the spot where he'd been touched. He could still feel the pressure of hard metal links scratching against his flesh in the exact spot where Elena and Seraphina had been—

Leave. Leave now, while you can.

He wanted to, more than anything, but his body was not cooperating. It was as though his father's touch had sucked away all his remaining strength. Richard needed rest, but had no desire to surrender again to his subconscious at this particular moment. Who knew what other monsters might be lurking there?

I'll just stay awake and keep watch, then. He'd done that often enough through countless other nights.

Michael's eyes were closed now, and his head lay against Richard's chest. How comforting it was to simply hold him, to feel his intense little life warm against his own. So young he was, so vulnerable.

Despite his resolve Richard's lids grew heavier with every passing second, until his valiant fight was lost, and sleep swept over him, irresistible as a riptide at full moon, and carried him away. His head drooped forward to rest on the boy's, his breathing slowed and became regular, and his pain was finally, mercifully drowned by slumber.

Then came the nightmares.

Colors, sounds, merged and divided. The borders of his reality were torn down, mixed up in some hellish brew and thrown back up again, haphazard, all wrong.

Shapes flew by like carrion birds, close enough that the breeze from their passing ruffled his hair, yet never touched him. He grabbed at them, but his hands returned empty. One came directly at him, not a bird but some . . . thing . . . grinning, and Richard threw his arms up instinctively to protect himself, only to feel whatever it was pass all around him, through him, cold and laughing, like Montague with his sword.

Richard stood alone in some vast emptiness, buffeted by an unforgiving hot wind. He spread his arms wide and tried to face into it, but it kept shifting direction. Then slowly, like a wheel stopping its spin, the whirling colors and shapes began to settle and coalesce into something recognizable. Richard found himself in a house, familiar to him, but not his own.

It was the log house, the house that was now destroyed. Fully restored in his dream, but there was something not quite right in his perception of it. The ceiling seemed unnaturally high, the rooms longer and wider. Everything was so much larger than it should be.

He lay on his bed. He knew it was his though he'd never slept in it. There were posters on the walls, movie posters. Whatever actor it was that had last played Batman glared seriously at him from one, and a blonde supermodel unnervingly like a young Brigitte Bardot simpered at him from another. He sat up and looked around. Clothes were scattered everywhere, and toys. Mommy had told him to clean things up before he could play, but the lure of his brand new Spiderman comic was too much for him. He could sneak a few minutes and break off the instant he heard her coming down the hall and pretend to have been cleaning all along. She'd never know. He smiled to himself and settled in to read.

Then voices cut through his stolen pleasure. One belonged to his mother; he couldn't make out the other. She sounded scared, her tone high and cracked with strain. He'd never heard her sound like that before, not even when she argued with Daddy. She was shouting something, and it scared him. He had to find out what was happening, what was wrong.

He rounded a corner in the huge hall, hugging close to the wall, cautious of being seen. The voices were coming from Mommy's bedroom. His sisters were there too; he could hear them crying, but it was not their usual kind of fussing. They were afraid, so much so that it made his chest hurt hard, as though he wanted to cry himself.

There was another corner. He could see golden light from the big bedroom spilling around it. He didn't want to go there. Something horrible was there. Then suddenly his mother's words rang clear:

"No! For God's sake! You can't, not my babies, you can't, you can't—*NOOO*!"

She made an awful scream, and a balloon popped somewhere, scaring him, making him jump. It was a big balloon, because it made a big noise, and the air rang with the sound. Now his sisters shrieked like little animals, and two more balloons popped, the explosions echoing toward him.

Then all the noise stopped, and no more followed.

He shivered in the hall. Confused, afraid. He tried to call out, but couldn't make himself speak.

Who had blown up balloons? It wasn't Christmas or a birthday. There'd be trouble for bursting them. Daddy didn't like that. He hated any kind of sudden, loud sounds.

It was too quiet, something awful had happened. He didn't want to see it, but he had to. Maybe Mommy needed help. He moved forward. Then he peered around the corner, and he could see. Mommy was sitting in a chair. Her head was down on her chest. Maybe she was asleep. She must have spilled something because the front of her blouse was all stained . . . red.

His heart raced and his breath came short. He knew the stain was blood. He'd seen blood before, lots of it that time when he split his toe at day camp, and had to go to the hospital in an ambulance, and bled all down the hall. But this was much more. This was real bad. This was much worse than any of that.

His sisters were lying on the floor against the wall, and they were bleeding too from spots on their foreheads. Neither of them cried. But they always cried when they got hurt. Always. Now they just looked asleep, like Mommy.

Tears slid silently down his face and he started to rock gently from foot to foot. Wetness gathered at his crotch. What had happened to them and why? Was it still there? Would it come for him?

Then there was a gun. It was huge, black. It seemed to fill every space of the room, fill all of his world, as it slowly turned to point at him. The hole at the end of the barrel threatened to swallow him. Someone was speaking, but he didn't know who. All he could see was the gun; there was nothing else.

The finger on the trigger tensed, and the hammer began to move. He could see it clearly, hear the mechanism start its unholy journey.

"*Adios* to you too, you little bastard."

He should run, shouldn't he? Or maybe he should stay with Mommy. He tried to look at her but could not tear his gaze from the gun.

The hammer slid farther back on its inevitable journey, and then plunged forward. There was flame and a flash, the explosion crashing though the quiet, bursting through his ears, sending his mind spinning. He heard something fizz past him and thud into the wall behind. The gun had been jerked to one side at the last instant. Mommy had pushed it away.

She was on her feet now, weakly struggling with the gun, and the man who held it was hitting her and swearing at her, and through all this her hoarse terrified voice pierced through his own fear.

"Run, Michael, run, run, runrun*run*—!"

He ran for his life away from the scene. He barely heard the last balloon pop, cutting off his mother's shout. He tore through the house and out of the front door.

Bright morning light greeted him, nearly blinded him. He just ran and ran. He did not need to hear the man start after him to know he was there.

He ran across the bare front yard toward the beginnings of the mesquite scrub. Their fluffy-looking green concealed an endless number of long thorns. He ducked low, darting beneath the branches. The big man could not easily follow him here. The trees closed fast behind him and opened wide ahead into protecting darkness. He could hide there.

He ran straight into it, into the long dark tunnel that stretched endlessly before him.

He would be safe forever and ever if he could get to the end of the tunnel. He knew that.

He would be safe if only he could reach its end . . . if only he could . . .

Chapter Six

The tunnel was long, yet it seemed that he was finally coming to the end; he could see lights. He headed directly for them, but they were not to be reached, for even as he neared they swung away at the last instant, and darkness closed around him again. Would he ever find the end of it? He began to despair when more lights appeared in the distance. Again to his frustration, they swung away from him, but this time a strange wailing sound accompanied them. It rose and fell as it passed.

Too much like a banshee, Richard thought, stirring with unease.

The blackness slowly brightened, though, and Richard realized that he was sitting in an enclosed space, and there was something under his right foot that vibrated slightly. In fact everything vibrated slightly all around him. If only he could see more in this damned murk. He bowed his head, rubbing the glue from his eyes, and his world gave an unexpected lurch. He snapped up, all attention, found he could see perfectly well, and for a split second, panic seized him.

His car sped along, weaving gently from side to side, paying attention to neither the line down the middle of the road nor its ragged shoulders. No wonder the lights swerved away from his approach. They'd been other cars. Thank God he'd not caught any of them.

He grabbed hard at the steering wheel where his hands rested, and brought the vehicle under control. How in the name of all things had he gotten here? He could not remember. He must have left the house and been driving on autopilot for God knows how long—without bothering to turn on the headlights. It was a wonder he hadn't killed anyone.

Richard corrected the oversight and tried to get his bearings. He was still out in the country, and heading toward a glow on the horizon that must be Dallas. The clock on the dash pulsed green numbers at him, but he couldn't wrap his mind around the time it showed, only that it was very late. Or very early. Hours must have passed since his nightmare had begun. And he was apparently still in it.

He was sweating, and dizziness washed over him in waves, though the sea that tossed him was no longer in full storm. Memories came and went willy-nilly, refusing to stay long enough for sorting. Finding the bodies, the explosion, he could remember those clearly enough, but other details were muddy. He'd been sick . . . no, badly injured—

As if in response to the thought a sudden cramp in his stomach doubled him over, and the car swerved in violent reaction. He had to stop.

He hit the brakes a good deal harder than he meant, and the vehicle came to rest with its front end on the shoulder, its rear out on the road. No matter, it wasn't a busy highway. Richard cut the motor, pushed the door open, and staggered out into the night air. It cooled him, and he drank it down in great gulps like an exhausted runner. He remembered now. The damned animal blood. The hallucinations and shadows.

And . . . that vision.

He'd seen it all, seen how the murders in the house had happened. *He* had been Michael, been right inside his head, looking out through his eyes. Yet how could that be? Richard did not have the Sight. Sabra had told him often enough that it was not part of his Gift.

"It is given by the Goddess at birth. Even before birth, and to a very few. She chooses who will see, not I. And she does not give her reasons." And she squeezed his hand like a parent with a disappointed child.

He could feel her hand now, small, almost hidden in his grasp, warm and full of comfort. The feeling was so strong he had to look to see that she was not truly there. He was sorry for that, longing for the solace of her presence. She would know what to do, what to say to make things better, but she was miles away in her Vancouver wilderness.

The vision of the killings disturbed him deeply, not for what it was—he had expected such brutal violence—but for the fact that he'd seen it at all. He had the uncomfortable knowledge of having gone someplace dangerous where he was not supposed to venture, like a child swimming in a lake against his parent's wishes. There were certain things that were of the Goddess and should not be tampered with, and Richard had a chill feeling in his gut he'd somehow done exactly that. He'd swum deep in the forbidden lake, and looked up at the world above through its changing waters, and seen what he should not. A shiver crept its slow way up his spine at the very thought. Damn the animal blood for taking him where he was not meant to go.

But it *had* shown him what Michael had seen, felt, and thought, which could be . . . Michael. Where was he?

The car's interior illuminated as Richard opened the rear driver's door, and in the harsh light he could see the boy was sitting safely belted in the back seat. He slid partway in for a better look at the child.

"Michael, it's Uncle Richard. Can you hear me? Michael?"

No response. The silence rang deafeningly through the still night air. Those dead blue eyes gazed straight ahead, quite unaware of him. Richard stroked the boy's hair, whispering his name again. Still no response. Little wonder, considering what he'd been through. The vision had been disturbing enough for Richard, but poor Michael had witnessed the real thing. Richard would have to get him help.

He eased out and closed the rear door, the abrupt darkness swallowing everything. No streetlamps this far away from town. Usually he didn't mind the lack of artificial lights, but craved them now. Lights meant that he wouldn't feel so damned alone.

But before he could get inside to drive, the cramping nausea hit again, and Richard folded over with the hurt, leaning desperately against the car, sweat breaking out in great drops on his brow and falling to mix in tiny muddy puddles on the dry earth. His body ached in every pore, and his vision swam. God, but this was too much. He'd have to look after himself before he could look after the boy. He still needed human blood to dispel the last of the alien poison. He had to get back to New Karnak. Quickly.

After an age the pain eased, and Richard was able to stand upright and get in the car. It slipped easily into drive, and he set the rental right on the pavement, heading south. Driving was a huge effort. At first he thought the power steering was out, then realized it was simply his own physical weakness that made holding the wheel such an exertion.

He was healed for the most part, though. That was something to celebrate. The broken leg felt normal again, and the angry red skin marking his burns had faded to a less alarming pink. Even his torn-out nails had grown back. The blood had done its miracle, but the aftermath was still playing a devil's game with his insides.

His hands trembled, and whenever a wave hit he leaned forward toward the windshield, unable to sit up straight, resting his chin on the wheel. The car wandered alarmingly, and he found himself having to ease up on the gas during bouts so as not to go off the road before he could correct things. He was doing no more than twenty. At this rate it would take hours to get home.

He wiped sweat from his eyes. Tried to concentrate. He kept drifting in and out, always unaware of the onset of the dark mist, and waking with alarm at its retreat.

He wrenched the car over once more from the wrong side of the road. *I should stop,* he thought, but knew he could not. His sight blurred fitfully, and he shook his head in a feeble attempt to clear his vision. Then he noticed bright lights in the rearview mirror flashing red to blue, red to blue, and gave an inward groan. Why were they always there when you didn't want them? He heard the siren wail a short, imperious warning, and obedient to the law, he eased the car onto the shoulder and coasted to a halt. The police car did the same, leaving its headlights on. Richard could just make out the vague form of the officer inside and his heart gave a small leap. His initial dismay at the intrusion evaporated. This might be exactly what he needed.

But he was so weak. If only he could sleep. The steering wheel was mercifully cool against his forehead. His eyes fell shut.

He heard a car door slam and slow footsteps on the gravel of the shoulder. Then a flashlight beam shone red through his lids. He rolled his head to one side and squinted out the open window. It was a woman, clipboard in one hand, flashlight in the other, her uniform and badge proclaiming her to be a member of Addison's finest.

"Good morning, sir," she said in an overly loud voice. The sort of voice law enforcement professionals always used to command attention. It did not jibe well with the polite words. "How are you doing?"

There was nothing to be gained trying to form a reply to that query. He was doing rather badly, thank you very much; she should be able to see that for herself.

She shone the light around the interior and caught a good long look at Richard. He stank of smoke and sweat. His clothes were mostly torn away and what remained was either scorched or covered in dried blood. Her breath escaped in a non-professional hiss. "Jesus!"

Richard could see her silver name tag now against the dark blue of her shirt: Henebry.

"I'm just a little tired, officer . . ." Good God, what lunatic had answered for him just then? He could do better than that.

"Sir? Sir, I'm going to ask you to get out of your car."

Very well, ask away.

"Sir—I want you to get out of the car. Can you do that?"

I'd really rather not if you don't mind.

"Come on. Get out right now." Still speaking loud and clear. She had a no-nonsense quality about her that in other circumstances, Richard was sure he would find appealing. But here and now it irritated the hell out of him. It was probably the way she acted as though he were slightly deaf and somewhat backward mentally. Perhaps she thought he was drunk.

"Maybe I should rest here for a little while . . ."

"I said get out of the car, sir, and I mean right now." She was new. Richard could tell that without asking. There was an edge in her voice that gave her away, that and a bead of sweat on her upper lip. "Come on, open the door."

She was starting to grate on his nerves, ordering him about so politely, but he could also be teeth-grittingly courteous. Richard attempted what he hoped would pass for a smile of compliance and pulled on the handle. It took some work to push the door open, then turn and get his legs out. He finally managed to boost clear, standing more or less upright facing her.

Officer Henebry was solid and fit in her uniform. He towered over her.

Henebry backed off a step, still holding her clipboard. Her other hand rested on the big semi-auto strapped to her hip. Considering his appalling state he couldn't blame her. "Are you all right? You want to tell me what happened to you?" she asked, spacing the words.

Not in this lifetime I don't. Richard shook his head, gathering his scattered thoughts. He should have taken care of this by now. His usual time for dealing with traffic violations was less than a minute. Ah, but this was no simple avoidance of a speeding ticket.

"Are you injured? What happened to you?" she demanded, shining her light on him. "Who's the little boy in the back seat?"

The reminder of Michael snapped him to full alertness. For the moment. How long would it last? *Never mind that, get to work.*

"I want to see some identification. You got a driver's license?"

"Yes, officer. It's in my wallet." He slowly reached toward his back pocket. Henebry, on guard, tensed. Her grasp tightened on her gun, ready to pull it free.

Richard turned slightly, so she could see his every move, and took out his wallet using two fingers. He could not fault her for her caution. Aside from domestic disputes, the most disagreeable calls cops generally faced were investigating driving violations. Especially at night.

"Take it out of the wallet, please," she told him. The whole situation was wearing thin. Could this downturn possibly be another unpleasant hallucination? He wasn't certain. Better to play along. A docile attitude might reassure her somewhat. Things would work better for them both if she was relaxed.

He glanced back at her car to see if she was alone. She was. Better and better. Then he noticed something that would put a decided crimp in things. The vehicle had a surveillance camera set in the grill. The picture would likely be of poor quality, but enough to later identify him. It would have recorded his rental's tags as well. The paranoia of the twentieth century was often defensible, but now it was just bloody inconvenient.

He pulled his Canadian driving license clear and held it out to her. "Here it is, officer. I think you'll find it all in order."

She was intent on taking it from him, but for a moment, for a very crucial moment, she looked him in the eyes.

All he had to do was smile. He summoned enough strength to make a profound impression.

The wrong kind, as it happened.

Her service semi-auto appeared almost as if by magic in her hand. It was a Glock, its dark plastic surface dully reflecting first the blue, then the red of the prowl car's flashing lights. Henebry pointed it steadily at him. Right between his eyes to be exact. He felt a sudden tightness in his chest as the memory of Michael's horrific vision superimposed itself on the present time. Richard had to fight to maintain control, to keep himself from running away.

"Put your hands on your head!"

Funny, his smile was usually enough to win anyone over. But then he usually wasn't clad in burned, bloodstained rags and . . . oh. Oh, dear.

His corner teeth were out. No wonder she'd reacted so strongly. His beast could have that effect on people.

Henebry slapped the clipboard on the hood of his car, and shook out a pair of handcuffs. Richard was as adventurous as the next man, but he didn't think she had any intention of putting them to some sort of erotic use. "Lean on the car. Place your hands on the roof and lean on them."

"How can I do that and still have them on my head?" he inquired, annoyed again.

"Just turn around and put them flat on the roof." She said it with a sense of satisfaction, almost as if quoting from some obscure training test.

Richard grimly struggled to think of how to delay things. Once she got those cuffs on him he'd not be able to break free of them; he was too weak for that. Then he would be stuck in the endless quagmire of officialdom.

"I've done nothing wrong, officer." He was too weak for some things, but his beast gave him one last little reserve to draw from.

"Don't argue with me; turn—"

He could yet move very fast.

She had no chance to finish. Between one eye blink and the next he snagged the gun from her grasp. He caught her before she could react, swung her around, pressing her against the rental car with his body. She recovered quickly, though, and started to struggle, but abandoned that when he made her aware the gun was pressed hard on her temple. He hated doing it, but it was a necessary compensation for his feeble state. It also commanded her undivided attention.

The scent of her sudden fear jumped at him. How tantalizing *that* was to his beast.

Control. Keep control.

"Now, Officer Henebry—" No, such an address was too awkward, too formal for what he had in mind. "What's your first name?"

She glared at him. Scared as she must be, she was also mad as hell.

He asked the same question again, this time using her gun for emphasis.

"Kath," she spat out. "Kath Henebry."

"That's lovely. Suits you very well."

"Listen, mister—"

"I think not. You must listen to me, Kath. What I have to say is very important; you need to hear every word. Are you listening, Kath Henebry?" He looked her hard in the eye. An uncomfortable silence stretched between them when she did not answer. "Are you?" he asked, his tone softer, more seductive.

"I hear you." She practically sighed out her reply. There was a definite blush on her face, but he wasn't sure if it was because of him or a product of her anger.

He continued to look hard at her, but spoke mild, soothing words, and almost imperceptibly she slipped under his sway. Her eyes glazed slightly, and her breathing became even. Richard reached up and tucked a stray lock of hair under her hat. That done, he stepped back, holding to the car to keep his balance. The effort had taken a lot out of him. She remained in place, staring at the empty fields. Excellent. He held the heavy firearm out to her.

"I want you to put the gun away and not move until I tell you to."

The only sound was the smart snap of plastic against leather as she obeyed. She continued to stare, a wonderfully serene expression on her face.

"Thank you." He quickly checked on Michael who was as he'd left him, belted in the back seat, still unresponsive. Mindful or not of the world around him, he certainly did not need to see what was about to happen.

Richard turned back to Officer Henebry and reestablished their connection. "Come around here with me, Kath, there is something we have to do. It will not be unpleasant for either of us."

He took her hand. It was very small in his, freshly manicured and warm. He lifted it in his and brushed his lips against it. She smelled of roses, and he closed his eyes and breathed in deeply. Her veins lay pale blue under the skin, and in the silence, he could hear her heart fluttering.

The stimulus had its welcome effect. The sickness, the aches of his body, fled for the moment as deep in his gut, his groin, he felt his need for her. It was more intense than usual. He would have to be careful and take her now while what self-control he possessed was still in place. Gently, he led her around so that her patrol car lay protectively between them and the road. This was a very open place, and he did not want to be disturbed by any passing motorist. He glanced quickly both ways, but everything was clear.

Kath stood facing him, mouth slightly open, lips moist. She wore lipstick, and Richard idly wondered if that was allowed on duty. He took off her hat. Her shining brown hair was curled up in a knot. How lovely it would be to take it down and twine between his fingers . . .

Steady on.

"Roll up your sleeve."

She obeyed.

"Now hold out your arm."

This she did too, and Richard moved closer. He knew what he looked like at this moment, and was glad she had no conscious perception of it. His eyes were red, wolflike, and his teeth long and razor sharp. A low growl, pure animal, rose from him, and his beast impatiently stirred as Richard braced her against the car.

He took her arm in his hand, and brought it up to his mouth. The scent of roses was heavy at the wrist, then diminished as he moved along toward the elbow. His sense of smell was heightened, and the fragrance almost brought water to his eyes, it seemed so potent. He slid his other arm around her waist, and despite his best efforts at self-restraint, pressed himself roughly upon her, feeling the firm length of her body with his. He ran his tongue slowly along her neck, tasting her, feeling the veins there throbbing so quickly. Ah, if only he had more time and was not in such sore need. He would have to forgo this sweet contact in favor of one less dangerous to her.

He bowed his head down, and bit into the soft skin on the inside of her elbow. His teeth cut through the flesh easily, and the blood flowed strong into him, pulsing in time with her heartbeat.

He sucked hungrily, hardening, pushing himself urgently against her. Her head fell back and, loosened in the moment, her hair cascaded down. To Richard, it smelled of heaven. He caressed her, feeling the fine texture of her hair, the smoothness of her temple, her cheek. Her mouth opened as his fingers brushed over her lips and a low moan escaped her.

He wanted this to go on and on as he had all those years ago with the servant in Sabra's tent, that first time. More than that, he wanted this woman, wanted to be inside her, to be one with her. Kath's heart beat faster—he could hear it—and her breath came in small gasps. Her breasts pushed hard against him, and he could now smell her musk, heavy in the air with her own arousal.

He supped heavily and well on her strength, her sweetness, her very spirit. If he could not be in her, then she must surely be in him. He felt the rush of her vitality flooding his own veins and welcomed it, reveled in it.

But he had to stop. It would cost Kath her life if he did not. So he pulled back, reluctantly kissing away the remaining traces of blood, eyes closed as he savored the last shreds of ecstasy. He could feel it coursing through him, healing and reviving as it went. He had fed enough to last until he got home.

After a few moments he came back to himself. He lifted her face to his and kissed her long and deep. Then, looking her in the eye, he told her what he always told his partners. She'd been to a blood donation center and would feel a little light-headed for the next day or two. He always carried adhesive bandages in his back pocket for just such occasions, and by some miracle they were yet clean in their wrappings. He taped them over the small puncture marks he'd left, rolled her sleeve down, and fastened the cuff.

"You will remember nothing of what has happened here," he whispered in her ear.

"I will remember nothing," she obligingly confirmed.

Then Richard leaned forward and whispered once more, getting rather detailed. Kath immediately went to her patrol car, and in a very short time he had the highly incriminating surveillance tape in hand. Officer Henebry would simply report that by some mistake the recorder had not been loaded prior to her patrol that night.

"Your hat . . ." He gave it to her.

After a quick rearrangement of her tumbled hair, she replaced her visored cap squarely on her head. "Thank you."

"It truly was a pleasure," he replied, quite sincere.

She threw the car into gear and sped off, executing a smart U-turn and accelerating back in the direction Richard had come from. As she passed, she waved, and Richard heard a long throaty laugh as she disappeared down the road. Yes, it had been an enjoyable experience for them both.

In the distance, her siren started its ominous howl. She would get to what was left of the house and start the whole process of investigation. She wouldn't remember how she'd gotten there or why, but those explanations were her problem, not his. He must be on his way. Her fresh blood had improved his state; the dizziness and cramping had cleared, and his vision, though not steady, was better than it had been. But he was still far from well.

He retrieved his wallet and license from where they'd fallen forgotten on the road shoulder. With some chagrin he noticed her clipboard with its attached paperwork still on his hood. Yet another mystery for the good officer to ponder. Just as well for him to have the thing: she'd recorded his tag numbers. He tossed it on the passenger seat with his drover's coat and hat. There would likely be some record of them with the dispatcher when Kath first called in her stop, but without the car tape and clipboard as support there was a chance the minor mystery would be dismissed. He'd covered that as well while filling her head with instructions. After all, so far as she was concerned, she'd never even seen him, and in less than an hour the police would have far more important matters demanding their attention.

Once inside again he checked on Michael. His head drooped and his eyes were closed; he seemed to be sleeping. Hopefully that was a good sign. There was no point disturbing him. Snapping his seat belt, Richard started the car and pushed it into gear. The sooner home, the better. The last thing he wanted was to be caught out in daylight.

He could sense the sun dragging itself toward the horizon, the sky changing from black to dark blue; the night all but gone.

The rest of the journey proved uneventful, and he was glad for small favors. Driving almost lulled Richard to sleep again, but he came fully awake in time to swoop under the amber lights marking Midway Road. He hurried past gas stations, shopping centers, and light industry, past a restaurant row and office buildings toward the distinctive shape of New Karnak.

Engulfed in its welcoming shadow, he hastened into the underground parking lot. His space next to the elevator was empty, as it should be, and he slipped in and killed the motor. The silence after it died was disconcerting after the long drive. He listened with all his preternatural ability to detect if there was anyone else about at this too-early hour of the morning. He preferred not to have witnesses and thankfully none were apparent.

Getting out, he opened the rear door and reached in. Michael did not wake, and Richard lifted him easily. He'd forgotten how light children were. Holding the boy protectively close, he kicked the door shut and headed for the elevator.

The soft hum of its ascent was comforting, signifying the end of his journey. He leaned back against the wall, tired to the bone, yearning for sleep. The car rode upward uninterrupted to his apartment, stopped with its customary subtlety, and Richard stepped out. The doors closed behind him, the car automatically plummeting back to the garage level. He carried the boy to the master bedroom in the back of the big flat.

Except for spare clothing and some framed photographs, he kept few items of any meaning to himself here. Having been professionally decorated, it was rather like a luxury hotel suite possessing all the basics—and those being of the finest quality—but ultimately impersonal. Still, there was a soothing quality to such surroundings. Passing a mirrored wall on the way, the only chaos Richard perceived in the beautifully coordinated calm was himself and the ragged, dirty little boy in his arms. Scarecrows, the both of them. He turned away, not liking what he glimpsed in his own face.

In the master bedroom Richard turned down the coverlet and sheets with one sweep of his arm, and laid Michael down. The boy did not wake, and his breathing continued normally. Oh, to know that kind of utterly abandoned sleep again. Richard took off the child's shoes and socks, and decided to wait a bit on the rest. Except for some minor scratches on his arms and legs—which Richard knew had come from the flight through the thorny mesquite scrub—he appeared physically unharmed.

There was no measuring the depth of damage done to his mind and spirit, though.

Looking down at Michael's sleeping form, the stresses of the night started to rush at Richard, demanding attention, but he pushed them back. He was in no state to cope with them now. He bent to kiss the boy lightly on the forehead and dragged the covers over him.

Straightening, Richard found the room swaying in a too-familiar manner. The strength he'd taken from Kath Henebry's blood was nearly spent. He needed more. Thank the Goddess for the supply he'd obtained from Dr. Sam, sitting cool in his refrigerator.

He drank down two entire bags before he felt anywhere near to normal again. Their boost gave him enough momentum to strip and stand under a scalding shower. He put it on maximum pressure until the supply in the water heater gave out, then stood dripping before the mirror in the bright light of the bathroom. He again glimpsed the expression on his face, this time able to confront it, to stare himself down. After awhile, its corpselike aspect faded to the less alarming mundanity of simple exhaustion. He took stock of what remained.

The worst of his wounds had completely closed up, though the scars were red and sore. They would soon fade. They always did. Only those he'd achieved before his change remained, like the sword cut on his shoulder that had nearly killed him, and the one where his ring finger had been severed then restored.

The angry raised blisters left by the fire ants had subsided, and the aching pain in his body had eased, but he was not fully recovered. He wanted sleep, and could see no reason for putting it off. He would need all his energy for what was to come.

Wrapped in the loose ease of an oversized terry robe, he made a quick round of the flat. His prime concern was being sure the doors were secure and that the metal blinds over the windows were sealed shut to block out the day. He lay on a sofa in the gentle darkness of the bedroom so as to be close should Michael wake.

Richard shut his eyes, waiting, hoping fatigue would allow him swift oblivion. Hoping he would be spared further dreams. Further nightmares.

Somewhere in that strange place between waking and slumber he realized that the worst was not yet over. Bourland would have to know. How would he tell him?

The vision of Michael's experience placed the time of their deaths in the early morning. Richard had been on the plane then. There was no way he could have arrived in time to prevent any of it.

Cold comfort, that.

Icy cold.

Chapter Seven

Britain, the Beginning, Five Years Later

"King's Champion indeed," said Elaine, rousing from her doze. "I think you've ridden more oft for me."

Richard smiled and shifted his weight from her. "And you've ridden me enough to be the Queen's Champion."

She chuckled softly, moving so he could lie on his back with her cradled in his arms across his chest. Hers was a virgin's narrow bed, but he had no complaint for the warm closeness of it. "The queen would not be pleased to hear that," she said. "All the court knows she loves you."

"But no more than the court does itself," he countered, well aware of his own popularity. "I do not seek her favor."

"Yet she would give her heart to thee as easily as I have, as would the other maids and dames."

" 'Tis none of mine what they would do. Why speak of it?"

"Because, sweet Lancelot, it is my greatest pleasure to know that above all those others *I* am the one you chose to bed."

In reply Richard brushed his lips against her temple, and kept the truth to himself of just how many of those ladies he'd bedded in the years since his arrival at court. He'd been discreet about his various liaisons, so much so that many thought him more chaste than a monk. For some reason, this distinction made the women all the more fascinated with him.

Elaine was as unaware of his many mistresses as they were of each other. A delicate juggling act, but Richard managed it quite well, perhaps too well. Though a dear girl, Elaine possessed dreams for him of a future with her he could never fulfill. Already she had been hinting about his speaking to her father for her hand as though it was an inevitability.

"In my memory," he finally said, "it was you who chose me."

"What matters so long as we are together?" She sighed with vast contentment, burrowing snugly against him. "What matters so long as it lasts forever?"

That she spoke thus told him he would have to soon conclude things with her. He'd heard such from other girls when he walked in the sun, and with no small chagrin knew it would be so with future lovers. Why did some of them have to make a simple union so much more than it was? Even when they professed their understanding that a tryst was to be no more than a satisfying of mutual desire, they would change their minds afterward. Sabra had troubled to explain all the reasons to him. Several times. Still he was mystified. Sometimes it was just easier to simply pay for a woman's favors—and the blood that he took—than to deal with the complexities of mutual seduction.

He would have to soon supplant his will over Elaine's wishes and make her forget about their stolen nights together. Or at least persuade her from this dream of marrying him. That could never be, and the sooner she accepted it, the better for them both.

Not tonight, though. They'd enjoyed each other thoroughly here in her chamber in her father's keep; no need to vitiate the current good feeling with base practicalities. Richard had gone to some effort to gain entry, hoisting himself up the timbered sides of the building—his vampire's strength making the task easy—to climb through her window. Elaine had enthusiastically welcomed him for some months now, prettily delighting in their secret sport as though she'd never known its like. Well, she'd never known Richard's like, that was a surety.

She slept still in a virgin's bed, but had probably not slept as a virgin since her first moon as a young woman; her skills in love were too certain for him to believe her claim that he alone had received her maidenhead. The only blood he'd seen from her was that which he'd taken from her veins when they loved. As with the others he fed from, he was ever careful to remove *that* from their recollections. Other memories and intents required more effort and care.

But still . . . Elaine was such a lovely girl, fair of face and with a lushness and grace of form as to stir a statue to life. Even now he felt a decided stirring within from the thought alone . . .

Enough. He would soon have to bring this intimacy to a close before anyone found them out. Elaine herself might let something slip—more likely on purpose than by accident—in an attempt to achieve her fantasy of marriage. Her father would be annoyed at her seeming deflowering by Lancelot, but not so much as to deny himself the status of having the king's rich champion for a son-in-law.

Elaine reached across to the little table by the bed. Richard thought she might thirst, but instead of taking the wine cup, she picked up a small crockery jar.

"What's this?" he asked as she settled back again.

Her bright eyes danced with mischief. "A love potion."

"Oh, really?"

"Yes. An old wife at the tourney fair told me that no man could withstand its power."

"And so you wish to test it on me?"

"Indeed. If it gives you no pleasure, then I will know her for a liar."

"Am I to drink it then?"

"Only from my lips." She sipped a little from the jar, then placed her mouth over his. On her tongue he tasted honey and cloves and other rare flavors before she drew away. "Is it working? Are you in love with me yet?"

There was no harm in playing along with her new game. He could always change things later. "I'm not sure. Perhaps you must try again."

Instead of kissing him, she moved farther down his body. "Yes, perhaps I shall." He watched with amused interest as she let fall a fat thread of her potion onto his manhood. She spread the stuff with her fingers, enjoying his swift response to her touch. "The old wife told the truth it seems."

"So far as it goes, yes." He put no credence in love potions, only in Elaine's presence and what she was doing to him.

"Then must I test it a little more." She bent her head, her mouth enclosing him, capturing his full attention. He lay back with an appreciative sigh and gently stroked her hair, his heartbeat quickening as she worked on him.

Some time later she paused to inspect her results. "Indeed, she told the truth. You do love me."

For this night at least, sweet girl, he thought. He sat up and took the jar from her. She sat up in turn, facing him, smiling. He smeared a few drops onto each of her breasts, then did his best to lick and kiss them clean again, until she shivered and moaned in her need for him.

But he held off, knowing that some delays were better for the wait.

They passed the honey concoction back and forth, laughing, each hushing the other lest someone hear. It would not do to have Elaine's father or brothers bursting in upon them.

Richard cherished the taste of her, the salt essence beneath the honey. Her skin was cloud-smooth, her least reaction to his questing fingers adding immeasurably to his own excitement. How precious it was, how rare, and yet so brief.

These fragile children abide with us but a little while and then are gone.

Sabra's words came to him even as he embraced Elaine. The girl in his arms would die and go to dust while he lived on. He faltered, looking long at her young face, as though to discern if death's shadow already lay upon her.

"What is it, Lord du Lac?"

He shook his head. A thousand words or none were equally inadequate. It was not something she could ever understand. "Time is so short," he murmured. *Short for thee, my pretty one.* He held her close, as if to keep her mortality at bay by his will alone. Futile gesture, but it made her gasp with joyance for his eagerness.

She will think her potion worked. Perhaps it has, for this night, for this hour.

When their want became near unbearable, they coupled once more. She wrapped her strong legs around Richard, heels locked at the small of his back, her hips rocking hard against his. He kissed her mouth and her eyes, his hands moving on her until the first shudder of her climax began to take her.

Only then did he bite hard into the firm flesh of her throat.

She started to cry out, but he pressed his palm over her mouth, smothering the sound. Her breath came fast and harsh as he supped, drawing out the red ecstasy of her life even as she took his seed from him. He made it last for them both until she lay half swooning in his arms from sheer exhaustion.

"None," she whispered, her head lolling on his shoulder.

"Mm?" He was fair exhausted himself, but not for long. Eyes shut, he savored the heat of her blood flowing within him, renewing his strength.

"None pleasure me as do you," she murmured.

So far gone was she that she'd forgotten her claim that Richard was her first. He smiled and caressed her thick hair, letting the moment be.

He left a few hours before dawn, dropping to land silent in the dewy turf beneath her window, then looking round to make sure no one had seen. He wore no armor, nothing that would make a noise, but the moon was high. Its silver light could be deceptive to normal human eyes, but would serve to reveal an intruder; he kept to the shadows. To Richard it was like a sunny day, and he made use of his advantage, slipping across to the outer wall, his passage unnoticed by the sleepy sentry watching the gate. It was the work of a moment to take the man from behind and persuade him to blind obedience. Blind insofar as Richard's presence was concerned. The guard would have no recollection of letting anyone out through the small door set in the gate.

Richard could have climbed the keep's curtain wall and thence to the dry moat below, but saw no necessity for the extra effort. His powers to influence were harmless to others and most advantageous when he was on the hunt. Though he could have more safely fed from any number of servant girls, he had yet to tire of the sport of seducing—and being seduced by—their mistresses. Besides, a hasty feeding in some dark corner of a hall with a giggling wench was not nearly as satisfying as a slow loving of a giggling lady. Of course, there had been occasions when he took his time with the wenches as well. . . .

His horse still waited, ground-tied where he'd left it in a hollow just out of sight from the walls. The dogs, Prince and Merlin, kept it company, better guards than the one he'd just influenced to let him out. They yawned hugely, shaking themselves awake for the lope home. He tightened the saddle girth and mounted, kicking the horse to a canter. The clean night air cooled his face and cleansed his spirit. He would sleep until the forenoon, then ready himself for the coming day's tournament.

Light showed in his tent by the lake. Nothing remarkable in that; his people were accustomed to his night rambles, but as he dismounted and gave the reins to a waiting servant, he saw he had company.

Sabra stood holding open the door flap, smiling, her dark brown hair undone and hanging freely to her waist. How he loved to play with it.

Prince and Merlin bounded forward to welcome her, tails fiercely wagging.

"Such good boys," she said, petting them before they knocked her over in their excitement. "Did you care well for your master?"

"You've turned them into lap warmers," said Richard affably, watching as his great and deadly hunters fawned upon her like puppies.

Sabra laughed once and pulled him inside, their kiss of greeting long and warming. The dogs snorted and stretched themselves on the tent's carpeted floor to finish their naps.

"I thought you would yet be with the queen's company," he said.

"She decided to see the tourney after all, and the cortege arrived an hour after dusk. She gave me leave to depart. I was told you'd left before then."

"I hungered."

"Ah. Is it still Elaine, or has another caught your eye?"

"Elaine it is. Do you mind?"

Sabra shook her head, not as a reply, but to express fond patience. "Richard, you know well that I don't. There's no need to ask."

"It concerns me, so I will."

She kissed away his concern. "You'll want sleep. Come to bed." She took his hand, leading him to the broad spread of furs, pillows, and blankets he was accustomed to resting on during the day. Much wider than a normal bed, he could fair sprawl on it, his big frame unencumbered by the limits of an ordinary pallet. Some thought it a sinful excess on his part, having such an extravagance solely for the repose of his body, but he ignored them. He fought hard on behalf of his new king; it was only his just due to have a comfortable place to recover himself.

Sabra put out the oil lamps and helped him undress, her hands lingering familiarly over him. He caught them, bringing them up to kiss.

"I've sorely missed you, my lady." And he wanted her. Always.

"And I, you, but you've much to do on the morrow."

Regrettably, she was right, but the weeks she'd been away traveling with the queen's party had been weary to him for lack of her company. No matter whom he bedded, or how many, none could fill his heart as Sabra did.

"Do you hunger?" he asked, slipping her loose robe from her shoulders and drawing her onto the bed with him. He pulled a coverlet over their nakedness, to protect them from the cool of the late spring night.

She nestled comfortably against him. "I've fed."

"Who was it?"

She chuckled. "In truth, I know not. Some lad whose duty was to fetch water for the horses. On one of his trips he took a little longer than usual to complete his errand, and he will not be able to say why."

"Handsome?"

"Oh, yes, like a young god he was."

"Do you love him?"

"No more than you love Elaine."

He took the gentle point with good grace and kissed her brow. Once upon a time he'd have burned with inner rage, but no more. This was how life was for them, and he'd dealt well with what had been his most difficult adjustment to it, rooting out all jealousy over Sabra having lovers to feed from. Certainly she showed none toward him for his conquests. They did have an unspoken rule, though; both took care to keep out of each other's way when on the hunt. It was one thing to speak of other partners, but quite another to witness the seduction itself.

"What if they were like us?" he asked, staring up at the dim roof of his tent. "Able to live beyond their years, ageless and young forever?"

"What of it?"

"Their lives are short, so we must not love them too strongly, but if they also had the Goddess's Gift, would it make a difference to us?"

"You know it would not."

And she was right. He'd only wanted to hear her say it.

"Were you thinking to share blood with any of them?" There was concern in her tone. They had many freedoms, but bestowing the Gift to anyone they pleased was not one of them. Sabra had made clear to him that doing so was rare; the choosing came from the Goddess herself and no one else.

"No," he quickly assured her. "Nothing like that."

"Why then do you wonder such a thing about them?"

"Because the sadness of it came to me when I was with Elaine. One day she will die. They all will die."

"Ah." Sabra touched her lips to her fingers and placed her hand upon his heart. "Sweet Richard, in that you are not alone."

He took solace in her words and held her more closely.

She murmured and sighed, settling in, but a moment later raised herself on one elbow. "Richard . . . *why* do you smell of honey?"

He burst forth with a low laugh. "Elaine tried a love potion on me."

"Did she now? Are you enspelled to her, then?" Sabra gave him an arch look, eyes sparkling.

He grinned back. "Oh, yes. I'm quite certain of it."

"How terrible for you. I shall have to break that spell sometime."

"Now would be perfect, before it has a chance to grow in strength." His hand stole around her waist, pulling her back.

"But the tourney . . . you should rest . . ."

"Damn the tourney. I can always sleep." He rolled on top of her, pinning her arms.

She struggled briefly against his play, laughing too much to effectively fight off his kisses. Soon she was returning them. "You taste of honey," she remarked. "All over. Just how did she use this potion?"

"You really want to know?"

"Oh, yes. Please acquaint me with—"

And so he did. At first he repeated the course he'd taken with Elaine, but Sabra's reactions and wants were different, and his desire for her urgent. He quickly forgot the game, so caught up was he with the loving of her.

"You speak of growing in strength," she said, stroking him. "I had no idea the spell was so potent."

"There's more, much more," he said, and showed her that as well. God, but he'd missed her. The others were nothing, less than nothing, compared to her. He held Sabra like salvation itself, loving her until at last they both lay spent and gasping from the effort of it.

"You seem to have overcome her magic," she murmured sleepily.

"There is no magic for me but yours."

"None?" She unknowingly echoed Elaine, but made a question, not a statement.

"Were they all changed to be as we are, not in a thousand times ten thousand women could I find any like to thee. All that is life to me is the world in your eyes."

"Ah."

"You are my heart, Sabra, my soul, and I love thee more with each breath I take."

At this, Sabra made a small noise in her throat. An instant later he felt a wetness on his chest where she'd lain her head.

"Why do you weep?" he asked.

"For the happiness you give me, my Richard. No one can, has, or ever will move me as do thee. Your love is the breath in my body."

They clung tightly to one another in the darkness.

It was yet dark in the noontime, for the day of the tourney had but a feeble dawn. Gray clouds shrouded the spring sun, and the air was damp and cool, but so far there had been no rain.

"Is that your doing?" Richard asked with a short nod to the ominous sky.

Sabra only smiled.

"Some are taking it as a bad sign, that there will be death on the field ere nightfall."

"'Tis only a little weather wizardry," she explained. "This is an important tournament for you. It would not do to have the King's Champion blinded by too much light or fainting from sunburn."

"I'd give you a proper thanks for the boon," he glanced sideways at her, "but neither would it do for the King's Champion to be seen kissing one of his squires."

She erupted into giggles, then hastily smothered them, schooling her face to sober lines as befitted a humble servant. Her slim form was such that she could disguise herself in boy's clothing and succeed with the deception. For those seeing through it, she had other ways of making them forget their discovery. She stood at Richard's side, dressed in his colors, her coil of hair hidden beneath a close-tied cap. Her delicate features were overshadowed by a thick cowl. She held one of his swords at ready. Behind them, the other servitors looked after the rest of the weapons. Before them lay the tourney field.

It was a wide span of acreage, surrounded on three sides by tilled fields, the fourth by a lake. Elaine's father owned the land and forbade his people to plant on it, keeping it instead solely for the practice of warfare. It increased his reputation to have so many famous fighters gathering here, all with the king's blessing, of course.

The king had been effective in keeping the peace, wisely maintaining its preservation by seeing to it his subjects knew how to fight. Though a force of armed men was a good hedge against outside enemies, more often than not they would fall to warring with each other. The tournaments, however, provided the nobles with a means to disburden themselves of tendencies to rowdiness. Here they had the opportunity to display their courage at arms without laying waste to the countryside or one another.

There was profit to be had as well. Richard had ever taken advantage of it when he'd fought on behalf of his father's house. Defeating and capturing a fighter for his gear or ransom was the custom, and an accepted method of enriching one's purse. But some of the noble combatants were wealthy enough to eschew the money altogether. Richard had not been one of them when in Normandy, but that was changed. He now could afford to be generous to those he defeated. Many in the court had come to follow his example, treating their captives as esteemed guests who had fought with skill and courage, and making a great show of returning the ransoms. It was a game of honor to some; to others it was survival.

To Richard it was practice and a way to judge the worth of a man. How an opponent conducted himself on the field revealed much of his inner face. Was he a thinker or did he let his passions rule? Did he plan his moves or trust in luck? Did he fight for himself or let others take the brunt first before stepping in? All this was useful to Richard, who might one day have to face any one of these men in earnest battle, whether on the field or across the Round Table in a council session.

Here the squires would also test themselves, close observed by their elders for signs of cowardice. Until they'd been through at least twenty such tourneys, most young men were not considered seasoned enough for a real battle. Broken teeth, broken heads and bloodings were common, as was death, by accident or on purpose if things got out of hand and tempers flared. No blunted or wooden weapons would be used in this combat. This was true training for war.

Yet there was no dearth of participants; too much profit was to be had to discourage anyone.

"I count many more than a hundred men," said Sabra. "Twice more than at the Michaelmas tourney."

"The news traveled far about the prizes and the purse the king offers."

"And about yourself, I'm sure. The bards have been kind in their praise of your battle skill."

"The skill is there, but I've advantages to make a pass of arms unfair to any who would challenge me. You saw to that, my lady."

"You've more strength than any, but take care, for there will be those who will test you on it."

"As I've always been tested. I will win out."

She shot him a look of amused warning.

"I know." No need for her to say aught, he understood well enough. One fault he'd always had difficulty controlling was his damned overconfidence.

Richard watched as two sections in the field were roped off. Tall poles with long streamers proclaimed neutral ground, where the wounded or captured were to take themselves or be taken if they were too injured to walk. Most of the time no one intentionally set out to kill or maim anyone here, but misadventures took place more often than not. It was well to be prepared for the worst. Both healers and priests stood by, ready to receive whichever came their way.

At last the field was cleared and a loud fanfare of horns and drums was struck, signaling the beginning of the tourney. A cheer went up from the watching crowds surrounding the field as the fighters marched past the pavilion where the king sat with his queen. Each man paused to have his name announced by one of the heralds and to bow to the sovereigns. The tourney's host, Pelles Bernard—Elaine's father—sat on the king's right. The old warrior, grim of face, made a particular show of bowing once at Richard, picking him out from all the others in the line for the honor. He was the King's Champion after all, but it was an unusual enough gesture to raise an eyebrow or two.

Returning the courtesy, Richard bowed back, furiously wondering if Elaine had said anything. It hardly seemed likely for he'd cautioned her to silence before leaving and could trust the efficacy of his influence upon her. Perhaps one of her serving maids had heard or guessed. Household gossip traveled faster than a winter gale and could do more damage.

Bernard bowed again, this time to his youngest son Lavaine, who had placed himself just a few paces down from Richard.

This was bad. If Bernard reserved such a courtesy only to those within his own family . . .

He did not bow to any of the other nobles.

Elaine sat with a group of ladies at the far end of the pavilion and did not meet Richard's gaze as he passed her. Pale as she was after his feeding, she still managed to raise a blush, showing two fiercely pink spots high on her cheeks. She worked her sweet mouth, as though trying hard to suppress a smile.

The subtleties of their combined messages were clear enough to those with eyes to see. Certainly the king and queen had noticed something of the byplay.

Damnation!

"What is it?" Sabra asked, whispering. She trudged next to him over the uneven turf, still carrying his sword. She'd sensed his sudden discomfiture as though he'd spoken it aloud.

"There's mischief afoot with Elaine. I think her father is planning to welcome me to his hearth as his new son."

Sabra made a choking sound and nearly stumbled.

"This is no time for jollity," he snapped. "I've no wish to take the minx for a wife."

But Sabra was too consumed to wholly check her mirth. She pulled her cowl well forward to hide her face and for the most part kept her laughter internal, though she seemed like to burst from it.

Annoyed, Richard held his peace, until she returned to a fit state to speak, which took quite some while. She was nearly recovered as they assumed their place on the far side of the field, waiting for the rest of the men to make their bows to the king.

"What's to be done?" he demanded.

"Nothing for now. For later, we shall both do much. If Bernard asks for a private word with you—and I think he will—then you deal with him. I'll find a way to get to Lavaine, then we can dice to decide who is to speak to the girl."

"This is no little sporting, Sabra," he said, rankled at her levity.

"I know, but we can make it such before the day is done if we hold ourselves strong. Remember who you are and who I am. None may win against us if we so choose. Consider yourself lucky that Bernard did not make a declaration of the bans here and now."

"He's probably waiting to see if I live through the contest," Richard muttered. "Elsewise I might be tempted to forfeit on purpose to avoid marriage."

"Your pride would prevent that," she said, but in a way so as to restore his good spirits. She pushed the cowl back now that they had some distance between themselves and the rest of the field. "Fight as you always do, then—" But the rest went unsaid as she stared across to the pavilion.

"What is it?" He followed her gaze, trying to pick out what had so arrested her. "Is it Bernard? What does he do?"

"Sweet Goddess," she breathed. "Not here."

"Sabra?"

She swayed, dropping his sword and clutching at his arm for support. He caught her, his heart swooping at her abrupt weakness.

"What is it? A vision?" Sometimes they were intense enough to collapse her, but those were rare. What they signaled was always grievous.

"Aye, a vision . . . Oh, Richard, hold back, do not go forth today."

"Why? What do you see?"

She shook her head, fighting it. "Death. I see death."

"For whom? Me?" But that was nigh impossible. He could get nothing more from her, though. Her eyes had rolled up in their sockets and her body had gone rigid like some poor sufferer from the falling sickness. The nearest of the men drew away and crossed themselves after an uneasy glance at the dark sky; others came forward for a better look. Lavaine was one of them.

"How fares your squire?" he asked, half curiosity, half concern. At least he did not seem to be the outraged kinsman looking to avenge his sister's honor. Not just yet.

" 'Tis nothing toward," Richard replied, searching Sabra's face for distress, but she was gone from this world for the moment. "He has these fits when he gets overexcited. I expect he shall grow out of it once his voice changes."

"We've a healer if you wish one."

"I thank thee, but my people know how to care for him. I'll take him away."

" 'Tis not a task for a noble. My squire will do that for you." Lavaine's was a broad strapping lad who appeared strong enough to carry Richard himself.

"You honor me, but this is my charge. 'Twill be enough if he would guard my sword until my return."

Lavaine nodded and signed to his squire to retrieve the blade. "We'll wait for you."

Richard thanked him, then swept Sabra up, carrying her with long swift strides toward his tent. Before he'd gone a quarter of the way, she began to wake and struggled a little.

"Be still," he said. "Rest first."

"No, I must tell you—"

"Yes, but only where none may hear." They'd garnered enough attention. If word got out that Lancelot's squire was subject to visions, the outcome would mean either sainthood or a public burning.

But she would not be put off and pointed. "Look to the line, Richard. *See* him!"

He looked. The nobles were nearly through with their march. Last in their number was a man who stood to be more than Richard's match in height and span. He wore familiar colors, so familiar that Richard stopped in his tracks from the shock of it.

"Dear God, he's from Normandy—he's the champion for d'Orleans."

"More than that."

"You don't mean—" Richard now broke off, staring in near disbelief before puffing out a short, bitter laugh. "It is. He's the young bastard who defeated me, the very one. By God, but he's come up in the world."

"Take me from here," Sabra pleaded. "*Now.*"

He shifted his attention to her and quickly finished the journey to the tent, setting her down on the bed. Servants hovered close, but she banished them with a sharp gesture and a sharper word. This was highly unusual behavior on her part; Richard sat next to her as they hurried out.

"What ails thee?" he demanded, worried for her agitation. "What was your vision?"

She put a hand to her temple. "Why did she show me this now? Why not before?" Thus did Sabra refer to the Goddess and her Gift of the Sight.

He held her other hand. "Just tell me. What is it that troubles you? What did the Goddess show you? Death? Death for whom?"

A tear spilled down her cheek. "For him. I saw a glimpse of his doom that day five years past, but clearly now. Too clearly. His fate is set; nothing may change it."

"Why does it affect you so? Men die. 'Tis the way of things." He tried to say it in such a manner as to give her comfort, but it had the opposite effect.

She slammed a fist ineffectually against the giving surface of the bed, snarling frustration. "Because I know now *who* he is!"

"Who, then?" Though bewildered, he kept himself patient with her.

"It cannot be changed—chance, fortune, and fate brought him here."

"To meet his death?"

She nodded, swiping impatiently at her eyes as more tears streamed forth.

"What of it then? Am I to be the one to kill him?"

"*No!*" She all but shouted in his face. "That you must *not* do!" She seized his sword arm, gripping hard even through the mail with a strength to make him wince. "Richard, if you love me, promise you will not go near him. Promise me you will raise no weapon to him even if it costs you your honor and place at the king's side."

"It's that important?"

"Yes!"

"Then I promise. Now tell me why."

She eased her hold and wilted. "I have not the words. The Sight told me all in an instant, but why not earlier? Why did she wait so long to show me?"

"Sabra . . ." His patience had limits.

She swung off the bed, pushing past him to go to the door of the tent. The servants lingering there hastily scattered. He followed, looming over her as she looked across to the king's pavilion. The heavens were darker than before, clouds churning as if in response to Sabra's turmoil. In the still air that preludes a storm they heard the herald's clear call as he presented the bastard to the crowd.

"Michel d'Orleans, champion of the house of Duke Montague d'Orleans of Normandy!" he shouted.

"My father yet lives," Richard murmured. *What a terrible old man he must be by now.* He'd not thought of the ancient tyrant since leaving home.

But Sabra took no notice of his observation, her gaze fixed on the young man. "Look to him, Richard, and remember your promise. I know not why she held this truth from us."

"Can you speak it?"

Her shoulders drooped. "Aye, and the words burn my tongue. This Michel d'Orleans . . ."

He'd never seen her waver so. "*Tell* me. Sabra?"

"He's—he is your son. Your bastard son, bred before your change."

What? He gaped, staring across the field. "What . . . what say you?"

"You heard. And it is the truth."

Hands on her shoulders, he turned her to face him. Her expression told all, but he could not bring himself to take it in. Blood pounded behind his eyes like a club.

"Richard—"

"No . . . oh, it cannot be. I'd have known. That day in

Normandy, seeing him then—when we fought—I'd have *known*."

She puffed a little, hopeless laugh. "With all my gifts, only this moment did I realize it, only when I was shown . . ."

"This cannot be. I'd have *felt* something from him, seen my blood in him, and if not that, then his mother would have sought me out while he was yet in her womb."

"Perhaps. If she knew you to be the father. You had many women in your youth in the sun. 'Tis like that they in turn had other lovers than yourself."

"Yes, but . . ." Indeed, he'd enjoyed the company of dozens of wenches in those days. Any one of them could have mothered a babe and not been able to name its father. "Know you his history? Who she might have been?" Richard wanted—needed—to remember. Which, if any, of those girls had kept his seed and made a child?

Sabra shook her head, helpless. "But you've only to look at him—his face and form tell all."

Richard looked and saw his younger self mirrored there. Michel was now a strong young man of one and twenty perhaps, with a proud carriage beyond his rank, and those eyes . . . like chips of winter blue ice. They stared over the short distance, meeting Richard's gaze, challenging, arrogant.

Dear God. He caught hold of a tent pole to steady himself. "I've no words. No thoughts." Only feelings, a terrible roiling mix of them. "What am I to do?"

"Nothing."

"But you said he's to die this day?" He spoke less to Sabra than to himself, his voice so thin he did not recognize it. "*Why?*"

She spread her hands, still helpless.

"Why tell me now? Is this some cruel joke?" He could scarce believe the Goddess would be so petty.

Sabra shut her eyes, as though to look inward for an answer. After a moment, she took a deep breath, like a swimmer starved for air. "To spare you. The Goddess would spare you."

"From what? From ever knowing I had an heir of my body?"

"From . . . from being the one who kills him."

He released Sabra, falling back a step. "What mean you?"

"If you'd gone on the field in ignorance . . . There are two paths for him; both lead to death. Richard, one of them led to *you*. You would have been the one to kill him."

"Where leads the other path? Name me that man!"

"I cannot—she denies it to me. This is his fate. I know not why it must be so; she has reasons beyond our wisdom."

"That shall not be."

"It shall, Richard. There's naught to be done to save him."

"Fate be damned," he snapped, and set off. Sabra cried his name—his real name—out once in anguish, then he heard no more.

Michel d'Orleans squared himself as Richard approached. The young man's expression was guarded yet amused. "Come for a second trial at arms?" he asked, impolitely speaking first. He made no bow.

Richard stopped before him, searching this stranger's face for signs of recognition. "Michel . . . do you know who I am?"

"I know who you *were*. You've made a good place for yourself since that day you yielded all to me. Defeat served you well in the end."

"But do you know me?"

He shrugged. "You are the King's Champion here, by another name than your own. Many hold you in high esteem. I'm not one of them."

Now was not the time to reveal his paternity. He would not be believed. "How came you here?"

"The duke sent me. When news of this tourney came to the keep, I asked his leave to champion him. He granted it. He warned me that I might meet you again. He knows what you've been up to all these years."

That was a surprise. "He cares what I do?"

"He cares to keep watch over his enemies, and he gave me enjoinment on what to do should we meet."

"Which is . . . ?"

Michel smiled unpleasantly, hand straying to the sword on his hip. It had once been Richard's own blade. "You can answer that for yourself . . . old man."

The jibe held no sting for him now; it inspired only desperation. "You may kill me as we stand here, Michel, I care not, only please, *listen* to me."

"What trickery is this?"

"None. I bear you no malice over that day, boy. The past is gone; the present is all, and you *must* listen to me . . ." Richard put forth his will, pouring it out like a river. "Hear my words . . . and obey them, Michel."

Above them, thunder crackled threateningly. The Goddess was not pleased. Then damnation to her. He could not stand idle.

"Obey you?" Michel questioned, fighting off his influence. "I have my liege-lord. You are nothing to me."

"I am your way to life; hear me out!"

Michel glared at him, sullen. His face was flushed. There was wine on his breath. Had he had too much to be susceptible?

Richard focused hard. "There is a seeress here, a prophet. All that she says comes true. The king himself will swear to it. She foretold that your path on this field goes straight to your death."

That took him aback, but he quickly recovered. "You lie. You just don't want to meet defeat again from me."

"By Jesu's wounds I am charged to keep you alive!"

Despite the force behind the words, Michel held to a stubborn face.

Dear God, he is *my son. How could I have not seen?* Richard tried a different tack. "I ask—*ask*—that you simply not fight me this day, just this one day. In return, you will have *all* that is mine as your prize." He gestured at his tent, far richer than the one Michel had originally taken from him. "Everything is yours, horses, weapons, all, if you retire now. I will vouch for you and say you took sick. None will question your honor or my word."

His gaze strayed to the tent, but Michel caught himself. "You mock me. I owe fealty to my lord Montague—this is some ruse to insult him and disgrace me."

"Not a ruse! Run me through now if it will please you and Montague, only promise you will not fight this day. Should you wish it we can make a test of arms later, but—"

Michel snorted. "You're bewitched! The duke warned me you'd

been enspelled into madness by the lady of the lake. Seeress! Sorceress more like. I'll not be caught in her web—"

Enough was enough. He'd sworn to Sabra not to raise a weapon to Michel, but had made no promise concerning his fists. He clouted the younger man solidly on the jaw, knocking him flat. Michel lay like a stone and would stay that way for some time to come.

Their exchange was seen by many, and now the herald hurried over. Several others came with him.

"What means this, Lord Lancelot?" He was highly offended at such a gross breach of conduct, but restrained himself before the King's Champion.

" 'Twas a private quarrel, nothing of import."

"It is here, before this throng. What am I to say to the king?"

"Whatever you please. I'll speak to him later on it." Richard walked away quickly, leaving the man and his foolish questions behind.

In the tent he found Sabra slumped on the bed, still in her squire's clothing. She raised up when he came in. Her eyes were red with spilled sorrow. "He did not hear you," she stated.

His mouth twitched. "Yet I made him listen."

"Richard . . ."

"No! Not one more word. I have obeyed the Goddess in all things, but not this. She asks too much."

"There are destinies even she cannot command. This is one of them."

"Who commands is nothing to me. The boy will be spared this day, I pledge my life on that."

She went bone white. "Take care, Richard." There was fear in her whisper.

Thunder. A deafening roar and crack of it, that made them both flinch.

Richard looked up, as though to see the sky through the tent's ceiling, as though to see the face of the Goddess herself. "Be angry with me as you will," he shouted. "Strike me down if you must, but let him live."

You don't even know him.

The voice was unexpected. His heart faltered at the sound. It was *in* his head, like a whisper of doom.

From Sabra's stricken look, she'd also heard.

He mustered himself, bolstered by righteous anger. "I don't *have* to know him! What do you expect of me? Did you think I would do less? If so, then you know me not at all!"

The thunder without rumbled, going on and on, yet no rain fell. Eventually, the noise faded. The air grew thick and hard to breathe.

"Has she more to say?" he asked Sabra.

"I don't know."

"*None* of this is your fault," he declared. "I hope she understands *that*."

"Nor is it yours. You are who you are, Richard."

"You may have to explain that to her. I must go now."

"Godspeed," she blurted, as he reached the tent flap.

He turned and came back, just long enough to frame her face with his hands, then kiss her. He wiped her tears away with his fingers, touching the salt wetness to his lips. "Here do I wear thy tokens, Lady du Lac," he said, then left.

He fought as one struck mad, as Lancelot had never been seen to fight before.

Gone was consideration of his opponents' moves, gone was planning; he fought recklessly, taking sword blows like fly swats, beating down all who dared to test him. The crowds cheered him, but he heard them not. One after another, he disarmed or knocked them unconscious or wounded the warriors in his frenzy. The fallen were taken away to the safe areas cordoned off between the flags. He fought on.

He was dimly aware of Lavaine sometimes being at his side, sometimes at his back. Richard was neither thankful for the alliance, nor against it; it was simply part of the day's ordeal. All he wanted was to end the melee quickly. If Michel recovered himself too soon . . .

No, he'd taken a well-judged knock. Enough to keep him out, but not permanently. Richard had had years to practice; he knew his craft.

"Here's another charge for us," huffed Lavaine.

Bors, Ector, and Lionel had formed a temporary alliance with nearly a dozen of their kinsmen, and were making havoc against the lone fighters on the field.

"Shall we break them?" Lavaine asked, grinning. Despite the cool of the dark day, he streamed sweat. His mail was rent from various cuts, his shield scarred from use, his helm battered. Blood crept down his neck where someone had shaved off a slice of his earlobe.

"Do what thou wilt," said Richard, not caring.

His manner had no ill effect on the always cheerful Lavaine, who shouted challenge to the others. Bors heard and raised his spear overhead in acknowledgment. He and his men would come when they'd seen to their current task of clearance. Lavaine waited them out, resting while the others tired themselves.

"Soon," he said, all anticipation.

Richard used the pause to survey activity off the field; this included Michel's tent. Throughout the contest he'd kept such watch as he could manage in that direction. There was no sign of movement yet. Good. If it held so until the hidden sun truly set . . .

"That big Norman you felled is back," said Lavaine, pointing in the opposite direction.

Richard whirled. *No!*

Michel, looking fully recovered, had armed himself and was in the process of hurrying toward them. There was murder in his eye.

Richard stepped in front of Lavaine. "He's mine. Touch him and I'll kill you."

Lavaine snorted, nettled by the threat, but gave way. "As you please. What is your quarrel with him?"

Richard made no answer, busy meeting Michel's rush. The boy was better than before, but then he'd had five years to hone his talents. He ruthlessly pressed the least opening, but took care not to overextend himself. Richard used his sword and shield to deflect what came to him, but nothing more. This puzzled Michel, who dodged return strikes that never fell.

"Afraid, old man?" he taunted, holding his arms wide. "Fight me, damn you! Let me take back my honor!"

Richard held his sword blade downward, and slammed it against Michel's shield. The force staggered him backward a few paces, but not off balance. He returned the attack, withholding nothing, roaring out his fury. Still, Richard managed to keep clear of harm. He retreated a step, as though beaten back. Michel followed. Richard continued to retreat, not being obvious about it, but slowly drawing Michel away from the main knot of fighters. Once they were clear, he'd step in and knock the boy out again.

He thought of surrendering to him, but then Michel would only rejoin the battle. No. He had to be taken from it completely; then later, with cooler heads they could talk. Richard had no idea what he would say, but knew that he must—

With savage cries, Bors and his people bore down on them.

Lavaine, thrust aside in the rush, was trying to regain his ground while fending off Ector and two others. He shouted at Richard for help even as he swung the flat of his blade against a man's legs to trip him.

Richard had no mind for him. He lowered his head to get under Michel's guard and butted him clear of the charge, using his shield and sheer muscle. Michel grunted a curse and lost his footing, flying back to roll down a slight rise. One of Bors men went after him, sword raised high.

Richard got between them just in time and with the edge of his shield hit the man's helm hard enough to break it. He dropped. Another Richard beat back using his sword in earnest, surprising the noble with his energy. Bors intervened, his spear shaft taking what would have been a death blow. Richard's blade bit deep, cutting it halfway through, close to the spearhead.

"Retire, Lancelot!" he boomed. "Retire before you kill someone!"

Ignoring him, Richard wrested his sword free, making a stand before Michel. He took out one man after another, not holding back, cracking bones, shattering shields, fighting to win no matter the cost to others.

Lavaine threw himself into the press, smashing his sword

pommel into a man's helm to clear his way. He shouted something at Richard, hurtling recklessly forward.

Richard half turned, just in time to see that Michel was up and coming at him. He led with his sword, about to run it through Richard from the back. Richard sidestepped at the perfect instant to avoid it, parrying it skyward. Michel's arm shot up, then out of nowhere a blade caught him in that unprotected spot beneath his arm, driving in deep. He made a brief low grunt of pain, then fell, blood spurting.

No!

A wordless shriek and Richard brought his blade down on the other. There was a flash as the metals struck sparks like flint, then both shattered. He stared madly into the face of Lavaine.

"He was going to kill you!" he screamed at Richard. "The coward would have taken you from behind!"

Richard fell on him like death, hands closing on his neck, but the milling men around them kept him from getting a solid grip. Then something struck Richard hard in his left side. He heard the scrape and felt the tear of links as whatever it was sheered through his chain coat. All the breath went out of him. Suddenly the cloudy sky was before him, the earth at his back. He smelled his own blood as it flowed out to soak the turf.

"Lancelot is down!" yelled Bors somewhere above.

"See to the Norman," Richard told him. "See to him, for God's sake!"

"They're coming. My lance slipped and caught you by chance, be still!"

Squires were racing in from the sides with litters to carry off the wounded. Most of the fighters paused now, catching their wind, trying to make out just what had happened to cause the indestructible Lancelot to fall. Richard hardly knew himself, only that the pain flared each time he tried to breathe. Looking down, he saw Bors's spearhead—the shaft fully broken off—sticking out from his side just below his ribs. More than half of it was yet buried in his flesh. Impatiently, he clawed at it to draw it out.

"Don't, man—you'll bleed to death!" Bors made to stop him.

Richard struck him away and continued to pull. The effort

dragged a scream from him. When had this last happened? That night in his father's keep . . . only then it had been a dagger in his thigh. He'd lived then, would live now.

The spearhead came clear, mostly. The top third of the tip was gone. He threw the head away and rolled over to look at Michel.

He lay panting with pain, his d'Orleans colors stained through with his blood. No one was with him; all were crowding round Richard. He crawled forward toward him, shrugging off help.

"See to him! Get a healer to staunch his wound! God's death, leave me and see to him!"

Two of the squires went to Michel, moving him onto their litter, then lifting and bearing him away to the cordoned-off ground. Only then would Richard allow himself to be helped. Lavaine. It was Lavaine who came forward and hauled him up. Richard glared at him and got only noncomprehension in return. The man still thought he'd saved his life. Rage was pointless. His arm around Lavaine's shoulders, they staggered after the bearers.

Dizziness seized him. His legs began to give way to the blood loss. His will alone kept him walking.

Michel sprawled flat on the grass, a healer on one side, a priest on the other.

Don't do this, Goddess!

The squires had cut away Michel's tunic, and were working to remove his chain shirt. They manhandled him roughly, trying to pull it over his head. Lavaine let Richard go, and he fell on his knees, pushing the others away. He took hold of Michel's shirt in both hands and ripped it in two as easily as if it'd been made of thin cloth. The priest crossed himself; the others stared.

"Fire!" Richard snapped, tearing off the padded tunic beneath. "Bring a torch."

One was put in his hand. He touched the blazing end of it to Michel's gaping wound. The stink of burned flesh and blood columned up. Michel screamed and struggled as the men held him down. Still the blood poured out.

"Not enough," said the healer. "You'll burn his arm off and still not staunch it."

"Wine, then."

Someone gave him a skin. He sloshed a stream into the wound, then set that ablaze. Michel bucked and shrieked under the hot blue flames.

And still the blood poured out. The big vein had been cut through.

The fire dwindled, died. Richard pressed his hand into the wound, to halt the flow. He looked at the healer. "Get your needle, sew this up."

The man knew better than to argue, but his long face held no hope for this patient. He went to work. Michel had fallen into a daze, his eyes open and wandering, and he began to shiver. His skin was gray and icy. Richard called for blankets.

"He must live," he told the healer. "I had such a wound as near took my arm off and survived. You will do that for him."

"If it please God to grant me the skill, my lord," he muttered back, working the needle and gut string like a seamstress. "He's Norman, as are you—a kinsman?"

Richard choked, his eyes blurring. "Yes . . . a kinsman."

The healer glanced quickly at him. "Someone see to Lord Lancelot—he's like to faint."

He felt gentle hands drawing him back, and he had not the strength to fight them. He was laid next to Michel. His overtunic was cut away, his chain shirt and the padding beneath pushed back so they could examine his wound. It was open and seeped steadily. Strange, it should have closed by now, the pain stopped, but—

Sabra's face came into his view. She yet wore her squire's guise. No weeping now, no time for it. "Lie still," she whispered.

"How is he?"

She shook her head, one hand palpating against his wound. "The spearpoint broke off inside you. You won't heal until it's out."

"Do what you must, then look after him."

"Yes, I swear it."

Reassured, Richard lay back. Sabra motioned for several men to come close. "Hold my lord fast."

Lavaine sat on his legs, another half knelt on his chest, two more on his arms. They marveled, though, when Richard moved not a muscle as Sabra dug into his side, fingers probing. It was an agony, but strangely distant; his heart and mind were elsewhere.

One of the men laughed. "Your squire will have a new name after this, Lord Lancelot. We shall call him Thomas after the one who doubted our Lord Jesu's return unless he could put his hand in the Holy Wound."

The others shushed him for blasphemy, but grinned at the joke.

Sabra made a small sound of triumph. Slowly she worked the spearhead free, finally holding up her bloody prize: a wide triangle of metal the length of her palm. She tossed it away and swiftly lay a thick pad of clean linen over the freshly bleeding gash.

Richard sighed out his relief. It would knit up now.

The men rose, foolishly asking after Richard's health. He shook his head and looked across to Michel. The boy looked back at him, his expression calm now, even rested, his blue eyes free of pain and pride. Richard spoke his name, but got no reply. It was then he saw that the only one in attendance was the priest, who crossed himself one last time, then laid a cloth over Michel's face.

Overhead, the thunder drummed throughout the heavens, and the black clouds finally broke. Silver sheets of the long-withheld fall streamed down, drenching them. Richard's hot tears mixed with the cold rain, and he stretched forth his near hand, trying to take Michel's, but couldn't quite reach . . .

Chapter Eight

He sat up fast with a sharp intake of air, heart thumping, his right hand crossing to his left hip as though to draw a sword.

Old habits . . .

He listened in the cool confines of the dark room. He heard only Michael's soft breathing from the bed and the distant hum of the air conditioning.

What had awakened him? He concentrated and finally determined it had been nothing at all. He'd simply slept enough, and it was time to face the day, or what was left of it. His watch told him it was almost noon. It might have been midnight in this dim sanctuary.

He felt better. Getting up was not an effort. The aches in his body were gone, and he sensed his final restoration was complete . . . at least on the physical level.

Michael was exactly where Richard had left him. The covers were kicked off, but he still slept deeply. Maybe too deeply, but surely it would help, it would heal him, and God knew Michael needed healing. Richard replaced the bedspread, quietly chose fresh clothes, then left the boy alone, closing the door softly behind him.

In the living room, Richard dressed slowly. It was time to deal with responsibilities and he had no spirit for it. Going back to stand watch over the child in the easeful dark was more preferable than facing reality. He sat heavily at the desk, a bleak stare for the telephone as he put things off for one more minute. No matter how much he wanted to avoid this, he couldn't. Waiting would not make things better. He picked up the receiver and, since it was Saturday, punched in Bourland's home number. A woman answered, the live-in housekeeper, and at Richard's request went to fetch her employer.

"Hallo?"

Bourland's voice was polite yet puzzled. Richard had not said who he was, and few people had this particular number.

"Philip . . . it's Richard."

"Richard, how are you? It's been months. What on earth have you been up to?"

Such warmth in Bourland's drawled greeting. Richard could not make himself respond. The words stuck in his throat and an uncomfortable silence stretched over the lines.

"Hallo? Are you there? Is something wrong?"

Yes, my old friend, I'm about to put a knife in your heart and twist it.

"Richard?"

"I have very bad news, Philip. Please sit down."

"What—" Bourland bit off the rest. Along with the ominous words, he'd have picked up on those subtleties of tone that indicate something truly serious had happened.

"I'm in Dallas."

"What is it? Is Stephanie—"

"I'm sorry, Philip." There was no way to make the news less brutal. Best just to say it, get it over with. "Stephanie is dead, and so are Elena and Seraphina."

A very small strangled sound came over the line, cut short. "What . . . what happened? An accident?"

"No. Not an accident. They were murdered."

There came a soft exhalation of breath, not quite a word, not quite a sigh, then a long silence, and Richard could sense his friend bowing under the sudden burden. He heard the scrape of wood against a bare floor. Bourland was sitting down. When he spoke, his voice was tight, stretched, hardly recognizable. "Are you sure?"

"Yes." *Yes, I'm sure. Dear Goddess, I'm sure. I saw the blood, the bullet holes, the awful gaping smile of their slit throats.* He shook his head sharply, disrupting the image.

"But they . . . they . . . oh, God." Another long pause.

"Philip? I'm right here, Philip."

His response was a whisper thick with tears and pain. "Sorry . . . I—I can't. I'll call you b—back."

The disconnecting click was sharp, abrupt. Bourland would be completely devastated. Stephanie had been like a second daughter to him. He had loved her in that hopeless, helpless way that older men do when their own daughters have left the nest. He'd once confided his wish that Richard might marry her and give him surrogate grandchildren to dandle on his knee in his old age. He had eventually gotten them, but now that happiness was gone. Ripped away.

Richard sat by the phone, waiting until Bourland's first terrible rush of grief abated enough so he could talk again. His own anguish hovered close; he willed it away. Nothing would be served if he lost control now. A scant ten minutes passed when the sharp warble broke the silence. Richard picked up.

Bourland's voice was steel. "Was it Alejandro?"

"Yes."

"You saw him?"

"If I had he'd be dead."

"What about Michael? And Luis?"

"I don't know about Luis. Michael's alive and safe here with me. He's sleeping."

"Thank God, thank the dear God for that. Are you all right?"

"I'm . . . coping."

"What happened? Tell me everything."

Richard poured out the whole story from the first alarm call on his computer to walking into the too, too quiet house and finding the bodies. He gave the simple facts, carefully keeping out all emotional embroidery. It was the only way he could get through it.

"There must have been devices set all through the place," he said. "I smelled something odd under the propane, but didn't identify it as Semtex until it was almost too late. I think the gas was on to cover the smell and add to the damage. There was nothing I could do for them, so I ran. I got clear just as it went up, but something knocked me flat. Must have been flying debris. Didn't quite pass out, but I couldn't do anything for myself. It was like being drugged. Took hours before I was able to wake up enough to move."

"Hours? But the explosion must have drawn attention. Didn't anyone call it in?"

"The property's isolated, miles from everything, and the house is far from the road in a low spot in the land. That would muffle the blast and hide the flames. The smoke would have blended into the general darkness."

Bourland swore once. "Go on."

"I don't remember much. Just being thirsty. I crawled to the pump house for water and that's when I found Michael. He must have been hiding there the whole time, scared out of his wits."

"How is he?"

"Just some scratches and a bruise or two. He's asleep."

"You're hedging. How *is* he?"

"In some kind of shock."

"What do you mean?"

"He's not said a word since I found him. I'm hoping all he needs is rest—"

"He needs a doctor."

"I know a good one here; I'm taking him right over."

"Do. Keep me informed."

"Of course I will."

"What about Luis? Where the hell is he?"

"I've no idea. His car . . ." He trailed off into silence, his mind working rapidly.

"What is it? Richard? Do you know something?"

"Luis's car wasn't there when I arrived. Suppose he drove in after it was over, saw what happened, then fled."

"Without trying to find out if there were survivors?" Contempt seeped into Bourland's tone. But then he'd not seen the total destruction wrought by the blast.

"It was very bad, Philip. One look and you'd know how hopeless."

"But if he'd been there, then how did he miss spotting you?"

"He might not have gotten close enough. It was a fearful mess. He could still be alive, hiding somewhere." Richard's thoughts churned with a new realization. "Look, by the condition of the—of things, the murders took place in the morning. The killer had all day to set up the bombs. He was only waiting for Luis to come home from work and find what was left. That's the sort of retribution Alejandro would arrange. He would want Luis to see what he'd brought upon himself and his family for his betrayal."

"Damn him."

"When I got there the killer must have slipped out the back and hid, allowing me just enough time to find the bodies—or rather he meant it to be Luis. We're about the same build, and it was dark. He mistook me for Luis, detonated the bomb, then left me for dead. It would certainly explain the perfect timing."

"My God, then he really could still be alive."

Yes, they might yet salvage something from the disaster. "There's a chance of it."

"What about the police down there?"

"Sorry?"

"What are they doing about this?"

"I've not spoken to them."

"For God's sake, why not?"

"Philip, stop and think about it. If I bring them in, I won't be free to act in a manner I deem . . . appropriate."

Bourland caught on instantly. "I understand. I'm taking the next flight out."

"No, please, I need you exactly where you are."

"But—"

"I need help. *Your* kind of help."

A pause, as Bourland took in the implications. "Anything. Name it."

"Information. I need free access to the databases of the CIA, FBI, DEA, Interpol, and anyone else you can think of at the highest clearance you can manage. All the major law enforcement agencies, the local police, too, the airlines, Immigration. Get me their access codes."

There was a long silence at the other end of the phone. "I don't know if I can."

"Philip, for Stephanie's sake you will. I must have them if I'm to find Alejandro."

That shot hit home. "I'll see what I can arrange . . . and Richard?"

"Yes?"

"Alejandro or whoever did the killing for him may well know Michael is alive. That child is in extreme danger."

Richard's gut lurched. Damnation, why hadn't he thought of that? Of course the killer knew the boy had gotten away. And would be looking for him. "He's safe, and I will keep him that way. I'm going to be on the move, so use my cell number. Just get me the information I need."

"Soon." Bourland hung up with no further comment.

Richard sank back in his chair, his gaze hard on the closed bedroom door.

Ah, Michael. Poor Michael. What would become of him? His family dead or missing, the absolute loss beyond his young comprehension, he might never wake from his withdrawal.

Across the room on a table Richard caught sight of a gold framed photo of his twin goddaughters. It was one of the few personal items he kept here. Elena and Seraphina had been seven at the time and laughed at the camera as they sat on their pony.

Oh, God, those poor girls.

And suddenly the grief welled up in him once again. In a desperate stolen way, sweet Elena and Seraphina had been his daughters, his innocent, helpless children. It was mere technicality that Luis was their father. Had Richard not been there at their christenings, holding them tenderly, grinning into the camera with a parent's absurd doting pride? He always remembered their birthday, knew every tiny, immensely important event of their young lives. Photographs his cherished Stephanie had taken were in his wallet, creased with wear.

And now some bastard had murdered them all.

Richard had seen much over the long centuries and of necessity had learned to maintain a certain amount of emotional distance from those few and fragile souls that he loved. They died. He lived on. That was the way of things. He had had to pull back time and time again to survive the years with any sort of sanity intact. Yet now, with the events of the past twenty-four hours crowding upon him, he could not pull back far enough for this.

His sight blurred, his breath shortened. Great heavy sobs began to rack his body, and he did not fight them. He let them take him, for this was the only way to deal with the grief.

Try as he might, wish as he might, he would never be too old or too stony of heart not to weep.

Richard splashed cold water on his face, wishing he could as easily wash away the sorrow along with his tears. The grieving was not over, he was fully aware of that, but he'd vented enough to be able to push it to one side, allowing him to focus and function. He would give himself time to truly mourn only after he'd caught Alejandro.

He padded to the bedroom to check on Michael and was surprised to see the child seated cross-legged in front of the TV there. Michael stared, empty-eyed, at a dark screen, for it was not turned on.

Damn, damn, damn. He suppressed an inner groan, then got down on the floor to be in the boy's line of sight.

"Michael?"

No reaction.

"Michael, it's Uncle Richard. Will you look at me?"

Nothing.

He fought back a twinge of panic. The boy needed and would get professional help. Now. Richard donned his daylight coverings, gently gathered up Michael, and headed for the elevator.

Some thirty minutes later, child in arms, he bulled through the door of the Med-Mission Clinic, startling the patients in the waiting room. Helen Mesquita buzzed him straight through the second door and pointed. He'd called ahead on his cell phone to give Dr. Sam some warning, sketching out what was required.

Richard found the examination room, and eased Michael down on the table there.

Helen came in, a clipboard in hand, dark eyes wide with unvoiced questions. "Well, who have we got here?" she asked, addressing Michael. His lack of response didn't seem to bother her, giving Richard to understand that she'd been primed about what to expect.

"This is Michael, my godson," Richard answered.

She wrote the name down on the form on the board. "Last name?"

"No paperwork for this one. Sam will confirm it."

This was unheard of. She started to object, but after a few seconds of eye contact Richard persuaded her to forget the matter. She put the form aside and turned to the child, smiling. "Hi, Michael, I'm glad to meet you. My name is Helen. We're just going to check you out and make sure everything's running fine. Is that okay with you?"

The boy's eyes moved, downward. It was the first sign he'd given of being aware of anything.

She glanced at Richard, taking in the mixed emotions on his face. "Sure it is."

Richard felt a hand on his arm and repressed an urge to flinch. It was Sam, only trying to push past. He murmured requests to Helen, and the two of them proceeded to make a swift and efficient examination of the boy.

"Who's his pediatrician?" asked Sam. "You might want to notify him."

"I don't know."

Sam gave him a sharp look, head-to-toe. "Richard, you look like hell."

"How's the boy?"

"Dehydrated, some scratches, bruises, needs food, a bath, and clean clothes. How'd he get this way?"

"I'll explain. Can you do all that here?"

"We can manage."

Helen smiled at Michael. "Yes, we're old friends now. I'll look after him if you tell Ruth to keep holding the fort out front for me."

Sam saw to it, then took Richard back to his office. Sunlight blasted harsh through the window, warming the place past the limits of the otherwise efficient air conditioning. Richard shut the blinds and dropped his long frame into the same chair as before.

Sam perched on the edge of his desk. "So . . . what is going on? What happened to that boy? Why come here instead of to an emergency room?"

"Because I can answer your questions; I wouldn't have been able to answer theirs."

"Don't tell me you've kidnapped him." Sam was only half serious, the other half was plainly alarmed.

"No, nothing like that, but any official notice of the child could put him in danger."

"Why is that? What's happened to him?"

"Yesterday morning he saw his mother and sisters murdered. The killer is still loose and probably looking for him."

That stopped Sam's questions for a very long minute. He shifted from the desk to his own chair, looking at Richard the whole time. "I think you know what I'll ask next, so please . . ." He gestured, palm up, for more information.

Richard kept his story short, the barest of bare bones. It was the only way he could get through it again.

"My God," Sam whispered. "I heard something on the radio when I drove in, but I never thought . . ." He glanced at his watch, then swiveled his chair so as to turn on a small black-and-white portable TV jammed onto a crowded bookshelf.

The picture was fuzzy, but served. The images and sound marched their slow way through the credits of a sports show and some ads, then the local carrier station news center broke in with the day's headlines. They gave a full thirty seconds to the mysterious explosion of a house in Addison. A helicopter view of the area was shown as the narrator spoke of arson.

Richard made himself look at the near obliteration of the house, made small by the screen, but still naked and awful in the daylight.

The TV voice continued, " . . . and an inside source has revealed that some type of powerful explosive was involved. Police, FBI, and BATF agents are searching the site for clues and bodies."

And if I don't come forward now and they discover I was there . . .

But the likelihood of that was slim, very slim. Yes, the authorities would not be happy with him, but he couldn't allow himself to be restrained by the limits of the law, or allow Michael to be taken from his custody by well-meaning strangers who could get the boy killed for lack of security.

A commercial suddenly replaced the blackened wreckage on the screen.

Sam shut the thing off. "He was in *that?*"

"Not quite, but close."

"And the murders . . . they were killed just to make an example?" Sam shook his head. "I don't understand that kind of evil. I see it all the time, but his own brother? He would kill *children?*"

"Sam. Believe me, you don't want to understand it. This is the kind of corruption found in gangrenous limbs. Alejandro had his face rubbed in it when Luis turned on him, and he swore vengeance."

Sam shook his head. "Damn, but I try most of the time to forget how awful the world really is."

"With your line of work? With what you do here?"

"I've got a selective memory. It helps me get through some of the bad days." He sighed, frowning at his desk. "Now what?"

"Now I go after the man behind it."

"You? Why not the cops?"

Richard made no reply.

"Why? You're going to talk to them about this, aren't you?"

"The less you know, the better you'll sleep."

"Richard . . ."

"No. Anything I say about it will just upset you."

"But you're a security expert, not any sort of a sanctioned law officer. If you get in trouble with them what happens to Michael?"

"You don't need to worry about it." Richard held his gaze a moment, allowing his friend time to settle.

Dr. Sam relaxed infinitesimally; it was enough.

Richard continued. "Michael needs to drop out of sight for the present. As soon as you're done treating him, we're going elsewhere to safer ground."

Sam shook his head. "The kid's not a car you can just bring in for a tune-up then drive out again. For the kind of shock he's had, he will need round-the-clock help. You should get him to a hospital, find a good child psychologist—do you see where I'm going with this?"

"Yes, Sam, but I can't. The people behind this are professional killers. Michael is a witness. If they find him, they will murder him and anyone else with him. I'm taking a risk with your life bringing him here."

"Then get him police protection."

"No. I do not trust the police to be able to take care of him; there are too many ways his presence can be leaked to the wrong ears. The man responsible has money enough to buy kings, much less anyone else."

"Even when he murders children?"

Richard fixed him with a "what do you think?" look. "You said you don't understand that sort of evil."

"All right, I get the point, but just where do you plan to take him?"

Richard had no ready answer. He had some idea of calling on the local security man for Arhyn-Hill and taking it from there.

"You can't just leave the boy off at a day care center," Sam argued. "Not in his condition. Any good one would be the first to phone the authorities. Keep him here."

"I can't ask you to volunteer."

"No, but I will anyway. It's what I'm good at, remember? I'm Crusader Rabbit with a tongue depressor instead of a lance."

"You don't know anything about dodging bullets."

Sam snorted. "That wet-eared kid you rescued way back when has since picked up a few survival clues by osmosis, though I'm open to suggestions."

Richard hesitated, but no better option presented itself to him. And he could trust Sam and his staff to be bribe-proof. "All right, but you absolutely have to keep him out of sight, smuggle him home in a laundry bag if you must, but *no one* sees him."

"I think we can manage. How long will this take?"

"Not sure, but I'll be making arrangements to get him away from here in a day or so." Richard wrote out Bourland's name and number. "This man is your emergency guardian angel, should you need one. He's in Toronto, but he has a long reach. I'll see to it he knows who you are."

"Emergency, okay. How much can I tell Helen? I'll be needing her help."

"As much as you deem necessary. Tell her the boy is a witness to a crime and needs to disappear. I had my eyes open on the way over; I don't think I was followed, but the killer may know the connection between Arhyn-Hill Oil and this place and could come calling, just to be thorough."

"You're not exaggerating, are you?"

"Not one bit. I think once you're done here for the day you should close up as usual, then overnight elsewhere." Richard got his wallet out and peeled off half the bills in it, putting the stack of hundreds on the desk.

Sam's eyebrows jumped at the amount. "Come on, you don't have to pay me—"

"Operating expenses . . . and for the extra blood I need. Is it . . . ?"

"Yeah, in the fridge."

"Good. Have you a cell phone?"

"Helen has one. I have a pager."

"I'll want both numbers; you've still got mine? It's for emergencies only, though. And if it's that bad, then you call Bourland, too."

Sam had a short discussion with Helen, who had no objection to looking after Michael for the next few days. Details were settled out, then Richard went to see the boy again.

With the dirt off, Michael was several shades lighter than before, now dressed in a faded, but otherwise clean shirt and shorts that were more or less his size, rubber beach thongs on his feet. Apparently the clinic dealt with a number of children being brought in possessing only the clothes on their backs and kept a donation bin for such emergencies. Another bin held toys. MedMission was a thorough place.

Richard pulled a low stool over to the examination table and sat before Michael. "You're looking better. How are you?"

The boy would only stare at the floor.

With one finger, Richard slowly tilted Michael's head up so he could see his pale blue eyes. Empty eyes. He focused hard, trying to touch the mind behind them. Helen somberly stood close to one side, but he didn't think she'd notice what he was attempting. "Michael, it's all right. You're safe. No one will hurt you any more. You can speak now. You are safe."

God, he was so young, much too young for such a burden.

As if in response to the thought, Michael's chin crumpled a little.

"It's all right . . ." Richard concentrated, hardly daring to breathe. "I know what happened, but you're safe."

A tear seeped out and rolled down Michael's cheek, dropping cold on Richard's hand. With it, a feeling of overwhelming sadness came over him—so strong that it was physical, like a blow; he felt ready to weep anew himself.

"It's all right," he lied, fighting to keep his voice from cracking.

"*Mommy*." One word from the boy, whispered so soft as to barely be heard.

Helen shifted slightly in reaction.

"Yes, Michael, I know—"

"*Mommy!*" This time, he screamed it. He pushed violently away from Richard and threw himself at Helen, wailing uncontrollably. She caught and held him close like a baby, rocking him back and forth.

"He needs a little time," she told Richard, tears trailing down her face in sympathy. "This is good, what's happened. He just needs a little time."

He nodded, squeezed her shoulder, and backed off to where Sam stood in the doorway.

"Let's give them some space," said Sam, herding him out.

"I should be there for him."

"You already have been, but he's not ready for more. He's probably regressed a bit. He's a scared little boy who only wants his mother, and Helen is a close enough substitute. Let him have that for now."

Richard nodded acquiescence. Reluctantly. He could still hear Michael's sobbing.

Sam gave him another once-over. "You won't do him any good the state you're in. You need rest—or at least a time-out."

But Richard's phone warbled before he could reply. He fished it out.

Bourland was on the other end. "Get a pen," he said. "I've got some of those codes, and God help us both if you lose them. Only their own agents are supposed to have these."

It seemed best not to warn him about the cell phone. The risk was small that anyone was listening in; besides, agency access codes were always being changed. Richard found pen and paper, printing everything out carefully on one of Sam's prescription pads.

"That's for the FBI and DEA only," said Bourland. "I might be able to get more on Monday, but everyone I know that I can trust to keep quiet is off for the weekend."

"It's a start. Thank you, Philip. Can you filter it in to someone the possibility that Alejandro may be in this country? An alert sent out by the proper channels . . ."

"Already done, but it'll be a matter of pure luck if he's spotted. If he ever was in Texas, he's probably well gone by now."

Too true. Alejandro was a smart man. Not the sort to put himself at risk, according to his brother. Anyone else was fair game, though.

"What about Michael?" Bourland asked. "Have you—"

Richard filled him in on the boy's condition and change in situation, giving Bourland names and numbers. "Dr. George will look after him very well; he's in first-rate hands, I promise."

"I'm still coming down there. Monday."

"But—"

"I can pull strings from anyplace with a phone. I need to be there . . . to make arrangements. For them."

Poor Bourland. This was all he had left to give Stephanie, to take her and her daughters home for burial. "Yes, very well. Stay with me at New Karnak. I've plenty of room. I'll tell security to expect you and let you in."

"Won't Alejandro know about your penthouse?"

"At this point I don't know if he's even aware of my existence, but the place is listed as a corporate expense for Arhyn-Hill, and access is extremely limited. It's safe." *Safe enough for me, old friend.* Perhaps not for Michael, but that worry was off his shoulders for the time being. "Philip, what can you organize concerning Michael?"

"Organize?"

"I want to get him out of the country. He'll need a passport, won't he?" Richard's knowledge about international travel for children was hazy.

Bourland understood instantly. "Yes, I'll get right on that. Excellent idea."

They rang off. Richard folded the phone and tucked it away. He tore off several of the top sheets from the pad and tucked those away as well, shrugging an apology to Sam for the misuse of office supplies.

"You're not going to rest, are you?" asked Sam.

"Later. I've work to do."

"Meaning you'll be hunting this Alejandro?"

"Yes."

"You going to kill him?"

Richard thought a moment, realizing that only the truth would serve for his friend. "Yes. With great pleasure."

Sam nodded, apparently expecting just that answer. He wasn't happy with it, but knew better than to argue. "They've got a saying in this neighborhood about that sort of thing."

"Yes?"

"'Have fun . . . but don't get caught.'"

Chapter Nine

Richard slipped the bags of blood into the vegetable bin, slapped the refrigerator door shut, then shed his coat and black Stetson onto the kitchen table. He went straight to his computer in the living room, hitting the power buttons to wake it up, going through the technical rituals necessary to access the databases he needed. It seemed to take forever. As he waited for the information to appear, he considered an upgrade. It used to be every year was enough, then every six months; advances were now coming so fast and thick these days it was impossible to keep up. He'd not been down here since last fall, more than sufficient time for this machine to become antiquated, given his special requirements.

He thought about the mundane, rather than the fact that his last Dallas visit had little to do with company business. He'd appeared at Stephanie's door with a stack of pizza boxes, a bottle of good wine for the adults, and some toys for . . .

Damn.

He pushed the memory away. Hard. The touch of it on his heart was too cold and heavy to bear.

The DEA screen came up, asking for a password. He carefully entered the code Bourland had provided and was gratified when it worked. After that, it was only a matter of delving into what they had on the Trujillo brothers. He traced Luis first just to see if there was anything new on him. Their interest in him mostly stopped the same day that Richard had gotten the whole family to disappear. Good. So far as it went.

Next, he concentrated on Alejandro, with mixed results. The latest report was three months old, placing him firmly and unreachably in Colombia. He'd taken quite a financial setback when Luis turned on him, but seemed to be recovering. In the gap left by the other drug lords' arrests and confiscation of stock, Alejandro had stepped in, taking up the slack and raising the prices. According to some conservative estimates, he was making as much now as before and looked to be expanding his business geometrically. Such was the nature of demand and supply.

Much on Alejandro's habits and methods of operation were in his file, though the greater part of it was speculation. Some few bits were accurate. He usually had at least two bodyguards from home with him at all times, hiring others on when he traveled. He liked clubbing, fancied himself a ladies' man, and was a lavish tipper.

He would not have personally set the bombs; that was for hiring out. Alejandro had many such associates, mostly in Colombia, only a few in the States. Richard recognized some of the names, but they had to do with the actual business of transport and sale of product. What he wanted were the soldiers, the ones willing to do the dirty work. If he could find just one of them, he could find Alejandro.

After a search, two prospects presented themselves: Nick Anton and Jordan Keyes, both local. Anton was muscle, working as bodyguard, bouncer, or collection agent, whatever was needed for any given job. Alejandro was just one of his many employers. Anton had been questioned several times in regard to a number of killings and disappearances, but never arrested—lack of direct evidence. His juvenile records were sealed, but Richard hacked into them, turning up nothing too terribly surprising. It would have been odd if Anton had not come from a broken home and dropped out of school. He was bright, though; what time he'd spent in jail he'd put to good use in furthering his criminal education and making important contacts. After turning twenty some dozen years ago, he managed to keep himself, if not out of trouble, then at least out of jail for it. Anton was a thug, but a smart thug.

Jordan Keyes was quite a bit more interesting. He had no police record in the States or anywhere else in the world so far as could be determined. He'd resided in the same house in Fort Worth for the last twenty years, paid his taxes, his modest income clearly derived from solid and steady investments. He traveled, mostly to South America, ostensibly as a tourist. Whenever he visited a country, someone important connected with the drug trade died. The victim was nearly always an enemy or rival of Alejandro Trujillo. There had been about a hundred of them.

The method varied, sometimes a long gun, sometimes a bomb, sometimes close range with a small pistol jammed into the victim's spine. On several occasions, though, death was delivered by a crossbow bolt, the razor-sharp point coated with curare. Even a graze would kill. Dramatic, but effective.

Keyes was suspected of being the hit man, or at the very least arranging the hits, but so far no one could find anything even remotely resembling evidence that could be used against him. He lived alone, had no expensive vices. His past was wholly innocuous with its records of school transcripts, various mundane jobs, and promptly paid bills. But paper trails could be faked with the right know-how. The one photo of him, taken from a distance, showed a bald man in sunglasses, bearing a superficial resemblance to Vladimir Lenin, average height, average weight and build, the sort who would blend invisibly into nearly any crowd in the world. An excellent talent to have for such a profession. The report stressed the speculation that Keyes was probably not his real name, but investigations into discovering his true identity had been futile.

Richard snorted. Wonderful. Another exotic assassin with a predilection for symbolism. Jordan conjured up crossing over the famous river . . . and Keyes? Perhaps Keys of the Kingdom?

I'll ask him when I see him, Richard thought, writing down the man's address next to Anton's. It was his short list of people to interview and probably eliminate, should Keyes's slim connection to Alejandro prove solid. If so, then he would have been the one who made the bombs and murdered Stephanie and the girls. Such skills were thankfully rare, but if he was the instrument to carry out Alejandro's orders, he would suffer for it.

Exiting the DEA's database, Richard then tried the FBI. They had essentially the same information, just different details. He saved what information he deemed relevant, then closed down.

Now it was time for some on-site research. Richard took the elevator to the ground floor. For a quiet Saturday, there was plenty of activity in the vast lobby. Beyond a screening row of palm trees and other greenery, he heard the shrieks and splashings of children enjoying the indoor pool. The scent of food drifted on the cooled air from a small eatery situated halfway between the residential and business halves of the complex. He glimpsed adults at ease on a scatter of tables before the pool, watching their kids.

As it should be and too often is not.

He turned away from them, swiping his special magnetic key through a slot, then pushing open the glass door to the business side of New Karnak. He softly approached the large round reception kiosk there. One security man was seated on duty, a lean young fellow, his long hair neatly tied off at the base of his neck. In front of him was a stack of open college texts, but his attention was on the TV screens built into the desk below counter level. One camera's view took in the Egyptian-motif pool. In addition to children playing, the area was also populated by lots of young ladies attempting to push the envelope of brevity with their choice of bikini design.

"Yes, they do look very dangerous," Richard remarked, coming up behind him.

The guard gave a slight start, then grinned. "Just doing my job. May I help you?"

Richard took out his Arhyn-Hill identification. "I'm Mr. Dun, and I'm down from Toronto for a few days to check on things."

"Mr. Dun? *The* Mr. Dun?" The fellow gave the ID a twice-over, then goggled, apparently well aware of Richard's status as owner of the company. "Yes, sir. What can I do for you?"

"I need to be let into one of the offices, Mr.—ah—Ballard." He read the name off the man's pocket tag.

"Sure, I mean, yes, sir, and you can just call me Charles. Right this way. Which office?" He left his post, coming around.

"First I want to see your sign-out roster." He indicated a flat book lying open on the desk top. Ballard did an about-face and grabbed it, setting it before him like a gift. Richard flipped the page back to Friday's date. All employees and visitors were required to sign themselves in and out. The template for each sheet had spaces for names, times, and their reason for being in the building. The regular employees usually left the latter blank.

Among the scribbles in various hands was the strong signature of Luis Marcelja, the name he'd lived under all these years. He'd entered the building at 7:55, stayed in through his lunch, and departed at 5:17. According to the previous log entries, this was his usual routine, give or take a few minutes.

So why hadn't he gone straight home? Had he been ambushed on the way by Alejandro's killers? And if so, then why should the hit man have waited to blow up the house? Why even bother to set charges if the main target was already dead?

Richard frowned, mulling over the possibilities, the most likely still being that the hit man had mistaken him for Luis in the dark and followed through with his orders. If Luis had come home earlier he'd have died. If he returned after the blast, he'd have missed finding Richard.

Hell, I was probably unconscious in the pump house.

Richard shut the book. "Thank you. I need to see Mr. Marcelja's office now."

He knew the way, but let Ballard usher him along, summoning the elevator then opening doors with a wave of his master key. He flicked on the lights to a large, luxuriously furnished chamber on the fourth floor. They were hardly needed; plenty of sun blasted its way through the slanted glass of the outer wall despite its darkening glaze. Richard winced and sought out the control rod for the blinds, quickly shutting them.

"Sure heats a place," commented Ballard. "He must roast up here in the afternoons."

"You know Mr. Marcelja?"

"Just by sight. I'm usually signing in for my shift when he's on his way out. I do nights and weekends. Mostly he just says hello and bye, same as the rest."

"Do you recall him signing out yesterday?"

"Sort of . . . yes, because he left later than the rest. Usually on a Friday everyone can't wait to cut out early and try beating the traffic. I remember saying he'd have a tough time driving home. He just nodded and smiled like he always does, then went off to the employees' garage entrance."

"Anything odd about his manner?"

Ballard shook his head. He was clearly curious about being questioned, but held it in.

"How was he dressed?"

"Dark suit, I think. Dark tie. He had a laptop case, usually does."

"Did you notice any strangers hanging about the place? Did any of your coworkers?"

"We get lots of strangers every day, but we don't allow people to loiter. I'd have been told to look out for anyone if that happened."

"What about outside the building?"

"We make regular circuits—and we have the cameras. You want to look at the tapes?"

"Not just yet." That would take hours, and probably be futile. Richard was hoping for a straw to grasp, but wasn't to the point of desperation just yet.

He surveyed Luis's office. It was decorated in Southwest style with big comfortable chairs, landscape prints on the walls; a huge ceramic jar with a three-foot round of glass over the mouth served as a table. The credenza behind the huge desk displayed a scatter of business awards and trophies, an ambitiously creeping ivy, and a large portrait-style photo of Luis with his family. Stephanie beamed happily from it, her arms protectively around her children in a relaxed, informal pose.

Richard made his gaze skip over it, turning his focus on the desk, which Luis had left in a tidy state. The top was clear of mess, only some memos lined up by the phone, presumably ready for his attention on Monday. The computer was on, the monitor left running. A screen saver showed an underwater scene of drifting tropical fish in vivid colors.

"Is Mr. Marcelja in some kind of trouble?" Ballard finally asked.

"He might be, but not with me. I'm just looking for him."

"What, he's missing?"

"I think so. You may have been the last person to see him."

Ballard's expression indicated that he had no need of such a dubious honor. "Maybe he was in an accident. Have you called the hospitals or the cops?"

"Not yet." And for a very good reason. He didn't want the calls traced back to his own line. By now the authorities would have identified the owners of the destroyed house and be alert to anyone asking after them. "Will you do that for me? The hospitals only for now."

"What'll I say?"

"Just that his supervisor is trying to find him, you don't know why. You may keep my name out of it for the time being. If you have any luck, let me know. I'll be up here."

"Yes, sir." Ballard took himself and any further questions away.

Richard was unsure how many hospitals were in the area, but judged he had more than enough time to go through Luis's sanctum. He began with the computer. All the files were password protected, but there were ways around those, the most obvious involving a search of the desk. On a battered notepad shoved far in the back center drawer he found a list of random letters and numbers, the top dozen crossed through. He typed in the new string at the bottom. The computer opened up like a flower. He'd have been suspicious over his ease of entry but for knowing Luis. The man was careful, but only up to a point. He'd not taken Stephanie's fears seriously. Had that cost them their lives?

Scowling, Richard tore through all the files in the hard drive, then one by one went through every disk he could find. They all had to do with the business, and Luis was a good businessman. Even without the necessity of disappearing the family, Richard might well have hired him. All the work was up to date, nothing neglected or out of place.

Next he tried the e-mail, which was somewhat more tricky when it came to passwords. Richard referred to the string on the notepad and gained access by entering the last one backwards.

Interesting.

Except for some correspondence that arrived after five on Friday, the files were all empty. Most people held on to old mail for one reason or another, but not Luis. His on-line address book was also clean. Had he wiped that out or had someone done it for him? And if yes to either possibility, why?

Richard called up the undelete function and tried to salvage the files to no avail. They'd been erased beyond recovery. Damn.

The next search involved the office itself, inch by inch. The place was as clean as the computer, right down to the emptied wastebasket. Richard thought it might be so and was not overly frustrated when he found exactly nothing. The only puzzle was the computer. A virus could account for the erasure, but more likely Luis had done it himself. Had he a clue that something was wrong? If so, then why hadn't he gone home?

Richard attacked the keyboard and tapped out a note to Luis: *Am in Dallas. Michael is well and safe. Contact me.*

If Luis was alive and still had his laptop, he might check his mail. A long shot, certainly, but it never hurt to be thorough.

Quitting the office, Richard went back to the lobby to see if young Ballard had made any progress. He was seated in the kiosk, poring over the yellow pages, where he'd checked off a number of the listings.

"I called all the hospitals in the Metroplex," he said. "None of the ER rooms had Luis Marcelja or a John Doe of his description brought in since last night. Should I try the coroner's?"

"Not yet." Best to stave off official notice for as long as possible.

"Sir, has he been kidnapped or something?"

"Why do you say that?"

"Well, I used to see in the papers about oil company executives getting grabbed by South American terrorists. I thought maybe they'd migrated north."

"The truth is I don't know what's happened to him. Yours is as plausible an idea as any I've come up with."

"Or could he have embezzled from the company and be on the run?"

Richard smiled and shook his head. He came around the desk and took the second chair there to be eye level with Ballard. "I'm going to fill you in on a couple things, but you need to listen to me, listen very carefully . . ."

The young man proved to be an excellent subject for hypnotic suggestion.

"The police or FBI or BATF will be turning up here sooner or later," said Richard. "When they do you will cooperate fully with them, but not bring my name into it. In fact, you've never even seen me. You can refer them to Mr. Marcelja's immediate supervisor instead, all right?"

"Yes, sir."

"But if and when they turn up, you're to let me know. Leave a message at the penthouse extension; here's the number. If Mr. Marcelja comes in, you send him straight up there, no questions, then forget all about it."

Ballard, somewhat blank of eye, nodded.

That out of the way, Richard primed him to expect Bourland on Monday, leaving a note to that effect for the weekday guard shift to find. Arhyn-Hill's security did not normally have to deal with the residential side of the complex, but an exception could certainly be made in the case of the company's president.

As he left, Richard had to admit to himself, and not for the first or last time, that it was good to be at the top of the food chain.

At this hour of the afternoon the heat of the day was in full force, and the damned compact's air conditioning had yet to correct itself. Richard sought and found a branch of the rental agency and exchanged the small disaster for something larger that functioned efficiently. He had some driving to do and preferred to avoid bumping his head on the ceiling every time the road dipped. All the better as well to have cold air blasting on him; it made up a little for the pitiless sun.

Despite the blocking lotion and hat, his face was quite red and sore by the time he reached Nick Anton's apartment in north Euless. Situated near the center of the Metroplex, it was an excellent location for a man with work calls in both Fort Worth and Dallas.

The apartments were respectable-looking, the grounds neat, but not expensively landscaped. The cars in the lots indicated their owners to be average wage earners, with a few standouts at the high and low end of the market. A nearly new red Corvette nudged close to a rusted and decrepit Nova, the two vehicles conjuring the image of an automotive *Lady and the Tramp*. What would their little ones be? In-line skates?

Richard peered about for the block numbers, finally locating H-105. The corresponding parking slot was empty, meaning Anton was either without a car—almost unheard of in Texas—or gone on some errand.

He levered out and strode quickly along a walkway. Anton had a ground floor flat by the pool. Only a few determined, sunburned teens were using it. The heat was too oppressive for anyone else.

The balcony above Anton's flat made a shady overhang for his partially enclosed porch. Richard welcomed the relief, pushing open the iron gate, which shrieked protest. He paused. Anyone inside would have heard it, a built-in alarm system, perfect in its innocent simplicity. Well, he'd not planned to sneak up on the man, anyway.

He pressed the bell, but heard no noise of it within. He knocked, loudly. It was form only. He could get in easily enough. The door had glass insets; it would require little effort to put his fist through one and unlock the place.

"He's gone for now, cowboy."

A woman's throaty voice drifted down to him. Richard eased out enough from the shelter of the overhang to see the speaker. There was quite a lot of her standing on the balcony above, and it was all beautifully arranged under the cover of some very tight shorts and a halter top. From his low angle, her bare legs seemed to go higher than Everest.

"Excuse me?" he said, forcing himself to look at her face. Her eyes were hidden by sunglasses, and a huge mane of blond hair balanced precariously above. Several tendrils had come loose and clung to the damp skin of her neck. She looked quite delicious.

"Nick's gone to work," she informed him.

"Oh. I was hoping to catch him before then. I thought he said he'd be here."

"He says a lot of things. You a friend of his?"

"Not directly. Someone recommended him to me for a job."

"What kinda job? A club?"

"Yes."

"He might be too busy. He's working a security gig with some guy, but the rest of the time he's a regular over at Bubba Rob's. What kind of club?"

He smiled. "The kind he usually works at."

She smiled back. "You looking for dancers?" She punctuated the question with a remarkable shifting of her center of gravity, bending slowly at the hips to lean forward. The halter top proved to be a marvelous marketing ploy, the ample goods within on tantalizing display.

"Maybe."

"I'd like to—um—put in an application."

He reflected that Mae West would have been proud of the girl's delivery of that line. "I'd be pleased to accept it, but I'm in a bit of a hurry to find Nick. You said Bubba Rob's?"

"Yeah. He might not be there until later. The place don't start jumping until ten. He said they were having some kinda party then."

"They? Would that be his new boss?"

"I dunno; I guess. He works for a lotta different guys."

"You're good friends with Nick?"

She laughed, playing with a wisp of hair. "Not *that* good. Where can I get an application? I could fill it out . . . right now."

The girl has a natural aptitude for filling things out, he thought. "If Nick gets the job I'll have him pass one on to you. I'm sure you'll suit. You can carpool in together."

She grinned. "Cowboy, you're crazy! I like that."

Not much point in searching Anton's place. The girl's watchful presence, though decorative, was inconvenient for any attempt at breaking and entering. He could adjust her memory to forget, but it wasn't worth the effort. He had the information he wanted. All he needed to do now was wait.

And find out where the hell Bubba Rob's was located.

He retreated back to New Karnak, hiding from the furnace blast of sun. Texas afternoons, with their all-day buildup of heat, were near-intolerable to the natives, much more so to a visitor from Toronto, and infinitely more so when he happened to be a vampire. Richard gladly shut himself in and stripped, soothing his flesh with a tepid shower. He ran the cold faucet only, but the climate was such that even the groundwater was warm. How people survived here prior to air conditioning was a mystery to him.

His face was very red and itched, always a sign of sun damage. Much more and he'd have come out in bloody blisters. He made an ice pack with a damp hand towel and pressed it to the worst spots, his cheeks, nose, and chin, then phoned Sam. The receptionist, recognizing his voice, put him straight through.

"It's me. How's Michael?" he asked.

"Sleeping again. He's in the back room with Helen watching."

"Any sign of bad guys?"

"No more than usual for the neighborhood. Things are slowing down. I thought I'd close up and get us out of here on time for a change."

"Have you decided where to stay?"

"Helen has room at her place. And before you object I'll follow her home and make sure no one follows either of us. God, you've got me thinking like you, now."

"It's a good way to live longer."

The doctor's reply was muttered and not terribly edifying.

"Did you get Michael to eat anything?"

"Yes. He settled down a bit after you left, and Helen had some luck getting some fruit and peanut butter into him. He drank some juice and water, so I didn't have to do a drip on him."

"That's a good sign, isn't it? His eating?"

"I'd say so. Give him some time, Richard. He won't recover from this for a while, no matter how much we want it." After promising to call from Helen's, Sam rang off.

Sam was right about recovery taking time, but unaware of a treatment option Richard could offer that was outside of modern medicine.

Sabra would be able to reach the boy's mind . . . and heart.

She of all people could touch Michael's damaged spirit and bring him real healing.

Where are you, my lady?

Richard knew she would be well aware of his pain and turmoil. As far away as she was in her Vancouver retreat, it would have lanced right through her, especially what had happened to him the night before. Her Sight would have disclosed the whole terrible ordeal to her by now. It was an awful Gift at times, yet Richard could almost wish for it himself. Perhaps he then could have somehow saved them . . .

No. He'd been down that road too many times before, and it always led to sorrow . . . or helpless rage. He was in the here and now and must deal with things as they were, not as they should be. Learning that aspect of life and fate and death had been his bitterest lesson.

To keep the past at bay, he flicked on the living room set and sought out CNN for distraction. He had a feeling that the Addison explosion might be of interest to them and was not disappointed. It was the top story on their national report, containing the same helicopter views of the ruins he'd seen earlier. They had more details, this time giving the name of the home's owner, Luis Marcelja. Amid ground views of the house, they'd incorporated a shot of the body bags being carried out.

Richard made himself watch. And think.

The investigators would connect Luis with his job and be by Arhyn-Hill soon. If they took prints from his office . . . well, that would be difficult. Richard had wiped down everything he'd touched while there, marring Luis's by default. They might still turn up some latent prints, then run them through the system and learn his real identity. If any of them were on the ball, they would know about brother Alejandro and have their prime suspect. They'd put an alert out for him, for all the good it would do.

Had he been smart enough to stay out of the country for this? Richard hoped so. He would have the field to himself, able to deliver hard justice without having to stumble over legitimate authorities. He'd have to go to Colombia and track Alejandro down there: difficult, but absolutely possible.

Of course, much depended on the information Nick Anton would provide.

Bubba Rob's Texas Nights was an upscale topless place, lots of lights in the parking lot, a huge sign with more lights, a marquee to announce headliners, and plenty of grim-looking muscle roaming the area. At nine-thirty the lot was full and likely to stay that way. Richard parked half a block down in an annex lot, surprised that he didn't have to pay for the privilege. He could have gotten valet service, but eschewed that in favor of simplicity and a low profile.

With the sun gone, he was free of the encumbrances of his drover's coat, gloves, and Stetson, but still felt the heat as he strode toward the club. It was as though the concrete had absorbed it during the day so as to vent throughout the muggy evening.

He'd dressed to blend: dark new jeans over his boots, a dark shirt, and bolo tie. Texas chic, though he had a sneaking suspicion he looked more like a Jersey tourist than a native. He got something of a confirmation of this as he passed a couple of young women hanging about the front of the parking annex. The dark-haired one flashed him a winning smile.

"Howdy, honey, you looking for some southern comfort?" she asked, her lazy drawl thick enough to cut.

Her blonde friend—*so many blondes down here*—smiled as well, waiting for an answer. Both were casually attired in tight, but not too revealing clothes and restrained makeup. The only obvious giveaway to their profession were their too-high heels and oversized handbags. Fort Worth hookers were less gaudy than their Dallas sisters.

"Perhaps later," he responded, and he meant it. The blood he had at home was fine for survival, but not nearly as good as taking it fresh from a vein.

"We might not be here later, honey. Maybe you should stick around before the good times slip away."

"I could say the same thing." He gave them one of his charmer smiles, no real promise implied, but sufficient to take any sting out of his refusal. "It'll have to be later, though, sorry."

"You just remember Gail," she said as he walked on. "Like a tornado, but with an *i*."

"I will."

"And I'm Stormee, with two *e*s," added her friend, managing to drawl and sound breathless at the same time.

What interesting weather they have here, he thought. And, lord, but he loved their accents.

He reached the club's entry without additional distracting delays, paid the cover, and went in to an assault of lurid noise, light, and movement. A deep base drumbeat of recorded music provided a background for the current dancer on stage—yet another blonde—her hair swinging free as she went through her routine. He spared her a scant second of attention, intent on getting his bearings first.

The layout of the place was fairly standard, but large. A long bar ran along the length of one wall, open booths facing the center of the room took up another. The third wall accommodated the stage area and runway, the fourth had doors leading to the rest rooms and business offices. The floor, crowded with filled tables, had upper and lower levels so customers could enjoy a clear view of the performers. Hanging from the ceiling was a Southwest variation of a mirror-encrusted disco ball, this one shaped like a saddle. Vari-colored spotlights shot sparks off it as it slowly revolved. Red and black were the theme colors throughout, accented with streamers of silver tinsel and ribbons meant to conceal the sound system and other hardware.

Damned little else was being concealed here.

Men pressed close to the stage, eyes upturned to a dancing fantasy of paradise. The dancer had several bills tucked into her G-string and readily drifted over to any man looking to add to her collection. If she liked him, he might be rewarded in turn with a brushing kiss, a smile, and some special dance gyrations just for his benefit. The men here weren't allowed to touch back, though, which made this club rather tame compared to other such establishments Richard had seen over the centuries. The intent was unchanged through time, however, for here was the purest sort of relationship. It lasted exactly as long as the man had money. Hopefully, both parties considered the trade of feminine attention for cash to be a fair and balanced exchange. If not, then that was for the bouncers to sort out.

Richard found a place at the bar, paid too much for a beer he would never drink, and began a careful survey of the male employees. Nick Anton, from the statistics in his description, would be on the large side. His file photo showed a full-faced man with jet black hair, a beard, and dead eyes. No shortage of that type working here.

When a small table opened up, he took it, having another ploy in mind. Girls circulated over the floor, some doing lap dances, others sitting to chat with the customers, the unspoken objective being to get them to buy more drinks. Richard ended up with a lady who seemed intent on doing both.

She was a slender, well-muscled redhead, her hair falling straight to her waist. Her lithe body was clad in a spectacular, red belly dancer's costume trimmed with gold fringe, jangling coins, and bells. Wisps of transparent red fabric accented rather than hid her figure.

"I'm Vashti of the Flaming Tresses," she said, by way of introduction.

"You are indeed." Had she claimed to be the Empress of Russia he'd have wholeheartedly agreed with her.

"Would you like me to dance for you, or would you prefer another drink?"

"Both would be delightful," he said with a nod of encouragement.

She shot him a wicked smile and caught the beat of the speaker music with her hips. They seemed to function quite separately from her torso. Not just a girl in a costume, she knew her art and lavished a full minute of it on him, more than enough to leave him dry in the mouth and craving more. Men at the other tables looked on, grinning, her presence enough to take attention away from the D-cup on the runway.

Richard obligingly tipped her with a large enough bill to compel her to linger for that drink. She ordered an iced tea. Overpriced, of course. He stuck with his untouched beer.

"You're very good," he said.

"Thank you."

"You've too much talent for this place."

She shrugged. "Maybe, but the Renaissance Faires don't pay as well. The local ones are through for the season anyway."

"You usually perform at those?"

"Sometimes, but it gets so hot, and I burn easily." She pushed away a lock of russet hair, tilting her head so as to better expose her milk-white neck with its dusting of freckles. "See?"

"Indeed." God, but it was almost as though she knew exactly what to do to arouse him.

"Yes, a nice dark club is the best place for me." She fastened her gaze on him, oddly familiar in its force. "You new in town?"

"Not really. Trying to find someone who works here."

"Anyone I know?"

"One of the bouncers, Nick Anton. He's a big fellow."

"They usually are. Yeah, we got a couple of Nicks here."

"This one has black hair, maybe a beard."

She pulled back, eyes narrowing. "You a cop?"

He laughed. "No. Just a businessman."

"Then maybe you should talk to the manager."

His turn to fasten his gaze on her. "I prefer your company. Is Nick here tonight?"

Vashti caught her breath, rocking back slightly. "Wha . . ."

He repeated the question, stepping up the pressure.

"I . . . I . . ." She shook her head sharply, fighting it. "Hey, who the hell are you?"

That was unexpected. She should have been under by now. Instead she glared right back at him, eyes blazing and guarded. He found he could not get through to her again. Not drunk, could she be on drugs? They would make her resistant to—

"Listen, I don't want any trouble from you," she stated, her voice low. An ordinary man wouldn't have been able to hear her above the blast of music. "Let's just be a couple of ships passing in the night and leave it at that—no collisions. *No* complications. Okay?"

So *that* was it. "Yes, absolutely. I apologize for the presumption."

She gave him a long look, apparently sizing him up. "Accepted."

"Thank you."

It was enough to mollify her. "It's an easy enough mistake to make. Doing that stuff with them is one thing, but not your own kind. If it makes you feel better, I didn't know about you either."

He grinned. Encounters with other vampires were rare. He wondered what breed she might be. Probably not of his blood, else he might have sensed a kinship. "You were trying for me?"

"Sure, why not? Big healthy guy like you could spare a bit of the fresh for little old me."

Feeling flattered, he raised his undrunk beer. "To might-have-beens?"

She smirked and tapped her undrunk tea glass against his mug. They then set both containers back on the table. "You weren't trying for me, though, were you?" she asked.

"Regrettably, no. I really am looking for Nick Anton. Is he here?"

"Why do you want him?"

"It's about a job."

"What kind of job?"

"You said you wanted to avoid collisions."

She snorted. "Yeah, right. He's here, but in the private party room in the back. They won't let you in."

"They?"

"One of the boys is on watch at the door. It's invitation only. Lots of big spenders with grabby hands. I was invited but didn't like their energy. They look like Mob, but not as polite."

"You could handle them."

"Too much trouble. Besides, it's harder when they're drunk. You know that. I like it out here where the house guys keep an eye on me, and I can pick and choose who I want to be with."

By that she meant whom she chose to feed from. "Understandable. Where's this party?"

"Take a left at the rest rooms, door at the end of the hall."

"Thank you." He made to stand, but she put a hand on his arm. "Ladies first. It'll look better, and it's good for my ego."

He liked her style. "No problem."

"And one thing? Be careful with them. They're dangerous. Even for someone like you, they're dangerous."

"Someone like me?"

"Like us."

"Throwing in with me against them?"

"Your energy tells me you're a good guy. I like good guys."

"I try."

"You don't discount that kind of stuff, do you? Auras and things?"

"Never. It's a useful gift to have. Thank you for the warning. Professional courtesy?"

"Something like that. As one bloodsucker to another." Vashti of the Flaming Tresses winked, flashed her delightfully wicked smile—with just a hint of her retracted fangs showing—and gracefully rose, bangles and bells making their own music as she undulated away. Seconds later she was at work on another man, presumably someone who could provide her with more than mere cash to keep her well nourished for the evening.

Ships in the night, indeed. I wouldn't mind docking at her port.

When the next dancer took her place on the runway, Richard quit his table, heading toward the rest room area. Its arched opening led to a short hall containing better lighting, a phone, and a moderate respite from the noise. At the end of the hall was a red door with PRIVATE painted on in silver. Before it stood a large slab of a man with absolutely nothing better to do than watch the comings and goings of the patrons. He wore a loose tan sport coat, warm for the weather, but excellent for hiding weapons.

Though lacking in Vashti's gift for reading an individual's energy, Richard could tell at thirty feet that the fellow would not be readily persuaded to allow in a party crasher.

Not by ordinary means, anyway.

Richard walked up as though he had a perfect right to be there. The man shifted slightly, the movement reminiscent of a boulder settling itself more firmly in the earth. But all boulders could be budged—providing one had the right sort of lever.

Fortunately, the lighting was sufficient, and the man conscientious enough not to drink while on duty. A moment of quiet talk and he obligingly held the door open to let Richard pass through.

"Forget you ever saw me," Richard told him, by way of a final order, getting an affirmative grunt in reply.

He stood in a dim antechamber. Loud music, drunken whoops, and laughter beyond another arch indicated that the party was in full swing. Richard stepped forward, using the cover of an artificial ficus tree to delay notice of his presence. Through the silk leaves he saw a rousing orgy in the making. It reminded him of the goings on at the old Hellfire Club, but with fewer clothes to remove.

Booths lined three walls, the center of the floor given over to dancing. All the dancers were topless, and several of them were clad only in high heels, some jewlery, and a smile. He wondered where they stowed their tips. The men getting lap dances had seemingly forgotten the no-touching rule, and one couple who had slipped under a table was in desperate need of a hotel room. Though more than enough to get the whole club closed down, apparently the money going to the management made the risk worth it.

Richard scanned each man's face, looking for Nick Anton among the crowd of thirty or forty. In the bouncers there was a preponderance of shaved heads, tattoos, goatees, and sloped shoulders. The low lighting wasn't much of a hindrance, but it was erratic as it flashed in time to the music, making it hard to focus. Figures writhed in the gloom, or sat transfixed by the dancing or by whatever booze or drug they'd taken. The heavy sweet smell of pot was on the air, along with that of regular tobacco. The restless, too-bright eyes of some indicated there was plenty of coke to be had as well.

All the better for him, there was less chance of any of the guests noticing . . .

Time stopped. The hubbub of the party went still and faded. A frisson of pure shock struck him almost as solidly as a fist. Richard blinked, but what he saw remained firmly in place. He gaped, disbelieving his luck, then with an internal lurch accepted it as a gift from a benevolent Goddess.

Right in the middle of the drunken and drugged mob, like a king carousing with his sycophantic court, was Alejandro Trujillo.

Chapter Ten

Richard's first instinct was to surge forward, grab him by the throat, and gut the bastard bare-handed. The impulse, all fire and ice, roared over him. It felt good, but he could not give in to it, and made himself ride it out until he could think again.

Alejandro was unaware of his doom standing a scant few yards from him. He was grinning, enjoying a joke from the naked girl seated next to him, a half-smoked cigar in one hand, his other on the girl's thigh. His shirt was open, and the way things were proceeding it wouldn't be long before his pants went the same way.

It's a victory party. He's celebrating their deaths.

The sounds and movement of it abruptly resumed again in Richard's perception. He stalked slowly into the middle of it, heart pumping hard with pure rage. He went straight to the girl, gently touching her arm to get her attention. She paused in her laughter to look up, saw his face, and blanched. He gestured for her to leave. Not understanding the why of it, but clearly relieved to be excused, she boosted from her chair and tottered off, amazingly quick on her six-inch heels.

Richard took her seat. Alejandro's expression was a study in puzzled fury for the interruption. He brought himself under swift control.

"What do you want?" he asked. No need for the preamble of

demanding this stranger identify himself; any man making such an approach would always want something.

"Do you know who I am?" Richard asked in perfect Spanish.

Slightly older than his brother, Alejandro bore a sibling's likeness to Luis, but his good looks were dissipated, his expression remote, stony. He could smile and laugh as heartily as the next man, but the humor would never reach his shark's eyes. They were hooded over now with supreme caution. He raised his hand lazily. The people nearest to them drew back and several men materialized in their place. The brassy music continued, but the dancers faltered in their gyrations.

"I don't think it matters who you are," Alejandro replied. "You do not belong here. I will ask you to leave."

"Not if you are a wise man."

"Indeed?"

"A wise man knows the face of his enemy."

"And how have I offended you to make you my enemy?"

"You breathe. That is offense enough."

"I'm sorry you feel that way. You will be too, I expect. Very soon."

"As will you. For Luis."

That shot home. Alejandro's eyes flickered. "I know many named Luis."

"But only one you may call brother."

"What is your business with me?"

Richard made no immediate answer, putting forth his concentration to snare Alejandro's will and subjugate it to his own. "I want you to listen very carefully. What I say is important to you. Your life depends on it."

Alejandro had had drink, quite a lot, but the words, the soothing tone were having their effect. He blinked, eyes just beginning to glaze.

"You must tell me where Luis is. That's the most important thing in the world to you now."

"I . . ."

"Yes, you know where he is. You must tell me." Richard felt the veins in his temples pulsing as he pressed matters. "Where. Is. Luis?"

"He's . . . he's . . ." Alejandro wavered, fighting it.

"*Where?*"

"You—you're the one who . . ."

Richard kept his voice even and low. Velvet persuasion. "Never mind that. Tell me where Luis is."

His breath came harsh, sweat popped on his brow, but Alejandro could not pull away. He raised his arm, weakly, like one drowning.

"Tell me." Someone slapped a hand down hard on Richard's shoulder. He continued without pause. "You must tell me. You will tell me. Where is Luis?"

"*No* . . ." Alejandro won his struggle, his head jerking to one side as though to avoid being struck. He nearly fell from his chair, but one of his men caught and steadied him. It was a general signal to the others to do something.

They hauled Richard up and back. He recovered himself in an instant, but they were fast. More hands grabbed his arms, fists pummeled his body. He shook off two men and felled two more. Three took their place, hampering each other, but eager to get in on the kill.

Something slammed against the side of his head. It was meant to be a fatal blow, but only slowed him. He punched backward reflexively, his elbow connecting with a skull to judge by the bruising impact that shot up his arm. A gun was shoved in his face. He batted it away, breaking bones, and tried to force himself through to Alejandro, who was retreating toward the door, yelling orders.

Richard felt a terrible shock in his back, level with his right kidney; his legs suddenly gave out. The lot of them toppled, their combined weight pinning him to the floor. He tried to shoulder his way from under the pile, but could not. Then he couldn't move at all. He lay dazed and inert, his mind tardily concluding some minutes later that he'd suffered another strike to the head, this one decidedly effective. Somewhere above, his enemies caught their breath and discussed what to do with him.

"Who is he?"

"Man, I need a doctor."

"Gonna kill that mother—"

"What was that shit about Luis?"

"Goddamn fucker . . ."

"Man, I'm bleeding, gimme some help here . . ."

". . . busted my arm."

"*Enough! Shut up!*" Alejandro. Very much in charge. They subsided. "You—put that damn thing away. You think they would not hear a shot?"

Richard was turned over. His eyes refused to focus properly. He winced against the spin of too-bright lights and the flesh-colored blobs that were people. His primary sensations had to do with lack of air, bruisings, and an appalling burning in his back.

A blurred face came near, scowling. "It *is* you. I thought you were in— How in hell did you get here?"

"Who is he, boss?"

"Never mind." Alejandro snapped. "Everyone out! The party's over. Move! Now!"

A general shuffling took place, accompanied by muttered questions or grumbles at the fun cut short. Soon the room was cleared of all but a few of the crowd. Richard dimly recognized the oversized form of Nick Anton among their number.

Alejandro nodded at him. "You and your men, get this bastard out of here."

"What do you want us to do with him, sir?"

"What do you think? Get rid of him."

"Permanently?"

"Of course. And make damned sure you do not leave a trail—of any kind. If this comes back to me you are dead."

"Yes, sir." Anton was apparently unfazed by his employer's threat. "What about the manager?"

"I will make it okay with him. You do this."

Not one to waste time, Anton directed two of his people to see to Richard. He was roughly lifted and carried through a side exit. He registered the change from cool, smoke-filled air, to muggy outside air. Most of his attention was on the bonfire in his back. He belatedly recognized the distinct pain of a knife wound. It had gone deep. He'd be a little while recovering—if they gave him the chance.

They won't.

The men dropped him onto the hot, gritty concrete. One went off to get a car. Two remained. He'd never have better odds and, given his condition, two against one were more than enough.

Anton bent close, one hand holding an odd-looking knife. The thing was half a yard long with a viciously sharp Damascus blade, some sort of a custom job. He wiped the flat of it against Richard's shirt to clean the blood away, straightened, then apparently slipped it into his pants pocket. He must have removed or put a hole in it to allow him access to whatever hidden sheath he had strapped to his leg.

Once the knife vanished, Richard abruptly came to life, seizing Anton's ankles. The big man was just stepping away, and his forward momentum worked against him. He cursed and tried to right himself, but came crashing down, hands barely cushioning his fall.

His friend had time to turn and react, aiming a kick at Richard's face. He caught it with his hands and twisted hard, throwing him severely off balance. The man gave a hoarse yell of pain, not only for his jolting hit to the ground, but for his greenstick fracture.

Anton was quick. That long knife magically reappeared in his hand, and he made his thrust just as Richard was getting to his feet. The blade caught him across the back of his right knee, slicing easily through the tough denim to bite the flesh. He grunted as his leg caved. More fire shot through him as he dropped and rolled, trying to gain time. Anton followed with a backswing, but Richard dodged it, moving awkwardly.

He pushed upright, but could place no weight on his leg. Anton charged in, death in his face; Richard dove under his guard, tackling him. It was like trying to bring down a well-muscled refrigerator. He just barely managed, landing on top. Seizing his slim advantage, he smashed a fist into Anton's jaw with as much force as he could summon. The man stopped fighting. Thank God.

The second one was too busy moaning over his injury to do

anything. Good. Richard used the pause to assess his own damage. A bad wound in his back, yes, but starting to ease. His knee was far worse; the bastard had hamstrung him. He'd not felt anything like this since swords had gone out of fashion. Keeping as immobile as possible, he put pressure on the vein to keep from bleeding to death before he healed, his breath made short and shallow by the pain. He'd had worse, but it was still a bitch to get through.

The car was on its way. A third man inside, possibly more. Certainly well-armed.

Damnation. He was too vulnerable and weak for any chance of success against them. If he called for help, the club bouncers patrolling the outside would either throw their lot in with Alejandro's men or bring police, medics, and other unwanted complications. Richard despised the idea of retreat, but saw no other alternative.

His bad leg dragging, he crawled toward the darkness edging the boundaries of the club and prayed the hunters had no flashlights.

He found brief cover between two cars. It felt like the knife was yet cutting him with each jarring move, but he kept going, not daring to stop. He got over a curb into a patch of dried-out scrubby grass littered with empty beer cans and broken glass. A neglected lot between buildings. It stretched on for several yards, the grass growing higher with distance, until interrupted by the thick posts and crosspieces of an old wooden fence. He scrambled toward it, hearing activity behind him. The car had arrived. Men clustered about the fallen.

They'd start casting about for him and would not easily give up. Alejandro had no tolerance for failure.

Richard made it to the fence. The crosspieces were set very close together, making it almost easy to climb, but they were shoulder-high. The landing on the other side was singularly unpleasant. He bit off a cry and had to waste a precious moment before the agony released him enough to move again. To his dismay, he found himself trapped in a small enclosure. A cattle pen. From the look of age and neglect on the weathered fencing, it'd not been used in decades, a relic from the city's early years when beef on the hoof was money in the bank and this area was a true stockyard, not a tourist trap.

Though decrepit, the enclosure was yet strong enough to keep him in place. The overgrown patch of iron-hard ground within offered no concealment. He crept to the opposite side, not wanting another climb and drop, but found one of the lower slats was cracked across. He broke through, gaining another dozen feet of distance between himself and pursuit.

The next pen was in even worse repair with part of one side gone. The opening led to a narrow alley running between sections. Here, long ago, cowboys could drive the cattle in single file toward the slaughterhouse.

"He went this way; Hub tol' us—not over there!"

A man's voice, unexpectedly close, froze Richard. He had the visual advantage at night, but it was of little use when he couldn't stand to see.

"Hub also tol' us Nick nearly chopped his leg off, so no way could he climb that," another man countered. "He'll be along here, not in that mess."

"Then you tell the boss."

"No way."

The first man clambered up to survey the area. He had a flashlight. Richard rolled against the near side of the fence, face into the dust, pale hands under him, hoping his dark clothes would blend with the general gloom. He went absolutely still.

Was it fancy, or did he actually *feel* the beam of the light playing across him?

It danced and flickered along the fencing, making harsh shadows. Confusing ones, he hoped. He held his breath, listening for the least sound of movement from the hunter.

The man was thorough, his search lengthy. Richard's time sense distorted as the minutes stretched to infinity. He forgot his pain in the waiting.

"Aw, hell." The voice of defeat. The man jumped down—on his own side—and trudged off.

Richard sagged, sweating with relief, but remained in place. They might decide to swing back. At least this forced respite offered him a chance to heal.

And thirst. He'd bled quite a lot from both wounds. He swallowed dry, his throat aching.

They kept at it for twenty minutes, twice coming his way. There was some argument about searching the pens. Most were reluctant to venture in. They paused, uncomfortably near, their voices carrying well in the motionless air.

"Place'll be fulla rats," said one. "Or snakes."

Now they tell me, Richard thought.

"Nah, they's a lotta cats get dumped here; they eat the snakes," came another.

"All they gotta do is miss one. Ain't worth it to me to step on some rattler what got missed."

"You gonna say that to the boss's face?"

"Don't matter to me; I ain't gonna say it. Not worth it to do this."

"Huh. Don't like playing with the big boys?"

"Nope. Grabbing some ass inna titty bar is one thing, but chasing down some fucker who should be dead is another. I saw Nick stick him. Where he got it, he shouldn'ta got up again, but he did, an' he got away after decking Nick and Hub. That ain't anybody I wanna meet out here inna dark. What about the rest of you? Think it over."

They did. One by one, they departed. Richard thankfully marked their retreat as they crunched their way over the trash in the lot.

The threat of rats and snakes aside, he decided to remain a while longer. The burning in his leg and back was beginning to cool. It meant recovery, but was tedious. So bloody . . . damned . . . tedious . . .

He jerked awake, disoriented and strangely cold. He peered at his watch. Past midnight. He'd been out that long? Or that short? With the damage he'd suffered he could have lain unconscious until dawn.

With great caution, Richard slowly got up, using the fence to keep his balance as he tested his leg. It hurt like hell, but he could walk—make that limp—on it. Shivering, he made his way along the alley until finding a break in the pens that allowed him real escape.

From the look of the buildings fronting the lot, he judged himself to be just a little south of the club. His car would be close by, just off the main street. All he had to do was avoid drawing attention. Not easy, given the state of his bloodied and torn clothes.

God, but he was thirsty.

The walk was not amusing. The new-healed tendons were stretched tight and diabolically sore. Each step over the uneven ground was needed physical therapy for them, but it was much too soon to press himself. And it was all his own fault.

Damn it, why had he charged in like that? He could have waited for a better moment to take out Alejandro.

But the sight of that bastard laughing, enjoying himself, positively gloating over his success had been beyond endurance. Richard accepted that he was far too emotionally involved for common sense to rule, but *that* had been pure insanity.

And yet in reproachful retrospect, given the time to think, he knew he'd do the same thing again. Richard would not have been Richard if he'd stood by, stoically marking time until a reasonable opportunity presented itself.

Had Alejandro not been so drunkenly resistant to hypnosis, the whole business would have ended quite differently. He'd been sober enough to eventually recognize Richard, though. Disturbing, that. Was the New Karnak sanctuary compromised?

Alejandro would have been well aware of Luis's job at Arhyn-Hill, but Richard kept a very low profile there. Some of the employees had heard of him, but his name wasn't listed on any company directory. One of the reasons he'd chosen the job for Luis was its lack of an obvious connection.

Ingrained caution dictated that he not underestimate Alejandro's resources.

A desire to conclude things dictated that he turn this possible breach in his defenses to his advantage.

All I need do is go home and wait for him to find me.

Not the best of strategies. But then he was hardly at his best right now. Later—he would plan something out later.

The pavement resumed behind the buildings, beginning with an access drive for delivery trucks, the lighting sparse. He hobbled across to an alley that led to the brighter areas of the main street and the parking annex. The eateries were closed or closing, the shops dark, only the bars showed activity. And a police car was parked right in his path opposite the alley mouth. They'd see him going to his car, and at the moment he certainly looked to be a highly suspicious character.

He paused well back in the narrow space between aged buildings. Hidden by shadows, he leaned against the indifferent red brick, wearily wishing the officers would take themselves elsewhere before he collapsed.

Then he came abruptly alert, sensing another presence nearby. Just a few paces ahead he made out the form of a petite woman pressed into a doorway set in the opposite wall. She was also keeping a wary eye on the patrol car, shifting uneasily on her too-high heels, waiting for it to leave.

Well, well. If it wasn't Gail like-a-tornado-but-spelled-with-an-*i*. Her blonde friend Stormee was nowhere in sight. Perhaps busy with a customer. Gail was losing business with the cops in the way. Perhaps he could amend that.

"Hallo, Gail," he called in a soft low tone, hoping she wouldn't run away. "Remember me?"

She gave a violent start, whipping around to peer into the general darkness. "Who's that?"

"It's all right. We met earlier. Stormee was with you."

This reassured her. Slightly. "An' who're you?"

"Just a lonely man looking for some southern comfort." He noticed she had a small object ready in one hand. Pepper spray. In her line of work a girl couldn't be too careful.

"Why you hiding?" she demanded.

"I got into a scuffle tonight, and those policemen might wonder why my clothes are in a less than pristine state. I'd just as soon avoid official notice, if you know what I mean."

She chuckled once, relaxing somewhat. "I sure do, honey. You said you were lonely?"

"Exceedingly so. You may recall that I was too busy earlier."

With a quick look over her shoulder at the car, she cautiously stepped across to him. "You got some time now?"

"Oh, absolutely. Do you think we could come to some mutually advantageous arrangement?"

"Depends what you want, honey." Gail gave him a hard look, for all the good it did her in these dense shadows. "An' I'll tell you first off I use protection no matter what you want. You don't like that, then too bad."

"Not at all. I quite approve."

A big smile. "Then we should get along just fine."

"This is hardly the place, though."

"Yeah. If one of those cops decides to take a leak, it could get embarrassing. Come over this way." Gail took his arm. He tried to disguise his limp, but she noticed anyway. "You hurt?"

"Not much. You should see the other fellow."

A short laugh. "You men. Get a drink, have a fight, get laid."

He had to agree. In his fifteen hundred years' observation of human nature, nothing much had changed about that particular male ritual. He planned to shortly modify the ordering of the pattern for himself, though.

"Jeez—are you all right?" Her voice rose with alarm.

They'd come to a place with light, the outer nimbus being sufficient to reveal his severely disheveled condition to her. She gaped exactly one second at the dirt and blood and turned to run.

He caught her just in time, lifting and hauling her back.

"*Lemme go!*" Her voice was climbing to a full-blown shriek. Before she could vent it, he clapped a hand over her mouth and pressed her to the building to minimize her struggles. He did *not* want to do it this way, but had no other choice.

She brought up the pepper spray. He was expecting that and took it from her.

"Just hold still," he whispered, trying to catch her gaze.

Her eyes were wild and staring, flushed with fear and anger. She fought as best she could, kicking, clawing, screaming under the pressure of his hand. Very little noise of it came out.

"Gail, it's all right, I'm not going to hurt you."

She'd heard that one before, to judge by her frenzied reaction, and why not? Didn't killers and rapists always make such empty promises to their victims?

He had to get her attention, to put a quick end to her terror. Toward that goal, he gave her a good shake, not so much as to snap her neck, but enough so she'd know that he was very much in charge. With her feet dangling a foot off the ground it was easy for her to take the point. "Be *still*," he ordered in a no-nonsense tone.

He got an anguished look from her.

Eye contact. All he needed.

He focused the whole of his will upon her. "Hush now and listen to me. I won't hurt you. *Listen* to me, Gail . . ."

Fear could be almost as potent as alcohol as an impediment to hypnosis. She had strong resistance to suggestion, and did not readily accept his soothing persuasion. Some of them were like that, especially if they were on guard to start with, so he never forced the issue if he could help it. Much better for them both that he take what he needed from a willing woman, much simpler, much easier on his battered conscience.

He kept at her, counting each moment that she did not try to bolt as a victory, until at long last she went under and truly relaxed. Her desperate fight forgotten, she stood quietly—waiting and oh, so willing. Thank the Goddess for large favors.

His velvet soft words to Gail now had the effect of foreplay. He caught the gradual change in her scent, heard the quickening of her breath. He would never tire of it, never. She soon lifted her face to him as she would to a lover, wearing a smile of pure trust, eager, with demands of her own.

Southern comfort, indeed.

Some crates had been left stacked by a delivery entrance. He sat on one to rest his leg, drawing her toward him.

Richard hungered, but took time to kiss her ardently, his hands roaming her body, not restraining it. She responded in kind with an expert's skill, her touch making him hard with need. He lifted her easily onto his lap. She giggled, wrapping her legs around him, pressing her hips and breasts close.

His corner teeth budded. He wanted her, wanted to strip the

clothes from her well-muscled body and thoroughly lose himself in her. She offered love and solace and release from his cares and griefs. Only momentarily, though. It was ever thus with all of them.

Damnation.

He'd have liked nothing better than to be able to properly take her, to really make love with her. But this was not the time or place. He had to hurry, to feed his hunger rather than his desire. Not fair, but often what he had to settle for when circumstances were unfavorable. In instances like this, the lady always came out ahead of him in pleasure.

But not too far ahead, he thought, nuzzling the taut skin of her throat. He bit down, holding her tight. She made a long, gasping cry at this, then another as the first rush of blood left her. He drew strongly on its healing fire, so different from the burn of injury. The red heat instantly relieved his countless aches and bruisings. It was miraculous stuff. His wretched hunger fled; his torn flesh painlessly renewed.

Gail murmured something, arching strongly against him. For a second he thought she'd resumed her struggles, then realized she was climaxing. Her whole body shuddered in reaction. It was quite lovely, holding her as he was, feeling what was happening to her, knowing he'd brought it about. He drank deeply, drank until she finally wilted with exhaustion.

He pulled away, the small wounds he'd made still bleeding a little. He kissed them clean until they closed, then inspected her face. Her eyes were half shut, drowsy. She would sleep very well tonight. Perhaps she'd feel light-headed for a day or two, but nothing more serious than that. Good. He'd promised he wouldn't hurt her and preferred to keep his word.

As for those very visible marks on her sweet neck . . . well, the blood donation story would not suit. This time the blame must be placed on insect bites. The ruse went over rather better in Toronto, for even Texas mosquitoes were no match to their Canadian cousins when it came to size and sheer viciousness.

Richard primed Gail with that unlikely explanation after wiping the reality of their encounter from her conscious memory. He substituted a more mundane one in its stead, then raided his wallet. Knowing that she might not be recuperated enough to work the following night, he was generous, covering whatever earnings she'd lose, and putting an extra hundred on top. He felt badly for having scared her so much at the beginning.

No trace of fear from her now as they strolled back to the alley. They were able to continue on to the sidewalk, for the patrol car was gone.

"You look me up again sometime soon, honey," she drawled as he crossed the street. His limp was nearly gone. "That's Gail—like a tornado . . ."

"But with an *i*," he finished amiably. "I won't forget."

Richard went back to the club.

He was in no presentable state to be allowed inside, but did not plan a direct approach. He parked in a handicap space, killed the motor, but left the headlights on, blinking them several times. This was sufficient to catch the attention of one of the door bouncers, who sauntered over. He came close, bending to peer in the open driver's window.

"Can I help you?" he asked.

"I hope so," said Richard. "I'm having a problem with my contacts."

"Oh, yeah?"

He vaguely gestured toward his face. "I think one them slipped down but I can't feel anything. The light here is really bad."

"Why don't you put your dome on?"

Richard gave a self-effacing laugh. "It's a rental, I can't find the damn control."

"Might be on the steering wheel."

"Really?"

He leaned closer to point. "Try that one."

The dome came on, bright enough to work with. Richard caught the man's attention. "Would you look at my eye? Maybe you can see the lens. It's rather hard for me."

The man looked. After a long, still minute, Richard had him. He instructed him to find the manager and bring him out.

"Tell him it has to do with the large private party that left earlier. He should understand."

"Okay." The bouncer departed, pushing past his fellows at the door, obviously on an errand with no time to waste.

Richard watched and waited, refusing to allow his hopes to rise.

Presently, a dark-haired man in an open-neck white polo with the club's name stitched on the pocket emerged. The bouncer pointed out Richard's car to him. He came around to the driver's side, too.

"Yes, sir?" He possessed the grim, tired expression of one who expects the worst of people and usually gets it.

"You're the manager who dealt with the host of the private party?" He did not think Alejandro would have used his real name.

"Yes, sir. I'm Mr. Forestieri. I spoke to Mr. Gonzalas earlier. Is there a problem?"

"No. Mr. Gonzalas wanted to arrange another party, perhaps for next week."

"We may be booked. Why don't you come to my office? The schedule's there."

"No need to trouble yourself, if you'll just listen to me very closely . . ."

Forestieri proved to be a bit less of a challenge than the bouncer. It took only half a minute to hook him. He obligingly got in on the passenger side. Richard had many questions. Unfortunately, the answer to them all was "no." Forestieri only knew Trujillo as Gonzalas, had no address or number for him; the party had been paid for in cash. Lots of it.

"Who made the arrangements?" Richard asked, exasperated in spite of himself. He'd known this foray would probably not have a payoff. "You had to have talked to someone."

"Nick Anton set it up for him."

"When?"

"Last week."

That far back? Alejandro had been quite confident of success, then. "Anton was the only go-between?"

"He came in with the deposit for the room and entertainment. He's done that before for this guy and others." Forestieri, once started, had no trouble imparting information; the problem was finding anything useable in it.

"How often has Gonzalas been here?"

"Couple times a year."

"Where do you think he gets his money?"

"Oh, he's in drugs, anybody can see that."

"It doesn't bother you?"

"Money's money. He don't deal on the premises."

No, just shares in the bounty and bribes you to not notice, he thought, the sights and smells of the private room still fresh in his memory. "Where's Nick Anton tonight?"

"I dunno. Maybe with Gonzalas. The guy likes to have plenty of muscle around him. It's a status thing."

"Who would know where to find Gonzalas?"

"I dunno." Forestieri stared at the dashboard, indifferent. His clothing stank of cigarette smoke and sweat.

"Someone here must."

"I dunno."

Richard held his temper in check. "Then you will go out and *ask.* Talk to every girl who was at that party; talk to anyone who had anything to do with it or Anton. I have to know where Gonzalas is. Go."

Forestieri left, beginning his questions with the men at the door. One and all shook their heads or shrugged. He went inside. Richard cut his lights and ran the air to clear out the stink. After that, he had nothing more to do but stare at the club entry for the next hour.

Forestieri returned. What he imparted was a collection of conflicting stories of where Gonzalas *might* be staying. The guesses ranged from a prim bed-and-breakfast in Weatherford to several swank hotels in Dallas, to a private mansion at an unspecified location. There wasn't even that much speculation about Anton, as he didn't talk to fellow workers about his jobs outside the club. Little wonder.

Richard gave Forestieri his cell phone number. "When you next see Anton, Gonzalas, or anyone in that group or find out where they are, you will call me, no matter what the time. You will not speak of me to them or anyone else. Is that clear?"

The reply to that, of course, was "yes." It made a change, at least.

Nick Anton's Euless apartment was dark at this late hour. Richard moved quietly, eschewing the squawking gate, climbing over the porch wall instead. His instinct told him the place would be empty, but he had to be thorough.

His leg all mended, he landed lightly, crept to the door, and pressed his ear to its glass panel. His shadow would show against the closed blinds on the other side, but at this point he didn't care. He'd welcome the chance to engage Anton in a short, violent conversation. *That* would be extremely satisfying.

The door had a deadbolt as well as a regular lock in the knob. Richard's burgling tools were at home, and he didn't fancy the noise of breaking glass as an announcement of his presence to the other tenants.

Perhaps the would-be dancer in the flat upstairs might have a key to Anton's place. She seemed to know more about his doings than his coworkers.

She was also, alas, popular. Not at home to Richard's knock. Either working or on a date. Or both.

He gave up this trail for the time being. Anton probably wouldn't be back for hours, if at all. He could even still be out cold from the fight.

Cheering thought.

Richard headed east, swooping into his slot in New Karnak's parking garage just after two-thirty. Weariness enveloped him the closer he got to his refuge. When the elevator doors slid open, he was mentally prepared to go straight to bed.

Two messages were on his machine.

Bourland had phoned some six hours earlier to give his flight number and when he'd be arriving on Monday. He'd sorted out the details for Michael's travel as well. The boy would go back with him when the time came.

"There's one other thing," he added. "I'll be telling the police I'm Stephanie's uncle. If they think I'm next of kin, it will make the process easier—and yes, I'll have papers to prove that if necessary. My coming in will draw police attention to me and thus to you. I'll stop at your place, but it'll be better if I take a hotel room before I contact them. Call me if you've any news."

Considerate of him to be so cautious. Richard wondered what explanation Bourland would give to account for his knowledge of the murder victims ahead of anyone else. The media had not released any names yet, pending notification of family. Not to worry, the man was wily and charming as a cat; he'd smooth things over.

Dr. Sam left the second message. He announced that he and Helen had arrived safe at her home, gave the address and number and said that Michael's condition was unchanged.

"If he doesn't start to snap out of it tomorrow, I'm going to hunt down a specialist. That's not a threat, it's a necessity, so get used to the idea."

Sam was an easy subject for suggestion, but surprisingly forceful about getting his own way when it was important to him. It always had to do with the care of his patients.

Very well, so be it.

Richard stripped on his way to the shower, once more carefully trashing his ruined clothes. Damn it. He'd *liked* those jeans.

When he emerged, the night scrubbed from his once-bruised body if not from his spirit, he stopped cold, halted by an eerie, insistent sound. It was like a baby's cry, meant to get attention.

The awful déjà vu stole the blood from his face and strength from his limbs.

His computer was flashing the letter *S*. It had the same program as the one in his Toronto home.

Stephanie?

No. Utterly impossible, though an instant of hope had split through him like lightning. More likely this was an emergency call from another friend in desperate need.

He groaned inwardly, approaching the computer as though it were a bomb, and tapped in the access code.

The message that came through floored him.

This is Luis. Phone me. Please.

Chapter Eleven

He called the number, a local one. It rang only once before being picked up. Silence on the other end.

"Luis?"

"Richard?"

"Yes, it's me. Where are you?"

"Thank God. Oh, thank God."

He got the impression of Luis crumpling with profound relief. "Where are you?"

"He got them. He got them all."

"I know. Where are you?"

But Luis was unable to answer, choking into tears. He was not that weak of a man, but this was probably the first time he'd been able to speak to anyone. A severe reaction was only to be expected. Richard waited him out, quelling his impatience before it turned into anger.

"I—I'm sorry," Luis finally whispered. "I just—just . . ."

"It's all right. Tell me where you are. I'll come fetch you."

"What?"

"I'm in Dallas. I know what's happened. Where are you?"

Luis stumbled out an address and general directions to a roadside motel near Plano.

"I'll be there in thirty. Get ready to leave."

He got a meek, tired reply in the affirmative.

Richard dressed fast and shot down to his car, then pushed and repeatedly exceeded the speed limit. He pulled into the motel's lot five minutes early. The place was an ugly, no-frills model, its two stories overlooking only the freeway. It was a cut above a fleabag, but a very narrow slice. Richard drove slowly now, the window open.

A man broke away from where he'd been hiding next to a bank of soft drink machines, rushing over. He was in a rumpled dark suit, tie gone, clutching a leather laptop bag to his chest like a life preserver. He went straight to the passenger side and ducked inside. Richard gunned them away.

Luis sank down in the seat, his eyes shut. His face was flushed and sweating; he'd been drinking to judge by his breath. Quite a lot, apparently.

"Have you been there all this time?" Richard asked.

"Mm?"

"How long were you at that motel?"

"Since this afternoon."

"Where before that?"

"My car. I drove around. I didn't know what to do. My car's back there . . ."

"Leave it; you need to disappear."

A bitter laugh. "That does not work so well. God, Stephanie tried to tell me something was wrong."

And you didn't listen. But voicing reproach would help neither of them now. "Tell me what happened when you left work Friday."

"Friday?"

"You didn't go straight home after work. Where were you?"

"I had an appointment. I was looking at a horse for Stephanie. Her birthday present. The man and I got to talking; we had some beers. I called home to let her know I'd be late, left a message. I thought she'd just taken the kids out for pizza. When I phoned later, I got a recording that said the line was out of service. So I left. When I got there . . . it was gone, they were gone."

Luis spoke like a robot, dead-toned, dead-faced, then broke

down, trying to stifle his sobs. He couldn't speak, struggled to master himself. Finally he opened the laptop case and pulled out a nearly empty bottle of brandy and drained the last inch from it.

Richard understood the feeling. He'd want to get drunk, too. "Then what did you do?"

"I don't remember much. I drove. I don't know where. I drove for hours, was afraid to stop. Spent the night in the car at some truck station south of the city. Heard the news report on the radio. It felt like everyone was looking at me. I kept seeing Alejandro's face. My own brother. I never really believed he'd do it, maybe kill me but not my woman, not my children." He was out of liquor, but tried to take a pull from the bottle anyway. He didn't seem to notice it was empty.

"Then what did you do?"

"Drove some more. I was tired. The motel looked okay. They took cash in advance, and I used a false name."

"Why didn't you call the police?"

"Alejandro. He'd have people looking for me to do just that. He knows how to buy people; he can buy anything he wants, even death. No place is safe from him. You said we'd be safe. How did he find us? Where the hell were you? Did *you* tell him?"

That would be the booze, grief, and anger doing the shouting. Richard waited until the momentum faltered. "Don't be foolish, of course not."

"That bastard. I will kill him. Somehow, I will kill him for this, for everything."

"Do you know where he is?"

"If I did, I would not be here." Luis slumped even lower and went silent. He remained so until New Karnak came into view, then sat up, full of alarm. "We can't go here! He will know this is where I work. This is where he will look for me!"

"He won't find you, I promise."

"No! Let me out! He will have people watching this place!"

"Then don't let them see you. You'll be safe once we're inside. Get below the window line."

"You're crazy."

"Luis, please do what I say."

Luis responded less to Richard's soft order and more to the fact that he had no choice in the matter. He cursed and grumbled and slouched low, remaining that way even after Richard parked and got out. He held the elevator door.

"All right—now."

Luis scrambled over, head down as though dodging a bullet. "This place is *not* safe. It can't be."

"Alejandro will be looking for you to return to your office, not my flat. He doesn't know about me." Not the truth, but Luis didn't need to hear everything just yet. He did need reassurance and another drink. He wasn't thinking straight, and the sooner he got thoroughly numbed into sleep the better. By morning he might be useful.

In the harsh light of the elevator he looked worse than bad: two-day beard stubble, the whites showing all around his red-rimmed eyes, the air of defeat. Rest would help, but not cure him.

The door hummed open, and they stepped into the penthouse. It was as Richard had left it: no intruders lurked in the corners. Richard went to the bar and cracked open a fresh bottle of brandy from the store of assorted bottles in the cabinet. He always kept a supply for guests. He poured a triple and handed it to Luis, who took it without comment and drank.

He'd never been up here before. He looked around incuriously until spying the framed photo of his daughters on the desk. Then he turned away. "I'm sorry."

"For what?"

"You hurt, too. I forgot that."

Richard motioned at the couch. "Sit down. I've some good news for you."

He didn't sit so much as back into it, then drop. "Good news? How?"

"Michael is alive."

"Michael . . . ?" Luis shook his head. "What? But how? The place was leveled."

"I found him hiding in the pump house. Just a few bruises. He's safe with a doctor now, getting first-rate care."

Unlooked-for hope flooded Luis's face, replacing disbelief. "Where? What doctor? Take me to him!"

"In the morning."

"No! Now! I must see him!" He dropped his glass and boosted up, trying to cross to the elevator, but was too unsteady on his feet. He bumped into a table, nearly sending it and himself over. He caught his balance just in time and stood swaying.

"Luis, he will be asleep; waking him up will only frighten him."

"He needs his father; he won't be frightened of me."

"That won't be a good idea just now." *Not in your condition, my friend.*

"What do you mean?"

"He was very traumatized. I think he saw everything that happened, and it put him into some kind of shock. He's not been able to talk—"

"Then I *must* go to him."

"In the morning, first thing."

"But—"

"Look at yourself. Charging in the way you are now will upset him even more. He needs to know that his father is calm and in control of himself. When adults can't control their emotions, it frightens children. His world has been turned inside out; because of that you have to be strong for him."

"I can be calm." There was an edge in his tone.

"You'll be more convincing after you've slept. Clean up and get some rest. You've both been through hell. Show him it's possible to survive."

Luis framed his head with his hands, pressing hard on his temples. "How is it possible? Everything was *fine* yesterday. And now . . ."

Richard understood that all too well. He'd seen it far too often. "One hour at a time, then one day at a time, no more."

"I don't know if I can stand it."

"You will. For Michael you will."

"Yes." But his voice was dead. "Did he say anything to you at all?"

"No. He's cried a little, but he doesn't speak. The doctor will be finding him a specialist if he doesn't wake out of it soon. He'll need special care no matter what."

Luis took a step forward, seemed to think better of it and sank into an armchair. "And you found him? How did you come to be there?"

"I got an e-mail SOS from Stephanie early Friday morning. Like the one you sent me tonight."

"Yes, she taught me how to do that when we moved here. Made me memorize the code. For emergency. I didn't think to use it until tonight when I saw the motel had an access. I didn't know you were already here."

"I flew straight down." He'd not known that Stephanie had confided the code to Luis. Until now it had been his own private gift to her. For all the good it had done. "Just what disturbed her enough to call for help?"

He spread his hands. "Little things. The stable door was open one morning. I thought one of the kids did it. There were two hikers in the fields once. She said they hung about all day as though watching the house. That bothered me a bit, but only because I thought they might be burglars, so I just said to take extra care about the locking up. We each had a pistol in case of trouble. I was not worried. I wish I'd listened to her."

And I, too. "She told me to come to the house after dark as usual, but by then it was too late."

"How too late?"

"They . . . were gone by then. I arrived hours too late."

Luis looked steadily at him. "What did you see? Tell me."

"They'd been shot. It was quick. They could not have suffered. They likely never knew what hit them."

"Stephanie . . . was she . . . ?"

Richard instantly interpreted the unfinished question. "No. No one touched her."

"A small mercy from a man who knows none. An oversight, I'm sure. The news said it was an explosion, but you saw them."

"I was in the house, yes. I looked for you and Michael, then I smelled the Semtex. It went up just as I got out." Best to keep the truth short and the rest unsaid. Richard wished his own memory could be revised or at least softened.

"A wonder that you are alive."

"And you as well. I believe Alejandro's hit man was watching from cover and was waiting for you to come home. He mistook me for you and set the place off."

"My God."

"But I got clear, and he totally missed Michael. Alejandro is *not* all-powerful."

Luis shook his head, not ready to believe that.

"Tell me—why did you erase all the e-mails on your office computer?"

"What?" The subject shift confused him. He had to hear the question again. "You were in my office?"

"I was trying to find you. I noticed those files were deleted. Why?"

"I always delete everything at the end of a day. It means I've dealt with all the work. I don't leave until I've cleared it out."

"Your address book was clean, too."

"That I did later—at a coffee house."

"They had a phone line for that?"

"A public computer."

"At a coffee house?"

Luis shrugged. "It is a modern age. The young people go to such places. I was afraid Alejandro might somehow find the addresses, make trouble for the people, so I deleted that to be safe."

In the midst of his grief, Luis's survival skills had tardily kicked in. There was hope for his recovery, after all.

"Richard—have *you* spoken to the police?"

"Not yet."

"Why not?"

"I don't want them to know about me."

"They need to know who to look for. You can tell them."

"That's already happening. Philip Bourland is helping."

"God, I forgot about him. I must call him. I should have called him before now."

"After you've slept. He's made arrangements to get Michael to Canada. He can do the same for you. We'll make sure Alejandro never finds you."

"How?"

"Because he will be dead."

Luis almost smiled. "Again—how?"

"I'll find a way."

"You are a clever man, Richard, but even you do not have the resources to cut down someone like Alejandro. Many have tried."

"If there is a chance to kill him would you have me pass it up?"

"No, of course not. But I could wish to be the one to do it. He is not my brother. He is less than an animal. I would blot him out and pray God he burns in hell forever."

"Amen to that."

Luis's head drooped suddenly. Between the drink and the glut of emotional stress, he was overdue to collapse.

"Come on, you need to sleep." Richard stood.

"But this place is not safe."

"You won't be staying here."

"Where, then?"

Richard went to the desk and drew out another magnetic key from one of the drawers. "I've a special retreat within the building. It's not fancy, but you won't be bothered there; no one else knows about it."

Mystified, Luis slowly followed Richard into the elevator. He swiped the key through the slot and pressed the penthouse button five times. They went down one floor. The doors opened again to darkness. The air was circulated by the building's climate system, but had that stillness peculiar to lack of occupancy. Richard flicked on the lights. It was a small room, fitted out like a studio apartment, with a folding sofa bed and kitchenette. The two other doors, he explained, went to the bath and the one-way fire exit. From the slanted window there was a view of the Dallas skyline in the distance through the half-closed blinds.

Richard drew the heavy drapes. "You'll be fine here for the night. If you need anything, come upstairs for it. I'm afraid there's no food here—"

"It's all right. I'm not hungry. What is this?"

"A bolt-hole I arranged some time ago. Access is only through the elevator. You can leave, if you must, through the fire exit, but you can't get back in again that way."

"Why do you even have it?"

"Why not? In my line of business I never know what might happen. It seemed a good idea to have a safe haven, so I had this place fitted in while the building was being refurbished. None of the tenants know it exists. It's sound-proofed so you won't hear each other."

Luis almost smiled again. "This is wonderful. Quite brilliant."

"It serves."

Richard showed him the sequence again on the elevator button, opened up the bed, and wished him good-night.

"But should you not stay here as well? To be safe?" Luis asked.

"I've work yet to do. Come up in the morning. We'll go see Michael then."

"God bless you, Richard," he blurted, just as the elevator door slid shut.

Past four in the morning and there was no sleep in him.

This must be what coffee does to people.

Luis's appearance had stripped away all Richard's fatigue for the time being. There was hope for him that Michael would respond to his father's presence. They would find out tomorrow.

In the meantime, Richard knew he'd only pace restlessly and be quite useless here. He had to be out doing something, and one unfinished errand readily presented itself.

Along with the usual hammer, pliers, and screwdrivers, he had a collection of unorthodox tools in one of the kitchen drawers. In a thick plastic carry-case was a fine selection of lock picks; in another, a glass cutter, tape, and some very sticky putty. Most burglars these days just kicked in the door to grab what they wanted; Richard had more subtle skills.

Traffic was thin on his drive back to Euless. That would change in a very short time. He did not relish the prospect of facing the bright dawn on the return trip, pocketing more sun block against it. He'd lost his Stetson during the fight at the bar and had rummaged in his closet for a replacement. All he found was a black baseball-style hat with "Black Hat Productions" stitched on the front in black thread. A forgotten gift from a friend. It would have to do when the time came, and would likely make better cover. Half the casually dressed men in the state wore such hats.

Nick Anton's complex was not stirring yet as Richard pulled in and parked, though lights showed in flats belonging to early risers and insomniacs. He crossed the lot to the walkway, eyes and ears alert for observers. There were none as he again slipped over the wall onto Anton's porch.

The place was well shadowed and he very quiet as he worked on the locks. The doorknob one was no problem, but the dead bolt took longer, snicking loudly as it reluctantly surrendered. For a man in his line of work, Anton should have had better quality stuff.

Richard listened hard before entering, mindful that the place might be unexpectedly occupied. It was with both relief and chagrin that he determined it to be empty. He expected that, but had Anton been there it would have simplified his task. A few direct questions were much better than an hour's search through someone else's life.

He made sure the blinds were shut—there were no curtains—then flicked on a light. Anton had all the basics, but with an expensive, oversized TV and VCR. A large collection of action movies and porn was piled hodgepodge into a bookcase that had never seen a book. His reading matter was limited to picture magazines, their subjects consistent with his taste in films, and scattered throughout the small flat. Richard's initial scrutiny confirmed to him that the man lived like a pig and this foray would take time.

He began with the wildly untidy mess surrounding the kitchen phone, home to business papers and bills. There was no address book, but lots of business cards, old and new, matchbook covers, cocktail napkins, anything that would take a scribble. Many were not readily identifiable, consisting mostly of phone numbers and first names, usually of women. The business cards were almost as obscure, the matchbooks coming from various clubs and bars. The more important ones were attached to the wall by thumbtacks, or slid in between the wall and corner molding of a cabinet. Among them was one for Bubba Rob's Texas Nights.

There was a thick notepad with more numbers and reminders to buy foods and household items. Richard tore off the top sheet, then confiscated many of the business cards, taking most of the top layer. An inconvenience, perhaps, to Mr. Anton, but Richard did not think the man would live long enough to discover his home invasion.

Not if I get hold of him for five minutes.

The answering machine blinked patiently. Richard found a pen, ready to take down anything useful.

Three of the messages were from women, two from men. The ladies had only personal matters, it seemed, and did not leave numbers. One man was obviously a bill collector, the other was rather more oblique.

"I saw the news. You may tell our employer that I wish to cordially sever relations with him, so don't call me again."

No self-identification, no number. He spoke clearly, with precise diction, but possessing a trace of local accent, clearly expecting Anton to know him. Richard listened again to memorize the voice. The answering machine had a caller ID trace attached, but nothing came up for this particular message. The man at the other end either phoned from a public booth or had countermeasures in place.

His statement was cryptic, but given Richard's unique viewpoint, a possible meaning presented itself. The "news" might mean the excessive media coverage of the Addison explosion. If so, then the "employer" could be Alejandro. The man was taking a chance quitting him. Severance benefits tended to be rather violent and final in certain types of work.

A second go-through turned up nothing more of interest. The mine was exhausted, but he counted himself slightly ahead for these few vague leads, which he would soon look into on the computer. Tomorrow, after reuniting father with son, he could investigate Jordan Keyes. Richard hoped he'd prove to be a better source of information on Alejandro, else he'd have to camp out in Anton's grubby apartment against his return.

Dawn was just starting to become a real annoyance. He'd forgotten his sunglasses and was half blind from the glare as he drove to cover under New Karnak. He squinted and tried to rub away the pulsing afterimages from his vision. No good. He needed darkness and rest. A few hours of both could be had before Luis woke up.

Richard tapped the elevator control more from memory than sight, thought about making a quick check on Luis, then dismissed it. No sense in startling him awake, if he was even capable of waking. He'd had enough booze to knock him out for a goodly time.

The door hummed open; out of habit, he listened, mindful of the threat of Alejandro tracking him here. His eyes began to rapidly adjust to the gloom.

He went alert. He'd *not* shut the lights off before leaving.

The likely thing was Luis had returned, looking for food or more brandy or for Richard and had turned them off. Likely, but now was not the time to make assumptions.

He kept a gun in the bottom drawer of the desk, a Colt revolver bought decades ago. It was still there, loaded with wadcutters. The rounds would not easily penetrate the walls, being designed to create havoc on flesh instead.

He pushed away the small voice that said he was being too paranoid. He could deal with feeling foolish after he'd ascertained his caution was for nothing.

He sniffed the air, catching a slight difference from the usual filtered stuff from the vents. Booze and sweat. Traces left behind by Luis. He sniffed for Semtex, thankfully not detecting any.

Listening, he focused on the least little sound for a full two minutes before relaxing. If someone was in the apartment, he'd have heard their heartbeat by now and most certainly their breathing.

Lights still off, he eased over to the guest room and made a quick turnaround of it, the bath, and closet, then did the same for the kitchen. Last was his own bedroom.

Should anyone be hiding, this would be the best place, but

they'd not be able to see him in the dark. His night vision was fully restored by now. He pushed the door open with his foot, all his senses forward.

The universe began to break down into separate little bits of data: the door's slight resistance to his push, a strangely familiar, but quite incongruous, click and thump . . .

. . . something slamming violently into his chest.

He staggered from the force of it, the breath knocked from him. He fell with a grunt, strings cut.

Fire in his chest. The horrific burst of it stunned him flat. He gasped for air. A terrible weight pressed him down, squeezing the life from him.

His hands flapped frantically against something . . . in . . . him. Slender, like an arrow, but not as long. It had missed his heart, but only just. He obeyed his first instinct, wrapping feeble fingers around it. His strength was going fast. He'd have but one try.

No breath to scream as he tore it free.

He lay inert, unable to move, waiting for the roaring aftershock to subside. He could just manage a little air, keeping it slow, shallow. Any more and he might cough. He had enough pain without adding to it.

After a few awful moments he sensed a gradual fade in intensity as his body slowly healed.

Shot. But by what?

In the dimness of the room he made out the shape of a camera tripod. What was mounted on it explained the familiar out-of-place—and out-of-time—sound: a crossbow.

What the hell . . . ?

He was recovered just enough to reach up and claw at the light switch, getting a clear look at the booby trap. It was beautifully set—simple, but lethally effective. The tripod was a heavy model with extra weights attached to the legs to add to its stability, allowing it to hold the crossbow firmly in place. A length of what looked to be thin fishing line or piano wire ran from the crossbow to the inside doorknob. The door swinging fully open pulled the no-doubt-sensitive trigger. Whoever set the trap could safely exit the room so long as he didn't open the door too wide.

It was fixed at the right level to take out a man of Richard's height.

Jordan Keyes. His file had him linked with just such an exotic weapon.

Too bad for him and Alejandro that I survived.

Richard pushed himself up with an effort. It felt exactly like he'd been kicked by a very large angry horse. He'd been shot before by the damned things; depending on the bolt's point they usually left a much larger, bloodier wound. Not that this one was minor. There was quite a mess on the rug.

He opened his shirt and gingerly checked his chest. Blood there too, but no bleeding and . . . glass? He brushed tiny shards of it from his skin. The wound was closed and tender, but not as painful as it still should have been. It was less healing and more like numbness.

He found the bolt. The tip was odd, with a sliver of broken glass where metal should be. He sniffed for some trace of whatever liquid had been inside, but it was obscured by his own blood.

At least, I think I survived.

His head suddenly felt like it'd been stuffed with cotton, his limbs going heavy.

Poison. If the bolt doesn't kill, the poison will.

He had to dilute it. Quick.

His legs barely responded. He shambled to the kitchen like a drunk, reeling against the walls for balance.

He dragged open the refrigerator door, his hands clumsy and trembling as he scrabbled in the vegetable compartment for one of the blood bags. He tore it open, slopping some, then drank it straight down. He reached for a second bag, but his legs gave out. Gravity seemed to pound him into the floor. His arms refused to move.

The only light came from the refrigerator; the door, swinging to close itself, bumped against his body. Cold air flooded down on him.

The weight returned to his chest.

Curare. He uses . . .

The stuff had already attacked his voluntary muscles, now it was paralyzing the rest. Breathing became more difficult. His heart throbbed painfully, struggling against—

Then he no longer drew any breath at all.

His heart pulsed on for a few faltering beats.

He felt the exact instant when it ceased.

He lay inert, a live brain in a dead body, consumed with panic as it sent frantic orders to unresponsive flesh.

He couldn't even blink his eyes. Nor move them.

Strange black outlines edged his blurring field of view.

Then the universe simply shut down.

Chapter Twelve

The Beginning, Ten Years Later

Winter lay heavy on the land, like guilt on the head of a sinner. Snow covered all the great tor of the Isle of Apples; drifts taller than a tall man could reach buried its base. The surrounding fens had frozen solid; anyone with a mind to do so could walk across dry-shod like the Children of Israel.

Nothing moved on this dim dawn, though. It was too cold for even the woodcutters to venture forth. The sun hardly dared to show itself and wrapped up in clouds even as the shivering folk below wrapped themselves in blankets.

Richard drew away from the narrow window, pulling the shutter in and securing it. He let fall over the opening the thick woolen flap that was meant to cut the draft. Cold air came in regardless. A large brazier crackled with flames in the center of the round stone chamber where his servants huddled. Away to the side were the horses, dozing on their feet, lending their warmth to the gathering. Until he got quite close to their circle he could see his breath hang in the air. The fire made most of the light, though some of the pale gray sky was visible through the smoke hole in the thatch above.

Several skins of wine had been passed around in an attempt to find another kind of warmth. The morning meal had come and gone along with whatever work that had to be done. All were content to sleep the day through until time for the evening prayers and meal and then sleep again.

As would I, if sleep would come to me.

Of late, true rest was not an easy thing for Richard to achieve, yet weariness saturated him to his bones. Even the blood he supped on failed to rouse him for long from his lethargy. He'd departed from the king's court after that last tourney, claiming he'd been called to retreat from the world for the good of his soul. None had hindered him. Those with eyes to see had noticed the change in him. Some rumored it was du Lac's impossible love for the queen that made him leave. Others loyally maintained it was his dire wounding that had caused his withdrawal from all court life. Though he'd recovered miraculously quick, they said he still bled in his heart.

At first, he'd gone to the lands granted to him by the king for his service. There, Richard had a fine keep of his own filled with rich furnishings, men, and weapons, the surrounding farms growing bounty enough to support all. He stayed there, alone, shunning the company of his fellow lords.

Sabra had tried to console him.

But . . . he shunned even her.

And then she'd departed, and he was truly alone.

He left his private chambers only at night to stalk the fields and forests like a lost ghost. Any hapless wanderers who happened to see him, pale of face, grim in aspect, clad wholly in black, crossed themselves and fled.

The comforts of his own hall brought no succor. After the harvest was in, stored, and allotted, he gathered a company of servants to see to his needs and took to wandering. He pitched his tent near a road or in a fallow field, or sheltered in some abandoned villa left by the Romans, never staying in one place for more than a few days. When his presence was noticed by the local lord, he would courteously decline the offered hospitality and move on.

He thought the passage of time would lessen his pain, but contrariwise, it only seemed to increase.

For the Goddess had betrayed him.

His servants, long used to his habits, took little notice when he went to bed an hour after dawn. They placed a smaller brazier of coals in the curtained-off area he claimed for his own and withdrew. One of the girls was curled in the bed to warm it and await his pleasure.

Today it was Ghislaine, ripened now to a comely woman. Richard climbed in next to her, pulling the covers almost all the way over their heads. She burrowed against him, sighing with contentment. Her firm flesh pleased him, a little, but he was not hungry, having supped the day before.

"Why do you smile?" he asked, once they'd settled.

" 'Tis nothing, my lord."

"I can see 'tis something and naught to do with me."

"I mean no offense, my—"

"And none has been taken, unless you deny me your reason to smile."

She hesitated, then yielded. "I've a small happiness of my own, I think. The next moon will tell me for sure."

"You're with child again?"

"I think so, the Goddess willing."

In the years from their first meeting she'd borne two children, both of whom had died. "And this is a happy prospect to you?"

"Yes."

"How so is it happy?"

"It just *is*, my lord."

He could see none of it. In the short hours that he'd known fatherhood, he'd felt only shock, regret, agony, and grief. Since that time he'd felt little else but anger, which he held carefully in check.

Why did Ghislaine not feel the same? Had not the Goddess taken her two babes before they'd lived even a year? And now she longed for a third chance to add to her sorrows.

"Know you the father?"

She giggled briefly. "Of course I must *know* him, else I'd not be this way."

He was in no mood for jest, but she did not notice, so diverted was she by her own thoughts. "If the babe lives we may marry, if my lord permits."

If it lives. So, she was aware of the possibility of loss. "And if the Goddess takes this child from you?"

"We may marry anyway. 'Tis not good to be alone. He's a fine strong man. His get will also be strong, I'm sure."

How do they endure it?

Richard had been in this changed life for only a decade and already felt impossibly removed from the rest of humanity. To him, their lives seemed short and shallow as they toiled one day to the next, starving or feasting, living and dying, accepting such as their lot with few complaints, for that was the way of things, and it would ever be so.

I will live on, they will die. But how they waste their little lives! Their world is so small, they're like farm animals with speech. Can they not see themselves?

Ghislaine made bold to caress him, smiling her woman's smile. "Does my lord wish to be pleasured?" she whispered.

What he wished for was a lifting of the blackness from his heart. Even Ghislaine with her sweet body so willingly given could not do that. All that stirred within him now was despair and impossible loneliness.

"Sleep, child," he said. "Sleep and dream of heaven."

If she was disappointed by his reply, she made no show of it, obediently lying down again. Perhaps she expected some attention from him later to make up for it. True, he could go through the forms of love, mount and ride her to fulfillment, but would mock himself from beginning to end for his emptiness of spirit.

He lay still, holding her, until her breath lengthened into that of slumber. How he envied her that kindly rest. He'd not truly slept in months. He continued well in health; the blood he took kept him so. Would that it could as easily heal his soul.

When he thought he could move without waking her, he slipped from the bed and dressed. Gooseflesh plucked at him, but he hardly felt it. *I must be as cold within as the world is without.* But to avoid comment, he covered and cloaked himself, then quietly left. Though it was odd that he be up and about during the day, his drowsing people had long grown used to their lord's silences and night rambles and hardly stirred as he passed them.

The knife-sharp air made short work of his heavy finery, cutting its way into any careless opening. Well, a good walk would cure the chill and, he hoped, utterly tire him out.

It was hard going through the drifts. There were some paths trodden through this small village, though no one had used them much in the last few days. Richard's party had arrived just in time to shelter from the coming snowstorm in a hospice the nearby church maintained for travelers. It was a relic from the Romans, old now, but kept in repair. No one knew what they had used it for; it could have been anything from a temple for one of their gods to a granary.

The sun was well hidden, but the light still pained his sensitive eyes. He'd heard tales about how certain wild men of the north knew how to keep the snow glare from blinding them. They had a secret way of masking their faces, or was it just their eyes? No matter. Richard had nothing but his hood for protection. It would have to be enough.

In the distance he spied the humped shape of a church on a rise and set out for it. The village was an important one to have such a structure. That it was so close to the Goddess's sacred tor was interesting. The two faiths could work together if their believers tried even a little, but there were zealots on both sides that frequently prevented it, or so Sabra had said.

No. I've no wish to think of her today.

He did not wish it, but it happened. Often. Not an hour went by that she did not hover in his thoughts or that her name came to his lips. Sometimes, when the black despair all but consumed him, he thought he'd see her standing quietly in the deepest shadows, her beautiful face marred by that same sadness. Her arms would be stretched toward him, as though longing to relieve his suffering.

Then would he turn away.

He did not hold Sabra responsible for the betrayal, but she was still a servant to the Goddess. Her unquestioning faith was not something he could endure now that his own had been shattered.

But what has led me here to the Goddess's stronghold? In all his wanderings his steps always seemed to be drawing him to the great tor. He would resist and take another path, but as the seasons waxed and waned he would go south or east or west or north and eventually come within sight of it time and again.

Finally, this year, he gave in and came to the little village in its shadow. That was as far as he would go. If the Goddess really wanted him, then she could come the rest of the way herself.

But the days and nights passed with no sign from her. It was as he'd expected, so his disappointment was neither deep nor especially bitter. It simply *was*, like the weather.

The church was farther than he'd thought, until he realized it to be larger than he'd expected. Most were small and made of wood, empty inside, with perhaps a simple table to serve as an altar. This one looked comparable to the grand one in his father's keep, made of cut stone, built to last for centuries. As he drew closer, he saw some of the stones were not matched in color, meaning they'd probably been taken from older, unused structures and thrown together where needed. Sure enough, he saw some Roman lettering cut into one of them. Whatever word it had been was broken off in the middle and was upside down.

The door was of stout oak and fitted well. It pulled open easily, the balance indicating the hand of a master carpenter. He went in and pulled it shut.

The church was very large, a full thirty paces from the door to the altar, and fifteen from side to side, the thatched ceiling gracefully high. Two long, narrow windows, hardly more than a handspan wide, were placed on either side of the altar. At this time of year, they were covered over with oiled parchment, allowing in light, but keeping out the drafts.

On Sabbaths and feast days the building could hold a very large congregation indeed. Now it held only Richard, but he'd wanted to be alone. Though his servants usually kept a silent, respectful distance, it wasn't the same as true solitude.

He slowly approached the altar, pushing his hood back. Above hung a very large cross, nearly mansize. Cut into it was the crucified Christ, His tortured body twisted just so. The wood was stained nearly black, so that one had to come quite close to see the equally black figure emerging magically from the background. His wounds had been painted red. The one from the spear thrust bled profusely. Richard's hand stole toward his own long-healed wound, recalling the blasphemous jesting of the other lords on that bleak day. Unlike the Christ, he had no scar to show for it, not to see, anyway.

He'd come here, seeking comfort from the faith he'd been born to, but the crucified man had nothing to say to him.

Below was the altar table, bare now, but the sides were beautifully carved with scenes from the Bible. He recognized Abraham offering his son Isaac up as sacrifice, knife in one hand, the other holding the boy down, his face raised to heaven.

Richard backed away, suddenly sickened. *Can I never escape?*

He quickly turned to leave and was brought up short, colliding with a stooped old man who had been directly behind him. With a surprised cry, the ancient toppled over and would have fallen hard to the flagged floor had Richard not instinctively caught him.

"I'm sorry, old one," he said, righting him. "I did not know you were here."

The fellow chuckled at his obvious chagrin. "Nor did I, but I perceive that you must be gently raised to show a poor stranger such courtesy."

" 'Tis nothing."

"'Tis much in this harsh world, especially for me."

Richard suddenly noticed the thick film that covered the old man's eyes along with the long staff he held to steady and guide his faltering steps. What he did not understand was why he'd not heard him.

"May I ask one more boon?" said the ancient. "Would you show me to the altar? I'm turned around."

"Of course."

He took the old man's arm and slowly led him over. The staff tapped noisily now, his sandal-shod feet shuffling. "Here it is." He placed the man's hand on the table.

"Ah, this is a comfort to me, to be able to tell myself the stories again." His questing fingers ran along the carvings like spiders.

"I should think you'd know them well enough by now."

The man smiled, something he did frequently to judge by the hundred creases in his leather-dark face. "Ah, but does one ever tire of dancing to a favorite song?"

Richard made no answer.

"Who are you, good sir, that I may thank you?"

He could say Lancelot, but was weary of that fame. He wanted no distinction today. "I am Richard."

"I thank thee, Richard of . . . ?"

"Just Richard."

"Then I am just Joseph."

He was a courteous man to take no title, place name, father's name or trade, so as to be no better or worse than Richard in his life station. His apparel was ragged and humble, his white hair and beard untrimmed like that of a hermit, but fairly clean. Perhaps he was a holy man with this church. They wore their vestments only when required by their duties.

"Why are you out on such a bitter day as this, friend Richard?"

"My legs wanted stretching."

He chuckled again. "Not by much, for I judge you to already be an uncommonly tall fellow."

"So I've been told."

"Come and sit with me a little while, would you? Perhaps you will tell me a tale of the road, and I will tell you one of our village." Joseph eased himself down, seating his creaking bones on the one shallow step that led to the altar. He seemed very much at home and not likely to move.

Richard gave up all hope of reclaiming any solitude without seeming to be boorishly impolite. He sat on the step as well, knees near his chin, arms bridging them, hands clasped. "My road is long and has no ending."

"That is their nature, is it not? My village is small and has no ending—in its own way, of course. It is very famous for this church, though. This is the first ever built in the land, did you know? Many pilgrims come here to pray. Are you such a pilgrim?"

"No, my people and I are only sheltering in the hospice until the snow melts enough for us to travel again."

"But you did come here to pray?"

"I may have."

"May have?" he laughed. "I like thee, friend Richard. Few are so brave as to admit the truth, even here in God's house. Have you tried praying elsewhere?"

"Yes, my words go up, but my thoughts remain as in a grave. Heaven does not hear me."

"That sometimes happens."

The comment startled Richard. He expected a reproof that perhaps he'd not been listening well enough.

"It is an awful thing when heaven is silent to us. It's happened to me many times." He seemed strangely cheerful about it.

"Indeed? What did you do?"

Joseph shrugged. "I just went on until God took notice and spoke in such a way as I could hear. There were times when He was wickedly slow about it, but I always forgave Him."

"*You* forgave God?"

"Oh, yes, all the time." His seeming conceit was boundless. "Do you smile?"

"Yes." Richard could not recall when last that had happened. "I hope you don't let others hear you speak thus."

"Pah! I care not. What can they do to me that God has not done already? If I can forgive Him, then I can forgive them. What? Do you laugh?"

"Were this summer I'd say that the sun had touched your head."

"I've had that as well. A good, long life I've had so far. I'm sure whatever comes next will be just as interesting."

Richard thought the man's advanced years would preclude that.

"You think me too old?" he countered, as though he'd heard the thought spoken. "Fie on thee, good Richard. I've time left in me to do *many* things."

"What would you do, then?"

"I'm not sure, there's much to choose. I could walk the road like you and find out if it is truly endless. Think of the stories I would hear on the way! How the traveling poets would envy me!"

"Or you could stay and let them bring their stories to you."

"True. Come, tell me your story."

"All of mine are sad."

"For one so young? How wretched."

Richard had not thought of himself as being young for a very long time now. A decade had passed since his change, and though he did not look any older he often felt quite aged. But seated next to him was a man easily twice his years. Why did they not weigh him down?

"Tell me one anyway," said Joseph. "Perhaps the sorrow of it will make me more content with my lot in life."

"I would not burden you so—might I ask a question instead? You seem to know much."

Joseph, staring ahead and seeing naught, waved one hand, palm up. "Perhaps. Ask away."

"I have heard from the holy men that no one may serve two masters, but what of serving both a master and a mistress?"

"Are they of the same house?"

"I think so."

"Then I would say yes, if both are in accord with each other for your welfare. I'm sure you already knew that, though. Why did you ask?"

"Because my mistress betrayed me, and now I wonder if my master will do the same."

"It's been known to happen. How did she betray you?"

"She demanded too much of me and would not tell me why, so I left her service."

"You must love her deeply to feel such pain."

"I love her not now. I may even hate her. She gave me everything I desired, and much that was beyond any of my dreams, but then . . . what she then did was most pitiless cruel. She allowed someone important to me to die."

"And there is a hole in your spirit from that."

"Yes."

Joseph turned as though to look at Richard, then gestured at the figure carved in the cross behind them. "Did He not suffer a great betrayal—and forgive?"

"It was not my life sacrificed, but that of another. I could have borne it had I been in his place."

"You seem to have dealt with that grief, just not with the betrayal."

"Yes. I wanted to know *why*, and she had no answer for me. I was told she had no answer for herself either."

"So your faith in her died."

"And I came here."

"But He also gives you no answer, hm?"

"None that I can hear. If it must ever be so for me, then why should I live on?"

The old man nodded, thinking long. "I can speak for myself only. My future is as veiled to me as my sight, but I move forward, because I do *not* know what is in my path. I may stumble off a cliff and break all my bones, or I may happen upon a great treasure that will buy comfort to last me all my days. What I cannot do is hold myself mired in place. You are mired, friend Richard."

"I've a right to be."

"For a while. But that you came here tells me even you know the while is past. You wish to break free."

"I've wished it from the first! I wished it, prayed for it, demanded, begged, shouted to the skies for it. Why has it not happened?"

"Because until now it was not the right time."

Richard snorted, then sagged. An answer that was no answer. Not to him, anyway. "I thank thee for listening, Joseph. You have been kind."

"You think I've not helped you?" He laughed. "You will see, child." With some effort, Joseph boosted himself up. "Ah, but those flags are cold on my bones. I shall take myself to a good fire now. God keep thee, traveling Richard."

"And you. Here—take this token to remember my thanks."

Richard pulled a gold ring from his small finger and pressed it into Joseph's hand. "It will buy you wood enough to warm thee."

"An old man's blessing on thee in turn do I give. Be of good cheer. The road has many twistings." He bowed his head once, turned, and shambled from the church. Richard could hear the tap of his staff on the frozen ground for a time, then full winter silence fell. He was quite alone again, dwarfed by the emptiness around him.

It is too easy for me to feel sorry for myself.

Compared to blind Joseph, he had all there was in the world.

Everything but blind faith?

To that he had to answer yes. And he still did not know what to do about it. Falling on his knees before the altar would seem but empty posturing now. He had a disturbing feeling that he'd somehow moved forward, all without noticing. Well, he would see if the road had a twisting ahead soon enough, when the snow melted.

He departed the church, pushing the door shut. The day was still dark, but he kept his hood well forward and shrugged his sleeves down to cover his hands. Just because he could not see the sun did not mean it wasn't there to burn him.

He looked about for some sign of where Joseph had gone, spying footprints in the snow, leading back toward the hospice. They sometimes crossed the ones Richard had left. He wondered where the old man had come from, for there were no other tracks. Perhaps he'd been sitting in a dim corner near the door all along.

But such speculations left him about fifty paces from the church. On one side of the path stood a strong young sapling, its straight trunk nearly his own height. The same height, in fact, as Joseph's staff.

He cast about for Joseph, but the old man's steps halted here.

That the little tree had not been there earlier was strange enough, but what reduced Richard to gaping astonishment was the fact that it was thickly foliaged as though at the height of summer. The tender green leaves seemed to glow against the virgin snow, bathed in a light from a hidden elsewhere.

He touched one, and found it to be real. He plucked it away and smelled the fresh sap.

And on this sunless day a glint of gold winked brightly at him from the green. At the base of one of the slender limbs was his ring. It fit around the wood exactly; indeed, the bark was beginning to swell and grow over it.

The leaves rustled in the wind like warming laughter, but a chill seized Richard, and he ran the rest of the way back to the hospice.

He wanted to tell someone, but could think of none. There were many in his company, but servants all. They would accept his story without demur. He'd not be able to discuss its meaning or ask questions. They would only shrug and call him blessed and continue on with their own little tasks. Telling even Ghislaine would not be right.

For the first time in years he wanted Sabra with him, not to pour out his bitterness, but to share his wonder. She, of all those he knew, would absolutely understand. How he ached for her.

It was time to go home.

He pushed noisily into the hospice, drawing breath to tell them to get ready to decamp. They would obey willingly enough once they knew their destination.

But he never gave the order. Standing but a few paces inside was the richly cloaked figure of a woman. His heart stopped for an instant and a smile of true joy broke upon his lips.

Sabra?

She turned round, pushing back her scarf. His heart resumed its beat, but sank low. She was not Sabra, only some noblewoman also stopping here to rest.

Richard quickly gathered his wits, pushed his hood back, and made a low bow. "Greetings, lady."

She curtsied in turn. "Greetings to thee, Lord du Lac."

Damnation, she knew him. He wanted no part of courtly life just now. He had much to do and think about.

"I heard in the next village that you were traveling to here," she said. "I am glad to see they were right, for long have I searched for thee."

He had no ready reply, puzzling over the familiarity of her voice and face. "And you have found me." He hoped she had not sought him out for some errand, for he would have to disappoint her.

Her smile faltered. "You do not remember me? It's not been too long, I hope. Recall you Elaine, daughter of Lord Pelles Bernard?"

He managed to shut his gaping mouth, go forward, and bow over her hand. "Of course I do. I could not see you well coming in from the light outside. How fare you, good maid?"

She laughed—and he'd have recognized that sound at least—and touched her free hand to his cheek. "Maid no longer, my lord."

Of course, she'd have married after all this time. He saw something of the change in her, now that he knew to look. Her bearing was sedate, as befitted any dame past twenty. Her figure was more lush and there was a maturity in her eyes only experience brings. "My congratulations, good lady."

She retained her impish smile. "We are at cross purposes. Come without, I would speak with thee."

Which meant no servant was to hear. He held the door for her. She swept out, pulling her cloak tight. "Glad I'll be when spring comes. This is the worst winter I've ever known."

"What brings you out in it, then?"

"Something of import to you, I hope."

"What? A message from the king?" That did not seem right. If the king wanted him, there were other messengers to send.

"No, from me. I've been trying to find you for a very long time. You've wandered to and fro so quickly that any missive I sent to you was lost or arrived too late. Only a week ago a minstrel come to sing for his supper at our keep claimed to have seen you on the road heading this way, so we rode hard to catch you up."

"We?"

"My brother Lavaine is with me as escort and protector."

"And your husband?"

"I have none."

"Ah. So why have you sought me out? What message would you impart?"

"An important one. It is your own fault that it arrives so many years late."

"I'm sorry—"

"Never mind that, Lord Lancelot. Come this way and you will know all."

She had grown into quite the imperious lady, but then he recalled she'd been as sweetly demanding in bed as well. He followed her to where her party had paused on the road. It was a small group, half a dozen armed squires, their horses, and a supply cart. The latter puzzled him, for if they'd wanted speed, they should have had pack animals along. As he approached, he recognized Lavaine, who seemed no worse for wear for the intervening years. They exchanged greetings, Lavaine as cheerful as ever, Richard more reserved. It had been an honest mistake on Lavaine's part, but Richard found it damned hard to look on the face of the man who had killed Michel.

"Does he—" began Lavaine.

"Hush, brother," she said, waving him back. "And let me do it in my own way."

"I shall be here." The way he spoke, the statement would serve equally as reassurance or warning.

"What is this about?" Richard asked as Elaine drew him toward the supply cart.

"You are overdue to meet someone. I hope you will like him." She was positively enjoying herself.

"Who?"

The cart was covered over with woolen blankets and furs. She lifted a protective hanging and held out her arms, reaching in. When she drew back, she held a strapping child of four or five years, rosy-cheeked from the cold, but smiling. She whispered something to him, and he squirmed to be set down, which she did.

He looked fearlessly up at Richard, then executed a miniature version of a courtly bow. "God keep you, sir!" he piped. "My mother told me to say that!" Then he beamed, laughed at his own cleverness, and threw his arms around his mother's skirts. His hood got pushed awry at this, revealing a bright crown of sun-gold hair.

"God keep you, young master," he returned. "Elaine, what is this about?"

The imp had left her expression. She was most serious now. "I wanted you to meet your son and he, you."

"My son?" he said blankly.

"You've only to see his hair and eyes to know. He is yours and no one else's."

Richard looked, and did mark a certain surface resemblance, but no more than that. This land had many blond, blue-eyed children. He released a great sad sigh, bowing his head. Just when he thought himself beginning to break free of his sorrow and anger, the Goddess or Fate or whatever decided to heap another cruelty upon him.

"You are not pleased," Elaine said. She sounded as downcast as he felt. "I had hoped better from you."

"No . . . you misunderstand."

"Then explain." She seemed to be bordering on anger as well.

It took him a moment to master himself, and another moment to find the words. All the while he knew they would not be adequate. "You quite break my heart, Elaine."

"How so?"

"Because if this beautiful boy were my son, I would have a happiness beyond all measure and love and honor you forever."

His raw sincerity took her aback, but her clouded brow did not clear. "You say he is not?"

"I know he is not."

"But his face, his eyes—how can you deny him?"

"I wish to God it were otherwise, but I must be truthful with you. He cannot be my son. You had another lover at the same time, did you not?"

She colored deep red to the roots of her hair. "And what of it? The boy looks like you. He is your get as surely as the sun rises. I have no shame of him, why do you?"

"The only shame I'd have would be in lying to you. Were he my child I would shout it throughout all the world. You've no idea how I wish I could do that."

"Then why are you this way?" Tears choked Elaine's rising voice, and the boy looked anxiously up at her, his own face crumpling in sympathy.

Richard extended some of his force of will upon her. "Calm yourself. I will tell you, but you must not upset him."

The appeal to her mother's protective instinct had more influence on her than his will. She broke off and put her attention on the child. "There, now, all is well. Go find your uncle. Tell him to give you a ride on his horse."

This had an instant curative effect. The boy's face came alight, and he tore away on chubby legs calling shrilly for Lavaine.

"Lord Lancelot, what you say makes no sense. You want him but you deny him? Is that it?"

He came close and took her hand. "Elaine, listen to me and know the truth."

"What truth? That my eyes and heart have deceived me all these years?"

"Yes."

She shook her head, exasperated.

"Hear me out. Before I came to serve at court, before I met you, I suffered a fever that nearly killed me. I healed, but eventually came to realize that it had taken the fertility from my seed, burned it out of me."

"How do you know?"

"I bedded many women then. None of them conceived from me afterwards. None."

"It takes only one seed to make a baby."

"And had I that seed I would have chosen you to keep it." Easy words to say, and who knows but he might have proved them true once upon some other time. Here and now, Elaine needed an illusion for the sake of her pride.

"You give me that honor, at least," she said. "I so wanted—believed—you to be his father."

"Who was the other man? If I may ask?"

"It matters not. He was Grunaius. Lavaine's squire."

Her taste ran to large, muscular fellows, then. "Is he yet a squire?"

"He will always be so. He was knocked from his horse in battle practice that summer and broke his neck. I wept for days for him and for losing you."

"I'm sorry. Had I known . . ."

"It's past."

"How did you fare?"

"As well as may be. When the household noticed my belly I refused to name the father. I wanted to speak to you first and said as much. Lavaine took my side against the rest—we were always close as children—and eventually I was left in peace. But even before the babe was delivered, there was talk that you had known me. Afterward, once they saw the child, they simply accepted it. My father was even pleased."

Yes, Pelles would be, but then he was a most practical man. Having even the bastard son of Lancelot under his roof was quite a treasure, in both coin and prestige. "I'm sorry, lady."

"And I said it's past. But are you absolutely certain he's not your son?"

"Upon his life and mine I wish he were."

"But his looks? Grunaius was dark."

Richard shrugged. "I know not. Sometimes one's looks come from a grandsire—or great-granddam and not the parents at all. But you are fair yourself."

"Not that fair." She sighed. "What am I to do? What are *you* to do? I believe you, but no one else will. They've lived with it too long."

"We will find an answer in time. If it will ease things for you, then I'll claim him to anyone who asks."

"You would commit falsehood for me?"

"For all of us. My conscience will not be troubled."

"Would you . . . think perhaps to . . . marry me?"

"I don't know. What do you wish?"

"To give the boy a father. I'm not sure if I want to give myself a husband. To hear the other women talk, husbands are a terrible lot, always making more trouble than they're worth."

He laughed, for she spoke with weary honesty. "I'm sure the same could be said for wives."

"But if we did marry, then I could not give more children to you," she said.

"No. Yet there are children enough to be had in the world."

"Fostering others? That's not the same as having your own."

"How so is it not? If God casts some poor babe into your care what matters who bore him?"

She'd clearly not considered that before. "There is more to you than I thought, du Lac."

He nodded sheepish agreement. "More than I thought as well. You find me at a strange time, lady, but at the right time, it seems."

"Indeed?" She lifted her chin, expecting an explanation.

He did not want to share his story with her, though. Again, it would not be right. "Never mind. What is the boy's name?"

"Galahad."

He had to close his mouth again. "You jest."

"You don't like it?"

"I confess it would not have been my first choice, but I'm sure I'll grow used to it."

"You will come back with us?"

"Yes, but what is it you wish me to do? Acknowledge him as my own or speak the truth?"

"I think . . . speak the truth to my family. Let the rest of the world believe what it likes."

"So be it." To seal the pact, he bent and kissed her cheek, which delighted her. Then they both looked toward Lavaine, who had placed little Galahad on his charger and was leading him around.

Beyond them, in the distance, Richard saw the flash of green from the sapling tree, a reminder of summer out-of-time—and something else was there. He shaded his eyes, squinting. Standing next to the tree was a small, lithe form in a russet cloak trimmed in gold. It raised one arm high. An achingly familiar gesture.

His heart leapt. It was she, and no mistake.

As he stared, long-forgotten joy flooded him. The figure lowered her arm, turned, and trudged up the gentle rise to the church. She would wait there. He had much to do right now, but she would wait for him . . . as she'd done all along.

Chapter Thirteen

Dallas, Texas, the Present

The first breath was the hardest, like the first breath after being born. No one remembers that one, and it's just as well. It is a terrible struggle to inflate new lungs, to exchange the comfort of warm fluid for harsh, cold air, screaming at the unfairness and pain.

Richard wanted to scream, but was too consumed with the effort of trying to take a second breath.

He couldn't quite work out what was wrong beyond being paralyzed. His mind was separate from his inert body; he was a sleeper on the edge of waking, unable to move, and panicking at his helplessness. He could only focus on the absolute necessity to move. If he could shift but a finger it would break the spell holding him, and he'd wake from the nightmare.

Alas, it didn't work that way. He had to take a third breath.

Then a fourth.

Air shuddered reluctantly into him and too easily departed. In between, he endured the terror that he would stop altogether. That gave him impetus to try again.

Days later, it seemed, the process gradually became less of a fight. The panic receded.

After a month or so, he didn't have to think about it at all, only drift and dream. They were sad, those dreams, and always fled from him when he tried to take hold of one to find out why.

He wanted to turn over in his sleep, to interrupt the mild frustration of the not-dreaming. Eventually, he thrashed out with one arm, cracking his knuckles against something cold and hard. The floor.

It broke the spell.

He groaned, a clumsy, thick sound, his voice box responding sluggishly to express his discomfort. He was sprawled where he'd fallen in the kitchen, bathed in the cold downdraft from the open refrigerator. Its overworked motor hummed a loud complaint at the abuse.

Pulling himself together had a special meaning to him now as he strove to organize each limb to work with the rest. Now he knew what it was like to be one of those puppets made of hollow balls with a single string running through it. It would lie loose and disorganized until the string was pulled taut, then assume shape and function. He was doubtful about being able to retie things back to normal. An order to his leg set his arm to twitching. Trying to close his fist made his foot kick.

He gave up for a while and went back to breathing. At least he knew how to do that.

His second attempt met with more success, and he managed to peel himself from the floor. From there it was just a matter of time until he could stand and flex the rest of the numbness from his muscles. His fingers felt like they were encased in gloves. When he slapped them against a counter corner, he felt the impact, but not the sting.

And some people do this to themselves on purpose?

But he was past the curve. To speed things up, he drank more blood.

That helped.

How had his would-be killer gotten in? There was state-of-the-art security on the doors, but for every measure, a good home invader could devise a countermeasure. It had been a professional job, and Alejandro could afford the best. Like, perhaps, Jordan Keyes.

Richard checked the time. It was nearly three—in the afternoon. Where was Luis? He should have come up here by now.

Richard retrieved his revolver from the bedroom floor and went to the elevator. He punched the button five times and sweated through the short descent. The door opened to a deserted flat. Luis was quite gone, along with his laptop case.

What the hell had happened?

On the return trip, Richard worked it out. Luis had wakened, come up to the penthouse, and found the apparently lifeless body of his only ally. What he'd made of the blood bags if he'd noticed them did not bear thinking. He'd have fled, but where?

He'd want Michael, though. How to find him? Luis would have gone through Richard's desk, of course, hoping to find an address book with a listing for a doctor.

Richard looked there for signs of a search and found them. Everything had been hastily tossed. The computer, when he tapped a key to make the screen saver disappear, had been subject to an attempted search, but Luis wouldn't have had the luxury of a password to crack into the right file.

But . . . next to the computer were the prescription chits with the access codes Bourland had provided. One of them was gone. The codes would have been meaningless, but not the name, number, and address of the clinic printed at the top of each sheet.

Luis would have called the clinic and gotten Dr. George's home number from the answering machine.

That was a relief, but only for an instant. Once Luis had Michael he'd run far and fast, and it still wouldn't be enough for him to escape Alejandro. Richard immediately punched in Sam's home number, but got only his machine. *Damn, should have tried the pager first.*

He tried the pager, then called Helen's cell phone. No answer. A recorded message cut in to explain why. He tried information for her home phone, but the machine at the Mesquita residence was just as unhelpful.

The clinic. A long shot, but what the hell.

Miraculously, a live human voice answered. Instead of the usual business greeting announcing the clinic's name, he got a shaky sounding "Hello."

"Helen? Is that you? It's Richard Dun."

"Mr. Dun?" She seemed unconvinced.

"Yes. What's going on? Has Michael's father contacted you?"

"God," she said, then there was a clatter. Her shout rang loud in the hollow distance. "Dr. Sam! Come here! He's all right! It's Mr. Dun—he's on the line!"

Another clatter, then Sam's breathless voice. "Richard?"

"Yes, Sam. What's happened?"

"You . . . we thought . . . oh, God." He broke off as his voice caught. "We thought . . . are you hurt badly?"

"What?"

"You need to call 911 right away."

Richard realized what misapprehension they were under, and regretted the fact he could not hypnotize people over the phone to restore calm. It took him some minutes to convince Sam of his good health.

"But Luis said you were dead," Sam insisted. "That you'd been shot."

"He made a mistake. All I did was knock myself out when I ducked . . . oh, never mind. Luis took off. I presume to see you to find Michael."

"Yes, he tracked me down. I thought he might be a ringer and was careful to set up a meeting at a public place. We met at one of the malls; he showed me his driver's license and talked about what had happened. He was in pretty bad shape, took me a while to settle him down, then I had to find Helen. It seemed best for us all to meet here at the clinic."

"How's Michael?"

"He was the same."

"Was?"

"Luis has him now."

Damnation. *I knew it.* "You didn't talk him out of it?"

"Of course I tried to, but the man was scared. He insisted on leaving. I insisted he stay. Then things got out of hand."

"How do you mean?"

"He just grabbed Michael and walked. I tried to stop him, but he . . . well, he sort of decked me."

Richard sighed. It was understandable, but so bloody unnecessary. "Are you all right?"

"Just sore. Got me in the gut. Surprised the hell out of me more than anything. By the time I got mad enough to get up, he was gone."

"What kind of car was he in?" He feared Luis had taken the rental.

"A cab. Helen got the number."

"Brilliant woman. Remind yourself to give her a raise. Tell her to phone the cab company and find out where the driver dropped that fare, then get back to me."

"What if they don't give out that information?"

"Tell them it's a medical emergency, that the boy needs insulin or something. I have to track Luis before he completely disappears, so hurry."

Sam rang off. Richard used the interval to clean up, selecting a blue industrial-style work shirt and drab gray trousers from his closet. He matched these with thick-soled black work boots. By the time he'd dressed, the phone trilled.

"I got it," Sam said proudly. "Damn, I feel like a TV detective! The driver took them to the Anatole Galleria by the tollway, not too far from where you are. Said they went right in."

Luis must have opted for the better security of an expensive place over that of another fleabag. "You did very well, Sam. Want a chance for more?"

"What? Call the hotel?"

"Yes. They probably won't give information on guests over the line, so you may have to go there in person. He'd have used a false name . . . but they tend to want to see ID up front, though. He might be there under his real name . . . God, what a mess. Get the manager on your side; use the medical emergency story. Describe Luis and just ask to be put through to his room, then sort him out about my condition."

"Why don't you go there?"

"I have to track down the person who decked *me*. I think he may be my strongest lead to find Alejandro."

"But what if he decks you again?"

"It won't happen."

"But—"

"Even if it does, you have Philip Bourland's number."

"God, I'd forgotten what with all the—"

"Just tell Luis to phone him. He'll be flying into D/FW tomorrow morning. He'll know how to deal with everything."

I hope.

The rental, happily, was still there and functioning, though before starting it, Richard went over the thing looking for bombs. None present. Mr. Jordan Keyes must have been quite confident of his booby trap.

Richard put the crossbow and the bolt on the passenger side. If things came down to it—and he was certain they would—he planned to dispatch Keyes with his own device. It seemed only fitting.

The drive to the man's house was a tedious one. There were no fast ways to get from Addison to west Fort Worth in the late afternoon, even on a Sunday. Traffic was as dreary here as in any overcongested metropolitan area. An hour and a half later he was finally speeding along a clear patch of I-30, having spent a quarter of it in an inexplicable stop-start jam on the long bridge that spanned the downtown area. He'd have done better to brave a line of side street stoplights, but road construction had trapped him in. During the long wait, stewing and burning in the sun, he grew thoroughly sick of staring at the backside of a dump truck he'd gotten stuck behind.

By the time he reached the exit for Hulen he was in a fine mood to commit murder.

Keyes's neighborhood was a mild surprise. As a hit man for Alejandro Trujillo and others like him, he would have made enough to buy a palace. Instead, he resided in a quiet, well-tended neighborhood of seriously unpretentious houses built during the fifties boom. Some had been added onto over the years, but most were of the infamous shoe box design, cheap-looking and unfashionable to current tastes.

A few sun-tolerant teens glided noisily past on their in-line skates. No one else was out. This was the hottest, most sweltering portion of the whole hellish day. Blinds and curtains were drawn shut, their owners sensibly within watching their cable TV and drinking beer. Not a bad life at all.

Richard made a slow circuit of the meandering roads, fixing in mind the various exits available to him. The quickest led to the highway via a northbound back street. He marked that down as his primary escape route, should he require one.

The frame house he wanted was on a corner lot, one large tree shading the back yard, two aged cottonwoods deteriorating branch by branch in the front. It seemed rather vulnerable seated on a slight rise, but from the windows the occupant had a fine view of the crossroads because the building was set on an angle to them. This detail did not escape Richard's notice. Nor did he miss the fact that a security camera was neatly mounted under the eaves of the carport. Its viewing range took in much of the street.

He could admire the man's paranoia.

It looked to be that Keyes was home. A battered black Escort with a cracked windshield rested patiently in the carport. It had been new a good decade and a half ago. Amazing that the thing still ran. Perhaps Keyes kept his real money invested elsewhere. That, or he was a tightwad. Good God, the front grill on the little car was actually sporting duct tape to hold it in place.

I could have the wrong house.

Richard refused to consider that possibility just yet, and assumed the rest of the working-man persona he'd opted to try. He fitted his black baseball cap forward on his head, then reached into the back seat for a clipboard. It was the same one he'd taken from Officer Henebry, looking battered enough to sell the ruse. He parked his car facing north toward the highway, tucked his revolver under his belt, and got out, pencil in hand.

The heat. It wasn't the humidity that killed, it was the heat, the god-damned bone-melting *heat.*

The asphalt street radiated it up to him in waves as he crossed and went boldly up Keyes's driveway to the front door. The blinds were shut fast here, but for the sake of any hidden camera he'd missed, Richard looked at his watch, noting the time down on the clipboard, which concealed the presence of the gun.

Richard had a great respect for clipboards. Used the right way they could take a person anywhere. They made you important, yet invisible. They were one of the great unsung inventions of the world, like paper clips. A calm-faced man writing on one was a universally harmless man, at the most an annoyance, but never a threat.

The welcome mat had GO AWAY blazoned on it in bright red letters. Richard stepped up and tried the bell, just barely hearing an electronic version of the chimes of Big Ben within. No one answered. After a reasonable interval—made short by the blistering sun—he knocked, the sound booming through the house as he pounded on the sturdy metal door. He noticed the discreet sign of a commercial security firm shoved into the baking grass of a walkway planter. That was amusing. It was a company Richard himself had founded back in the sixties. He still had a controlling interest in the stock. Nice to know that Keyes wanted only the best.

One of the blind slats twitched. Richard caught the movement and stood up straighter, as though anticipating an answer. A little late, he wondered if Keyes had been provided with a photo or description of his New Karnak target. *Assume he has.*

There was a click of a dead bolt being drawn back and the door opened three inches. A soothing, air-conditioned draft hit him.

Then he hit the door.

He intended to smash it hard into whoever was behind, then take him down. Instead, all his force turned into an overcalculation. The door crashed wide open with no resistance at all, bouncing against a wall to come back at him. It struck his shoulder, throwing off his balance. Despite this, he kept to his feet, dropping to a crouch, his revolver already in hand.

The room was dark. His eyes weren't nearly well enough adjusted to see, but he sensed a presence behind and to his right and whipped around to meet it. At the same time, something cracked down mercilessly hard on his wrist and he lost his gun. He grunted once, too busy to worry about pain, and struck out with his leg in a back kick, connecting with a solid body. There was a crash as it fell.

Richard followed through, his eyes just picking out the shape of a man on the floor scrambling to right himself. In one hand was a baseball bat. He'd managed to retain hold of it. He made a short arcing swing at Richard's legs, but missed. Richard dove forward, landing on him before he could recover, driving out all his breath with a well-placed fist. The man gasped and dropped the bat, his hand open and palm up in surrender.

"Okay! Enough!" he wheezed out. "Stop wrecking my house!"

"Jordan Keyes?"

"Who wants to know?"

Richard recognized the voice from Nick Anton's answering machine. Interesting. "The man you tried to kill last night. Me."

"Oh, really? Good trick since I was home the whole evening. Who the hell are you?"

"All in good time."

"No, right now, asshole. Get off me. Now."

Richard felt a no-nonsense prodding in his left side. While distracted by the man's flapping hand and the discarded bat, he'd forgotten to check the other hand. It held a rather large gun. If it went off it would tear a sizable hole laterally through his chest, taking out both lungs and his heart. *That* would hurt.

He decided to be cooperative for the moment and carefully removed himself.

Keyes got to his feet first. "Face down, lie flat, arms out, spread your legs. Don't think it over, just *do* it."

Not one of my better days, Richard thought, obeying.

Keyes kicked the front door shut. "Start talking. Who are you?"

"My name is Dun, Richard Dun."

"And why the hell are you here?"

"I'm looking for a mutual friend, Nick Anton."

"Wrong. He's no friend of mine."

"A mutual enemy, then."

"Wrong again. I've nothing against him, either. One more bad answer and you win the fuck-you-and-the-horse-you-rode-in-on prize, and I can promise you won't like it. Do I have your attention?"

"Yes."

"Good. Now what's this about me trying to kill you last night?"

"Just what I said."

"Trust me, if I'd been trying you wouldn't be here. Who put you on to me?"

"You did."

"You trying to make things hard on yourself?"

"Not at all. The weapon used was a crossbow, the tip on the bolt had a glass vial with curare in it."

A brief silence from Keyes. "The hell you say."

"Missed me, though."

"Then that should tell you it wasn't me. I don't miss."

As the man was in full charge of the situation, he had no logical reason to lie. Richard did not always trust in logic; however, his instinct told him something was decidedly odd here. "Look, I think we've some talking to do."

"That's right. You stay there and talk."

"Mr. Keyes, you are a professional and so am I. Given sufficient precautions on your part, I'd prefer to be able to sit up and face you for this conversation."

Keyes thought it over. "All right. Slowly. You will stay on the floor and sit on your hands."

Fair enough. For him. More than fair enough for Richard once he made eye contact.

They'd not wrecked the house too much. A table and lamp were in pieces, and a big leather sofa askew. They managed to miss a large entertainment center in the low, rectangular box of a room.

Standing by the shaded front picture window, Keyes had his back to what light did seep through. In his thirties, medium in height, but with powerful shoulders under an innocuous brown polo shirt, he held a Walther P-99 in one strangely delicate hand. His alert stance smacked of military training, though there was no mention of it in his files. He matched the DEA's grainy photo, a bald man with a well-shaped skull, his fringe of remaining hair cut very short. He now sported a precisely trimmed goatee; close up, his resemblance to Lenin was positively uncanny, but without the facial hair he'd have been Mr. Invisible . . . except for the eyes. Richard recognized a fellow killer.

Keyes returned the study. "It's an okay cover," he said, with a nod to Richard's clothes. "Except for your car being wrong, the hat the wrong color and the fact it's Sunday, you might pass as a city worker to anyone else."

"I thought it worth the chance."

"You had a fourth strike against you. I was expecting someone like you to show up."

"Because you quit working for Alejandro?"

Keyes's eyes sharpened. "You know an awful lot. Tell me where you heard that."

"On Nick Anton's answering machine. You've a distinctive voice."

"And why was Nick letting you listen in?"

"He wasn't there at the time. I broke into his place last night looking for him."

"Keep going."

Richard smiled. "I think we may have a common enemy—Alejandro Trujillo. If you were expecting someone like me, then you know he doesn't like it when people leave his employ without his blessing."

"His retirement plan sucks. I figured if the news came through Nick it'd soften things. Maybe."

"Nick was your go-between with Trujillo?"

"Sometimes."

"I take it you didn't like what he arranged in Addison?"

"What do you know about it?"

"Quite a lot . . ." There. Eye contact. And Keyes was sober. His partial silhouetting by the window made it hard for Richard to be sure if his focus was working, but the silence between them grew profound. "Are you ready to listen to me, Mr. Keyes?"

"Yes."

That was a relief. "I'm going to stand up now. You will remain still. Got that?"

"Yes."

Richard stood and stretched out the kinks, rubbing his extremely sore wrist, flexing the fingers. He'd taken a good crack there; it might have shattered the bones on another man. As it was, he'd have full use of it within the hour.

He found his revolver, shoving it back into his belt, then turned on Keyes. "You may put your pistol down now."

He set it on the window sill.

"Mr. Keyes, you will start cooperating with me. You trust me. I am your friend. You will always tell me the truth. Is that clear?"

"Yes." His killer eyes were dimmer now, his stance more relaxed.

"Excellent. Now tell me where Alejandro Trujillo is."

"I don't know."

"Does Nick Anton know?"

"Maybe."

"Where might I find him?"

"He's got a place in Euless. Rest of the time he works at Bubba Rob's."

Shit. This was getting entirely too frustrating. "I want you to contact him again."

"Okay."

"You feel very comfortable talking to me; trust that feeling. Because of it you will do nothing to harm me or cause harm to happen to me."

"Okay."

"Now, how did you get into my flat?"

"I didn't."

"Then who did?"

"I don't know."

That was it, the situation was now officially *beyond* frustrating. Richard did not put his fist through one of the walls. He was still healing. But damn it all to hell, he *wanted* to. "All right, Keyes, let's sit down and have a heart-to-heart."

Keyes's expression changed in some subtle way, becoming almost good-natured. "Sure thing. Want a beer?"

"Ah . . . no thank you."

"I got some ice tea." He left his spot by the window and went into a very small kitchen, Richard trailing him. Keyes started to open an avocado-green refrigerator covered with magnet-pinned photos and food delivery ad cards, but froze, glaring. "Whisky! Soda! Goddamn it! Get out of there!"

Two gray-striped cats shot down from a counter where they'd been crouched over an open pizza box. They tore past Richard's legs and vanished somewhere deeper into the house.

"I'm gonna kill those two one of these days," Keyes muttered, checking on the pizza. "Okay, they didn't do any permanent damage. I should have shut the lid, but you came banging on my door. Want some supper?"

"No, thank you."

"Damn stuff got cold." He shifted two slices onto a plate and shoved it in a microwave. As soon as he hit the cook button, a loud mournful yowl went up, like a soul crying from hell. He interrupted the heat cycle and looked behind the oven, which was at an angle in a corner, creating a triangle of space. "Monster, what the hell are you doing there? Well, come on, babyness. Aw, poor Mr. Monster."

The unhappy white and black cat he pulled out lived up to its name. It had a small head compared to the rest of its body, which had to weigh at least twenty pounds.

"You stupid cat, you trying to get irradiated? You're already a mutant." He held the huge feline on its back, fingers digging into its vast expanse of stomach. The beast yowled again, a long, sad wail of protest. "Shut up and get some loving." Monster had other plans, though, successfully struggled free, and hit the floor. Suprisingly fast, he shot toward a cat door cut into a wall and, after a minor struggle, oozed through.

"He's not much for visitors," Keyes said. "Paranoid for some reason. You like cats?"

"More or less. You certainly seem to."

"I hate the little freeloading bastards, but they're more important to me than most of the people I know."

"How many do you have?"

"Enough to put me on everyone's weird list." He opened a cell phone sitting on a counter and started to punch in a number. Richard asked for an explanation. "I'm calling Nick, like you wanted. Change your mind?"

"Not at all."

The other line buzzed a few times, then the answering machine kicked on with a basic message. "It's me," said Keyes in a stern tone. "Something's happened your boss will want to know about. Call me back immediately. This is serious so don't fart around." He disconnected. "That should do it."

Richard waited as the man heated his interrupted meal and opened a beer; then they went back to the living room. Keyes put it on a foldout TV table, sat on the couch, and dug in. Richard found a chair opposite for himself, using the respite to massage his wrist.

"Sorry about that." Keyes said.

"Part of the job. I'd have done the same."

"So who are you, Mr. Dun?"

"One of Alejandro's targets."

"And you think I was trying to hit the bull's-eye? If they used a crossbow, I can understand you making that mistake. A very select few are aware of what I do with them, but the truth is I never heard about you until today."

"You weren't contacted to do a job here?"

"I didn't say that."

"What do you know about the Addison explosion, then?"

"Why do you want to know?"

Richard focused, giving him a slight nudge. "You first. Tell me everything."

Keyes blinked awake. "About two weeks ago Nick called to say Trujillo wanted a job done. A pretty big one, a business rival he wanted blown to kingdom come. I turned him down."

"Why?"

"Too clumsy, too spectacular. Use a gun, then it's only another murder for the cops. Use explosives and you've got the *Federales* and all their cousins on your ass. There are simpler ways to take people out. Besides that nonsense, it was local. I *never* do any job like that locally, always out of the country."

"Killing international drug lords for fun and profit?"

"Why not? Someone has to." He washed down a gulp of pizza with beer. "And the pay is good."

"Working for another drug lord?" Richard kept any and all judgment from his tone.

"If not me, then someone else. I'd rather the money come to me. I got a family to support." A slender black cat jumped onto the couch next to him, highly interested in the pizza. He pushed it off, growling. "Not now, Dot. Go away."

"You trust Trujillo?"

"Absolutely not. But I trust his agenda, which is to be the richest damn bastard down there by taking out the competition. He might make it, too, or would have. Without me running errands for him he's going to find it a lot harder. He doesn't have anyone else with my special skills that he can trust not to screw up. It's easy to find someone who can kill, but damn near impossible to find someone who's smart about it."

"Are you entirely out of work, then?"

"I never said that." Keyes's eyes almost twinkled. "There's plenty to be had, you just have to be careful who you work for."

"Meaning if someone contracted you to kill Trujillo . . ."

"Anyone come up with the money for it, I'd take him out just as easy as the rest. Nothing personal, just business. Since he's in the business, he knows that that's a possibility. So he's always paid me more. Call it insurance."

"How did Trujillo react to your refusal?"

"He wasn't happy, but I explained my reasons. He offered me a hell of a lot of money, but the deal smelled bad. I put that in his face, and said I wouldn't be able to do other work for him if I got caught. The forensic boys up here are pretty damn sharp. I might be able to get around them, but it isn't worth the risk for me to try. I never dirty my own back yard, that's one of my rules. Trujillo wasn't giving me much information, either, just that I was to wire up a house and set things off at a certain time, and that's all. That's what smelled to me. He's always got more information than a library on who he wants out of the way, but not for this one. So I backed right off."

"Did you sense he might put a hit out on you for that?"

"No, it was just business as usual. He didn't press things. I'm more valuable to him for those out-of-country sanctions. I figured he'd find someone else with less smarts for the job, and it turned out I was right. Soon as I saw the news report I knew that was what he'd wanted me to do and why he'd been so cute about not giving details. There was some woman and a couple kids in there; he knew I'd never have gone for it."

"An assassin with principles?"

"Call me old-fashioned, but killing women and kids is just *wrong.*" He leaned forward, tapping on the table with one finger, each tap emphasizing a word. "When you have a *job* on, you go in like a *surgeon* and take out *that* target. Collateral damage, as they call it, is just being *stupid.*" He sat back, face consumed with disgust.

"Then you severed relations with him."

"Business is run on trust, and he screwed up." Keyes made more pizza disappear. "Now you tell me someone went after you with a crossbow? No way would I do anything as damn-fool as that up here. The DEA is just looking for an excuse to turn me over and see what shakes out. I don't know why they're so anal; I'm doing most of their work for them."

"I may have an explanation."

Swig of beer. "I'm listening."

"Trujillo wants us both out of the way. He set up a crossbow booby trap to take me out. The idea being when my body's found the DEA traces the weapon to you. A very neat copycat frame to enrich your life."

"But it missed, so *you* come looking for me. Either way, one or both of us is taken out of the picture, and Trujillo gets a good laugh. Most neat. But how did you even know about me?"

"Computer search."

He grimaced. "Damn things. I'll have to retire before they lead to my downfall—unless that's already happened?"

Richard gave no direct answer. He'd not yet made up his mind on what to do with the man. "Your name and Anton's came up in connection with Trujillo. You were on my short list of people to interview in order to get to him."

"Why are you interested in him?"

"The house explosion. It's personal."

"How so?"

Richard frowned. "The woman was a good friend of mine. Her little girls were my goddaughters."

Keyes put his beer bottle down. "I'm sorry to hear that. Was he after you through them?"

"No. The woman's husband is Trujillo's brother, Luis. The one who turned evidence on him. Their deaths had to do with punishment, revenge, and to make an example to others."

"I heard about that case. The brother dropped out of sight a few years back."

"Yes. I'm the one who disappeared them all."

"Because of the woman?"

"And the children. But Alejandro found them. You saw what he did. Now I wish to find *him*."

"I don't fault you for that. Not much you can do until Nick returns my call, though."

"Then we'll wait." Richard's cell phone trilled. "Excuse me."

"It's me," said Dr. Sam.

"What news?"

"I couldn't find them."

"Damn," he muttered. "What's happened?"

"I don't know. Helen and I drove to the hotel and talked to everyone from the manager to the maids. A few people remembered seeing a man and little boy, but not where they went. I was very insistent about the need to find Michael, described them both a hundred times over, had the clerks check the guest roster twice, even called a couple of likely prospects in their rooms. Nothing. Then Helen and I split up and went to search the Galleria Mall and got the security people there alerted for them. When that didn't work I phoned the cab company again and asked if they had any pickup fares from the mall or the hotel. They had their dispatch talk to all the drivers. Nothing again. That's when I started calling the other cab companies. Helen's still in the manager's office working on it, but it's probably hopeless. Luis and Michael just walked in and disappeared."

"You were very thorough, Sam, not your fault." In fact, he'd been outstandingly thorough.

"Maybe he got a bus or hitchhiked . . ."

"Sam, it's all right. Some things can't be helped. When I've dealt with details at this end, I'll see what I can do. Chances are he will shortly contact that other friend of mine for help and we can sort it out then." Even with Keyes hypnotically persuaded to being an ally, Richard had no desire to mention Bourland's name in front of him.

"I hope so," Sam said unhappily.

"Perhaps you'd best go ahead and phone him first; let him know what's going on so he doesn't have to take news of my untimely death seriously. I've told him who you are."

Sam seemed to brighten. "Okay, I'll get on that."

"Good man." He rang off and hoped Sam talked to Bourland before Luis did. The man did not need news of anyone else's death unless it was Alejandro's.

"Where's that crossbow?" said Keyes, who had finished his beer and pizza during the interval. "I'd like to go see it."

Richard shifted mental gears. "No need. I brought it with me."

One eyebrow quirked. "May I ask why?"

"I had an idea about using it on you. Poetic justice."

Keyes looked at him awhile, lips thin, then slowly nodded. "Fair enough. I'm glad you decided to talk first."

"I'll go fetch it."

When he returned from the car, outré weapon in hand, Keyes had cleared away the TV table and was stowing the pizza box in the fridge. Two more cats appeared; they were white and black like Mr. Monster, but with longer fur. One of them *yowed* a plaintive question.

"Oh, shut up, Spot. Your food's right there." Keyes pointed to a bank of filled food bowls in one corner, and shoved the complaining cat in their general direction with his foot. The other, he swooped on and picked up. It also *yowed*. "Aw, Le Feline Nikita, wanna make funny noises? Let's make funny noises, babyness." He held the animal upside down, hand over its face, and indeed produced some strange squeakings from the creature.

"Le Feline Nikita?" Richard asked doubtfully.

"From my favorite movie. That little chickadee was most doable. She's the reason why I learned French."

"What about that TV show?"

"Now *she* is most tasty. Extremely doable." He glanced at the crossbow Richard had in hand.

"Look familiar?" Richard watched the upside-down squeaking cat furiously batting at Keyes, who paid it scant attention.

"Nope. That's a commercial model—a good one—I wouldn't mind having it, but I could never use it in my work. I build my own."

"You build your own?"

"Yeah, lemme show you. You'll appreciate this." He discarded the outraged cat, who landed on all fours, shook itself, and began to clean as though nothing amiss had occurred. "Short attention span. I dated a girl like that once. Good weekend, lousy week. C'mon this way."

Keyes had a very small house, three small bedrooms, one bath, minimal furnishings, all in keeping with his character of living on modest investments. The forces of officialdom would have a difficult time finding fault with him.

"Where do you keep your real money?" Richard asked.

"Some place real safe. You wondering why I live like this when I could do better?"

"Yes. Why not?"

"I like the neighborhood. I have what I need, which is a place where I can just come in and *relax*. Besides, it'd be a hell of a job trying to transplant this."

He went into a bedroom no more than nine by ten feet in size. It held only a chair, work desk with a computer, and two filled bookshelves. An eight-foot-wide closet with sliding mirrored doors covered the length of one wall: big storage space in compensation for the claustrophobic dimensions. He slid one four-foot-wide door aside to reveal a rack holding some plastic-wrapped suits, which he also pushed out of the way. On the floor were a couple of suitcases he pulled out. He activated some hidden mechanism behind the door jamb and a section of the closet floor popped like the hood of a car. He pulled it up.

"Interesting," said Richard, looking down into darkness.

Keyes hit a light switch just inside the cavity. The sides were composed of the house's cement foundation for a foot or so, then opened up. "C'mon." He made use of a metal ladder, quickly descending.

Richard followed, looking around, fascinated. He stood in a very efficient low-ceilinged workroom, not much more than ten by ten, but well-lit and fitted with a woodworking bench and plenty of outlets for the power tools hanging from the pegboard walls. The air was fresh, courtesy of fan-powered vents.

"You did all this yourself?"

"Yup. About ten years back I started. Took me awhile to chip through the foundation, then start hauling out dirt and limestone. For a year or so this place looked like something out of *The Great Escape*. I filled up dips and holes in the lawn with the extra dirt, used the rocks to decorate the backyard and build a barbeque. I tell you, doing it one bucket at a time sucks, but when I realized that I was too far along to stop. Had to go to an acupuncturist to put my back right again, but it was worth it."

"Why go to such trouble?"

"Why not? I got a hidden retreat that no cop's ever going to find. Makes for one hell of a tornado shelter, too. Couple of times me and the cats did a little duck and cover here. I hollowed out enough to give me the work space I needed, but not so much as to undermine the house. Poured in a second foundation down here, one cement bag at a time, running a waterhose from the bath tub—that was a mess. Put in those support braces to shore up the ceiling, then put in plywood walls and plastered them over so there wouldn't be any fresh earth smell coming into the house, and started hauling stuff down. I had to limit the size to things that would fit through the trap, brought the lumber down in pieces to make the bench and storage."

Keyes was clearly proud of his effort and accomplishment. This was likely the first time he'd ever had the chance to show it off.

"Very impressive," said Richard, and he was completely sincere. It was wonderful. He wanted one too.

"Thank you. *None* of this is going anywhere, least of all me. Not until I'm damned good and ready. If Trujillo thinks he's going to change that he's made one hell of a mistake."

"He's made several. Why are we here?"

"So I can show you what I build." Keyes then proceeded to give him a brief lecture on the construction of crossbows. He was quite the artist. He had several different sizes, all with various ranges and functions, all of them made to break apart into components. He took a number of small wooden pieces that seemed to have nothing to do with each other, and assembled them together with a small screwdriver. The only metal in it was a few brass screws. By the time he'd finished, a very wicked little weapon crouched on the workbench, only needing a string and a bolt to complete it. It was quite different from the large metal model Richard had brought in.

"I always use wood," Keyes explained. "The airport X-ray techs always see it as being part of my suitcase, so they don't make a fuss and pass me through. Once a job is done I take the bow apart and throw away the pieces."

"Hence the need to come down here and make more."

"Yeah, but it's a lot of trouble, takes time, and has become too much of a trademark pointing to me. Lately I've been thinking of switching over to blowguns for some jobs. Those are just hollow tubes, but you have to really practice to put the dart where you want it. Hey, check this out." He flicked on a closed circuit TV. It had four views, two covering the street, one the backyard, the last the front porch. "I can control the angle of the camera from here."

"Got a night vision adapter?" asked Richard, highly interested. He loved tech toys as much as the next man.

"Of course—and infrared backup."

He was starting to like the fellow in spite of himself. He'd had a bellyful of dealing with exotic assassins after his encounter with Charon some months back, but Keyes looked to be considerably more reasonable.

Keyes patted the set twice. "I got all the mod-cons. When I'm down here I don't want to be completely cut off from the world, so I ran in a phone line, cable radio. For some things I'm a gadget junkie. There's a lot of most *bueno* stuff out there, so I have to pick and choose—and what the hell have we here?" He tweaked one of the cameras onto a large car that had pulled parallel to Richard's rental, and zoomed in. "We got us a big-ass ol' Cadillac fulla drug muscle. Looks like I was right about Trujillo coming after me, but I thought he'd send in just a couple of guys, not a fucking army."

"How many?"

"Five—two in front, three in back."

"That's hardly an army."

"Count the five in that other car and it is." He shifted the view to the cross street, where sat a second large car crowded with men.

"In a twisted way, it's almost flattering. What do you think they're carrying?"

"Probably full autos. Trujillo likes to pass out MP-5s like party favors, and his boys love to play macho man. This could get ugly fast—son of a bitch, look at that!" Keyes zoomed hard on the second car. One of the faces in the back seat was . . . Alejandro Trujillo. "We got some serious shit here if the big boss wants to catch the fun. Okay, that's it. War is declared, but I'll be damned if I let those assholes shoot up my neighborhood."

Richard watched the car by the rental slowly cruise off. A moment later, the second car also moved out of camera range. "I think they're just checking things over first. They know you have a visitor, but are not aware it's me. As far as Alejandro is concerned, I'm dead. If I leave and make sure they *see* me, they'll follow."

"Not all of them. One of those cars will stick around to find out if you killed me."

"Then I suggest you get your Walther and prepare for them."

"No shit." Keyes went to a large wall cabinet. Inside, mounted on padded prongs hooked into more pegboard, was an assortment of firearms, enough to start and likely end a small revolution. On a shelf below were quantities of ammunition and cleaning supplies. Keyes caught the look Richard gave him. "Okay, so I was a little worried about the Millennium Bug. I had these on hand already. Pick out something."

"I've my revolver."

"Only six shots and no reload that I've noticed. You want more than that against these goofballs. Unless you got a problem with killing."

"Hardly. All right, I'll use the Glock then."

Keyes snorted and gave it over along with three extra loaded ammo magazines. "I thought you'd take that one."

"You don't like them?"

"They're okay."

"Why have one, then?"

"For guests, of course. They like 'em, but the Glock's never felt right in my hand. The grip on my Walther is set at just the right angle for me."

"That's the new James Bond gun, isn't it?" Richard always enjoyed those movies.

"Right you are—but I had the idea first."

"You don't like James Bond?"

"Oh hell, I'm a *big* fan, I just found the gun first is all. Come on." He stuffed more mags in his jeans pockets, switched off the TV, and went up the ladder. He left the trapdoor open and shoved the suitcases farther out of the way. "In case we have to beat a quick retreat here," he said, moving toward the living room.

"We may not have to."

"Why is that?"

Richard peered out through the front blinds. The sun was still bright and would be for another two hours. "They're probably covering the street exits from this area in case you should leave, but my guess is they won't actually come for you until well after dark. They're going to get bloody hot out there waiting."

"That just breaks my heart."

"Well, I'd rather not have them shooting up your neighborhood, either."

"Oh, yeah? You got another option?"

"As a matter of fact," said Richard, straightening, "I have a cunning plan. . . ."

Chapter Fourteen

Crossbow prominently propped on his shoulder, Richard practically strutted across to his car. The sun was waning, but there was plenty of light. And heat. It prickled like fiery needles on the back of his neck. He could almost feel the blisters forming.

He endured it.

He took his time putting the crossbow into the back seat, apparently having a bit of trouble getting it through the door. Once done, he gave in to a luxuriant stretch, the mechanics of which allowed anyone watching to get a damn good look at him. He took his hat off and ran a hand through his brush of blond hair to clinch things.

Even if Alejandro's men were half asleep, they couldn't help but notice and identify him. Alejandro himself would be livid that his target had survived yet again.

Richard got in the rental, started it, and pulled out, heading for the near-direct exit to I-30. He'd put his windows down to keep the interior from heating up too much. They were still down as he drove sedately past a Cadillac parked close to the corner of a side street. He did not look over.

That was the hard part, the truly dangerous part. If they got impatient, or stupid, they could nail him here.

He held his breath, and he did not look.

Then he was past them. Safe for the moment. But would they take the bait?

When he turned onto the access road that led to the highway, he saw the brown Caddie distant in his rearview mirror.

He smiled and hit a newly programmed-in speed dial on his cell phone. "I got mine hooked," he said when Keyes answered. "What about you?"

"I'm still in the neighborhood, heading south. They're behind me, but not too close."

"Can you lose them?"

"In this area? No problemo." He rang off.

Richard's job was to buy Keyes time. Not a difficult thing at all when he reached the downtown overpass. Yet another traffic problem had turned the freeway into a single-lane parking lot. He didn't mind this delay, though; it served a good purpose. Besides, the sun was down.

Once through the one-lane road-rage test zone, he phoned Keyes again. "How's it going?"

"I lost them. Where are you?"

"Just passed an exit for a Beach Street. Does that make sense?" There were no beaches anywhere near this city so far as he knew.

"I'm a couple miles ahead of you coming up on the 820 intersection. I'm going to take that north. You stay on I-30 east until Loop 12; you're a tourist, they won't expect you to know the shortcuts. That'll buy me more than a half-hour extra in case of delays at my end."

"You sure your car will get you there in time?" He recalled that model of Escort as being underpowered and remarkably fraught with troubles.

"You know what that guy in *Star Wars* did to his space ship?"

"Yes . . ."

"Well, I had about the same thing done to this little crate. It's a lot better than it should be. I'll get there in time."

Richard took him at his word and thought it a pity that they didn't have some sort of laser-type blaster guns to use on this expedition. Ah, well, give the inventors time. The evolution of weaponry he'd witnessed over the centuries was quite extraordinary.

Perhaps in five or ten years the actual technology would far surpass film imagination. Not available to him now, but how satisfying it would be to cut Alejandro in half the long way with a sword of white-hot burning light . . .

No. It wouldn't be all that satisfying.

That death was too bloody *quick* for him.

Richard made it easy on his shadow, holding to a steady speed, not passing anyone unless they were really slow. The Cadillac's lights were consistently in his mirrors, not too far back, but neither too close. He was grateful for that. It meant they'd decided not to shoot the hell out of his car while on the road. A drive-by at these speeds would probably be effective, but he'd survived two hit attempts; they would want to make sure the third time was the charm.

This was the long way to north Dallas and thence to Addison, so he felt safe edging up to seventy when traffic permitted. Keyes would still have his time window, and Richard would not appear to be in the least aware of the tail. While he couldn't assume the thugs to be stupid enough to utterly fall for the ruse, he only needed to keep them guessing about it.

He hoped the men also had cell phones—they probably did—allowing them contact with the second car. Ideally, they would link up at some point, their common goal being to turn Richard into tomorrow's headline.

Eventually he reached the point where the Loop intersected with LBJ and took the eastbound lane. They would know he was headed for New Karnak now. He had to slow once more along this corridor, but expected that, changing lanes a few times just to make the shadows work to keep up. He was positively grinning on his final exit. There were now two big Caddies trailing him.

New Karnak was very much in sight, its glass walls shimmering with reflections of the full moon. He sailed right past the great pyramid, heading north, wishing he could hear the commentary this was doubtless causing behind him. Was he aware of the tail, or just looking for dinner on restaurant row?

But he passed that area too, speeding up as traffic suddenly eased. The first Caddie allowed him to lengthen his lead. Good, they'd figured it out.

The traffic and street lights thinned then stopped; he was now in the undeveloped areas, the memory of his initial trip here coming sharply back to him, along with myriad regrets. He should have done a better job of hiding them. He should have told Stephanie to leave the moment her emergency e-mail had come through. He should have cut *all* contact with her, leaving no trace for Alejandro to pick up.

He should have killed the bastard to start with.

Richard had considered it, but it would have stirred things up too much back then. He'd not been prominent at all during the legal wranglings, but he *had* been present. If Alejandro had suddenly died, his underlings would have known where to place the blame and create murderous complications for all. At the time it seemed simpler to just hurry Stephanie and the family out of the line of fire. That had worked. For a while.

He hoped that the missing Luis had phoned Bourland by now and gotten some good news for a change. *I should call him as well.* But not just yet.

He sailed by the spot where he'd encountered the delicious Officer Henebry, and marveled that he'd driven so far in such a benumbed state. His dreams had been wretchedly vivid; it was amazing that he and Michael had made it home in one piece.

Phone. He answered.

"I found the place," said Keyes. "If I got the directions right."

"You took the fourth turn after the stop sign?"

"Yeah, and this road looks like Verdun on a bad morning—oh, there . . . okay. Yeah, I'm at the right place; the cops strung some crime scene tape right across the drive. It's not visible from the main road."

"Just as well, keeps the curious from looking in."

"You just better damn-well hope the *Federales* didn't leave a watchdog hanging around."

"Not likely, but if so, I'll deal with it."

"I'm pulling off now to hide the car. How far out are you?"

"About ten minutes."

"Cutting it fine, but I'll manage."

"I appreciate this, Mr. Keyes."

"Hey, I'm in this for my own self-preservation."

Rather too enthusiastically, Richard thought, disconnecting. For a man who never dirtied his own backyard, he showed remarkably little demur against going on a deadly snipe hunt for Alejandro.

Keyes had the equipment for it. As they waited for the sun to set, he'd pulled an amazing collection of combat gear from his hall closet. He had cammo fatigues in green, gray, and solid black, boots, matte black body armor, hand-to-hand weapons . . . Richard hadn't seen such stuff since he'd taken a tour of an SAS training facility.

"If you're worried about the DEA, why do you have all this?" he'd asked.

Keyes smirked as he shook out the black fatigues and started changing. "All of it is completely legal. I got it from military surplus stores and catalogues."

"But why have it if you don't operate in the States?"

"To keep in practice. This is my paintball gear."

"Paintball?" Richard noticed that the green cammos, though clean, had the remains of pink paint stains here and there.

"Yeah, great game. I always win."

No doubt.

Richard counted off the turnings, taking the fourth. He knew the area, but was starting to nerve up and wanted no mistakes at this point. He put his high beams on, less for his benefit than for Keyes and the ones following.

There were signs of traffic activity left along the drive. Tree branches had broken off where tall trucks had bulled through. Pale dust thrown up by dozens of official vehicles now coated the foliage and dead grass. He came up on the police line ribbon. It was snapped, the two ends lying listless over the baked ground where Keyes had earlier passed. Richard's car would get the blame for that.

He hoped.

His departure from the tract house, closely followed by Keyes . . .

they would wonder. They would wonder if some devil's deal had been struck between two men who should have been dead. They would wonder where Keyes had gotten himself to, and now they might consider the possibility of a trap.

For Richard to come out here at such an hour would strike Alejandro as odd, but he'd also see it as an opportunity. Richard's hope was that Alejandro would weigh the odds of facing at most two isolated men armed with only handguns, against ten. If Keyes was right about the MP-5s, Alejandro might feel very confident indeed, even if one of his foes was known to be an expert assassin.

But would he risk going in himself?

Phone again. "Yes?"

"I saw you go by, but they're hanging back," said Keyes, who was now on watch at the entry road.

"How far?"

"They're stalled at the turnoff. Corporate meeting. Looks like the memo is under discussion. I can't see past the window glare or I could try popping Trujillo. I don't know which car he's in. Damn, if I just had a launcher and two grenades I could take them all out."

"Give them a minute. Don't let them spot you."

"Huh. Fat chance of that. Damn city boys don't have a clue." His confidence was reassuring.

Richard kept on, topping the slight rise, dipping down again, the horrific wreckage now in view, stark in the moonlight. Absurdly, it looked smaller than he remembered. When he'd been struggling in the midst of the disaster, it had loomed impossibly large to him. Where had the horses gotten to? Probably rounded up and taken away by some livestock control service. He'd have to check on that. He couldn't allow Stephanie's beloved animals to be sold off or destroyed.

"Mission control, I think we have a go," Keyes announced, suddenly cheerful.

"They're coming in?"

"Looks it . . . yes, both of them. I'm on my way. Time to open a can of whump-ass and have ourselves a party."

Parking prominently in front of the ruins of the house, Richard quickly stripped off his blue uniform shirt. Beneath, he wore a lightweight black knit pullover, long sleeved, loose for Keyes, who had loaned it, almost too tight on Richard. His gray pants were gaudy in comparison, but would have to serve. He planned to keep his head down. Most of the time.

He left the car, the Glock in one pocket, spare clips in the other, the revolver in his belt.

The stink of burned wood was yet heavy in the air. Richard went to the debris, found a charcoaled stick and smeared the black powder over his face and hands. The full moon would make enough light to be useful to the hunters; he wanted to break up his profile.

Speaking of breaking up . . .

He located a sizable piece of wood thrown from the house, a section of charred log almost four feet long, as big around as a telephone pole. The weight was nothing to him, only a little unwieldy. He was more interested in mass than grace, though, and tucked it under one arm like an overgrown football, then looked for some likely cover.

He heard them coming. Saw the nimbus of their headlights.

He dropped flat by the fence next to the barn. Debris was all around him; he was just another unidentifiable lump. Their focus would be on his car. He'd left the lights on, aimed at the ruin as though he'd come here to scavenge for clues the police had missed. Crime scene tape ringed the area.

Before the first car topped the rise, the driver cut its lights and coasted the rest of the way, coming in slowly. The second car did the same.

When the first was within thirty feet of him, Richard surged up and charged right at it, holding the log like a latter-day battering ram. He could move preternaturally fast when necessary.

The driver had no time to react. He also likely never knew what hit him when Richard slammed the log directly into the windshield. It struck with terrible force, shattering the glass, breaking the wheel, smashing the driver's head to bloody pulp and taking out the man immediately behind him.

Richard didn't pause to look back, but flashed toward the second vehicle, which was just beginning to brake. The driver's side window was up. No matter. Richard put his fist through it. That hurt, but he hit the man inside so hard on his temple as to cave in the bone and snap his neck. Richard grabbed the steering wheel and ripped it from its column.

Someone fired shots, but missed wildly, the bullets tearing into the roof, not Richard . . . who was gone.

He darted behind the second Caddie—which rolled on to collide into the first—dropping to cover in the mesquite brush a mere ten yards away. Both vehicles were disabled, cutting off retreat, and the odds were now seven to two.

He phoned Keyes with the news.

"The hell you say," he whispered, approving. "Were those your shots?"

"No. Knee-jerk reaction. He missed. I'm clear for the moment."

"A three-round burst. I think I was right on the MP-5s. They're gonna burn ammo trying to find you now—they can afford to. See if you can spot how many and who's got what."

But Richard had to duck as men erupted from the cars, firing recklessly into the brush. They were cursing, screaming at each other, disorganized. The ghastly nature of his attack had had its effect on their morale, all of it in his favor, providing he avoided getting hit.

They seemed to run out of ammunition at the same time, having quickly burned through their thirty-round magazines. Richard, flat on his belly, picked his shot and dropped one, then rolled like hell to his right. His Glock had no flash suppressor. Sure enough, one of them had a round left. The bullet cracked into the spot where he'd been, kicking up earth and gravel. On all fours he backed away a few yards, then rose slightly for a look.

A tinny voice in the cell phone asked if he was all right.

"Four down, six left. Three have heavy power. I'm a bit busy, can I call you back?" Without waiting for an answer, he shut it off.

Of the six remaining thugs, two were still in the cars, the rest were starting to scatter out, yelling at each other and randomly shooting into the night. One of them was having trouble reloading his gun. He couldn't get the long magazine to lock in.

His bad luck. Richard took him out, rising up briefly, sighting down his arm like a duelist, then dropping to roll away.

That got the rest started again. They swung in his direction, throwing three-round bursts as fast as they could work the triggers, their aim random and wild. He made friends with the earth once more, deciding that the fabric of his shirt was entirely too thick, as it kept him much too far above the ground. He winced and grunted—something suddenly burning sharp over the back of one calf, something else scorched his shoulder blade, gouging flesh. They were getting close. . . .

Then from the second car he heard Alejandro screaming over the shots, calling for them to cease. He cursed them and told them to come back. They did—when they ran out of bullets.

Richard sagged, then checked his leg. Just a long scratch. His shoulder was about the same. He owed Keyes a new shirt.

Right. Three gunmen left, Alejandro and another man in a wrecked car, not daring to get out, unable to move.

One more gun fell. There was no sound of a shot, though. Keyes had gone to work, it seemed. This had a predictable effect on the others. They'd reloaded, firing in Richard's direction since that was the last place a threat had come from, but he'd rolled again. He reached the pump house.

Keyes must have opted for a silencer. It would throw off his accuracy, but if he got in close enough, that wouldn't matter.

Another man dropped with a gasp and sigh. One left standing, two in the car.

Alejandro was shouting again.

Shouting Richard's name.

Shouting *Michael's* name.

Shouting an utter impossibility.

"I have the boy!" he bellowed. "You stop or I'll blow his head off!"

The last man stared nervously about to see if this would work. It was Nick Anton, looking grim and afraid.

"Come out in the open or Michael dies," Alejandro continued. "This I promise. Come out or he dies!"

"Boss . . ." began Anton.

"Shutup!"

Ten seconds went by; no one moved.

"You think I don't have him?"

Richard prayed he did not. To no avail. Alejandro thrust the child from the car. Anton grabbed him up, holding him to his massive chest with one hand, his MP-5 in the other, braced on his hip and pointing outward.

"Come out, Dun!" Alejandro ordered. "You and your friend come out now!" Alejandro lurched from the cover of the car, the muzzle of his pistol against Michael's head. The boy was awake, face expressionless to the nightmare around him.

Richard groaned. *Please Goddess, not again. Don't take him again.*

"Now! I'm counting to five! One, two . . ."

No choice. "All right! I'm over here! Don't shoot!"

Futile hope. Of course he would shoot. Any time he wanted. He owned Richard.

As soon as he rose from cover, Anton's gun swung his way.

"Drop your gun, come forward," Alejandro ordered.

He obeyed, furiously hoping Keyes would be smart about things and hold back.

"That's it, come forward, you son of a bitch."

He was full in the first car's headlights. One corner of the car had plowed into the back of his rental, the motor in gear and still running, a hideous mess behind the broken wheel. He could smell the fresh blood.

Alejandro glared at Richard. "How many lives you got anyway, you fucker? Bomb don't get you, knife don't get you, goddamn fancy bow-and-goddamn-arrow don't get you—how you gonna do with a bullet?"

He made no answer, his gaze on Michael. "Go ahead and finish it, Trujillo, but let the boy go."

"I'll finish it, but he ain't gonna go."

"He's a child, he can't hurt you. He's your family. Your own blood."

"Hah! He's a son of a bitch and bastard, no blood of ours!"

This did not come from Alejandro . . . it was from Luis, who emerged from the back of the second car.

Richard stared. Forgot how to breathe.

"You think I never *knew*?" Luis demanded, voice shrill. "You ever think *that*?"

The world lurched. Somehow Richard stayed on his feet. "What?"

"You goddamn bastard! I knew! I *knew*!"

A portion of the veil tore away. Not nearly enough. Behind the rest . . . Richard did not want to go there.

Luis stood shoulder-to-shoulder with Alejandro. They looked much alike, their unity of face and stance tearing away more veil.

"You worked with him," said Richard. "You worked with each other."

"He's just getting it." Alejandro laughed once. "We always did. When the bust came, we decided Luis should play the poor victim of his big bad brother."

"You *arranged* the betrayal?"

"It worked good. All the stuff he gave the cops knocked out a lotta my competition and kept him outta jail. It worked *real* good. I make some noise so they think I'm hurting. Meantime, I'm cleaning up."

"Luis? Your own family . . . ?" No, that wasn't possible. Could *not* be.

Luis broke away, coming toward him, face mottled, ugly. "Not mine, you bastard! Yours! They were always yours!" He swung hard, fist cracking against Richard's face.

He felt nothing. His heart banged painfully. *No . . . it's too grotesque.*

"You were fucking that bitch behind my back every chance you got, the two of you passing off the bastards as mine. How stupid did you think I could be? Richard the big protector, the big, generous guardian angel, goddamn *fucking* Uncle Richard . . ."

Invective poured from Luis. He had years of it stored up. Bitter, vicious, obscene in its force, monstrous in its concept.

This can't be. "No." He shook his head. "Oh, God, no . . ."

Luis, the patient, kind, family man, loving husband, Luis the murdering butcher. In his mind Richard saw once more through

Michael's eyes, saw the truth the boy had blocked out. The man who had cut them all down and then turned his gun on . . .

Adios to you too, you little bastard.

Not just profanity, but a statement of fact. As Luis mistakenly perceived it.

"No."

"Oh, yeah. Time to finally pay, big man. Had to wait to set it up—"

"You were the one who called me down here, not Stephanie."

"Yeah, I got the place all ready for you. You go in, find them, see what you made for yourself, then *boom*!"

Only Richard had survived. He'd been the target all along. He shut his eyes.

"How's it feel? You hate me? Hate yourself more—you made it happen. It's all on *your* head!" Luis gut-punched him until Richard fell to his knees.

"You fool," he whispered. "There's no hell low enough for you."

"You'll be the one in hell, burning with that lying bitch."

"She loved you! Don't you *get* it?"

"Loved me? She fucked you, and passed off those—"

"*Your* children! Your daughters, your son! *Not* mine!"

"Goddamn liar—both of you lying for years. Who do they look like? They don't look like me, and never did, so don't lie anymore! You lie again and I'll blow the little shit's head off, you hear me?" He was screaming, shrieking down at Richard, hitting, kicking, frenzied.

Richard lay on his side, tasting dust. He felt no physical pain. Only loss, boundless, abominable loss . . .

Luis stood over him, chest heaving, insanity in his staring eyes. He backed off a step, then another, until he was next to Alejandro again. "Gonna finish it now. Nick—gimme that knife of yours."

"What for?"

"What you think?"

"We got no time for that; Keyes is out there still. Tell him, Mr. Trujillo. He's got a bead on us all right now, I know it. Only thing keeping him shut is this kid. He's crazy about those damn cats, so this kid will hold him off. It's our only way out."

Alejandro nodded, looking into the darkness. He still held the gun to Michael's head. "Mr. Keyes? We know you are there. This is not a matter to do with you. If you just leave, we will let the matter that *is* between us drop. I will match your last earnings with me and put half again as much on top as a bonus if you just walk away."

Silence.

Richard slowly pushed himself up, listening for a sign.

It came when Keyes called from somewhere to the side. "Double it, Trujillo! Double it and you leave me the hell alone forever."

"Deal! Want to shake on it?"

Keyes barked a short laugh. "The money's in my account Monday or I will be the *last* man you see on Tuesday. Got that?"

"Understood."

"Then I'm outta here and good riddance."

They all heard footsteps crackling in the dry brush, the snap of twigs. Then nothing.

Richard straightened, focusing on the trio by the car. He could reach Alejandro from here, but never be in time. An instant—less—and he'd pull the trigger.

"Don't," said Richard. "Please, Trujillo, let the boy go. I spoke the truth. He's your nephew."

"You would say anything to save him."

"You can always kill him later. Kill me now, but wait on the boy. Get a blood test done. You'll see. You want to take that chance?"

Alejandro looked hard at him, a tiny shade of doubt in his face.

"If there is the least possibility he is of your blood, give him that chance. For God's sake, don't make a mistake on this."

Luis had found a knife, taken from one of the dead. He stood behind and to the side of Alejandro. "I'll show you the mistake—his." He started to raise it to the boy.

Anton scowled. "Hey now, lay off. It's just a kid."

"You want some too?"

"Luis! Wait! Just a minute." Alejandro kept the gun in place. "We gotta think about this."

"Okay, fine, *you* think. I'm gonna kill this fucker." He started toward Richard.

Alejandro had no objections. "That I wanna see. You hold still for him," he told Richard. "You don't fight him, and I might not shoot the boy."

Richard thought he heard a soft cough almost directly behind him. He thought he felt something zing past.

At the same time Alejandro's head rocked back half an inch. He dropped straight down. It was instantaneous and almost soundless, only the collapse itself making noise.

Anton stared. Richard followed his gaze. The back of Alejandro's neck was exploded open, an unmistakable exit wound.

Anton's jaw sagged in astonishment and alarm; he glanced up at Richard, accusing. Then the big man collapsed as well, abruptly, in silence, as though by magic. His arms went slack, dropping both the gun and the child, and down he went, Michael beneath him. The back of Anton's neck . . .

Luis. The last one standing. His attention was on Richard, but he'd heard enough to make him turn and see and realize he was alone.

Michael galvanized to sudden life. Though still blank of face, he was squirming desperately to crawl free of Anton's dead weight. Luis closed on him, knife in hand.

Richard was up, rushing to get to them.

Luis grasped Michael's golden hair, pulling the boy's head back to cut his throat.

"Daddy!" The boy's voice was thin with fear. "Daddy—don't hurt them . . ."

"Adios to you too, you little—"

Richard tackled him from behind; the two of them went rolling. Luis bellowed, fighting madly, without plan, just striking out. One of his strikes connected, cutting into Richard's side. He grunted and hit back, catching the edge of a jaw. That slowed things. Richard made a second swing, more solid, and tipped it in his favor for good. Luis was out cold.

Pushing the body away, Richard took the knife for his own. He shook with rage, wanted to scream himself, rail at the useless, blind stupidity of the man, but most of all he wanted to rip him wide open.

For that he needed no knife . . . his bare hands would do . . .

"Daddy," Michael was sobbing now. "Daddy . . . don't."

He looked at the child's tear-and-dirt smeared face. Hesitating before those crystal blue eyes.

"Don't . . ."

His heart cracked. *He's seen one parent die. I'll be damned if that happens again. Doubly damned if I'm the one who does the killing.*

He crawled over, stretched forth his near hand to take Michael's . . . and this time reached him.

Chapter Fifteen

He gathered the child close, crooning to him, rocking him, letting him wail out his grief. Richard's eyes streamed tears as well in shared sorrow.

Eventually they were both exhausted. Michael went still, his face smoothing out. His eyes went dead and dull once more as he retreated into the sanctuary that appalling experience had created within him. Soon his lids drooped and he slept.

Richard stood up, careful not to jar him awake, and carried him toward the rental. He removed the absurd crossbow and lay the child out in the back seat. When he straightened, Jordan Keyes was standing a few paces away. The man had been damned quiet about it. Probably force of habit.

He seemed quite at home in his dusty fatigues and boots, his face liberally streaked with flat black paint. All he had to do to be invisible in the dark was shut his eyes. The gun in his hand was fitted out with a massive silencer. He was in matte black from head to toe, including the night-vision goggles hanging from his neck.

"Well, that got pretty intense," he said with a nod toward the fallen. He drew his arm across his sweating brow, shoving back the knitted skullcap to reveal some pale forehead. The ski mask-styled covering bore a cousin's resemblance to a chain mail coif, giving him a knightly air. "You okay?" His gaze dropped to the gash in Richard's side.

"Just some scratches. Nothing to worry about. I want to get the boy out of here."

"I'm all for it, but we got a hell of a mess. Can't leave anything behind that the Feds can track back to us . . . you hearing any of this?"

"Yes, I'm just a little tired."

"No shit, Sherlock, but get with the program, we've still got work to do. You need caffeine tabs? I got some."

"No, thank you." He drew himself up, shifting mental gears. They were rather rusty at the moment.

They walked to the center of things, surveying the battlefield. Richard looked at the fallen, scenting the blood, but felt no hunger. He was weary in spirit and sick. He had no conscience left when it came to killing killers. In the heat of necessity it was easy, but afterward doubts would creep in. *Who were they? Had they deserved their fate? And why was I the one chosen to deliver it to them?*

"Too much work and risk to try hiding the bodies," said Keyes. "But we're going to have to destroy all trace of our specific presence. With any luck, the *Federales* might think one of Trujillo's competitors caught up with him. And having him on this particular site won't hurt to keep them speculating. Just what kind of a link do you have to this place? Is that going to be a problem?"

"There's no paper trail to me from the land itself, but Luis worked for a company of mine. He's Luis Marcelja there, but his fingerprints are on file; the alias will be found out. A smart investigator will find me sooner or later."

"Trust me, they're going to have nothing but smart investigators all over this one once they identify Trujillo. Though if anybody comes after you, chances are they'll want to shake your hand."

With Bourland's help and his own hypnotic abilities he'd manage. He'd done so before. "I can weather it."

"Well, I can't. You and I don't know each other, never heard of each other."

"Of course."

"Let's start by moving your buggy . . . just what the hell did you *do*?" For the first time Keyes noticed the log rammed into the first Caddie. He looked at Richard. "There's a story here."

Richard shrugged. "Adrenaline."

"Impressive." He leaned into the open passenger door and gingerly twisted the keys, careful to avoid touching the corpse. The motor died. "Okay. She might roll forward—no way am I going to mess with the parking brake—but you get your crate out of there."

He did so, the bumpers scraping as Richard drove the rental clear and circled around the wide yard. He went halfway to the entry road and parked. Going back he saw Keyes had found a dead tree branch and was dragging it all over the ground, stirring their footprints and tire tracks back into the dust.

"Where did you walk, exactly?" he asked, pausing to wipe down the second car's ripped-out steering wheel. He had no question over how it had come to rest yards outside of its vehicle.

"There and there, and I went to cover there."

"Any sandy spots?"

"I don't know."

"Well, find 'em and sweep." He gave Richard the branch, then went to crouch before the bumper of the front car. He brought out a knife and a penlight and proceeded to scratch off paint traces that had transferred over from its contact with the rental. He caught the tiny flakes and pocketed them, then did the same for Richard's transport.

They worked like a rehearsed team, going through the effects of the dead, not for booty, but for any linking evidence. None presented itself. Richard found cell phones and beepers, taking them away in case anything inconvenient might be in their electronic memories. He'd make a good home for them in a dumpster later, after smashing them to pieces.

Richard saw to Trujillo himself, Keyes to Anton. Both were clean.

"Mouth shot?" Richard asked, indicating the back of the neck exit wounds.

"Little something I picked up from a commando. Blows the

spinal cord to hell and gone. The brain can give all the orders it wants, but nothing goes out. No reflex twitching that can kill the hostage."

And he'd done both with a silencer yet. "Impressive." A near-instant death. Too good for the bastard, but necessary. He returned the Glock to Keyes, who put it with his Walther.

"Hate to lose this one," Keyes said about the latter. "I just got it broke in."

"How will you dispose of them?"

"Probably take 'em apart, see what fun I can have with a blowtorch. I know ways to mess up a barrel without even trying. You use that revolver at all? Good. One nice thing about those, they don't throw brass. Any chance of you finding your empties? Never mind, there won't be prints on those anyway. It should be enough to just lose the weapons. The forensic boys can't trace something that doesn't exist any more. I think we've balled things up enough now; let's boogie. What are you going to do about Luis?"

"Kill him."

"You want a moment alone?" There was no irony in the question. He was aware that sometimes cold murder had to be a private act.

"Not yet. I've something . . . special in mind for him."

Keyes looked disappointed. "You're not going to set up some kind of Rube Goldberg thing, are you?"

"No, but I would like to ask about contracting for your services. I'll pay your normal fee."

"You haven't heard it yet."

"How much?"

He named a price. High, but Richard had the funds. "It's local work. I remember your policy against it, but this would primarily be a watchman's job. It can be done from a safe distance."

Keyes's mouth drew tight. "Well, I can see you've got a hell of a grudge on. Would you mind giving me the headlines about that first?"

He did so, his voice cold as he looked down on Luis's unconscious body. Richard had to be cold so as not to feed the rage. If he let it take him over, then Luis would die now, too quickly, deprived of a just punishment. In this creature's case, Richard had absolutely no conscience at all.

Keyes shook his head. "So he thought you fathered the kids, stewed about it for years, and then went postal with his brother's help. That explains why Trujillo stepped outside his usual box with the explosion stuff. Luis was the fireworks fan."

"Yes. For Luis it must have been a symbolic thing as well. His way of utterly obliterating the life he had here. I had no clue, not one hint of what was in his mind. If only I'd . . ."

"Hey, no way are you responsible for him being nuts. I want to know about the kids, though. The boy does look like you."

"It's genetics. The children took after their mother's side; her ancestors are all from Iceland. Luis was their real father. That's why Stephanie and I parted. I could not give her children or the life she wanted. He could." And ripped it away. "As for this job, all you need to do is make sure he stays where I put him."

"What have you got in mind?"

Richard explained it to him. In detail.

Under his sweat-streaked mask of black paint, Keyes went a little pale.

"It won't be easy to endure," said Richard. "And I don't know how long it will take. Are you willing?"

Keyes snorted, throwing a glance at the ruins of the house. "For a guy who did that to his own family? Hell, yes. And keep your cash. This one's on me."

He left Keyes to tidy up the last details and drove home.

This second trip was hauntingly similar to the first: the boy asleep in the back and Richard driving all battered and tired, his sheer weariness holding back the grief. It would need release and soon, but when? Tomorrow Bourland would arrive, and Richard would have to be there for him, if only to offer a drink and a listening ear. Other necessities would also arise, as the mundanities of the world closed in, demanding attention.

In the old days he could go off on his own and wail his sorrows to the forgiving sky. No more.

When may I truly grieve for you, my poor Stephanie?

His phone trilled. A wryly sardonic reply from the gods, it seemed.

"Richard, it's Sam. Any news?"

"Yes, and it's good. I've got Michael back and he's unharmed."

"Thank God for that. How?"

"It's a bit complicated. I'll explain when I see you, but I've sorted everything out. Michael's safe now with me. No one's going to hurt him ever again."

"How is he?"

"Same condition." *If not worse.* "I'll take care of him tonight, then we can see about that specialist tomorrow. Did you call Bourland?"

"Yes, and it was hell trying to fill him in when I didn't know anything."

"It's all right; he's used to me doing that to people. Would you call him again for me? If I phone he'll want details, and I'm too exhausted. Tell him what I just said and that he'll get a complete debrief tomorrow. A coherent one."

"What about Luis? Where is he?"

"Not in the picture," he said shortly.

Silence on the other end as Sam digested this. "Okay. You'll tell me everything?"

"I promise." Which, of course, was a lie. Richard had no intention of telling Sam the truth about Luis and his horrific betrayal. The man dealt with evil enough on a daily basis, no need to add another nightmare to his collection.

Nor would Bourland hear any of it. He'd been fond of Luis for Stephanie's sake. He did not need to wonder if he couldn't have done more, sensed something or anticipated the unimaginable, and have somehow prevented the butchery—all the things that were eating at Richard's soul.

This is my burden, my good friends. You're better off without it.

He would come up with a story to cover Luis's disappearance. Alejandro would get the blame. That would be the end of it.

But what of Michael, who knew the truth?

✧ ✧ ✧

He carried the still-sleeping boy gently, thumbed the elevator button, and waited for it to deliver him to a few hours of peace before the morning storm. As before, he laid Michael in the big bed, then padded about seeing to his own needs. Once clean, his skin flushed red from the heat of a scalding shower, he carried the crossbow tripod out to the front room.

No need to wonder now how Trujillo's hit man had gotten into the flat. Luis himself could have been the one to set up the trap.

At least it wasn't a bomb.

As soon as he thought of it, Richard made a quick, thorough search of the place, sniffing for Semtex in every cupboard, peering under every stick of furniture. Then he went down to his safe room and did the same. He felt ridiculous, but knew no rest would come to him until he satisfied his flare of paranoia.

That done, he stretched out heavily on the bedroom sofa, and listened to Michael's soft breathing, waiting for sleep to take him, too.

He was on the point of drifting into it when the sound of the elevator snapped him wide awake. *Who on earth . . . ?*

Then he suddenly *knew* and hurried forth, his heart hammering.

The doors parted, and he swept Sabra up into his arms.

"You knew to come," he said, quite some moments later. For a time it was enough to simply hold her. His fatigue vanished.

"How could I not? Your pain and need called me like a thunderclap. I'm only sorry I could not get here sooner."

He put her down, and looked at her. Outwardly, she was the same as ever, beautiful, delicate of frame and face, but there were changes in her that only he could discern. There was a new power within her now, carefully veiled to most, quite visible to him. She possessed a strange strength that went beyond the apparent limits of her small body, as though the woman before him was merely a projection of her real self, an ephemeral vessel to interact with the temporal world. He had the feeling that should the projection ever became a full reality, mountains would crumble.

The Grail had done that for her.

"You've suffered much," she said, having gazed at him in turn.

"You're here. I can bear anything now."

She smiled. "Take care what you say, my Richard."

"I know." He was long familiar with the universe's antic sense of humor. "But it's still true."

She dragged a sizable backpack in from the elevator, leaving it on the floor. Dressed in an old, oversized sweater, faded jeans, and jogging shoes, her long hair tied back with a bandanna, she could have vanished into any college campus, but for her eyes.

She could stop rivers with those eyes.

"Show me the child," she said, straightening.

He ushered her to the bedroom. She glanced down once at the surprisingly large bloodstain on the threshold carpet and looked up at him, one eyebrow raised. He shrugged sheepishly, then motioned toward the bed. The only light came from the open bathroom door, more than sufficient for them both.

She bent over Michael, touching a loving hand to his forehead. She was not his declared godmother—that honor had gone to Bourland's daughter—but was certainly his spiritual one for her link to Richard. She caressed the silken blond hair, then went still, her eyes closed. She remained so for a long time, then took a shuddering breath and pulled away, shivering.

He went to her. "What is it?"

"The child is dying."

His heart plummeted. *No. Not again. We've been through too much.*

Michael could not die. He was all that was left, all that remained of the beauty that had once been Stephanie, that had once held Richard so close, so wrapped in an unconditional, an undemanding love. "Is his fate sealed beyond all change?"

Sabra's smile was sad, yet it warmed his very soul. In that smile he knew that no matter what, all would be well. "Not quite."

He sagged with relief. There was a chance then, and if it were even remotely within his power, he would make it a certainty. "What must I do?"

She reached her hand up and gently touched his pale, unshaven face. "Ah, Richard, ever the knight, ever the protector. Indeed there is much, and it is such that only you can do. A man betrayed the boy, and a man must save him. Only another who has been so terribly wounded can heal his wound."

"I do not understand."

"Think back to another son despised by an unloving father, another so cast away, another wounded nigh unto death."

The inner vision was so strong, Richard saw it as though it were happening again: his father's face full of hate, the bite of the blade, and the tearing pain. Pain that went far deeper and continued longer than that of any physical wound; pain that had been his enemy and then his strange, awful friend; pain that had faded yet never quite disappeared. His most bitter companion. How unloved is a son unloved by his father, how desperate and unending his loneliness and despair. Such a great, unfillable void to bestow as a paternal legacy.

"Whatever Michael needs, that will I do."

"I knew as much. You must go and find his spirit. He is much hurt and needs your healing. Complete the circle before his soul drifts so far away that it can never return."

"Yes, of course I'll go; but where?"

Her dark eyes glittered in the cool dimness of the room. "Beyond."

When she explained what was to be done, Richard took her hand, leading her out.

"I've the perfect place," he said. "Bring all that you need."

Puzzled, but trusting his judgment, she went to her backpack and drew forth a bundle that made discrete clinking sounds. From it rose the dusky scent of herbs and incense. The second bundle was smaller, padded well, and wrapped in pure white linen that he recognized as handwoven. He knew Sabra would have raised, harvested, and worked the flax herself, weaving in magic with each pass of the thread shuttle. He had no need to ask what was inside, he could feel its serene force. She gave him the larger bundle, hugging the smaller one to her breast.

He motioned Sabra toward the center of the room where what appeared to be a square, free-standing closet had been built as a space divider. One of its four outer walls held an entertainment center, two had shelving or displayed artwork. He opened the door set in the fourth, entering a cubicle with a spiral staircase. It went up to a trapdoor in the ceiling, which he pushed open.

As she followed, emerging into the chamber above, he could not repress a grin. How good it was to know that even after fifteen hundred years he could himself surprise and enchant her.

They stood in the very apex of the great glass pyramid.

The slanting panels of glass met twenty feet overhead, the floor being an exact forty by forty feet. It was huge, but not oppressive with its space as in some structures. Fresh air circulated from hidden floor vents, which kept the heat from building up too much during the day, exposed as it was to the full sun.

He eased the trapdoor down, seamlessly enclosing them.

The floor was wood parquet, a light background with a dark red pattern stained into it. Within the largest framing square was a circle, within the circle a smaller square, its angles aligned to the compass points. The square-within-circle pattern continued until the final square. Unlike the rest of New Karnak, the measurements here were balanced and true. Richard had seen to that, drawing out the lines and painstakingly applying the stain himself.

But the focus was the construct in the middle. It was a step pyramid within the smooth-sided one and composed entirely of interlocking slats of thick, clear plastic. Free-standing, it rose to a platform ten feet up, the top in the exact center of the chamber.

"What do you think?" he asked, but was already delighting at the look on her face.

She finally found speech again, looking at him with bright, loving eyes. "You . . . absolutely amaze me."

"This is why I had to have the place." They climbed slowly to the top, his bare feet brushing the warm plastic, the sun energy flowing up into him in a form that did not injure. Standing there made it seem as though they were suspended, floating not only in the room but above the night-dark city.

Beyond the glass, the city itself was a distant fairyland, all lights and shadows. To the north were vast unlit fields and woods, yet untouched.

"It's my own world," he said. "I come here to meditate and remember how small we truly are in the universe and yet how boundlessly important."

She took his hand. Her love seemed to course from her fingers and into him like a rushing fall of water. "It *is* perfect. Let us begin."

Midnight, not of the clock, but the true mid of night when the moon was at her Zenith and the sun blotted out by the whole of the planet's bulk.

They sat cross-legged on the high center platform, facing each other. Sabra looked west, Richard east. Between them was a brass brazier on a tripod in which charcoal smoldered.

Sabra unwrapped the smaller, more precious treasure and reverently held it high. A small cup it was, very ancient, yet untouched by time. Richard fell in love with its simple beauty and all that it represented all over again. It was object and idea at once, promise and fulfillment, desire and satiation.

A *frisson* of its power went through him as Sabra placed it in his open upturned hands.

"Hold it gently," she said. "It will be there when you are in need."

He nodded, full well knowing the truth of *that.*

Sabra produced dried herbs from a leather pouch, casting them onto the redly glowing coals. The smoke swirled about them, a heady mixture of sage, sweet grass, and others he could not tell. They kindled, flames shooting up high and hot, but short-lived, guttering to extinction, releasing white smoke.

Magic was suddenly in the air. He could feel it all around, far more powerful than he, than even Sabra. Yet what was here was but one minute tendril drawn down from the whole of the core.

She cast a handful of incense into the brass vessel. The smoke doubled, trebled, pouring out to permeate every corner of the great chamber.

Absurdly, it occurred to him the alarm in the rooms below could well go off bringing heavy-booted firemen, all axes and purpose, crashing in on them. He almost said something, but

Sabra, catching his thought as she often did, merely smiled and shook her head. The Goddess would take care of such problems. He needed to focus on the task before him, to clear his mind of distractions. Michael's life depended on it.

The child still slept in the bedroom below, body intact, soul elsewhere.

Sabra began to chant, repeating over and over an ancient rhyme in a tongue he'd never heard before. She was calling out to someone, he discerned that much, and it was working. Softer than the touch of a shadow, other voices joined hers, one by one in the same key, female, strong, insistent.

The smoke thickened, whirling in a slow spiral around them.

The full moon was directly overhead, at first brilliant silver, so bright as to hurt his sensitive eyes. Then the silver darkened, the mottled markings on her distant face turned blood red, spreading across the whole of the disk. Its lurid light filled the room, melding with the smoke until he and Sabra seemed to float on a sea of blood.

Her chanting—and the chanting of her unseen sisters—grew louder; the sea closed in on them. It rose high until it filled all of Richard's sight. He concentrated on keeping his mind clear and calm. Fear would dispel everything.

Red darkness surrounded him, red moonlight bathed him from above, brightening again to hurt his eyes. It physically pulled at him.

He felt himself lifted toward the crimson light, drawn inexorably forth into its vortex. The chanting rang in his ears, rushing through his temples, roaring like a torrent in springtime. He stretched his arms high. Strong, invisible hands carried him swiftly upward; he passed through the barrier of glass as one might run through a curtain of strung beads.

His eyes were shut tight now; he strained for air, his breath coming in heaving gasps. He wanted to move but could not; something held him close in an iron grip along the whole length of his body. Panic-stricken, he tried to speak, to open his eyes. He was paralyzed again by the poison, only this time he would never wake from its spell. He tried to scream, but all he could hear was the chanting, the voices buffeting him like fists as he spun helpless and blind . . .

And then silence.

Suddenly released, he sat up as though from a nightmare, sweat cold on his brow, eyes staring. He could scarce take in what they showed him: a bright sunlit meadow, green under the midsummer sun, quite beautiful.

But slow, painful death if he did not find shade.

He saw a line of trees nearby. He stumbled toward their shelter, not understanding why he could not persuade his unsteady legs to more speed. They dragged like leaden weights over the thick overgrown grass. It took him ages to cover the ground, and when he fell beneath the shade of a friendly oak, he gasped like a dying fish. His side had caught a stitch and hurt like blazes. What was wrong? Was the poison still at work on him? He felt so weak and tired from the exertion. No matter, he would soon recover. Sabra said he had very little time left to find Michael, so while catching his second wind he took stock of himself, his surroundings.

He was no longer in his old blue bathrobe, but fully dressed in a soft woolen tunic and leggings the color of twine. Leather boots were on his feet, leather belt riding low on his hip, all handmade. He'd not worn such clothes for a thousand years. They felt strange to him, bringing back tactile memories long forgot. He wasn't just in another world but in very much another time.

The Grail was gone from his hands, but that did not trouble him. In this magical place intent was as strong as actuality. If and when he needed the Grail, it would be there as she'd promised.

What he'd first taken to be a meadow was actually a large clearing in the midst of a great wood. He recognized nothing about this place with no landmarks immediately visible. There was no sign of gaudy New Karnak. He certainly wasn't in Texas any more. Not with these massive trees. Some of the oaks here were a full ten feet or more in girth, ancient even by his standards, with shadows black as death gathered beneath them. Many raised their gnarled branches high to the sun, others were bent and twisted, taking perverse glory in their corruption, and some were divided, with new growth above, but their trunks split asunder to show rotting cores.

The day was warm, not burning hot, the sun shining gently from a pale blue sky. All around were the sounds of life. Birds sang incessantly, one taking over from the other unbidden, their calls filling the honey-sweet air with undeniable joy. Insects hummed along their busy way, drawn by the heady smell of wildflowers that drenched him, soothing as thoughts of love.

He leaned back against the trunk of the oak. Such a blissfully exquisite day he had not known for . . . how long? He couldn't remember. Had he ever? No matter. He did now.

He smiled, idly pushing his fingers deep into the grass until they reached the damp earth below, then raised them to his face to take in the wondrous scent of earth and green growth. It stirred his soul, that rich smell, he wanted to rest here and just breathe for a week. He knew that wasn't possible, but it couldn't hurt to steal just a moment. His eyelids flickered. He did not want to sleep, he would miss the beauty around him, but the heavy, lush air lulled him. The endless drone of insect and birdsong grew louder, shutting away all else, and his eyelids drifted shut.

"Richard!"

A voice cut through his semi-slumber.

"Richard!"

He knew the voice yet could not name it. It came from everywhere and nowhere.

"Richard, do not sleep!"

Something slapped him, hard. He twice felt the hot sting of a hand on his face. His eyes flashed open, alarmed. "Sabra?" His own voice sounded strange, thick and slurred as if he had been long abed, yet he had not dozed off. Or had he? He did not know. "I hear you, Sabra. What is wrong?"

"You must not sleep, my love. This is a dangerous place, treacherous. Time is not as it should be for you. Many have been here before and slept, some never to waken, some to return eventually to life but old, confused, swearing that they had closed their eyes but a moment. A moment here may be years elsewhere. Time is loosened and is your enemy."

He stood and rubbed his eyes. The air was cooler now, the birdsong more remote and less seductive. "Where are you?"

"Beyond." Sabra's voice was distant, fading. "This is all the help I can give, and then only by the strength of the Goddess and the Nine Sisters. To find Michael you must follow the signs as in the old days."

"What signs?"

"You will know them. Trust in that. But beware, there is danger for you that I did not foresee."

"What danger?"

"In this land you are an ordinary man once more."

"Ordinary? How can that be?" He could not believe such a thing.

"The magic demands balance. The blood of the Hounds of Annwyn was the price of your passage here. I did not know the Guardians would take it from you. In this place you are a fragile mortal man. You can die here. Truly die."

No—that was impossible. He felt no different. Or did he? "Sabra . . . ?"

"Take care, my love, for there is danger all around. Hurry, do not tarry. *Find* him!"

And the voice was gone.

Nerves taut and all his senses alert, Richard stared around with fresh eyes. Mortality? How? The first rush of terror froze him a moment, then eased as he thought things through. Danger was all around, true, but he'd survived in a tougher, much more demanding world than this for thirty-five years before his change. He could deal with this summer land for however long it took.

At least now he understood why his run to the shelter of the trees seemed to take so much effort. And why his senses seemed so muffled.

He would indeed take extra care. Yet there was one advantage to this return to mortal frailty. He stepped into the sunlight, raising his face like a supplicant for a blessing. It shone full on him, and for the first time in many, many centuries, all he felt was its warm healing caress. No blindness, no acidlike burning. He closed his eyes and spun slowly in a circle, arms outstretched, a game he used to play as a child, though he could not remember what it was called.

It was in truth a blessing, and he would remember it forever.

A sharp, cracking sound. A careless footfall? Richard dropped to his haunches, jolted from his reverie. He would remember forever . . . if he lived that long.

Something moved in the woods across the clearing, and he could not pierce the thick shadows under the trees to see.

There, again! A twig snapping and the rustle of dead leaves. It was closer. Richard, mindful of his new-vulnerable state, slipped back to the shelter of the trees on his side. There was silence once more for several long minutes. All he could hear now was the pounding of blood in his brain. Dear Goddess, but he'd forgotten the feeling of this kind of fear. Terror and exhilaration at once. He'd lost the memory of how *alive* it made him from one instant to the next.

He strained his eyes searching the trees opposite for any sign of whoever or whatever it was but could see nothing. He abruptly heard the sound again . . . there . . . yes, something white moved there. But what?

It emerged slowly from cover; delicate, shy, huge eyes innocent yet wise, a pure white hart stepped out into the sunlight, graceful as a dancer.

He slumped and tried to steady his still-racing heart. Relief flooded through him so strongly that he wanted to laugh; instead, he held himself quiet, not wanting to startle the animal.

The hart came a few paces into the clearing, standing quite still, only her ears flicking nervously for sound. And then she saw him. He would have sworn that it was not possible for her to know he was there. He'd been quite silent, and was mostly hidden behind a tree. Yet as he watched she turned deliberately, and fixed her great brown eyes upon him.

Come.

He gaped in response to the flower-soft whisper. It could have been a trick of the wind. Merely the leaves above shifting and not—

Come!

The voice was clear in his head this time. Then the hart turned and walked daintily back whence she had come. At the edge of the clearing she paused, as though waiting, looking once over her shoulder at him.

Follow the signs as in the old days, Sabra had said. The white hart had ever been a sign, a very powerful one, leading to adventure and danger. Richard's nerves tingled at the thought. She could only be here for him, to lead him to Michael. If his soul had retreated to this sanctuary, he might well have followed the hart himself. What child could have resisted?

Richard stood. The sudden movement startled the animal, for she skittered and seemed about to flee, but spun and stood her ground. He now stepped into the clearing, and they faced each other, man and beast united in common purpose.

"Where is Michael, good friend?" he murmured. "Lead me to him, if you will."

She broke away at once, ears canted to hear his progress as he followed.

Deeper in the woods the daylight faded, filtered by the dense foliage. The hart kept her distance ahead, and he did not try to close the gap. The white of her coat was easy to see as she picked her way, and Richard knew better than to try to hurry her, else she would leave him.

The journey was not easy. The trees grew close together here, often forming a barrier that he was unable to get through. Then he would have to circle around searching for a clear path. She would wait for him at these times, nibbling at tender leaves or snuffling the ground until he caught up, then she would head off again.

The exertion was beginning to have its effect on Richard. The day was still warm, and no cooling breeze could penetrate this growth. Sweat plastered his hair, and his clothes were soaked. Branches snapped and snagged at his progress, scratching him, and a myriad of insects clung in a hovering cloud. They got in his eyes and nose, biting, feeding on his blood.

So this is how it feels!

He swiped impatiently at them, angered that such small things could create so great a hurt.

When he looked up, the hart was gone. She'd ever been in sight, but no longer. The forest went unnaturally still. No birds, only the insects remained to continue their torment. He was quite alone, deep in the tangled trees and undergrowth with no idea of where he was or which way he must go.

He looked around desperately, cursing himself for a fool for having followed the animal unthinkingly. He looked for the path that he'd broken through the trees, but it had vanished as well. Fear began to rise up once more, for it was in dark places as this that panic was first bred and birthed. This forest was an enemy, terrifying in its vastness. He had to fight the urge to shout for help as he looked desperately around; who would hear him? Should he stay or go, and which way? He could not see the sun to mark a direction.

It would get dark all too soon. He had no wish to spend the night in this place. Blindly he set forth, snapping branches as he went, going as fast as he could in the close surroundings. At least he was moving. That certainly made him feel better. Then he spied a strangely gnarled tree just ahead and knew he'd seen it before. His heart sank as he realized that it marked the spot where he'd stood when the hart disappeared. Without her guidance he'd walked in a circle.

He sank to the ground, his heart hammering as he gave in to a moment of pure terror. He was lost, utterly, utterly lost. He wiped his brow and held his head in his hands, cursing the price he'd unknowingly paid to come to this hellish place. What he would give for his vampire senses now. Tears of frustration welled in his eyes, and he rubbed them away impatiently.

"This is not for me, but for Michael!" he called out. "Take me to him! Please!"

Movement.

A flash of white barely glimpsed through the tangle ahead. A pale gleam like a ghost.

He hauled himself upright and with fresh hope staggered forward through tangling vines and tree roots. The forest seemed against him, trying to hold him back, branches reaching forth to twist about his arms and legs, slapping his face and neck, leaves rustling with cruel laughter. He pushed and fought his way through. It had to end eventually. It must. He thought of free-flowing air and escape from the damned blood-sucking insects.

But when he finally burst through into a clearing, the white he had glimpsed was not that of the hart. It was the tattered dress of a woman leaning with her back against a tree. Her head was bowed as though praying or asleep, her long, rippling hair hanging free.

The sight so surprised him that he forgot caution, standing in the open to stare.

She was not really leaning. Her arms were drawn back around the trunk. She moved a little, and across the space between them Richard heard the unmistakable sound of chains clanking, chains and her quiet sobbing.

She was not alone. Some twenty feet from her was pitched a knight's pavilion. His war-horse, in full battle armor, cropped contentedly at the sweet grasses of the clearing. A shield bearing no token to identify its owner hung from one of the boughs nearby along with a sword in its scabbard. A lance leaned up against them.

Follow the signs as in the old days. Sabra's words once more rang in his head.

This was definitely a knightly quest. The hart had led him here, and now he must rescue the lady. It was one of the immutable laws of chivalry. A test of his courage. But he was mortal here, so any conflict could be deadly, and this would be conflict against a fully armed and armored knight. He had no doubt such a one occupied the pavilion.

Well, I've learned a few new tricks since those old days. Let's see what happens.

Richard stole forward, his soft boots silent on the grass. The woman looked up at him, her eyes sad and full of fear. He signed for her to be still, then reached for the sword and shield.

That's when he heard the knight emerging from the tent.

Chapter Sixteen

He was a giant, half again Richard's height, broad of shoulder, and clad in blood red armor. Again, there was no sign or emblem of any sort on his things. His face was hidden by a tall, conical helmet with small, hooded eye slits. In one hand he held a mace.

"Come to test me, boy?" he boomed, his voice harsh, mocking.

Richard hurriedly seized the sword and shield—just in time. He barely got the shield up to block a devastating blow from the mace. The force of it cracked against his lower arm and traveled up his shoulder, knocking him to the ground.

Training from centuries past reasserted itself. He cast his shield arm to the side and rolled that way on the momentum, keeping his sword close to his body. He got clear and was on his feet before the return swing, circling to keep just out of the giant's line of sight. It would be severely limited by the helmet.

"Who art thou who gives no challenge?" he demanded.

"Thy life and death at once!"

The great man lashed out wide. Richard ducked, darting forward and thrusting up at the unprotected base of his weapon arm. The point of the blade connected and bit deep, raising a howl of pain and anger. Reaction was quick, though; he had to drop and roll again, feeling the breeze of the mace as it brushed just over the hair of his head.

I can't smell the blood, he thought. He could see it, glistening as it flowed over the armor.

The giant paused only long enough to shift the mace to his left hand. He strode forward, roaring. He moved very fast, each stride a match for two of Richard's, and as for his reach . . .

Richard used his shield again as the mace crashed down. The wood began to splinter along some hidden flaw. Richard chopped at the man's extended arm on the inside, striking sparks against the mail.

"Weak vessel," taunted the giant. "Unworthy! Think thou art a man?"

The mace swept down. Richard danced just outside the radius of the swing and went close again, this time trying for the back of a leg. He succeeded, slamming a strong enough blow to buckle the left knee, but failed to cut through the mail to break flesh. He blocked the return strike of the mace with the shield. He got his sword up and caught the knight hard on the wrist. The armor prevented him from severing it, but the weapon dropped.

"Yield!" he shouted.

"Never!"

"I would not kill thee. Yield and depart."

The giant seemed not to hear and struck out. The thick mail of his gauntlets saved his hands as he warded off sword blows, laughing as he pressed on.

The best Richard could hope for was to keep the giant at a distance. Though larger and much stronger, the weight of all that armor would tell on him sooner or later. When that happened . . .

But Richard had to keep backing away, step-by-step, his chest aching for want of air. He should not be so tired. In a few moments he'd be too exhausted himself to fight.

"Come, boy! Come and show me just how weak you are!"

Still backing, fighting defensively, trying to catch his breath and plan. He was faster and could see better than his opponent, about the only advantages left; time to use them before he was too spent.

He feinted to the left, then darted right, out of the giant's view. Before he could turn, Richard had reached the woman. He dropped the shield, using both hands to arc his sword down on the heavy chain.

More sparks. He struck again and again to no effect, then the blade snapped in two.

No time to curse the luck. The giant seized him round the waist, lifting him high. Richard struggled, swinging down and backwards, hacking at those massive arms. That helped; he was half-thrown, half-dropped to the springy turf. He'd forgotten what it was to take a fall from a horse, all bruises and disorientation; this was like that. He pushed upright, focusing to hold onto the sword. At a sound behind him, he instinctively dodged, whirled, struck. Metallic clank. Bellow of outrage. Something hit his shoulder. He spun and nearly fell.

He needed the lance. The length and weight of it called for much skill on horseback, which he possessed, but there was no time to mount the tethered beast, and certainly no room to maneuver in this all-too-small clearing.

Richard stumbled to the tree, discarded the sword and grabbed the lance. It was heavier than he expected, more clumsy to balance than he remembered.

But now he was reduced to ordinary strength.

He'd have only one chance with it, too, for there was no way he could prevent the giant from taking the weapon. To him, it would be as light as a jackstraw and as easily plucked away.

Point control. One of the hardest things to master. Difficult enough on the back of a galloping horse, holding balance, keeping the lance steady and level, placing it precisely in one telling spot, all that while another man is charging at you with the same intent—and yet it was still easier than trying to do the same thing on foot.

He held it crosswise over his body like a spear, quickly moving on as more laughter erupted behind him.

"Think you to defeat me with that?"

He turned. The giant was in the center of the clearing, and except for the blood coming from his wound, seemed little the worse for wear.

"Come and charge me, boy! Unhorse me with that twig." He

shook both his fists. There was less movement in his right arm.

Richard hurried to his right, the giant's left, causing him to turn. Sluggish he was, and there was pain in that booming voice. All his effort was in intimidation and insult. He was in midword, when Richard suddenly cut left, bringing the long staff to the horizontal as he rushed forward.

The sharp point ran true and caught the giant in the same wound. The impact was not as devastating as it might be for a man full tilt on a horse, but it was enough. The giant screamed now and tried to fall back and escape, but Richard kept pushing on.

Then the giant's feet tangled upon each other, and down he dropped.

Richard let go the lance and hurried to retrieve the sword. He returned just as the giant began to right himself. Richard threw a side kick at the helmet. That hurt his foot, but it resulted in the giant's sudden collapse.

"Yield!" he cried, standing over him. He pressed the broken sword up under the helm, past the chain mail coif, the shattered end on the vulnerable flesh under his jaw. "Yield and live."

"Never! Kill me and be done!"

"As you wish!"

Richard drove in solidly with all his remaining strength, driving the broken sword deep. The great body flailed in its death throes; one massive arm caught Richard, sending him staggering.

His legs gave out, the earth jarred his back. He shut his eyes against the spinning sky above and lay inert on the grass, striving to breathe again. God, but he was tired. And how he thirsted. How strange it was to thirst this way, without hunger, without the strength of his beast to carry him forward to hunt.

When the dizziness passed and he could trust himself to walk without falling, he rose and went to the giant. Blood had fair gushed from him, soaking the turf. Richard felt no hunger for it; indeed, he was repulsed and wished to avoid contact, but hanging from the man's belt was a key.

He took it away and went to the lady. Though he must have been a fearsome sight himself with his batterings, torn clothes, bloodings, and doubtless wild eyes, she did not shrink from him. Instead, once he'd unlocked her bindings, she gathered him close to give comfort.

"I thank thee, good Richard," she whispered.

He had no surprise that she knew him, for he seemed to know her. He pulled back to look at her, but there was something odd about her face. It seemed to change like an image trapped in water, shifting as light and shadow played over it. He shook his head, rubbing his eyes.

She left him a moment, then returned with a water skin. He eagerly drank; though warm and tasting of leather it was yet sweet on his parched lips and dust-dry throat.

"Who was that knight?" he asked.

"He was your life and death. Ending and deliverance."

Richard twitched a smile. "That wants explaining."

"You will find the answer with him."

"Who art thou?"

"Your death and life. Beginning and continuance."

And perhaps she would give a more clear reply, when the time was right for him to hear it. "Why did he treat you so?"

"He did love and seduce me once upon a time. Fate and his own cruelty made him hate me."

An old story, he thought, and went back to the knight. He dragged off the huge helmet.

The man's eyes were open, giving the world one last angry glare. Though definitely dead, there was still a movement about him. Like the lady, his face seemed to change, rippling.

In that face Richard recognized the features of many men; his father, his brother, Luis, Alejandro . . . they and more like them shifted skin and bone like malleable clay. Hundreds of faces, callous enemies all, some he'd killed himself, others he'd simply outlived.

He thought he understood now, and returned to the lady. She was also one of hundreds, perhaps thousands. For a few seconds she was Elaine, then Stephanie, then Ghislaine, then Elena and Seraphina, both grown to the womanhood they'd been denied—all were beautiful to him. One face he did not know, yet she above the others drew him the strongest.

"Do I know thee, lady?"

"You have always known me."

How can such ice-blue eyes be so warm? he wondered. Then the answer came to him and he was on his knees, arms around her, holding her like life itself. He had no tears, for he'd wept them out centuries ago, wept them for the mother he'd never seen, the mother who had bled out her life delivering him . . .

She crooned to him, gentle hands caressing his hair. "You cannot stay, good Richard."

"I know, but 'tis sweet. There is so much I would say to thee, so much I would hear."

"Then speak to me in thy dreams, for I have always heard you."

"But I shall not hear you in turn."

"Nay, but you do. Thy heart has ever known my voice. I love thee and am proud of thee."

He'd thought himself exhausted of tears. Fresh ones sprang to his eyes.

"You must find the child, now," she said after an all-too-brief moment. "And quickly."

"Yes, I swear it. Come with me. Guide me to him."

"You know the way yourself. Though you walk in the darkness, the light within has ever guided you. Let it guide you again."

"Mother . . ."

"Fare thee well, sweet Dickon."

And she was gone. He remained on his knees, arms out as though in prayer. Between them was a shaft of sunlight from a summer out of time. It flared brightly, then faded. The wood around him dimmed for want of her presence.

His heart ached, his whole being ached. Pierced right through he was, yet he took a strange comfort from it. She loved him, had always been there, though he'd known it not.

That was changed. "I will speak with thee again and soon," he promised.

No reply came. Saddening, and he could not linger to mourn. He got tiredly to his feet, looking around for the next sign to follow.

The big war-horse snorted and stamped as though to mock his lack of perception.

Richard boosted onto its back, dug his heels in, but held the reins loose. As he presumed, the big beast knew its own way, taking a trail from the clearing. A sudden turning around a stand of beech trees marked the end of the wild forest and the beginning of open fields. He was on a rise, his road leading down to a lake and a shallow fording.

Of course. It had to be.

Beyond the lake was his father's castle. No reflection of it lay on the water, yet he knew it to be real. To himself at least. In *this* place.

He kicked the horse forward to a gallop, splashing over the ford, surging up the next rise and thence to the gates and through. Within, all was silent. No armsmen called a challenge, no servants scuttled up to attend him; he was quite alone but for his stamping mount.

He threw a leg over its neck and slipped down. Untethered, it trotted off to the stables, there to vanish, he supposed, as the hart had done, as had his mother. This journey, he now understood, was less to do with Michael than with himself. His prayer was that he'd not been delayed too long.

Ignoring his stiff muscles and bruises, he pushed into a shambling run, going through the tall doors that opened to the feasting hall. It was also empty, having no sign that anyone had been there in centuries.

He took the door opposite into the winding hall. No light shone here, but he knew the way, had walked it often enough in nightmares. It ended, as the dreams always did, with the door to his father's chamber.

He pushed through.

The great throne was yet there, next to it a simple table. The air stank of fat from the burning torches along the walls. Their light was red, unsteady, the smokes rising black to layer the sooty ceiling.

On the throne . . . Michael, looking very small and frail. His dead eyes gazed out, all unseeing. He leaned wearily against one arm of the chair.

To his horror, Richard saw that the boy was bleeding from his side, a deep wound, the blood flow slow but steady. The terrible stream marched down the base of the throne to the floor, where it pooled, growing.

Richard rushed to him, but the closer he got the thicker the air seemed, until he was unable to move forward at all.

"Let me go to him!" he shouted at he knew not what.

"Would you heal him?" a voice asked. It was neither male nor female, kind or cruel. It just *was.*

"Yes! Of course!" he answered, looking wildly about for the source. "Let me pass. Please!"

"You know him not."

"I don't have to!"

"Then learn."

Michael's face changed, his form shifted, grew. No longer a little boy, a grown man sat in his place, the same agonized posture, the same dead eyes. Such eyes Richard had last seen on Michel when they both lay wounded on the grass that day so long ago.

He could not breathe. Before him was the truth he'd always known in his heart, but never dared to speak. *How many lives have you had, boy? How many woundings? Could I have spared you?*

"Do you forgive?" the voice asked. "Do you forgive what had to be, what you could not help?"

He shook his fists in frustration. "I forgave, years past I forgave. You know it to be so."

"You never forgave yourself. You still carry anger within for not doing more to stop the impossible."

"My anger is nothing to his need. Please, let me pass."

The man's form shrank in upon itself to that of the desperately hurt child. "Wouldst heal him of this living death?"

"Yes!"

"You know not the price."

"Name it, I will pay."

"See it first."

The form on the throne shifted, grew. Richard saw himself seated there, face gray and gaunt, eyes hollow and lost, but wretchedly aware. He was old, ancient, hair and beard gone so white as to be transparent, his wrinkled, spotted flesh hanging loose from aching bones. One skeletal hand was pressed to his bleeding side; the pain like cold fire, unable to consume itself and die. His shrunken body trembled from relentless weariness; he could not lay himself down. There was no escape, no rest, only the unending torment of an injured soul.

"Thus will it come to pass, thus will it be for you forever," said the voice. "To save the boy, you must take his place, assume his hurts. You will live on in this agony until the last fall of night. And when that may be no one knows."

Richard swallowed hard. "Never to die and find release?"

"Never. The cup of life will ever sustain you."

On the table was the Grail. Its presence alone, he knew, had power enough for miracles. But that the miracle of life could be so twisted . . . how could they ask so much of him? To leave him perpetually dying, yet alive, without hope, alone . . .

But such was what the boy now endured, where he was trapped, and unlike Richard, he had no understanding of *why*.

Richard was himself again, standing before the throne, looking at Michael—and just able to step forward. The resistance was less than it was, but still strong. "I've seen your price and it matters not. Do what thou wilt with me, but save the boy. Restore and heal him, I beg you."

"Are you certain, Richard d'Orleans?"

In answer, he pushed closer until he could reach Michael. As soon as he touched him the thick resistance ceased. He gently gathered the boy into his arms. Precious burden. The last time he would ever hold him. It would have to be enough.

He reached for the Grail. Picked it up. There was dark red wine in it, or something that appeared to be wine.

He put the cup to the boy's lips, persuading him to drink. Michael did so, then shut his dead eyes, seeming to sleep.

God and Goddess, help him!

Richard searched his face for some sign of change, then held him close. "There is so much I would say to thee, so much I would hear. Speak to me in thy dreams, my son. If the gods are kind they may let me listen. They may let me reply."

The voice around him was silent to this. No sound was within the chamber except for his own breath and the hiss and burn of the torch fires.

He felt a wet warmth on his hand. Michael yet bled.

No! No more!

He put the holy cup on the table, then stepped away from the throne, taking Michael clear of the pool of blood at its base. With nowhere else to put him, he had to lie on the cold flags, no covering, no pillow. Richard peeled off his tunic. A wretched blanket, torn, bloody, and sweat-stained, but better than nothing.

He wrapped Michael with it, kissed his brow, and backed away. "Sleep, boy, and may heaven have pity on thee."

Richard approached the throne. A memory of his near-fatal childhood punishment came to him. He tiredly thrust it away, turned, and sat.

It was worse than in the vision. The wounding he'd taken in the field in the far past was negligible to this. In that same spot as the spear thrust, his flesh parted from within to without in a gash longer than his hand. He gasped as though struck, clutching his side as though to stave the blood flow and agony, all for naught. The pain devoured all his senses. Nothing else existed. Weak unto fainting, he leaned against the arm of the throne to wait until the first shock of it passed.

Only it did not.

The bitterness held undiminished. Each time he shifted to ease himself only added to his suffering.

I chose this. I will endure. Better me than him.

So he did not cry out; he bit off all complaint. He remained in place, and watched as his blood trickled down the same path as Michael's to merge with the pool already there. In the hours, the years to come, it would cover the whole of the floor, spread to the rest of the castle, be soaked up by the earth outside, cloak the world.

He shivered. How could such a close-aired chamber be so chill? The gooseflesh plucked at his bare back and arms like knife points. He dared not move to rub warmth into them, lest his pain increase.

He wondered if his face and form would also shift before the eyes of any who saw him. Would a visitor someday come and take pity on him, try to ease his pain? He doubted it. This was his world from now on, this drab, cold chamber with the smoking torches, season beyond season unchanged forever. In unbroken solitude he would count the stones of the walls and listen to his own heartbeat and groans of anguish. Sabra had warned him of danger, but not the depth of it, not the permanence. There were worse things than dying. He hoped she would forgive him for leaving her. Perhaps she would wait for him as she'd done before, but this time he would not return.

But Michael . . . there, he was waking. All would be worth it if he could live free.

The child did not see him, his gaze was fixed on the open door. Pale light shone there, pale, but growing stronger, brighter as something approached in the passage beyond. Richard held his breath as one by one several women slowly filed in. They were of a kind with their serene faces, and unadorned white robes. Their bare feet whispered over the flags. The light they carried was their own, shining out from their smooth flesh. Eight in all, eight of the nine sisters of Avalon, they surrounded little Michael, who showed no fear of them. Three of them—they looked much like the boy's mother and sisters—lifted him up and carried him away. Their light went with them, dimming with distance, then vanishing altogether.

None had marked Richard or shown any sign of his existence.

Richard was alone.

He slumped, accepting it, accepting everything. Wincing, he leaned back in the chair, knowing the pain would keep him from ever sleeping again, but wishing for a respite all the same. He wished only. Here, there was no more hope.

He felt the blood seeping past his fingers. He'd borne a thousand such woundings and worse and survived. They'd always healed, physically. This, though, represented not only all of Michael's hurts, but the inner wounds Richard had endured over the centuries, the ones whose scars yet bled when his thoughts touched on them. He would have much time now to think.

He closed his eyes.

Let go. The agonies of the past imprison and torture us all, but only if we allow it. Let go.

Indeed, were it only that simple.

It is. You cannot have the past you wanted, only that which you had. Accept that it made you what you are and move on.

How? he wondered.

Just let go. Move forward.

I want to. How? Whose was this out-of-time voice? Was it part of the room or within his mind?

Release the past. Let go.

Then sleep stole over him after all . . . and dreams.

He dreamed that he was able to sink back into the chair and find true comfort, true rest. His cares slipped away, spiraling off into sweet darkness.

He dreamed that gentle arms were wrapped around him, a soft hand caressed his brow, a softer voice called his name.

"Wake now, Richard. Come to me. Move forward and come to me."

He drew a great breath, like a diver just surfaced, and struggled to sit up. The pain clutched at him, holding him down.

" 'Tis over," Sabra whispered close to his ear. She cradled his shoulders and head in her lap. "Waken, my love."

He saw a black sky and full moon, glass and metal framing above, none of it seemed real, not at all solid as this chamber. One vision was hard upon the other, each wavering, fighting to assert itself.

"Come to me," she said.

Her voice drew him like a lifeline. "But I must stay . . . for Michael."

"He's here. Come to us."

Richard shook his head, trying to force his eyes to open on the right reality, the right time. The chamber of pain faded; the torches winked out. Sabra was with him instead, holding him. And there was a weight on his chest.

He sat up a little. Michael was unexpectedly in his arms, curled against him, his small fists hanging tight to the fabric of the old blue bathrobe. He slept, but with that wonderful abandon that only children know. His little face was relaxed now, at peace.

Richard fiercely tightened his embrace around the child and kissed the top of his blond head. He looked at Sabra. "Is he well? Truly well?"

"He is. You delivered his soul from its darkness. He will be able to heal in this world, now."

"But I thought I had to stay."

"Your willingness to do so was enough. The difficulty was persuading you away. You're a man of duty, my Richard."

"I saw my mother there."

"I know. Michael saw his, and long they spoke."

"They may still be speaking, if he dreams."

She nodded. "As it is for you. He is a special child."

"Michel come back to me."

"He's done so before, only you knew it not. His soul has been in many vessels over time."

"If only I had known."

"Nay, but each life must be what it is, not what it was before, else there is no learning, no growth. You must prune off limbs from a tree so that the trunk sprouts new ones more lush."

"And sometimes the cutting is harsh?"

"But what must be. You and he have endured much, learned much, he through many lives, you through this one. I think you will each understand one another better now."

"What do you see for him?" He thought better of the question as soon as he'd asked it. Her Sight was a terrible gift.

"His mother and sisters are close, you cannot see them, but he will know and they will comfort him. They will speak to him in his dreams and guide his waking steps. He has much power and must learn to be wise with it."

"Power?"

"He has gifts from the Goddess even I cannot grasp."

"Like the Sight and the giving of visions?"

"Yes. Those among others."

Richard thought of the nightmare vision he'd had of the house, the killings, the chase into the fields, and looked down at Michael in wonder. The animal blood had not forced that imagining. It had been Michael, reliving the memory, projecting it into Richard's mind as a reality. Dear God. "He is waking to them. But so young."

"He needs teachers, you and I, and more, many, many more."

"You will take him north with you, to the tribe there?"

"They will help with his healing as no others can."

"I thought as much."

"Perhaps you will come?" she asked.

Richard knew he needed healing as well. He would find it in the shadows of those tall woods with a wise people who yet understood the Old Ways. "Yes," he whispered. "As soon as may be."

With Michael still enfolded protectively in his arms, he leaned back against Sabra and, for a time, slept with that same peaceful abandon.

Relentless sun, blistering heat, muggy air. High noon in Texas.

Richard ignored those annoyances as he left his rental in the dust of a little-used lane and stalked through the scrub oak. He carried a heavy rucksack slung over his shoulder. Now and then he checked his compass. When the tangle of trees and briars opened up to a field, he saw the hill he wanted a quarter-mile ahead. He used the mirror on the reverse side of the compass and caught the sun in it, aiming the reflection at the trees on the summit.

A moment later, two flashes returned to him.

He kept close to the edge of the field, walking as quickly as he could manage through the trees. His new hat and old drover's coat helped shield him from the sun, but the additional shade meant he could stay out longer.

The last few days had been busy. Bourland had arrived, still weighed down with grief and in need of work to ease it. He efficiently took on the red tape of local officialdom, claiming the bodies, running interference for Richard's part in things, and generally smoothing the way for Michael to leave the country.

Seated in the air-conditioned shelter of the New Karnak flat, a drink at his elbow, Bourland had listened somberly to Richard's version of things. He'd frowned hard over Luis's disappearance from the Anatole hotel.

"My guess," said Richard, "is that Alejandro had people watching all the major hotels in town, waiting for Luis to surface. As soon as he walked in with Michael it was all up and they grabbed him. There must have been a hell of a reward out."

"That seems a pretty massive effort on Alejandro's part. Quite a long shot, in fact," said Bourland, doubtful.

Richard fixed his old friend with a long look. "Nevertheless, that's how it must have happened. Alejandro took them both, killed Luis, then tried to use Michael as a lever against me. Thankfully, it didn't work." He delicately released his mental hold.

Bourland shook his head, still frowning, but oblivious to what had just happened. "Poor Luis. You and Michael were damned lucky to have escaped that mess. The police are still trying to sort out what happened on the property. All those men dead? Alejandro, yes, he can rot in hell forever, but so many others?" He looked across at Richard, as though finding it hard to believe that so quiet and controlled a man was also capable of such savage violence. He knew it to occasionally be Richard's business, but had rarely seen evidence of it. The police crime photos had been most graphic.

"It's an ugly world, Philip. I did what was necessary to save Michael. Let the police form their own conclusions so long as he's left out of them."

"Oh, absolutely. But what could have happened to poor Luis?"

Richard shrugged. "We may never know."

"It'll be hard on the boy."

"He'll deal with it. My friend Sabra is an expert at grief therapy. She'll be there for him. We all will."

"Yes. My daughter is already working on the custody papers for Michael. After that, it's a short step to adoption. Michael Bourland is a strong name, don't you think?"

"Very strong. A good one."

Richard gave the same story—and hypnotic nudge—to Dr. Sam and Helen. Both were astonished at the change in Michael, going from near-comatose withdrawal to subdued but close-to-normal interaction with the world again. Both were delighted.

"He just needed a little time," said Sam after a final examination. He, too, was being shielded by Bourland's influence. The police knew nothing about Dr. Samuel Ross George's part in things, and it would remain so.

Richard's own story of going to the house to visit an old employee friend, then finding Michael wandering about the ruins in shock was also accepted. His delay in coming forward got him a stern rebuke from the investigators, but nothing more.

"They're not going to bother you again?" Sam asked, surprised.

"No. I explained my reasons about wanting to protect the boy by keeping him clear, and they accepted them. They're thinking that after the explosion, one of Alejandro's men defected to a rival, who simply caught up with him."

"But that's a Federal case! It's still being run on CNN."

Richard had shrugged, unconcerned. "You just need to know how to *talk* to people, that's all."

Sabra stayed with Richard and would be flying back with Michael and Bourland when the time came. She and Bourland became fast friends within minutes of being introduced, but that was only to be expected of her when she wished it. She also knew the value of cultivating important contacts. Bourland was certainly in that category.

And he was a big, handsome man.

"Please don't break him," Richard advised her *sotto voce*, well aware of her preferences. But she merely smiled.

One last detail remained for Richard to see to; Sabra alone knew of it, but said nothing either way of what she thought.

This was strictly his business.

Drenched in sweat and red of face, he reached the top of the hill. In the shade beneath the trees he thought he could risk removing the heavy coat, but the hat remained in place. At least now he could feel the wind, even though its source point must have been an oven.

"Over here," said Jordan Keyes, quietly.

It took a moment for Richard to spot him.

He was again dressed to blend with the background, this time in green cammos, with a matching bush hat. Except for the sunglasses, it all looked to be army surplus, well broken in. Richard gave him a once-over.

"What, no face paint?" he asked.

"The damn stuff gets in the beard." Keyes had not shaved in several days, nor bathed, indication to Richard that he'd been constantly on the job. He looked tired, but gave no sign of leaving his post just yet. "All I have to do to be invisible is keep low and not make noise," Keyes said. "No one comes out here, though."

"So it would seem. How do you know of this place?"

"Deer hunting range. Owner of the property's out of the country."

"Friend of yours?"

"Nope. He's never heard of me. I found this acreage awhile back, liked it, and looked up who had it. I keep tabs on him. If he ever decides to sell, I'll be first in line."

He and Keyes walked to the summit. It commanded a fine view of the woods and fields below. Here Keyes had set up something resembling a hunting blind. He'd strung camouflage netting around an area just large enough for him to lie down in and high enough to be above his head while seated. Within, he'd set up a folding camp chair and brought some paperbacks to read. Near the chair was a rucksack similar to the one Richard carried. It held empty food wrappers, depleted plastic water bottles, insect repellent, and a roll of biodegradable toilet paper.

"Glad you found the place," said Keyes. "I'm down to my last shot of water."

"How are things progressing?"

"About what you'd expect. He was pretty noisy the first day, but the duct tape took care of that. He can't talk any more, tongue's too swollen. Probably won't be too much longer, a couple, three days. Want a look?" He offered up a pair of very powerful binoculars.

Richard took them, peering down the hill toward a tree some fifty yards away. The figure by it sprang close in every awful detail.

Luis Trujillo was chained with his back to the tree, collapsed at its base. He was naked, but covered in patches of vicious red skin that seemed to clothe him. His body occasionally twitched, and he kept shaking his head as though trying to dislodge something. His face was puffed, his eyes sunken and bordering on madness.

"It's a wonder he's not passed out yet," Richard commented.

"That little refinement you wanted . . . I added to it."

"In what way?" Hanging from a limb in front of Luis was a large plastic bag holding liquid. A flexible tube extended from it, the end of which was within easy reach of his mouth, allowing him to drink whenever he wished. The bag was nearly three quarters gone.

Keyes took a liter-sized bottle from his sack and twisted it open. "It struck me that just putting water down there to make him last longer was a good start. I substituted some sports drink, and just to improve the taste mixed in a good dose of antihistamines and some uppers."

"The drink I understand, but the rest?"

"I'm figuring the antihistamines to help counteract anaphylactic shock and the uppers to make sure he enjoys every fun-filled moment."

"Very creative. My compliments."

Richard held himself steady, staring hard through the lens, adjusting the focus. He could just make out minute lines creeping over Luis's flesh. He writhed under them. Flies dotted his face and he shook his head again. If he groaned or cursed, it went unheard in the distance.

"Of course," Keyes continued, "if he really goes into serious shock then the fat lady's done with her chorus. That's when I pack up and boogie."

"But not before—"

"Oh, hell no. Can't let the fire ants get all the glory."

"What have you got for it?"

"Party favor." He pointed to an MP-5 on the ground by his chair. On top of it, a pair of surgical gloves. "Still has Nick's prints on it. I can pop three rounds in the skull, leave the gun, then it's home for Stoli time."

This was also the plan should someone happen along and find

Luis. Keyes was to kill the prisoner to silence him, then vanish. In this heat, so far from anywhere, the happenstance was remote, but both men believed in preparation.

"What'd you bring me?" Keyes asked, reaching for Richard's sack.

"More water, more food bars. The kind you said you wanted."

"Great, I ran out this morning. I was getting hungry." He tore the wrapper off one, taking a healthy bite. "These are most *bueno*, but they stop you up like a summabitch—though out here that's just as well. What's happening in the rest of the world? I take it no one followed you."

"Not to worry. I was careful and your directions were clear." Richard gave him a summation of events. Most of it was even true. "No one knows what's become of Luis. The general assumption is that Alejandro killed him."

"That's fine. Just what you wanted."

"You had no trouble getting Luis out here?"

"Not too much. I kept him drugged in the car until I found a good spot for each of us. I knew about this hill; it was finding the right tree close enough to it that was the problem."

"Right tree?"

"One that had fire ants. I lucked out, though, and turned up a mound next to that one. He woke up pretty fast when I sat him down on it. Had to be quick with the chains to keep him there, then he started hollering, so we had fun with the duct tape. He was freaking out for most of the day, then settled down. Too damn tired to keep it up. Next morning I could take the tape off so he could drink. That's when he tried to buy me off. Tried to say he had the locations of some of his brother's accounts. Like I could believe that. He got pretty crazy, babbled a lot. Just to humor him I wrote the stuff down. Doubt if anything will come of it, but I can play hacker and see what I turn up. If you hear any news about me buying an island you'll know I nailed it."

Richard rather hoped he would. "All this is rather above and beyond."

"Maybe so. Indirectly, he cost me a steady paying customer. 'Cause of him I had to bump Trujillo before he bumped me. Now that would have probably happened sooner or later, but it's annoying all the same. But what really chaps my hide is what he did to his family. That was *wrong*."

Agreed, Richard thought. *But is this not just as wrong?*

Even lowering the binoculars could not remove the sight of the dying Luis from his mind's eye. Richard had thought long and hard about the punishment he would inflict on Stephanie's butcher. It had seemed just. Certainly he'd done worse things to enemies in the past, but this time it was different.

The righteous satisfaction was not there.

He understood and had often reveled in its sweet, raw heat. But now . . . nothing. He couldn't feel pity for Luis, but could summon horror within for his own actions.

I've changed. This vengeance I thought so important is no longer necessary.

"Have you plans for after this?" he asked Keyes.

"I thought about buying a ticket to Aruba for the summer, but the cats'd hate it. They wouldn't have me around to bitch at. My neighbor who checks on them isn't as much fun."

"Perhaps it's time you went back to them."

Keyes finished his food bar and stuffed the wrapper into one of the sacks. "You wanting to cut this short?"

"He looks too far gone for anything more to matter to him."

"I expect so. The ants would have stopped biting sometime back. They're eating on him by now. Different kind of intense, but his mind . . ."

"You've other things to do, I'm sure."

"I can think of a few. You gonna do the honors?"

"Yes."

Richard helped Keyes break camp. It took but a few moments to roll up and stow away the camouflage netting. Richard hiked down to the tree and unhooked the plastic bag, draining it out on the return trip. Luis was so far gone he did not seem to notice his presence.

Keyes had folded the camp chair and put his books away. He hooked the bundle straps over one shoulder then stuck a hand toward Richard.

They briefly shook.

"It's been a pleasure," said Keyes. "Let's *not* do this again sometime."

God forbid.

Richard waited until Keyes was well gone. Before too long he caught the faint sound of a car motor turning over. He waited, spying a cloud of dust rising along the line that marked the road into the property. He waited until the dust drifted lazily back into place.

Then Richard put on the surgical gloves.

He raised the gun, sighting along the barrel. He could see no real detail without the binoculars, but they weren't necessary.

An easy enough shot.

Who was he? Did he deserve his fate?

An easy enough answer.

The figure down below moved fitfully, as one in the torment of a nightmare. Richard waited until the man went still again.

And why was I the one chosen to deliver it to him?

That one was easy as well.

Richard squeezed off a three-round burst. The cracking of the shots echoed briefly, then the summer silence reasserted itself once more over field and wood.